Book One
The Eagle Scout Picture

By

Gary Kidney

In memory of Frank Albert Elliott (U.S. Army, 1940-1945)
and Donald J. Kidney (U.S. Army, 1943-1946),
my brothers whose war stories inspired
my interested in World War II.

In memory of my wife, Debbie (1954-2008).

In memory of the old man by the bay, who claimed
to have lived this story.

For my sons, Brand and Josh, and my partner,
Mary Helen Lowry.

The World War II's rapid expansion caught the U.S. unprepared in several areas, including intelligence and espionage. Planners estimated that "no American could survive in the ruthless fascist police state." The British claimed, "no allied agent could avoid capture by the Gestapo." But one spy did. This is his story.

Quotes from John Mancini in OSS in Germany

"Be careful who you pretend to be. You might forget who you are."

—Hoda Kotb

CONTENTS

CHAPTER 1

Arrival

24 February 1941—Brenner Pass

Back on the farm, when I was Fred Brown, I wished for a life of adventure. And today, he thought, *I wake to the nightmare reality of the dream as Frederich "Zelly" Zellner.* Zelly inhaled deeply the frigid Alpine air, slipped from the bed, and wrapped a throw blanket around his nakedness. Eying the diplomatic pouch on the table, he decided—*If I'm to spy, I might as well start.*

Listening intently, Zelly waited for the telltale snore from his traveling companion, Vincente Testanuevo, to know for sure he was still sleeping. When it finally came, Zelly angled a wingback chair toward the potbellied stove and stoked two logs through the grate. As the railcar began to glow and warm up, he quietly worked a lockpick into Vinny's leather bag.

Extracting a sheaf of papers, he read them in the stove's light. The German pages were easy, as that was one of his native languages, but the Italian records forced him to guess words beyond his school studies. Only one paper intrigued him—an agreement pledging the Italians would join Germany's attack on Greece. Zelly thought about what that could mean for the war, the possibilities it opened up, as he carefully returned the papers to the pouch.

A sudden eerie sense of being observed made him shiver. A glance at the bed revealed Vinny completely covered by the thick duvet, including his head. Zelly's eyes moved to the luxurious Pullman belonging to Galeazzo Ciano, Mussolini's son-in-law and Italy's Foreign Minister. There, in the middle of a mahogany-paneled wall, something shiny caught the light—an eye. It vanished quickly, the hole closing with a scraping sound, leaving behind only a small knot in the wood. *Seems like the porter, who came with the fancy railcar, was watching me,* he concluded. *In fascism, isn't everyone a spy?*

Zelly recalled when Vinny and three men—whom he'd later nickname the butcher, baker, and candlestick maker—had recruited him straight out of high school. In May 1940, Zelly had become an American secret agent headed for Germany. The Third Reich was just ahead of the locomotive. The old country of his parents. A place he'd never been.

The land where I'm to spy.

Where you must fit in... or die.

As the son of immigrants from the German-speaking community in Fredericksburg, Texas, his mission was to become part of the SS at eighteen. Like a mole, Zelly would burrow deep into Nazi society and awaken to aid America in the coming war. For nine months, he had trained for the job with Vinny, an Italian from Brooklyn, New York. Vinny was his handler in the realm of espionage, posing as a cultural attaché at Italy's embassy in Berlin, a posting that included traveling in the unique coach.

Zelly considered whether he should feel guilty for rifling through Vinny's consular secrets, but he quickly shrugged it off. Every small piece of information might have value, even unexpectedly, and the paper about an attack on Greece was a candidate.

A shift in the train's steady noise and the flattening of its climb then caught his attention. Recalling the route map, he surmised that the Rome- Berlin Express had neared the summit of the Wipptal Valley, high in the Alps, a place known as Brenner Pass.

With the stove burning low, the bedcovers looked more and more inviting. And so, Zelly slipped beneath them and poked an icy foot against Vinny. In German, he whispered, "The porter peeked through a knothole."

Vinny shrugged.

Despite the cozy bed, Zelly's thoughts raced. Adrenaline, from his first spy act wasn't going to let Zelly return to sleep.

Vinny didn't catch me.

But the attendant did. You snooped on your friend. What will he think?

There's no need for him to know.

Thirty minutes later, the scraping sound returned. Zelly sprung from the four-poster bed with the arrogant haughtiness Vinny had taught him. He barked Italian orders at the paneling's knot. "Gabinetto! Fretta!"

Vinny jumped at the shout as the cabin door flung open. The porter hurried to pull the chamber pot from the cabinet, and Zelly and Vinny sprinted to the porcelain bowl. Zelly stretched his foreskin before pissing, as Vinny had coached. The American habit of retracting it wasn't something a Nazi would do—one of many habits requiring relearning for life in Germany.

Their streams splattered everywhere, sending the attendant for a mop. When he came back, Zelly eyed him with a sneer. "Put more wood on the fire," he ordered. Then, as the worker stoked the stove, Zelly demanded, "Breakfast, washing water, and clothes."

The two waited, wrapped in bedclothes, in the wingback chairs. Vinny's elbow grazed the diplomatic pouch, resulting in

Zelly's smile. The servant looked like he had something to say as he brought a tray of rattling cups and assorted pastries. He placed it on the table between them and poured coffee.

Vinny snagged a cream-filled cannoli and dangled it from his lips like a cigarette. In German, he asked, "Sleep well?"

"Hungover from the Fiano di Avellino that Primo served for my birthday." Zelly dunked a chocolate brioche in his java.

"Enjoying being eighteen, are you?"

"Well, could have been better." Zelly winked.

"Hmm...? Carlotta didn't like your anteater?" Vinny asked with a smile.

Zelly blushed at the teasing about his long foreskin. "The chaperone kept it from appearing."

"Since I'm twenty-one, Isabella and I didn't require an escort."

Zelly got the hint—those girls weren't at Primo's party but were from training in San Antonio. He took it as a chance to practice making conversation with an unexpected listener. "After the two of you sneaked off, I had only the wine for company and performed my duty to finish it."

The porter brought a bowl of warm water and towels, offered Vinny a shave. While Zelly washed, he discreetly observed the man's razor techniques, aware that he would start shaving soon. In the mirror, he studied the soft fuzz on his cheeks, comparing himself to his friend.

Both were slightly less than two meters tall and lean. Farm labor had toned Zelly's muscles more than Vinny's city-boy-next-door physique. Zelly's undercut blond hair and blue eyes made him look like a Nazi recruiting poster. Vinny's black locks were in a pompadour, towering above his dark brown eyes and hooked nose.

With the shave finished, Vinny washed. "Teaching Carlotta the dance surprised me. It enabled her to guess your background."

Zelly accepted the rebuke as a warning. In San Antonio, he had taught her the Texas Two-Step, unknown in Germany. Tiny mistakes—the wrong music or a different way of pissing—could be fatal in the Third Reich.

Vinny pushed blond strands from Zelly's forehead, his sharp gaze catching a hint of lipstick. "You've been busy," he said, his words light, but his tone edged with reproach. "How many kisses did you snag?"

"I don't share my lurid secrets, but I lost count at twenty-seven when the wine kicked in."

The porter brought their freshly laundered clothes—a winter-blue Hitler Youth uniform for Zelly and a brown Merino wool suit for Vinny. Zelly marveled at the martyr's badge on his uniform pocket—a simple golden party pin but with a black wreath of mourning.

The porter checked his pocket watch. "2:45 AM, and we're approaching Brennaro. Expect an hour for customs and border control."

After they dressed, the man pulled their luggage from the armoire and placed it by the door. When the train slowed, Zelly inhaled deeply. As the steam brakes hissed, he remembered practice time was over.

What am I doing here? An American, a Texan named Fred Brown. Dad fought for the U.S. Army in the Great War's trenches—the one to end them all. And I'm joining one that hasn't started.

In months, the blitzkrieg finished Poland, Holland, and France. You listened to Churchill's Dunkirk speech on the shortwave you built. You are Frederich Zellner, a Nazi boy. Sieg heil.

They shoot spies, don't they?

Vinny shrugged into his trench coat, and Zelly wore his jacket and ski cap. The carriage door opened to the frigid, brutal wind and mountains of snow. Vinny descended the steps to the wooden platform.

The porter lingered, his expression inscrutable. "What you did will be reported," he muttered, his words heavy with the cold authority of someone well-versed in the mechanisms of fascist loyalty.

Have I already made a fatal mistake?

Weather colder than the worst ice age in Texas slammed Zelly's face. When Vinny noticed the wince, he said, "Zelly, welcome home."

Once-distant threats became immediate and terrifying. The swastika flag draped over the station's door. Armed with automatic weapons, Wehrmacht troops surrounded the platform. A leashed German Shepherd sniffed at Zelly and let out a low snarl.

Can the dog smell an American?

Fit in... or die.

How can I?

A second train waited on another track. With mismatched railroad gauges, passengers had to switch trains. As travelers to Italy exited the station to board, those bound for Germany hurried inside. Before Zelly and Vinny reached the door, a Gestapo officer stormed through, nearly bowling them over.

He pointed at the departing locomotive and blew a whistle. "Stop them!"

Following the officer's gloved finger, Zelly spotted two hunched figures bounding through snowdrifts, chasing the last car.

The agent saw the double-diamond pips on Zelly's shoulder. "Sergeant, apprehend them."

Zelly sprinted across the wooden platform with boots pounding like kettledrums. Plotting an intercept angle, he vaulted into a thigh-deep snowdrift. Running through them required leaping from one heap to another.

"Shoot them!"

Without a weapon other than his Hitler Youth Knife, Zelly continued pursuit. He sucked for air, and his lungs burned—a sea-level boy sprinting in high mountain snow. In closing with the pair, he discovered one figure was a woman carrying a bundled baby.

"Juden!" The Gestapo called.

Realizing they would never catch the train, the family veered for a stand of pine trees. The man took the bundle and led his wife toward the woods.

The single bulb on the station's pinnacle extinguished, and blackout curtains darkened the windows. Around Zelly, the snowfield shone with a blue phosphorescence reflecting the stars and moon. He lost sight of the runners as their silhouettes blended with the tree trunks.

Bullets sprayed from an unseen machine gun, so he slowed to avoid the field of fire.

The couple tumbled to a drift. The snow seemed black when Zelly arrived, but the flicker of a flashlight revealed it was crimson. He noticed movement in the pile at his feet. Flailing arms and kicking legs cast aside the blanket and swaddling clothes, revealing a Jewish boy. The baby's fresh circumcision was still red and swollen.

Nine months ago, Zelly had been clueless about circumcisions because he and all his friends still had foreskins. Then, the Army introduced him to Carl Gettler and Bob Silberman, boys from Wittenberg, his pretend hometown. They taught him about life in National Socialism, shared their stories, and showed him the cuts of the mohel.

Still, tales of Germany's treatment of Jews were no preparation for the dead bodies at his feet. The automatic weapon had mangled the couple unbelievably, splattering blood and tissue over the snow. During his training, he had killed a man, but this scene made his stomach revolt. Blinking away tears, he reached for the baby. As the flashlight's glow approached, the infant smiled and quieted.

The Gestapo centered the light on the child. "Kill him."

Murder a baby? The thought shell-shocked Zelly.

"Stomp his head," the agent ordered.

When Zelly hesitated, the officer slapped him, the sting spreading like fire across his cheek. He recoiled, startled by the casual cruelty, as the officer flicked away the snot. Zelly's stomach churned, torn between fear of defiance and revulsion at obedience. How had things to quickly come to this—being asked to kill an innocent?

"Trample him."

I must be a perfect Nazi and live up to my uniform. Follow his order.

No. I won't murder. God won't forgive me, nor will I.

Zelly raised his leg and willing his boot to stomp, but his muscles refused movement. A pistol discharged, and the child disintegrated at his feet. He inspected his sole, poised inches above the child's head, to find blood, brain, and bone. As bile rose into his mouth, he pivoted and spewed.

The officer turned away. "Your disobedience squandered a bullet. I'll deal with you inside."

Zelly wiped his face on his sleeve. A handful of snow eased his stinging cheek. As he reached the platform, he scraped his boots against the deck's frame, smearing the baby's tissue and causing his stomach to churn again. Vinny's expression accused him of failure.

Zelly said, "I couldn't hurt the baby."

"You've been in the glorious Reich for eleven minutes and fucked up everything. Consequences might be extreme."

Zelly sniffed, catching death's stink, as he brushed snowflakes from trouser cuffs. The misstep brought memories of the three men who had recruited him. Major Donovan was the butcher who desired knowledge of the Nazi war machine. Professor Koehler was the baker who lusted after Germany's technology. Dr. Otto was the candlestick maker who snipped the tips of wicks and wanted proof of the terrible news relayed by escaping Jews.

Vinny led him into the station and stopped at the BDM girls' table to buy coffee. Zelly knew the Bund Deutscher Mädel was the female equivalent of the HJ, short for Hitlerjugend or Hitler Youth, the organization of which he was a member. When his stomach objected to a drink, he lingered in the stove's warmth.

The baby smiled at me.

He was a Jew. And you're a failure.

Since the other passengers had finished processing, Vinny stepped up to a bank-teller-like cage. A jovial Italian asked, "What is the reason for your departure?"

"Posted to the Berlin embassy." He passed his passport through the narrow opening.

The man sighed. "A prestigious job while I stamp official seals." After affixing the symbol, he returned the booklet.

"Grazie, signore," Vinny said, moving to the luggage inspection table.

The Gestapo officer from outside manned it. Zelly thought he resembled Paul Henreid in the movie *Night Train to Munich*.

Vinny covered his suitcase with a protective hand. "I'm a diplomat."

The inspector frowned. "Open!"

"I have diplomatic immunity." Vinny ignored the officer's glare and hurried to the cage, holding a sour-looking German who stamped his document.

The agent focused on Zelly as he neared the friendly Italian. Breaking into a sweat, Zelly slid his passport through the opening, afraid the forgery would not withstand scrutiny.

The man only cast a fleeting glance at the phony documents. "Why are you leaving Italy?"

"My exchange program ended when I turned 18, so I'm going home to enlist in the SS."

The man's nose curled at the mention of the Schutzstaffel, but he punched the seal. "A late happy birthday."

Zelly opened his suitcase for the scowling Gestapo officer. Black-gloved hands rifled through his belongings until they pulled out a cloth bag. The inspector removed a glove and loosened the drawstring before pouring vacuum tubes, wires, and assorted electronics into his other hand.

Zelly reached for the components but stopped himself. "Please be careful, as they break easily."

The Nazi gleamed at his luck, drew the pistol that had just killed a baby, and poked it in Zelly's chest. "Possession of radio parts is illegal." At his gesture, a Wehrmacht sergeant leveled a machine gun at Zelly. A Cheshire- cat grin covered the Gestapo's face. "Smuggling is a capital crime."

The weapons and commotion drew every passenger's attention. Their collective gasp seemed to consume all the air inside the cramped building.

Zelly choked on an explanation. "I make electrical things, so I took components with me to Italy and bought more in Naples." He pointed to a gold lightning bolt patch on his uniform sleeve. "I'm Nachrichten-HJ, the signals branch."

The sergeant recognized the insignia. "He's C-level—quite remarkable."

"What can you create with these pieces?" the Gestapo probed.

"Circuits, telegraphs, radios, and more."

At the admission, the staring passengers gasped again.

Zelly dug his HJ book from the jumbled suitcase and located the page of signatures for his specialty. He passed the document to the sergeant. "At C-level, I have full access to electronics, including specialized equipment."

The soldier slung his weapon and examined the booklet before giving it to the officer. "Sir, the documentation confirms it. In military service, his advanced training will be valuable."

The man dropped it into the luggage without a glance. "Give me all of your papers."

Zelly unbuttoned his tunic pocket and extracted his Ahnenpass, establishing his German ethnic genealogy, the kennkarte ID card, travel orders, and his Reichspass, previously stamped by the Italian. As he offered the bundle, his breath caught with the forgeries firmly in the Gestapo's hands. The agent compared the identification photo to his face. It was his senior pose from the Fredericksburg High School yearbook.

The memory of an early June Army staff car ride to San Antonio's Fort Sam Houston—just a week after graduation. The butcher handed him a thick envelope containing the documents now clenched in the Gestapo's fist.

"A perfect blond-haired, blue-eyed boy," Major Donovan had said.

"Forging was easy, but putting supporting material in place was harder," Doctor Otto had said. "Complementary records had to appear in file cabinets at your schools, Wittenberg's town hall, and other places. We are what Hitler fears most—an international conspiracy of Jews."

As the Gestapo perused his papers, the idea of global conspiracies echoed in Zelly's thoughts. Growing impatient, he read the man's name badge. "Herr Stengler, is there a problem?"

The agent showed some blank pages in the Ahnenpass. "You mentioned joining the SS, but requirements have changed. You need two more generations of genealogy on your father's side."

Zelly took the documents with a crestfallen expression. Shit, the Jewish cabal hadn't thought of everything. "I'm adopted and doubt anything more is possible."

He studied Stengler's close-cropped fair hair, sporting hints of gray and eyes of black tinged with amusement. A slight scar beside his ear twitched when he smirked that cat-like grin.

Stengler chewed for an instant before opening a Schmalzler tin, pinching some, and sniffing it up his nose. "Sergeant Zellner, step into the office, where we'll deal with your disobedience."

Sweat came like a waterfall over Zelly's forehead and down his sides. He shook as he shuffled into a tiny enclosure. Vinny's worried face followed his progress, and fellow passengers scowled at the delay.

In the cramped space, Stengler perched on the desk, leaving Zelly only inches between his knees and the wall. "Adopted?"

Zelly offered his cover story. "My birth parents were Friederich and Marta Just. He was an ardent National Socialist and one of Hitler's first followers. When I was seven months old, he died in a bomb blast intended to spring the Führer from prison. Faced with a baby and no husband, she abandoned me at her sister's farm in Wittenberg. August and Freida Zellner raised me and gave me their family name."

"Friederich Just, I recall from the list of martyrs." Stengler touched the martyr's badge pinned on Zelly's tunic pocket—a black laurel wreath ringed the gold center circle and a swastika. "Not for wear by a living person."

"It is all I have of him. The mayor and HJ leaders allowed me."

The officer's forehead furrowed. "What puzzles me is why a distinguished martyr's son would refuse to kill vermin."

"I didn't want the stinking baby's blood on my uniform. We could have let the dogs finish it." Zelly used the subhuman pronoun as he stared at Stengler's blemish.

"You disobeyed an order. Are you a weak boy or Jew-lover?"

"I've killed one before, sir." The tiny office closed in around Zelly, choking him with the stink of the man's apricot snuff.

"So, share the story."

"In the November Progrom, a Jewish man resisted orders. I finished him in a fight, but he left a mark."

"In the SS, scars are a mark of honor. Show me."

"It's under my trousers, sir."

Anticipation sparkled in the officer's gaze. "So, lower them."

"Ladies are present." He thumbed to the window where Vinny's scowl and the faces of passengers and BDM girls stared.

A guttural chuckle came from the Gestapo's throat. "They have brothers and sons, or do you hesitate again?"

He followed Doctor Otto's advice and dropped his slacks. Giggles penetrated the door as he raised his tunic and shirt to expose the scar arcing around his scrotum.

"A Jew got you by the balls?" Stengler's snort turned into a guffaw. He cupped Zelly's testicles and traced the blemish with a finger.

The touch revolted Zelly, but his only option was to stay at attention and let him continue. "I killed him for it."

Stengler's eyes were inches away from his groin while he inspected the blemish. "Details."

Zelly invented a lie. "On the night before Martin Luther's birthday, my HJ squad was to harass a jeweler, but somehow, he received a warning because the expensive stuff was in a safe. Still, the display case had some charming rings, so I broke the glass with my dagger. The Jew rushed out, and his hand lunged up the leg of my shorts to clutch me there. When I turned to stab him, my skin ripped, but my blade found his heart. I chose rings for my mother and girlfriend while my group took the rest. Since the train is waiting, may I dress?"

"The scar's discoloration isn't right for two years of healing. Your story sounds suspicious."

Zelly shrugged and made himself presentable.

When they left the office, the conductor hurried passengers aboard. Zelly caught up with Vinny, but his open luggage stayed behind. At the platform's edge, they waited where engine noise would mask conversation.

"Why were your trousers down?" Vinny asked.

"To solve the problem with the baby, I said I had once killed a Jew, but it left a scar. He insisted on seeing it. I told him it was from before Italy, but he didn't believe me. I've already fucked up."

"This isn't your first mistake. Your mission might end here and now."

"Murder! I never imagined things would be this horrible. God, I want to go home."

"Didn't you figure an SS member would have to kill Jews? Isn't that what they do?" Vinny pulled a red eagle pack of Regie 4 cigarettes from his coat pocket, lit two, and gave Zelly one.

****

Oskar Stengler checked the stationmaster's clock—4:30 AM. He caught Zelly's furtive glance at the inspection table and monitored him and his traveling companion going to the tracks. Picking up the desk phone, he clicked for service. "Berlin's HJ headquarters." He waited minutes until the call rang back.

"Heil Hitler!" a sleepy voice said.

"This is Herr Stengler from the Gestapo. Do you have a Sergeant Zellner in transit from a youth exchange program?"

"Let me consult the board." After a brief pause, the answer came. "Frederich Zellner is due late today with the Rome-Berlin express. He is with Vincente Testanuevo, a diplomat from the host family in Naples and a member of Gioventù Italiana del Littorio, the Italian Fascist party."

"How long was the boy in Italy?"

"Since December of '38. Have you encountered a problem?"

"No, Brenner station reports he's on his way." Stengler clicked off and gave the boy's suitcase a more thorough search. He located a curious tool tucked inside a sock. The device had two blades and a dozen other fold-out arms for other functions. He pocketed it.

Beneath everything was a snap to open a compartment in the luggage. Within, he discovered some items that demanded attention—two nasty Italian magazines and an American technical book. Since the Reich had banned pornography and few Germans knew English, his curiosity increased.

The stationmaster came to Stengler's shoulder. "The Pullman's porter sent this to Rome concerning the HJ boy."

Stengler scanned the transcript. 'Early in the night, while the Italian slept, the German picked the diplomatic pouch's lock and perused the contents. Most of their conversation was about sex and girls, one named Carlotta. But the Italian complained she guessed the German's background when he taught her a dance.'

"Danke." Stengler assumed the device in his pocket was the lockpick. Why would the kid spy on his friend? How could dancing betray his circumstances? Growing more suspicious, he closed the suitcase, intentionally leaving clothing pieces askew between the clasps and the literature from the compartment exposed. "Have the conductor take his bag aboard." He summoned the Wehrmacht sergeant with the machine gun.

When they entered a third-class car and found the passenger, Stengler gestured for the conductor to throw the luggage at the kid's feet. The fasteners popped open, spilling the contents across the floor. A shudder rippled through the boy—a palpitation of fear Oskar relished, like when the first tug comes on a fishing line. Stepping amidst the pile of clothes, he got in the boy's face. "Did you think I would miss your secret compartment?"

Zellner stuttered, "Only a p-p-place for papers."

He knew this kid would crack easily and pictured in his mind ripping a fresh scar around his testicles. Reaching into the junk, he extracted a textbook. "An English book?" Such a volume was about as common as a humpback whale in the Alps. "What's this?"

"A technical manual, written by an American expert in radio detection and range finding. The title is *The Design of Audio Amplifiers Using Regeneration*."

"You know English?" Oskar probed, understanding nothing about the volume's subject.

The kid nodded almost guiltily. "I'm self-taught. I often find novel insights in foreign books."

Oskar reacted with shock and lofted the book so the other passengers could see. "Who speaks English?" Only the Italian diplomat's hand raised while most people waved their hands over their faces at the silly question.

The diplomat supported his friend. "Is having an English manual illegal? Or is speaking the language?"

Stengler ignored him. "You should read German material instead of these!" Oskar pulled two nasty publications from the pile and displayed the pornography to the others. One fancy lady two rows back fanned herself at a cover—a girl in black gloves, heels, and the tiniest string panty posing with a leashed leopard beneath the caption 'Pet my pussy?'

"Those are degenerate!" she shouted.

"I used them to help him learn Italian," the diplomat said.

Oskar's mouth formed an 'O', and he switched to Italian. "Sergente Zellner, parli italiano?"

"Italian was my second language in school," he replied in the language.

Stengler returned to German. "You've mastered three languages at eighteen?"

"I'm not that good in Italian or English," the youth said. "There are far too many words."

Oskar switched directions for the interrogation. "Where did you qualify C-level in signals?"

"Army school in Halle."

"Perhaps you recall an acquaintance of mine—Theodor Von Brincken?"

"Of course, the colonel was headmaster."

The conductor waved his pocket watch. "To keep schedule, we must depart."

The Wehrmacht sergeant tapped Stengler's elbow. "Sir, his achievements explain the parts and manual. As for the pornography, I've indulged, and I'd bet you have." He left the carriage.

"To avoid further delay, we'll visit on the way." Stengler took the seat across from Zellner. He established physical contact between their knees to intimidate the youth. When the touch revealed the boy trembling, he smiled.

The conductor leaned out of the car and blew his whistle. With a hiss of steam, the train began to chug forward.

****

Zelly shuddered at the unsettling cat grin on Stengler's face and cursed his decision to bring that book. Vinny had recommended leaving it behind on the British submarine that delivered them to Naples.

Stengler stretched a leg, forcing it between their thighs.

Zelly prayed he had the answers to the questions he knew were coming. He would have to rely on the stories Bob and Carl had told him.

Stengler lost no time in beginning the quizzing. "Sergeant Zellner, the Bann number on your shoulder boards is for Wittenberg, which has two gymnasiums. Which one did you attend?"

Zelly took a hard swallow. "I attended Wittenberg, and the other one is Melanchthon."

The correct answer stunned Stengler. "Did you study Italian there?"

As soon as Zelly gave a nod, the officer's eyes popped wide. "Before the war, I was Wittenberg's only Italian teacher."

Though his heart raced, Zelly felt like he would faint. Vinny gasped.

Sensing their tension through his leg, Stengler chortled at their discomfort. "I can recollect every student, yet I find nothing familiar about you. A Zellner never appeared on my rolls."

Zelly forced his eyes on Stengler's face. "I don't remember you either, sir. I was in classes for only two months until the international exchange took me away. The headmaster let me graduate early by counting my time in Italy for the Arbitur. After the years away, I'm sure I've changed, and that's probably why you don't recognize me. If you plan to ask, the man was Doctor Bischoff, but the boys called him Klammerbein because he'd lost a leg on the Somme. His slogan was 'Young bulls for the Führer.'"

Stengler gestured towards the mess between benches. "Stow your junk."

****

Zellner's face was pale, almost ashen, as he stuffed things into his suitcase, but Oskar knew his answers about Wittenberg's school were correct in every detail. Perhaps I'm mistaken or suffering from a faulty memory. Maybe he's changed enough, or his time in my class was too short to be remarkable. As the heap on the floor shifted, Oskar spotted a scrapbook and grabbed it.

After the kid shoved his luggage on the overhead rack, the conductor flicked off the lights, and the passengers settled for sleep.

Oskar illuminated his flashlight and opened the book. The first picture was a dinner party with fancy tablecloths and fine china. The table in the foreground seated the boy and his Italian friend, among other boys who wore black berets. On the dais, Mussolini stood gazing at his guests.

"You met Il Duce?" Stengler asked.

Zellner gave a disinterested nod and pretended to nap, so the diplomat responded. "That was at the welcome banquet when we made Zelly an honorary member of GIL. Did you notice his beret in the luggage?"

Stengler flipped the pages—a newspaper clipping about the exchange program, the youth shooting a Mauser Karabiner 98k, and the two tossing a young kid into a gaping volcano. "Where was this one taken?"

Again, the diplomat answered, "That's Turtle, my cousin, on Monte Vesuvio, which is near his house in Napoli."

Oskar tried a random page—Zellner embracing a girl. "Chi è la ragazza?"

"Carlotta, Zelly's girlfriend."

"What dance did he teach her?"

Vinny stiffened, realizing the porter who overheard the Pullman conversation relayed it to the secret police. "Der Ländler, a precursor to the waltz, and I'm sure you know it."

Returning to the album, Oskar found two unmounted pictures and examined them with a lecherous grin. "These are as indecent as the magazine cover."

"I expect Zelly would say those are his private memories." Vinny shrugged dismissively at the nudity they depicted. "That's us wading from the river after skinny dipping and with our girlfriends, Carlotta and Isabella, on the blanket."

Oskar returned the shot of the two couples before inspecting the picture of the two guys.

As I thought, the kid lied. This shot offers a clear view of his genitals. At the scar's location, the skin is perfectly smooth. There are several inconsistencies with Herr Zellner, and his explanations are too glib. Instinct tells me he is not what he is trying to be.

He stuck the snapshot in his tunic pocket. "This one I'll keep."

****

They slept until the blackout curtains opened to spill sunlight through the carriage. Snow from the German Alps sparkled beyond the windows.

"Buongiorno, guten morgen, or should I say good morning?" the Gestapo officer smirked.

Zelly rubbed his sleepy eyes and yawned.

Stengler pulled something from his pocket. "I found this device wrapped in a sock in your suitcase. What is it?"

"It's like a Swiss army knife but specialized for electronics projects. See that wing? It folds out to hold solder, saving you from burning fingers."

Stengler unfolded some tools from it. "My guess is this is a lockpick."

"Why would I need one of those?"

"That's an excellent question." Stengler turned to Vinny. "Why does he need one?"

"He wouldn't," Vinny said, wondering why Stengler would reach that conclusion.

A service cart clattered through the aisle, offering breakfast. The coffee's aroma helped Zelly clear his head as he snagged a cup and a raspberry streusel pastry.

Stengler let him take a sip before springing his next inquiries. "Zellner, you say you attended the Wittenberg Gymnasium?"

"Correct, and I suppose you were my teacher, but I can't remember you." Zelly tried a friendly smile.

"And how long did you live there?"

"About fifteen years."

"So, what is at the end of Collegienstrasse?"

"Everyone knows—the famous oak tree where Martin Luther burned the papal bull of ex-communication." Zelly pulled the answer from Bob and Carl's training about Wittenberg.

"So, disclose something unique—a thing you think few people might know."

Zelly was at a loss as he searched through Bob and Carl's stories for esoteric knowledge. He thought of the Wehrmacht sergeant's comment about pornography and found the perfect match. "Did you know the gymnasium had a Wichsenhalle, a place for masturbation, and the teachers were clueless?"

Stengler reacted with astonishment. "I was aware of the rumors. What was the location?"

"In the jungensumpf's last stall. Loose tiles covered a shelf carved in plaster behind the commode's tank."

"How did you keep the ceramics from falling?"

"Papier mâché made with…."

A Luftwaffe major interrupted. "Obviously, he knows the school better than you. Welcome him home instead of berating him with your endless questions."

****

Stengler rode in silence for thirty minutes before disembarking in Munich. As he strode to the station, he spotted Zellner peering from the carriage. *He has the right answers but too many contradictions, disobedience, and at least one outright deception.*

Inside, he flashed his badge and used the stationmaster's phone to make some calls.

For the first one, he asked for Wittenberg gymnasium's headmaster. A familiar voice came on the line. "Herr Bischoff, Oskar Stengler here, remember me? A language teacher until the service called."

"Yes, you went to the secret police—always had a nose for snooping."

"Did you ever find where the boys kept their nasty material?"

"Two years ago, a janitor's mop handle hit a wall, and the tiles fell."

"Where?"

"It was behind the flushing box in the last toilet stall."

"I'm planning to pay you a visit."

"After your old job back? I haven't had a linguist in years."

"I want the records of Frederich Zellner. He finished school mid-year of '38 or '39."

Stengler clicked off the line and bounced the hook to gain the operator's attention. "Gestapo headquarters, Berlin, please." When a secretary answered, he said, "Oskar Stengler, here. I'm interested in Frederich Zellner, who recently turned 18 and has committed to enlist in the SS. He's returning from Italy on an HJ exchange program. Also, he claims to be the son of the martyr Friederich Just. Can you locate his file? I'll be in Berlin this evening."

"Of course, sir, I've submitted your requests."

Exiting the stationmaster's office, he saw the train pulling away. Dashing across the platform, he caught the last car. During the trip to Berlin, he composed his notes, trying to organize facts that seemed incompatible and illogical. The list for further research included the scar and the process of opening the diplomatic pouch. Though the disobedience, nasty magazines, English books, and unusual tools weren't enough for criminal charges, the short hairs on his neck told him something wasn't right with the kid.

When he closed the notebook, his eyes focused on the glass overlooking the gangway leading to the next carriage. Zellner's friend stood there peering at him. Immediately after Oskar spotted him, the man darted away.

****

When Vinny returned to his seat on the Rome-Berlin Express, he beckoned Zelly to the toilet. "Stengler got back on board, so he has unfinished business with you."

They relieved themselves into the metal commode, watching their streams splash against the rocky bed beneath the rails.

"I can't have the answer to everything he asks. He could have as easily been a grocer as a teacher and asked where my aunt shopped for groceries."

"True, but you held your own with what Bob and Carl taught you about Wittenberg. One question, though: did you use your lockpick on my diplomatic pouch?"

Zelly nodded sheepishly.

"The porter reported it. Stengler knows. Another of your life-threatening mistakes."

The coffee and breakfast pastry churned in Zelly's stomach.

Once they came back to their seats, he recognized Nürnberg from *Triumph des Willens*, a movie about Hitler and Germany he'd viewed in training. He took in Halle, where he'd attended signals school. After crossing the Elbe River at Rossau, the tracks followed the water to his hometown, Wittenberg.

He gazed east on Dresdener Strasse, the route to his family's farm. A small, white station appeared with high-arched windows and doors. From the view, he would guess a second story, but Bob and Carl had explained the clerestory. He took mental pictures of an unfamiliar location, hoping they might save his life.

Jumbled thoughts occupied his mind. *My future is nothing more than dumb luck encounters, like driftwood on the waves. Wittenberg boys should know me from the gymnasium or the HJ, but they won't. Now, the mission seems so foolhardy. How can I survive?*

Why didn't you consider that back in Texas? You're committed now.

What are my odds of going home?

Infinitesimal. Most likely zero.

Lost in thought, it took the steam brakes firing at Berlin's Anhalter depot to bring him back to consciousness.

They disembarked and hustled toward the S-bahn tracks for the #2 train, but Zelly craned his neck every few steps to glance behind.

"You'll spot the Gestapo back here, maybe even Stengler. They trail diplomats as a standard practice. I bet they've already bugged our room in the Adlon."

Vinny's embassy provided an excellent suite at the hotel with room service. They ordered dinner, took baths in a claw-footed tub, dried in luxurious robes, and slipped into a feather bed.

With the duvet over their heads, Zelly whispered in Italian, "Everything would have been easier without him."

"He fastened his talons on you at the scar story. Couldn't you devise a better lie?"

Dread made Zelly's sleep fitful with images of firing squads, hangman's nooses, and torture.

****

When Oskar Stengler disembarked from the Rome-Berlin Express, he watched Zellner and the diplomat queue for an S-Bahn train. A five-minute stroll took him from the depot to SS Headquarters. After climbing the stairs, he approached a blonde receptionist with her hair pulled into a bun. "I'm looking for the file on Frederich Zellner."

She checked some notes. "It is with Heinrich Müller." She escorted him to an oak door and knocked. In seconds, an imposing man, block-faced with piercing gray-blue eyes, opened it.

"Heil Hitler, Gruppenführer," Oskar said.

The edge of Müller's lips tried to smile. "Our records mark him as the son of a party martyr. That's an unlikely place for a communist, don't you think? What's your interest in him?"

Oskar took the offered chair. "I've found several curious inconsistencies about him." When Müller passed a file across the desk, Oskar said, "This seems rather thin."

"For an eighteen-year-old, it's quite complete. What concerns you?"

Stengler scanned the file. "I told him to kill a Jewish infant, and he didn't obey. He covered his disobedience with a tale of once killing a Jew who left him with a scar. He claimed the wound stemmed from a fight during the '38 progrom, but the mark was still fresh and healing."

"So, he lied?" Müller chuckled. "Isn't that normal for Gestapo questioning?"

"Yes, but he had a highly technical English book and a bundle of electronic parts in his luggage."

"He distinguished himself in the Nachrichten-HJ, which explains the electronics. These days, technology fascinates boys—radios, signals, airplanes, automobiles. Why are you suspicious?"

"Few youths know English. He said he was self-taught, but reading such a book? He also speaks Italian and is from Wittenberg, where I was the only language teacher. I can't recall him in class."

The Gruppenführer took it lightly. "Memory can fade. So, he misled about a scar and knows languages. What was the title of the scientific manual?"

"I don't recall exactly, but it was something about audio amplifiers and regeneration," Oskar said.

"Do you have anything else?"

"The boy is traveling with a diplomat. During the journey, the valet spotted him picking the lock on the diplomatic pouch and studying the papers."

Müller raised an eyebrow and snatched the folder from Stengler's hands. "Your German kid spied on the Italians? That is curious."

"Honestly, I feel my suspicions justify putting him under surveillance."

"Then do so, but with this warning—Der Führer considers the relationship with Italy strategic. Don't create a diplomatic crisis."

After Stengler saluted and departed, Müller added a fresh sheet of paper to the folder and scribbled furiously on it. He wrote—Nachrichten C-level, reading an English book on audio amplifiers and regeneration, and spied on his Italian friend. With a grin, he thought this might be a perfect fit for Himmler's special project. He buzzed his secretary and gave her the file. "Himmler's eyes, immediately."

CHAPTER 2

The Picture

25 February 1941—Berlin's Adlon Hotel

In the morning, Zelly rose from the comfortable bed and padded barefooted across the plush carpet to open the drapes. The sunlight brought a groan from Vinny, but Zelly relished the astounding view—Pariser Platz, named to commemorate the Prussian defeat of Napoleon. To the left was the Brandenburg Gate, topped by four horses pulling a chariot containing Victoria, the Roman goddess of victory. An Iron Cross and imperial eagle rested on her staff. As part of his training, he had read several history books.

Below the window, Berlin teemed with life—vibrant, dominant, and luxurious. Any enormous city might captivate a farm boy, but he'd been to Houston, Washington D.C., Baltimore, Belfast, Naples, and Rome. In those places, he'd never felt so touched, like he belonged or was at home.

A strange sensation coursed through his body. His muscles tensed, his back straightened, and his shoulders squared as Vinny approached. He raised his arm and clicked his heels. "Heil Hitler."

"God, you gave me the shivers," Vinny said. "Tag along for my appointment at the embassy?"

"I'm expected at HJ headquarters afterward."

Dressed in a suit and winter uniform, they breakfasted in the lobby restaurant. Zelly examined pictures of dignitaries at parties and official occasions, decorating their booth's wall. He recognized one—Otto von Bismarck and President Ulysses S. Grant, shaking hands at the entrance to some grand palace.

"Order two coffees," Vinny said.

When the server arrived, Zelly held up his thumb and index finger, the correct gesture. "Zwei Kaffee, bitte." Two fingers, as in America, would be a deadly mistake.

People at other tables gossiped about the war, so Zelly listened in on a conversation.

A lady's white-gloved hand lifted her teacup. She said, "Last evening, we viewed *Mein Leben für Irland,* and the newsreel was exciting. The footage showed a U-boat sinking a British vessel named *Beachy.*"

Zelly gasped, spurting coffee up his nose, as he recalled the ship was in the convoy that ferried them to Gibraltar.

With breakfast finished, they passed through Brandenburg Gate and walked Hermann Göring Strasse beside the famous Tiergarten. The park resembled a country estate nestled within the bustling city. Snow-filled footpaths led between barren stands of linden and maple trees.

Since the Italians were constructing a new embassy, Vinny took them to the older structure. In the lobby, a receptionist's long, shapely legs caught Zelly's attention as Vinny presented his letter of introduction.

"I'm Ambra." She handed Vinny a packet, and he kissed her hand. "First, find an apartment, and I recommend Kreuzberg." She unfolded a map, marking two circles a block off Friedrichstrasse. "These are within walking distance and close to trains."

They took the U-Bahn to Kochstrasse station and walked two blocks to a corner where they found two five-story stone and brick buildings with 'To let' signs. Both structures featured round turret-like corners, like medieval castles.

At the first location, the superintendent's wife offered a three-bedroom penthouse. Fancy classical furniture filled the flat, and pictures adorned the walls. In a large family portrait, the men wore Jewish skullcaps.

"What occurred to the previous occupants?" Zelly asked.

"They left after their Kaiserdamm antique shop closed some years ago." Her hands quivered, like leaving was common.

Zelly ascribed it to the November progrom that Bob and Carl called Kristallnacht—the inspiration for his fictitious story of acquiring the scar. "They took nothing with them?"

Her expression was incredulous. "They owned the entire building, so what could they take?"

Vinny frowned. "I only need one bedroom."

"But for an Italian diplomat, the price is negotiable."

Zelly tugged Vinny's sleeve. "Nazis stole these places."

At the second apartment, an elderly woman had the key. They followed her up to a third-floor flat with a sitting room in the round turret. A compact kitchen and private bath were on one side, with a sleeping room and tiny closet on the other. Furnishings included an upright piano in the circular room and a sway-backed double bed. Sheets covered everything like someone would return.

"Is the renter coming back?" Zelly asked.

"The single man studied music and played wonderful songs. Do you play?"

Since she dodged the question, he repeated it.

Her hands flitted about like the previous landlord's. "Gestapo took him."

"Jewish?" he asked.

"Communist."

When Vinny asked for the price, the rent was 100 Reichsmarks less than his housing allowance, and he grinned at the savings.

As he tendered the money, her face brightened to a smile. "Give me a couple of days to clean and air it."

"My turn to report," Zelly said.

They followed the map to Hitler Youth headquarters. The eight-story building was draped in red, white, and black bunting hanging from the top terrace to the cantilevered second floor. As they walked in, lobby speakers played youthful voices singing *Fahnenlied*, the HJ banner anthem. Zelly's heart fluttered with excitement at the song. He'd first heard it during training in San Antonio and loved it.

"I'm Scharführer Frederich Zellner from Wittenberg, Bann 356, returning from an exchange."

The BDM lady took his achievement book and letter from Italy before checking a clipboard. "Leader Koch wants to see you. Please wait."

Forty or fifty DJ boys, the younger branch of Hitler Youth, burst in. Their shouts about having visited Horst Wessel's grave in St. Nicholas's Cemetery echoed through the lobby. As Zelly waited, he shuffled through old magazines on a literature rack. One caught his eye—the March 1938 issue of *Hilf Mit!*

That's my picture featured on the cover! My Scoutmaster took it for my Eagle Scout Court of Honor program when I was fifteen.

How did it end up printed in a Nazi magazine two years ago?

They said they'd been watching you.

For how long?

The chaos provided a moment, so he stuck the page in Vinny's face.

Vinny's eyes grew with surprise. "That's you!"

"Look, right now, I'm expecting some explanations." He folded the newsprint and stuffed it in his trousers under his shirt.

The Army lied, and so did Vinny. This mission didn't happen as they said.

How could you be so stupid? Believing everything the butcher, baker, and candlestick maker said.

As the DJ boys collected grave-site pilgrimage stamps, Zelly's anger boiled. When they left, peace came to the lobby but didn't calm him.

I wanted freedom and adventure—no milking cows and baling hay.

And they used it against you, playing you like a fiddle.

What can I believe?

You shouldn't trust anything.

The lady called Zelly's name and guided him to Koch's office. After stepping inside, he saluted. "Heil Hitler."

Koch offered a handshake. "Welcome back, and a late happy birthday. If you had spent those two years in Germany, your rank would be higher."

"Sir, the SS is what matters now."

He opened the achievement book to the pages documenting promotion and scribbled and stamped. Next, he placed two silver bars in the fold. "Congratulations, Herr Oberscharführer."

"Thank you."

He punched holes in the letter from Italy and added it to the brads in Zelly's file. "This is quite a commendation. It says the Bannführer asked you to spy on your host."

Zelly nodded. "I lockpicked his diplomatic pouch."

"You'll thrive in the SS."

With the meeting concluded, they took a train to Kaiserhof and chose a corner coffee shop. As they sat at a table for two, Zelly pulled out *Hilf Mit!* and shoved it between Vinny and his cup.

"How's life, cover boy?" Vinny joked.

"Finding this made it beyond disturbing." He browsed it, discovering stories about Madagascar and lions and essay contests. "I can't tell the truth from all the lies."

"In spy work, they blend, don't they? And you're mastering the recipe."

Zelly pounded his fist on the picture. "I was only fifteen. Have you researched me for years?"

"Not me. I was building background in the Foreign Ministry at Rome."

Zelly's stare was hard. "That was a plural you—you, the butcher, baker, or candlestick maker?"

"Nice metaphors from the nursery rhyme." Vinny chuckled. "First time I've heard you use it."

Vinny's laughter pushed Zelly beyond his ability to cope. Gripping Vinny's wrist, he pulled him across the table until the Roman nose touched his. A flicker of fear crossed Vinny's eyes. "Answer my fucking question. Did they think I wouldn't discover this?" Rolling the booklet, he thrust it like a sword against Vinny's chest. "This was going on longer than I've been told or even guessed."

Vinny dropped his chin and fixated on his coffee cup, but Zelly perceived the truth in his eyes.

Upon their return to the Adlon, the desk clerk waved and handed them envelopes, each with their names written in flowing calligraphy. Inside, Zelly found an invitation to Fasching, German Mardi Gras, set for tomorrow night in the hotel's ballroom.

He punched Vinny's shoulder. "Congratulations, Herr Diplomat, you've made the embassy's social circle." Near the bottom, the invite called for formal uniforms. "Mine is too shabby."

The clerk passed him a business card for Wertschers at Friedrichstrasse 165. "The gentleman who delivered those expected the problem. You have a fitting at 2:30—go in uniform."

They got haircuts from the hotel barber, walked Unter den Linden, and located the store a few doors away.

When Zelly flashed the card, the salesperson started measuring him. Soon, the mirror's reflection showed a new Hugo Boss outfit and a wardrobe of underwear, socks, and shoes at his feet.

"Is there a rental fee?" Zelly asked.

"No, someone settled the account."

On the route to their room, Zelly pulled Vinny into a dark alley. "Is my secret benefactor you, or is it the embassy?"

Vinny's head wagged. "Neither. Some powerful person has become interested in you."

Who? I'm trying to follow orders—fit in and be a perfect little Nazi.

No, you're not. You should have stomped on the baby's head.

He was innocent. Not his fault he was Jewish.

He was a cockroach.

I'm amazed you thought that. You're not fitting in. You're joining them.

As Donovan hoped, some German has plans for me.

They don't know you. How could they?

I picked the lock. Spying isn't hard. I'm better than Mata Hari.

A French firing squad killed her for espionage—don't you remember the Greta Garbo movie? You could meet the same fate.

****

25 February 1941—The Tiergarten

As they approached the Adlon, Zelly's mind lingered on the old Nazi magazine and the lies. "Vinny, I need to consider things."

Vinny remembered the time in training when Zelly first confronted the stories of Jews in Germany. He took off on a sprint, and they found him hours later, passed out in a field ten miles away. "Then I'm going, too."

They dressed in athletic gear and jogged from the hotel through Brandenburg Gate. Soon, Zelly recognized the Reichstag from footage of the famous fire. They trotted along the Spree's banks, passing a small boat harbor and the central train station. At Schloss Bellevue, they turned on Spreeweg and went deep into the Tiergarten. The massive park grew progressively emptier. A path beside a thawing stream took them to a lake, where they rested on a bench.

The surroundings were cold, stark, and barren, yet beautiful for the promise of renewal and rebirth hidden within. They were alone—nobody walking nearby, no place a Gestapo agent could hide, only glassy water.

"Vinny, why did you lie?" Zelly asked, using English. The jumble of facts made little sense. His picture adorned the cover of a Nazi publication from years ago. Dr. Otto had mentioned a global conspiracy. One conclusion was obvious—Vinny and the butcher, baker, and candlestick maker have manipulated him. Who else is in the scheme?

"Lie? What lie?" One of the puppet masters asked, far too innocently.

"My scoutmaster takes a photo for my Eagle Award. Somehow, it reaches Berlin and appears in a magazine. Two years later, you, that's plural, recruit me. The timing is inexplicable."

Vinny's expression confirmed suspicion but contained an element of bemusement.

Instantly, Zelly hated him for it. The pain of betrayal coursed through his veins. He wanted to beat Vinny senselessly. Anger and frustration brought tears, but he refused to let Vinny see them. He sprang to his feet and ran.

Could Ma and Da be part of the cabal?

Your questions will linger, frozen like the Tiergarten.

Vinny chased after him. "Nothing has changed. You can't go home."

Zelly didn't hesitate; instead, he thought of a way to repay the anguish he felt. "I'll run to the Gestapo. Tell them you're recruiting me to be a spy. You'll never find me when I disappear into the city, but I'll come witness your execution. I'll go to war. One day, the lying fuck of a major will show up in my rifle's crosshairs, and I'll put a slug in his brain."

Zelly turned toward a park exit—the route to the secret police. He crossed a footbridge beside a statue of King Friedrich Wilhelm III.

Vinny had not closed the distance. "I never thought you'd be a quitter."

Tears hit like a thunderstorm. "I don't quit. Never have, no matter how daunting the task."

Zelly ran past the monument to the beautiful Queen Luise. When the monument appeared again, he realized he had circled a small island. At the bridge, he found Vinny waiting.

Vinny's face revealed panic and fear. "I'm sorry for the lies and things not making sense." His voice broke. "But, for six thousand miles, I'm the only one who cares about you. Your only friend. Don't run away from that."

Zelly froze as if he were the water in the stream when he remembered the story of the statues. The artist intended the sculptures to stand together, sharing a panoramic view. Instead, the city placed them on opposite sides of the water. Their purview was now separate but always connected.

Does truth exist, or is everything merely a perspective?

I need both truthfulness and friendship.

Zelly plopped on a bench and softened the wild anger consuming him. "I need a relationship that is both accurate and brotherly."

"I'll tell you what I know, but there's more to it. Some details may be hard for you to take." Vinny crossed the bridge.

Too tired for more fight and pain, Zelly said, "Go on."

Vinny joined him on the seat. "You've guessed some. After Kristallnacht, the American Ambassador to Berlin went home. Journalists sent back unbelievable stories of horror about the Nazi treatment of Jews. An exodus of Germans, like Bob and Carl, painted a gloomier picture. Planting a mole was a way to get unfiltered information. They chose you for your language fluency, whiz-kid electronics, and more. People groomed you for this mission—your scoutmaster, teachers, and coaches. The major lied about being able to use any blond-haired, blue-eyed boy. It was always you. Aren't you exactly what you pretend to be?"

"Was I born to do this? Were my parents in on the grooming?"

Vinny shrugged. "That I don't know, but doesn't Berlin feel like home? Minutes ago, you said you could disappear into the city, admitting as much."

How can he peer so deep into my soul?

You belong here. Almost like you've lived here all your life.

"Honestly, Vinny, I can't do this job—not terrible things like the Germans do." He shuddered at the memory of the innocent Jewish baby splattered on his boot and clothes.

"Follow Dr. Otto's advice. Lock Fred away, and don't release him until you reach home. Be Zelly, always."

"Doing it in training was hard and now it is nearly impossible. What if I had refused the mission?"

"Could you have? I think they had you before they even asked. Building your background—the documents in files, the family you'll meet in a few days, the magazine picture—took a long time to prepare. Don't waste the work. You can do this— whatever is required."

Zelly dried his tears. "I always want to do my best."

"The Scout Oath." Vinny curled an arm across his shoulders.

"On the day they recruited me, the major asked Ma for pictures of me at various ages. She gathered them too fast, like she had them ready to go in the Rexall drugstore sack." Suddenly, Zelly's sense of self and family shattered.

Zelly's life turned icy, like the landscape surrounding him. He doubted whether spring would ever thaw in his heart. "When my scoutmaster took that picture, he offered me a black neckerchief and sliding knot. He said they were particular for Eagles, but I'd seen no one wear them."

Vinny nodded. "Do you grasp the effort required to get the photo to Germany and make you a Nazi cover boy?"

Zelly wagged his head. "I'm cold. Let's finish this run."

When they jogged past the Propaganda Ministry where Herr Goebbels wove his web of lies, a thought struck Zelly—America's deck of falsehoods has the same cards. A short distance from the Adlon, they passed the British Embassy, vacant and shuttered by the war.

After returning to the room, Zelly undressed for a hot bath while Vinny turned on the radio.

With the sounds of music playing and water splashing, Vinny used Italian. "Even when you are alone, stay in character, and be what you pretend." He cupped his hands over his ears, warning of listening devices.

Zelly added bubbles from a bottle and settled in the foam.

Vinny removed his clothes and shared the tub. He pulled Zelly's ear to his mouth and whispered. "Here's the brilliance of their plan. Soon, you'll be in military training. New documents will replace many of your forged papers. That's why they sent a boy."

Vinny turned off the faucet, leaving the radio for background noise. "Are you angry at me?"

"Frustrated and depressed. Knowing the entire story might help."

"I had an old aunt who always said, 'Be careful what you wish for.'" Vinny pointed at the Hugo Boss uniform hanging on a hook. "You'll be the hit of the party."

"I wonder who my benefactor is."

"He… or she… will be the one who asks you for a favor."

****

25 February 1941—Berlin's Schöneberg district

Oskar Stengler woke in his tiny Berlin apartment. He had bought the flat in the summer of 1934 for a pittance, so he had a place to spend the night in the capital. As he dressed, he recalled the circumstances surrounding the purchase.

In the years before the Nazi rise, this district had been infamous for its seediness, including the building now housing his apartment. Once owned by the SA, it had survived the purge of the 'Brownshirts' during the Night of the Long Knives. That history lingered in its walls, an ironic backdrop to its current owner.

Oskar took a pinch of his apricot snuff and relished the sniff as the tobacco hit his brain. Slaloming through the hallway trash, he strolled to an underground stop at Nollendorfplatz and boarded a U-2 train. A delay convinced him to grab breakfast at Alexanderplatz before the ten-minute walk to his appointment.

When he entered HJ headquarters, the lobby was nearly empty. He provided his credentials to the receptionist. "I called last night."

"Zellner's file is with Leader Koch." She picked up the phone and dialed an internal number. "Gestapo agent Oskar Stengler is here to see you concerning Scharführer Frederich Zellner from Wittenberg." She looked up with a smile. "Shall I show you the way?"

"No need. I know the way." He found the office on the third floor and stepped in with a "Heil Hitler."

Koch echoed the salute. He waved the visitor to a chair, already positioned beside the open folder.

Oskar perused the document. "Do you find anything unusual about this HJ member?"

"Two years in Italy took him out of the HJ's normal structure. If he had stayed, I'd bet he would be commanding the Wittenberg boys."

"Wrong choice?"

"We let the boys choose something of interest. This one took to radio and electronics, earning the C-level certification. In all of Germany, we have less than fifteen guys of that caliber."

"I found his bag of parts in Brenner."

"I hope he explained his qualifications to you."

Stengler gave a curt nod and tapped the section for birth. "Is he really the son of a martyr, quasi-adopted by an aunt and uncle?"

"That's not unusual, but it is remarkable," Koch said. "We have more than one hundred boys and girls with martyred parents in the organization. Some of them have already gone to their duty. Every day, we enroll the children of prominent National Socialists. Zellner is on my calendar for this afternoon if you would like to meet him."

"I know where to find him." Stengler stood and parted with a handshake rather than a salute.

Leaving the building, he retraced his steps to Alexanderplatz. Since the U5 to Brandenburger Tor ran on a 10-minute cycle and he wasn't in a hurry, he chose a nearby Biergarten. While he enjoyed a creamy tomato soup, a small cheese and bread plate, and dark beer, he considered young Zellner.

His story has checked out, and he has an excellent, if not exemplary, record. Maybe he picked the exchange program to avoid the adopted family—abusive stepparents or feeling overworked on the farm.

Still, when my instinct triggers, my suspicion gets aroused. Why disobey my order? A witness saw him use the lockpick, so why not admit its purpose? Did he claim to kill a Jew to impress or distract me? Why lie about the scar? And why don't I remember him?

But matching issues arose just as easily. Can I trust my memory? I probably scared the piss out of him with my shouting and orders. In Italy, he wouldn't have had faced Gestapo yelling orders or much understanding of Jews. He called me on my accusation about the electronic parts and told the truth, which I've recently verified.

By the time he'd finished eating, the conundrums remained.

He caught the U5 to Pariser Platz and entered the Adlon's grand lobby. Of all the times he'd visited Berlin, this was his first time inside the city's cultural icon. Beneath a Murano glass chandelier, he wandered among dozens of armchairs and lounges and the overly-dressed crowd lounging around an elephant fountain. Though he doffed his fedora, he felt sure everyone pegged him as a Gestapo officer. The commercial wing turned away near the marble staircase, and he strolled it while gazing into the multitude of shops.

Soon, he spotted Frederich Zellner in the barber's chair and the young Italian diplomat waiting his turn. Sitting in an over-stuffed armchair across the hall, he lowered his chin and hat to leave only his eyes uncovered. The eerie feeling of disquiet returned. Something just didn't seem right.

But as he studied their camaraderie, the shared jokes and laughter, he decided they had bonded well in Italy. He rose, left the Adlon, and strolled down Wilhelmstrasse toward Gestapo headquarters.

Passing Albert Speer's New Reich Chancellery building, Hitler's seat of government, a sign drew his attention—Special exhibit: Martyrs of the National Socialist German Workers' Party. He veered through the massive two-story-high doors and followed the traffic to the courtyard of honor. The display started beneath a statue of a muscular man bearing a sword, a symbol of might and power.

Bronze plaques displayed pictures of fallen comrades alongside brief biographies. He hurried past the first fourteen men, all victims of the shootout between the Munich authorities and Hitler's Beer Hall Putsch. Their names and stories were familiar to him, having taught them for years. The next two also died in the uprising but at other locations. Soon, he arrived at the commemoration of Friederich Just. He stopped to study the plaque's photograph, but the detail wasn't sufficient for him to see a resemblance to the boy. The brief story was beneath.

With Adolph Hitler convicted of high treason and imprisoned at Landsberg Prison, ardent supporters attempted to free their leader. Friederich Just constructed homemade explosives for that purpose. Using information from a visitor to Hitler's cell who had paced off the distance along the outer wall, Just found the location and put the bomb at the precise spot. When Just connected the timer, the device exploded and killed him. The blast did only minor damage, blackening some bricks in the resulting fire. It was later determined he had placed the explosives on the wrong wall. Anyway, he gave his life to free the Führer.

****

Stengler chuckled at the comedy of errors in the tale—like father, like son.

CHAPTER 3

Investigation

**26 February 1941—Fasching at the
Adlon Hotel Ballroom**

For Fasching, the Adlon's ballroom gleamed in gold, green, and purple, overshadowed by the red, white, and black swastika flags that covered the walls. The men were dressed in uniform—a Soviet general had metal stars and sunbursts from belt to golden shoulder boards, while the Japanese ambassador's tuxedo and tails featured a sash dangling a pair of samurai swords.

The ladies dazzled in splendid evening gowns. One, in a cream-colored dress with a short train, caught Zelly's eye. Her bodice was strapless, and her breasts hid behind an ermine stole. Another, in a long milky gown covered with blue chiffon ruffles, was his favorite. A pearl choker adorned her neck, from which a tear-drop diamond of incalculable worth hung.

I'm embarrassed to be so young—the only Hitler Youth uniform present. The only boy among the nation's rich and powerful.

And an American.

Tables were scattered across the room, piled high with dozens of hors d'oeuvres and champagne flutes stacked in pyramids. Vinny approached the leggy Italian Embassy receptionist and secured his date. Not in a partying mood, Zelly played the wallflower. Still troubled by his appearance on the cover of a Nazi magazine, he braced for a shitty evening. He carried a plate of delicacies and two flutes and made his way to a distant chair.

Soon, a trumpet blared, and a man announced, "Ladies and gentlemen, dinner is this way."

Amidst the shifting crowd, Zelly couldn't spot Vinny. He joined the reception line and learned that people shook hands instead of saluting.

At the line's start, he offered his name to the gentleman, and the man introduced him to the first dignitary. "Doctor and Frau Goebbels, may I introduce Herr Frederich Zellner?" He bowed.

"HJ," Magda Goebbels remarked at the uniform. "Helmut, my five-year- old, wants to join."

The doctor spotted the martyr's pin. "I don't remember a martyred Zellner."

"Friederich Just was my father. He died when I was a baby."

"I recall him. Perhaps I'll do a story about you." He passed Zelly to a man he recognized from newsreels.

"Reichsführer." Zelly made another bow.

Heinrich Himmler extended his hand with a laugh. "Ah, here is the boy with the English book, radio parts, and a strange tool."

Zelly's jaw dropped, but he shook hands without missing a beat. "You know?"

"I keep myself well-informed." He turned to the lady beside him. "This is Emmy Göring, wife of Kamerad Hermann. She is this evening's hostess." She was the one with the blue chiffon ruffles over her white gown.

"A pleasure to meet you," Zelly said before his brain blanked and his hormones said, "You're beautiful."

Her smile was radiant. "And you're a handsome rascal." When he blushed, she touched his cheek with her gloved hand. "Mein Liebchen, I didn't mean to embarrass."

"Nor I to be so forward."

"Perhaps a cavort later to atone?"

He bobbed his head like an excited puppy.

Dinner featured roast duck. The Pinot Noir churned in his stomach as his mind lingered on Stengler's conversation with Himmler about the English book. During dessert, Dr. Goebbels delivered a brief speech.

After the meal, Adalbert Lutter's orchestra filled the ballroom with music. Zelly took a wallflower chair in a back corner and continued sulking as Vinny spun and swirled with Ambra.

He brought her over. "She would like a twirl with you."

A pity dance—the thought worsened his mood. "Listening is fine." Her frown reminded him of his manners. "Fräulein, it'd be a pleasure."

The band struck up *Bel Ami*, and they danced the foxtrot. She was an excellent dancer, and they flowed with elegance and sophistication, parting the crowd. They promenaded with an underarm turn and a corner grapevine.

"Thank you." He returned her to Vinny with a bow.

When a tap came on his shoulder, he turned to find Dr. Goebbels. "My wife would like a trip around the floor with you. She admired your skill."

As he took the Frau in his arms, she whispered, "With his foot, my husband finds dancing difficult."

The musicians played another Rudi Schuricke song.

What small talk do you make with a Reichsminister's spouse? He said what popped into his mind. "My first visit, and I love

Berlin. The city is so vibrant and alive. The Tiergarten must be spectacular in spring."

"I share your sentiment, but some don't. Margarete Himmler hates these social events."

"Why would someone not enjoy a party?" When the music stopped, he escorted her to the doctor. "Your delightful company was a pleasure."

Other ladies fancied cavorting. It was considered improper for them to ask; rather, always, a man asked on behalf of his wife, fiancée, girlfriend, or acquaintance. A Luftwaffe Major came beside Zelly. "A lady requests you as a partner." He followed the officer to Emmy Göring's chiffon ruffles.

She took his hand. "It's time to twirl with a handsome rascal." The band struck up *Bum! Bum!*

"Your party is as wonderful as you are beautiful," he said.

"Your skill and attractiveness are the talk of the evening. Oh, you've blushed again."

"Soldiers shouldn't blush."

"It's a part of your alluring charm. Give yourself a few more years?" "What convinces you I'm such a scamp?"

She winked. "Intuition. I'm sensitive."

The music broke into a faster jazz beat.

"Have you ever danced swing?"

Her eyes grew narrow. "Teach me?"

He swung her on a tuck-turn, and she responded. Next, he tried a swing- out roll. In a reverse underarm, the ceiling mirror ball reflected on the tear- drop diamond dangling from her neck. A kaleidoscope of colors played before his eyes. He wrapped her in a cuddle. Repeating the sequence, she followed every step. On the hold, a flashbulb popped, blinding him with white. A photographer had snapped their picture.

When the music stopped, Emmy floated away. He snatched a drink and some cookies and returned to his seat.

Vinny clapped his back. "Buddy, you've cut a broad swath at this party." Taking a knee, he frowned and switched to Italian. "Remember at Gruene Hall when you taught Carlotta a dance?"

Zelly blanched. She realized he wasn't German. Did Emmy come to the same conclusion as they danced steps prohibited for being Black and Jewish?

****

27 February 1941—Berlin

Oskar Stengler left his Schöneberg apartment, heading for Potsdamer Platz. In passing a magazine stand, he spotted a picture above the fold of the *Morgenpost,* Berlin's morning newspaper. The photo stopped him in his tracks, and he bought the paper. It was from last evening's Fasching party, but the surprise was that it showed Zellner dancing with the wife of Hermann Göring, the commander-in-chief of the Luftwaffe and possibly the second-most-powerful man in the Reich.

The kid gets around. Doesn't he?

He took the issue and ducked into a phone booth. When the circuits connected him to Heinrich Müller, he spoke. "Heil Hitler, Stengler here. Have you seen the morning news? The boy we discussed is on the front page, prancing with Frau Göring."

"She was the hostess for the event. I was there, but gyrating to some jazz bars isn't grounds for arrest."

"The official tale of martyr Just doesn't mention a baby."

"I've mentioned your curiosity to Himmler and gave him a copy of the paper. He would like to discuss the matter with you. Can you drop by the office tonight around six?"

"Sure." When he disconnected, he hopped a train toward central Berlin.

I wonder what happened to Just's wife?

He disembarked the coach at Friedrichstrasse station and quickly slipped into a drugstore to grab a pocket tin of aspirin. Purchasing a cola-flavored Fanta from the cooler, he swallowed two tablets and hoped his headache would subside before he had to return to meet Himmler. As a lowly SS officer from the hinterlands, he'd never met the Reichsführer but recognized the man's ruthless reputation.

Continuing south, he used his Berlin visit to buy presents for the family. An American Formfit Life bra and panties for his wife. A scale model of Unterseeboot 29 for his youngest son, Heini, and a used set of books by Edmund Kiss for Max, an HJ Streifendienst who hoped to follow his father's example to the Gestapo.

A revolving turntable in a photography store's window caught his eye. It displayed a miniature Minox Riga, a tiny device that would fit in a palm and easily slide into a pocket. Intrigued, he entered, and the salesperson convinced him he had to own one. He knew what picture he wanted to take first—Zellner's scar.

With his shopping complete, he strolled to Prinz-Albrecht-Straße 8, Gestapo headquarters. Local officers occupied every desk, so he borrowed a corner. He beckoned a clerical worker. "Would you wrap these presents for me? And bring me the file for the wife of Friederich Just, one of the party's martyrs. I believe her original surname was Bauer. He died in Munich, so that may be the best place to start."

"I'll make the calls, sir," the young lady said.

He wandered through the building until she returned with the gift box and a thin folder.

"Marta Just, née Bauer, received the martyr's badge on the death of her husband. Their marriage was both short and tumultuous, with police responding several times."

"Was there a son?"

"He grew up in Wittenberg with his aunt, her sister, and uncle using the name of Zellner. His 18th birthday was last week."

Stengler frowned and took a pinch of snuff. "What happened to her after?"

"Originally, her family came from Austria, so she returned in 1924 after her husband's death. I called Vienna, but they have no records of Marta Bauer or Just."

"Perhaps she remarried shortly after her return," he speculated.

"Before the Anschluss, local parishes handled marriage data. The Bauers were from Freistadt in Gau Oberdonau. I spoke with the Gauleiter and the priest at St. Catherine's, but neither had information to provide."

"So, a dead end?" Stengler scowled.

The lady shrugged. "You might get more from the sister in Wittenberg."

Stengler took his package to the mailroom and shelled out Reichsmarks for postage.

****

27 February 1941—Adlon Hotel

Vinny woke to a noise at their room door. When he investigated, he found a newspaper. After one look at the front page, he tossed it to Zelly. "You made the cover again."

He groaned at the photo and flashed Vinny a look of worry. Publicity isn't healthy for a spy.

"You could have been a less skillful dancer."

Zelly nodded to admit the mistake.

They packed their suitcases and moved to the Kreuzberg apartment, leaving behind the comfort of the posh hotel for a sagging double bed and a hot plate. A vase of blue and white cornflowers sat on top of the piano, a housewarming present from the downstairs lady. Above the radiator, she had added the official portrait of Hitler.

The apartment's radio wouldn't work, but Zelly's skill and parts from his bag fixed the problem. He shelved the Leica camera, a gift from Carlotta, beside the set. The device had taken each photo in his album, proof any photography expert would accept without question. He thought of the snapshot Stengler had kept with concern.

Evidently, he reported the English book. Did he report the picture, too?

Your mistakes bring you one step closer to a firing squad.

But Emmy Göring wanted a dance. Refusing would have been a mistake.

But why swing?

They spent the day setting up housekeeping.

****

27 February 1941—SS Headquarters

At six in the evening, a lieutenant escorted Oskar Stengler to the back stairway and pointed him toward the back entrance of Reichsführer Heinrich Himmler's office. They met in a small antechamber of a larger room. Clicking his heels, Stengler's arm rose in the required salute, his movements precise, almost mechanical.

Himmler acknowledged it with a tired nod and waved at a chair. "I encountered your young man at Fasching and didn't find him suspicious."

"Did he lie to you? Disobey one of your orders? I was the only Italian teacher in Wittenberg. He should have been in my class, and I remember every student, but not him. And that scar isn't two years old."

Himmler smiled to calm his guest. "I'm sure you are investigating. Have you turned up anything?"

"His life story seems to check out."

"I knew his father in the early days. I met Marta, his wife, and held the baby."

"Do you know what happened to her?"

"To me, the boy has his father's chin and eyes."

"Still, I find something off-kilter about him."

"And I intend to give you the chance to investigate."

Stengler's heart skipped a bit at the opportunity. He pictured having the kid confined in one of the building's basement cells. Making him suffer and inflicting scars worthy of a man. One thought dominated, though, viewing the exposed testicle dangling outside the sack.

"He'll be here in minutes because I have a use for him. Stay in this room and listen, but don't reveal your presence." The Reichsführer hurried through the interconnecting door and closed it.

****

27 February 1941—Vinny's Kreuzberg Apartment

As Zelly and Vinny ate a hotplate dinner of brats, the recently fixed radio played Adalbert Lutter's *Schottenparade.* The screeching tires from the street cut through the music, prompting Vinny to peek from the window at the darkening avenue. "Gestapo—stopped below with soldiers."

Zelly turned down the music's volume and listened to the footfalls on the stairs reverberating like kettledrums. He prayed the boots would continue beyond their floor. When the drumming switched to pounding on their door, Vinny went as white as the sheets once covering the furniture.

Zelly's anxious gaze locked onto Vinny. With heart racing and sweat pouring, he answered the door. Six Waffen-SS and a sergeant wielding a machine gun bulldozed through, crowding the cramped sitting room. He snapped to attention and saluted. "Heil Hitler."

A plain-clothed officer sauntered into the room. "Papers, please."

"I'm an Italian diplomat." Vinny held his passport out like a Catholic cross to ward off evil.

"My identification is in the bedroom." Zelly pointed.

"Fetch them," the agent ordered.

The gunner shadowed him closely. When he pulled the documents from his uniform pocket, the man grabbed them and hurried toward his superior.

The agent compared them to his orders. "You will come with us."

Zelly glanced at the upright piano—the resting place of the newspaper and a symbol of the Gestapo's arrest of the previous resident.

Worry covered Vinny's face. "I'll come, too."

"This is not one of your diplomatic parties."

Zelly donned his tunic and followed the squad downstairs, passing the old lady who clicked her tongue.

A soldier pushed him into the back of a black Mercedes waiting at the curb. The sergeant took the seat beside him with the machine gun's barrel poking Zelly's hip. As the soldiers piled into a long-bed truck, the officer sat in front.

Zelly's list of mistakes cluttered his mind. *The English book, dancing swing, the newspaper's picture, stolen photo, a wrong answer, hesitating to kill the baby, forged documents?*

The car screeched to a halt at SS headquarters, a tall and intimidating building as the architect had desired, with arching windows on the lower floors. Once inside, Zelly was struck by a cathedral-like atmosphere, the high ceiling and arched support beams, but employees hustled through the halls. A staircase confronted him. Years of foot traffic had worn valleys into the stone steps, more going down than up.

Instinctively, he expected offices to be up, and dungeons and torture chambers were down. His fate hung in a simple change of elevation.

When the squad climbed to the second floor, Zelly sighed with relief. He marched the marble flooring in the escort's cadence to a wide doorway opening to a business center. Uniformed men and women, not much older than he, worked at file cabinets and typewriters. They didn't glance away from their jobs as the guards took him to the next entry. The agent instructed, "Inside."

When he entered, the door's closing pushed the knob into his spine. A smallish man huddled over a writing table. "Herr Reichsführer, Heil Hitler."

The man lifted his eyes from his work and appraised Zelly with dark blue eyes behind rimless glasses. "In the SS, we drop 'Herr' and use only the rank. You'll learn our customs, won't you?"

"I hope so, Mein Reichsführer. Before I went to Italy, I enlisted. My training comes soon."

"Aren't you certain?"

"It's possible I'm not acceptable. Gestapo Agent Stengler claimed I must document two more generations on my father's side, but getting the information may be impossible. He's dead, and I haven't seen my mother since she took me to live in Wittenberg."

"You introduced yourself to Doctor Goebbels at Fasching as the son of Friederich Just." Himmler's eyes fell on the martyr's pin on Zelly's tunic. "I knew your father, and you have some resemblance. Your Ahnenpass, please." Zelly produced the booklet.

Himmler found the blank pages and scribbled, speaking what he wrote, "I was a friend of this young man's father and grandfather. His father was an original party member, martyred for the cause. His racial purity is unquestionable." He signed and affixed his stamp.

"Sehr dankbar, Reichsführer." Zelly's smile gleamed.

Himmler rose, took Zelly's shoulder, and led him to a settee. "Formality isn't necessary." He touched the badge. "Truly, your father was a comrade in the first days, and I'm glad you honor him. You're a Sohn der Bewegung and represent the future of the Fatherland."

Reddening at being called a 'son of the movement,' Zelly said, "The pin is all I have of him."

"You are dashing in the Wertschers uniform. No wonder the ladies wanted a dance."

"Thank you." He recognized his benefactor.

Himmler strode to a side door and opened it. Zelly wondered if someone was beyond and listening to the conversation.

Returning to the couch, he sat and crossed his legs informally. "May I inquire about a delicate matter?"

"Reichsführer, I'm yours to command."

"Oskar Stengler reports you bear a scar in a rather unusual place and that you lied about it."

Zelly blushed completely. "I made up a story from the Programs of 1938 because the Bannführer in Italy ordered me to never reveal the real circumstances."

"Does it apply to me?"

"I suppose not. While I was in Naples, I stood on the steps of Garibaldi's statue to view Rommel's Panzers driving through the city. A Jew from a step below took offense at my uniform. He yelled about how der Führer had sent his parents to a concentration camp. The lunatic reached up my shorts and grabbed my testicles. We fought. He scarred me, but I broke his back."

"Why not be truthful earlier?"

"The commandant feared mentioning the event might cause an international incident." Zelly rose and worked his belt buckle. "Would you like to see the scar?"

As Himmler laughed, his eyes danced. "No, I'd rather hear your impressions of Italy."

"I made a scrapbook."

When Zelly handed him the book, he glanced through the pages. "Mussolini's getting older and fatter."

"I had a glorious time. The host family's treatment was excellent. I visited places I'd only dreamed about, like Mount—"

Himmler's steel-blue eyes cut like razor blades. "What about the war?"

"Finding Panzers in Naples surprised me. From the desert paint, I guessed they were Rommel's."

"Your file says you once met him."

"It was at summer camp, but I doubt he'd remember."

"I read his letter about you. Why was the armor unexpected?"

"I expected them in Genoa because of a rumor about a German harbormaster. So, I went to the city."

"And what did you find?"

"A British fleet attacking them. I guess somebody hoaxed the Brits."

A grin formed beneath Himmler's glasses, and his laughter was like a schoolgirl's giggle. "I enjoy keeping the old bulldog off the mark. What did you glean from the crowd watching the Panzers?"

"Swastikas were everywhere, and the Germans cheered and waved, but the Italians glared with tired eyes. Sometimes, my uniform made them rude, like it provoked the Jew to attack."

"What do they think of the war?"

"They were furious when the *HMS Sollum* sank and killed Italian prisoners. The bombing and shelling of Genoa caused dismay. I think the people are weary of conflict."

"I have a snapshot, too." After wiping a smudge from a lens, Himmler retrieved it from a desk.

Zelly gazed at the picture, recognizing himself standing on Garibaldi's statue and waving at a tank. He chose a portly man on the step down from him. "That's the Jew I fought. Did a Panzer driver take this?"

Himmler nodded. "I know something else about you."

Zelly felt his heart cratering as a basement visit loomed. He expected soldiers to rush him through the open door. "What, if I may ask?"

Himmler's smile turned coy. "You spied on your Italian comrade."

Zelly blushed, wondering how much he already knew. "An officer from the German embassy in Rome asked me to keep tabs on what the Italian foreign service was doing. I did, and on the way to Berlin, I picked the lock on my friend's diplomatic pouch."

Himmler's eyes sparkled with mischief. "What did you discover?"

"Most of the papers were uninteresting, but one promised the Italians would join in a campaign against the Balkans and Greece."

His blue eyes deepened. "Ribbentrop has mentioned nothing. What makes you sure?"

"The paper gave a date—April 6th."

Himmler's grin spread. "You risked the anger of your friend?"

"He never suspected."

He patted Zelly's knee. "Well done. It is one reason you are here. Once you complete the training, we will have many opportunities to share secrets. I have an extraordinary favor to ask."

"Anything, Reichsführer."

"I will have you posted at a place of interest but where I have little authority. You can keep me informed of events and activities there."

Zelly nodded. "You mentioned one cause for my presence. Are there more?"

"When I learned of the English book, I had your file pulled. You finished gymnasium early, are C-level in signals, love electronics, and are unknown."

"I thought you summoned me for punishment since I didn't obey Herr Stengler's order to stomp a Jew baby."

Himmler detected the relieved sigh. "I have other people to handle the Jews. Can you tell me about radio detection and ranging?"

"You broadcast a beam at a specific frequency and listen for it to bounce from an object. The reflection is faint but predictable. The time between the sending and receiving allows one to calculate the range of the target and sometimes its altitude and speed."

"Invented by Germans."

"Of course, I've read the papers of Hertz and Hülsmeyer. They used enormous and expensive antennas to pick up the weak signal. The English book follows a fresh approach, amplifying the data and eliminating noise, making things smaller and cheaper."

A gleam came to Himmler's eyes. "You are the one."

Too many people have plans for my future, Zelly thought. "Is that what I'll work on at your important place?"

"No, we're too far along to switch directions. I have another project of interest."

The door opened, and Himmler pointed. "Please keep this conversation between us."

Zelly nodded agreement but secretly yearned for details. *Don't press your luck.*

You're walking out despite odds to the contrary. He saluted, pivoted, and hustled outside. Without a car, he walked with footsteps of elation as his mind churned.

I'm an American spying on Germany. That turning cog spun another one.

You're a German snooping on the Italians. A third gear rotated.

I'm a spy for Himmler.

You have enough gears for a fucking clock.

Vinny's blackout curtain was askew, so Zelly assumed his friend was watching. He lingered at the curb, and within minutes, Vinny came down.

"What happened?" Vinny asked.

"Let's walk." Zelly led them south, beyond Berlin's southern gate, toward Halle. In history, this had been the only city entrance Jews could use. He stepped onto a park footpath along the Landwehrkanal's water and strolled beneath the elevated U-Bahn line, where the noise of passing trains masked their conversation.

"The benefactor is Reichsführer-SS Heinrich Himmler," Zelly grinned.

"What favor does he want? Snooping on me and the embassy?"

"After I'm trained, he'll send me somewhere to spy for him."

Vinny's eyes shot open. "You're in, man, deeper than the butcher, baker, and candlestick maker could have hoped."

A group of Heinkel He-111 bombers flew overhead, banking toward Templehof Airport. Zelly stopped and stared because flying had always been a life dream.

Vinny disturbed his reverie with a shoulder punch. "You have a mighty fish on your hook."

****

27 February 1941—SS Headquarters

As soon as the outer door of Reichsführer's office closed, Stengler stepped from an antechamber where he'd been. "You're placing a lot of trust in the kid."

"He's perfect for my plans. I find nothing suspicious about him, and he covered the lie."

"Well, that wasn't all."

Himmler shrugged. "Continue to develop a full profile on the boy. When he completes training, I'll need a courier to move information between us."

"I'd like to stay on the case."

"Very well. Prepare your family for deployment in the Baltic."

Oskar saluted and left. He called his wife and told her about the transfer.

"You sound pleased with the new assignment," she said.

"Finally, they'll realize my skills are more valuable than luggage searches. Give my love to Max and Heini. Presents are on their way. I miss you."

He checked out a car and driver for the impending trip to visit the Zellner farm in Wittenberg. On the drive to his apartment, he felt a tingling sensation on his scalp. Something unsettling lurked just beneath the surface of his thoughts. A minor detail concerning the scar emerged. At Brenner, Zellner said he'd killed the Jew with his HJ knife, but he told Himmler he broke the Jew's back. His lies persist, and I'll expose each of them.

CHAPTER 4

Wittenberg

28 February 1941–The Zellner Farm

Two hours into the drive from Berlin, Oskar Stengler turned the 1938 Volkswagen onto Wittenberg's Dresdener Strasse. He planned to visit the Zellner family two times. Today, he wanted to meet the boy's aunt and uncle and then return after his arrival by train tomorrow. He found the steep driveway with an open gate and parked near the house. The structure was two-story with dormer windows upstairs, a wrap-around porch, and gingerbread trim along the eves. It could have benefited from some carpentry work and paint.

A German Shepherd stood on a small hill between the car and the front door. With ears raised and hackles up, the dog stared at him and tilted its head. As he opened the door, the animal bared its teeth and snarled. Oskar stopped movement and honked the horn, making him bark.

When a lady came to the door, he rolled down the window. "Can you chain him?"

"Here, Rolf," she said. When he moved beside her, she fastened a clip to the collar. Though he quieted, he continued to stand and stare.

Oskar climbed out. "You have a beautiful view of the Elbe River." It was still majestic, even though it was muddy brown. Across the water, a golden meadow spread as far as the eye could see.

"Frau Zellner, I am Oskar Stengler of the Gestapo. Your son, Frederich, is joining the SS. I'm preparing some documentation and would like to ask you some questions. I assure you, nothing is out of the ordinary."

"My husband is in the fields," she said.

"The first question is for you. Do you know the current location of your sister, Marta?"

"She is dead, killed in a crash on mountain roads in Austria, but that is only by rumor. I haven't seen or heard from her since she left him here eighteen years ago."

"What a shame because I must document a few genealogical details to begin your son's service."

"She was hardly a mother and was never happier than when she abandoned the baby. We gave him our name and loved him as we could, but he was only interested in making electronic things and going on adventures."

"When was that?"

"For his whole life," August Zellner said as he came around the house. "He went to Italy on the HJ exchange program two years ago, leaving me to handle the farm by myself."

"Do you have pictures?"

"The parlor wall is her shrine to the boy," August opened the door to allow the agent inside.

About two dozen portraits adorned the parlor's flowery wallpaper. One caught his attention—a large close-up of the boy. It matched the kid he met at Brenner Pass but was maybe three years younger—his age as an Italian student. The jaw was softer, the cheekbones and brow were less prominent, and the shoulders were more rounded.

"When and where was this taken?" Oskar was certain he'd never seen this face in his class.

"In Halle at summer camp when he was fifteen, only a few months before Italy."

Oscar scanned the other photos, finding a blond-haired kid of all ages ranging from the cradle through puberty. He pulled out a small camera and snapped pictures of the parlor wall. "I believe I was his teacher at the gymnasium, but don't remember him. Was he always interested in electronics—maybe instead of his Italian lessons?"

"Two years away is so long, and I worry I won't recognize him when he arrives," she said.

"He always shirked his chores," August said. "I needed him on the farm but lost."

"Shame on you," she scolded. "He sacrificed for the Fatherland—as you did in earning the Honour Cross. We are proud of him."

"I'm curious about how he got that name. Few nicknames come from shortening the last."

"You realize he came to us with a different one—Just," she said. "We told him his entire story so he would know about his father, the martyr."

"As he learned to talk, he combined them in a rhyme—Zelly Jelly," August said.

Stengler realized he would have to search elsewhere for clues.

****

1 March 1941—Zellner Family Farm

The next day, Zelly's train arrived at Wittenberg's whitewashed station. After stepping off, he bought a pretzel with mustard from a cart. The dread of the impending visit weighed heavily on him. He'd meet Uncle August and Aunt Freida Zellner, the ones who raised him but had never seen him. He had a colossal question— Why have they risked the Gestapo's wrath to join an enormous conspiracy? Every thought of the huge cabal controlling his life was terrifying.

He gripped his suitcase and followed the directions provided by Bob and Carl. Rushing across the tracks, he entered the cemetery among the tombstones and linden, beech, and oak trees. His path through the burial grounds paralleled the street and the banks of the Elbe River toward the farm. The red stone cathedral in the cemetery's center hosted a funeral service as he strolled. He climbed a small hill and gazed over the river to a golden meadow. At the tip of the river's bend, he spotted his home. The two-story house was nearly identical to the one in Texas.

Ma and Da didn't leave Germany. They built a part of it in the States.

Before leaving the graveyard, he stopped at the Zellner plot to find two generations of pretend ancestors lay. Soon, he turned up the farm's driveway toward the gate, where a barking German Shepherd met him.

He hesitated, figuring the animal would maul him the instant he entered his territory. Still holding a few bites of pretzel, he tossed it to the dog.

A strange touch of cold came over him—not unusual for March, but the sun shone warm, and the air was full of spring. The hairs on the back of his neck stood at attention, but he shook it off. The canine bounded up, sniffed, and sat, blocking the entrance.

He reached over the gate and scratched the dog's ears. "It's nice to meet you, boy."

The hound lunged at him, but the tongue was out and reaching for kisses. "Why are you so friendly? Do you think you recognize me?"

When he stepped onto the lawn, the dog tackled him and showered him with affection.

"Rolf, save a piece of him for me." His aunt rushed down the steps. As he rose, the stocky woman who reminded him of Ma engulfed him in her blue gingham dress.

"Hello," he said.

She planted a huge kiss on his cheek. "We've been expecting you and are so glad you're home." Her embrace took him to the porch with the canine beside him. He couldn't decide what to say. For her, this could be a performance, but not for the animal.

She guided him through the aroma of cinnamon apples to her warm, homey kitchen. A basin of soapy water waited on the counter, so he rolled up his sleeves and began scrubbing the dishes. Everything felt like his Texas farmhouse.

She grabbed a towel and dried. "I can't wait to hear about Italy?"

"This evening, Mutter? Where's Väter?" He froze at his words as he'd planned to call them aunt and uncle.

"He's cleaning the barn. Getting too old for a farmer's life."

"Berlin is a spectacular city teeming with life. I stayed at the Adlon and went to a party in its ballroom. The Tiergarten was beautiful in winter, but I bet it's glorious in the spring, full of flowers and boats on the lake. I danced with Frau Göring and met people like the Goebbels family and Heinrich Himmler."

She stiffened at the National Socialist name-dropping.

With the dishes finished, he dried his hands. Like in Texas, work clothes hung from pegs beside the back door. "May I help Väter?" He removed his shoes and stripped off his shirt and trousers.

A farm mother would have seen her boy in underwear a thousand times.

But you're not her son.

Could be I am...

The overalls, jacket, and boots were small, making Zelly curl his toes. He headed to the barn, and the dog came running when the screen door banged.

"Rolf, you're strange," he said. The Shepherd winked like he was the weird one.

He worked with his uncle, pulling muck from stall floors and separating the dung into a wheelbarrow. The man's hunched back and limp caught his attention. "Väter, I can do the rest."

August labored for breath as he studied Zelly's farming skill with a grin, amazed that the boy had so much experience. As Zelly washed the stalls, he tended the tack and rubbed cream into the saddles and collars. He stood in shock as the kid cleaned water buckets and repaired two managers.

While Zelly scattered the fresh straw, August checked outside to ensure their privacy. "Gestapo came yesterday."

Nonplussed, Zelly pushed the dung-filled wheelbarrow into the field, dumped the manure, and pitchforked it around for fertilizer. As he returned, he spied a white cross beside the barn—hidden and out of place. He investigated, but it bore no inscription. Rolf stretched nearby, and Zelly stopped to scratch the dog's belly. "Who's buried here?" The Shepherd kept his secrets.

August whistled, bringing horses at a gallop. With curry combs and brushes, they worked down opposite sides of each horse.

"Was it an agent named Stengler?" Zelly asked.

His father nodded. "He asked questions about your birth mother and studied your pictures in the parlor." Zelly poured oats while the man treated the team to carrots.

At sunset, they headed for the house. In underwear, they stepped inside and washed in the warm basin Mutter had ready.

"Not bathing in the Adlon, is it?" she asked.

"The hotel had a bathtub, running water, and bubble bath."

"Ah, to wash your entire body at once," Uncle August said as he reached for the soap. Zelly found the injuries that bent and hobbled him. His right side appeared withered, twisted, and scarred from his ribs into the boxers. Väter followed the gaze. "Want a war story?"

"If you don't mind telling."

"In 1914, the French attacked us in the Lorraine. We fought like devils, forcing them to retreat to Nancy. When we chased them, our army took a small corner of France. The next morning, they came to retrieve their land. A bullet hit me in the back, shattering my spine, and came out above my hip. I fell, unable to move, paralyzed. To make sure I was dead, the frogs bayoneted my belly." He showed the ugly triangular cut. "A day later, Germans took me to the field hospital for seven surgeries. What's left of me is the result."

Mutter tousled Zelly's hair. "Too soon, you'll be the old man showing your war wounds."

They ate in the kitchen and took the apple pie to the parlor's blazing fireplace. Zelly studied the wall of pictures as Stengler had. Some were from the Rexall prescription sack his Texas mother had provided. In the center was the Eagle Court of Honor/ *Hilf Mit!* portrait in a frame. Among the others, he found photos of a younger guy—not him, but a damned close resemblance. In one of those, the kid smiled from horseback as Mutter and Väter watched from the porch. In another, the pre-teen boy played with a German Shepherd puppy near the river.

Does the dog remember back that far? Does he mistake me for his owner?

Could you be him? Is this my actual family who sent me to America before I can recall?

The size of the conspiracy surrounding him grew like a tornado. People assisted him for personal reasons, and he was certain this couple had theirs.

She didn't like when you dropped the National Socialist names.

She could be a passivist. Whose cross sits beside the barn? A dead son might be a reason.

Zelly pointed to the radio. "May I find music?" When Väter nodded, he turned the dial until Rudi Schuricke sang *Bel Ami.* "Beautiful lady, care to dance?"

Mutter took his hand. "I haven't danced in ages."

"You've missed a boy to keep you in practice. I'm home now."

She laid her cheek against his shoulder as they traveled the rug. Her tears wet his shirt.

Before the song finished, a car in the driveway caught their attention, and she peered through the curtains. "Gestapo." A panicked gaze passed between them, but she held up her thumb and a finger.

When the engine stopped, Zelly shouted loud enough for those approaching to hear. "I'll get it." He greeted them at the door. "Heil Hitler and guten abend. My family is in the parlor."

An officer and an HJ patrol boy entered. They were father and son, duplicated at a three-quarter scale except for the cheek scar.

"Oberscharführer, welcome home," the youth said. "We require your presence tomorrow for field maneuvers with you commanding the signals squad. We'll meet at Melanchthon Gymnasium at nine and march to Brückenzott."

"Orders understood. I'm Frederich, but call me Zelly. I've been in Italy for years." He offered his hand. "Friends?"

The kid's lips curled upward. "Comrade, I'm Kris."

Zelly figured him at fourteen as they shook hands. "Mutter makes terrific apple pie. Would you like some?"

The Gestapo agent nodded his approval.

With his arm over Kris's shoulder, Zelly steered him to the kitchen. The boy sat in the chair draped by Zelly's HJ uniform tunic. Zelly plated a slice. "I suspect you don't remember me. When I left, you were about twelve, right? I'm afraid no one will recognize me tomorrow. Most boys my age already fight at the front, and I'll be there soon."

Kris winked as he chewed. "I'll know you, and I'm in command of the patrol." His finger touched the C-level badge on Zelly's uniform sleeve. "I've never seen this insignia. Our best signals, guys, are only A. Isn't learning codes hard?"

"It took years."

"How old are you?"

"Eighteen and ready for the SS."

Grinning, Kris licked the apple filling from his cheek. "The same goes for me, like my father."

"Want to view pictures from Italy? I made an album."

Kris flipped the pages. "Here's you with Mussolini and shooting a Mauser."

"Want a nasty picture?"

Kris's eyes matched his plate's size as Zelly handed him the shot with Vinny, Carlotta, Isabella, and him naked on a blanket. "That's my buddy who works at the Italian embassy in Berlin, and this was my girl, and the other was Vinny's."

"Sweet tits." Kris grinned like a fourteen-year-old boy, glimpsing forbidden things.

"Time to go," his father called.

"Thanks for sharing. Goodbye, Zelly."

"Until tomorrow. Heil Hitler."

As the car drove away, Zelly said, "Would you like to view my photos from Italy?"

As they peered at his pictures, he told tales of Italy. When the fire dimmed, they turned in for the night, and he found the way to his dormer bedroom. Someone had made the room fit his interests with a Hanna Reitsch poster, the German pilot, hanging over the desk. The bookcase held electrical experiments that were intricate but non-functional. Quilting stuff filled the armoire, proving no male had lived here for years. The furniture was small, with the bed ending at mid-leg.

On the desktop, he found the name Frederich Zellner scratched with the four E's backward. The dresser's lowest drawer pulled out, revealing a two- inch secret space beneath where he found a child's treasures—metal army men, a toy revolver, and a shot of Tom Mix's horse and dog. He hadn't reached his teen years, as the stash included no porn or smokes.

He grabbed his DJ book from the suitcase and headed to the parlor. As he had suspected, the picture inside matched the boy on the wall— meticulous work from that international conspiracy enveloping him. A particular image drew him—the kid and his puppy playing on the riverbank.

Is this where you died?

I did?

Us, we, you, and I—who can tell the difference?

Vinny said that Major Donovan mentioned a lucky break. Could my doppelgänger be it?

****

2 March 1941—Field Exercise

In the morning, Zelly made his way to Melanchthon Gymnasium, where the only thing that differed him from other boys was his souvenir Italian black beret. As expected, he recognized no one and waited alone under an oak.

"Zelly," Kris called from his father's open car.

Smiling and waving, Zelly greeted him when he climbed out. Several guys crowded around, making Kris appear popular. "Hey, everybody, Zelly's got pictures from Italy."

The album was an instant icebreaker when Kris opened it to the banquet picture. "Zelly met Mussolini. See?"

"What was he like?" One asked.

"Was he as smart as the Führer?" Another asked.

"Reichsführer Himmler says he's getting fat," Zelly said, and the group laughed.

Kris's jaw gaped with astonishment. "You've encountered the Reichsführer?"

"Two times, and he welcomed me home with a party." He bragged.

A BDM girl found the snapshot of Vinny pretending to throw Turtle into Vesuvius's cone. "Who's this handsome guy?"

"My Italian comrade who's throwing his cousin into a volcano— sacrificing a virgin to avoid an eruption."

"Then you have nothing to worry about, Inga," Kris said.

She blushed as strawberry as her hair. "Zelly, I don't remember you."

"My parents didn't either because I was in Italy for years. You know, puberty and growing and all. Would you like to see Vinny naked?"

When he extracted the picture, she nudged his side. "He's spectacular, and so are you." She passed the photo around.

"You're too old for an Oberscharführer," one boy said. "I'm fifteen, and I'm already one."

Zelly shrugged. "I guess it was the price of meeting Mussolini and seeing Vesuvius, but well worth it."

"You're Zellner, right?" Another said. "We played football together like ten years ago, but I can't remember the team's name. Do you?"

He's recalling my doppelgänger, Zelly thought but was clueless until he spotted an imperial eagle above the gymnasium door. "Wasn't it the Eagles?"

"The Junge Adler, I recollect now."

Another teen arrived, riding his bicycle, and Kris waved him over. "Fritz, look! Zelly qualified at C-level, and he'll command signals today."

"Shit, I've never seen that badge," Fritz said. "I busted my ass to make A, but I'm your man for anything you need."

The band bugled them into formation, and Zelly recaptured the album.

Kris took him to his squad. "Be careful with Inga. She gave me crabs." His crotch scratch proved convincing.

When the HJ formed up, the drummers rolled them into a song, and everyone sang.

> Wir Jungen tragen die Fahnen zum Stürme der Jugend vor.
>
> We boys carry the flags before the storms of youth.

When the music ended, the Bannführer announced a training exercise. Wehrmacht recruits were assigned to capture the Elbbrucke Bridge, south of Wittenberg, supported by a dozen Panzers. The Hitler youth were to delay their advance and deny them the river crossing. The command post was to be Brückenzott, where five roads converged. An artillery battery was available on the Elbe's opposite bank. The girls were to set up a field kitchen for lunch and a hospital for the wounded. Zelly's job was communications, including radioing shelling coordinates. The Bannführer asked, "Who'll stop them short of the Elbe?"

They answered with deafening shouts, using the song's first words. "Wir Jungen."

"Who will kill the enemy?"

"We boys."

The band played the song, and they sang and yelled at the top of their voices, "We boys."

Zelly thought he was invincible, like he could do anything. He remembered being drawn to the HJ by the movie *Hitlerjunge Quex* when he viewed it in training. The comradery pulled him; his heart yearned for it, and music swept him away. So, he shouted as loud as anyone, with pride covering his face as he strutted with strength and power. No wonder Germany mastered the continent.

Heute Europa, morgen die Welt—Today Europe, tomorrow the world.

The senior cadre leader summoned him to the map for tactical planning. Between Wittenberg and the Elbe lay two areas of land—the Stadtgraben, a marsh crosscut by a drainage canal, and Der Anger, a wooded hill. Five streets left the city, passed through the swamp and forest, and converged at Brückenzott. "Zelly, how can I learn which street they choose?"

The story of Paul Revere and North Church lanterns came to mind. "Leave a spotter behind, someplace high, with a telephone. He'll phone with the chosen route."

"Cranachhaus—the view is perfect," Kris suggested. "I'd love to be the guy."

"How can we communicate the right avenue to the rest of us?" the leader asked.

Zelly thought of cavalry bugle calls from the American Old West. "The band can play a different song to show which road." He thought of Paul Revere's horse. "The guys can ride their cycles to the enemy when they hear the music."

"But Panzers go faster than bikes."

"Hit the tanks first," someone suggested. "We've trained with Panzerbüchse and can pick off the armor in the Stadtgraben."

"My squad qualified as marksmen," another said. "We can ambush them in the forest."

As the meeting broke up, Zelly found Fritz. "Set up the radio near a telephone in Brückenzott and test it for relaying artillery coordinates."

The HJ marched to the market plaza, singing *Die Jugend Marschiert* with the band.

The sight of a shop urged Zelly to leave formation. Weathered boards, painted with black swastikas and marked with 'Juden,' covered the broken windows. Though someone had covered the shop's sign, he could read the original lettering—Gettler & Silberman Jewelry. Bob and Carl's family store. He remembered their tale of Kristallnacht and how he embellished it for Stengler.

Peeking through the cracks, he had an odd feeling, as though he had been there before —an unsettling moment of déjà vu. The display case where he'd once stolen two rings, stood the back door where the Jews had hidden. Dust enveloped everything except his eerie recollections. The young army continued to march and sing.

It can't be. I twisted their story into my own.

Just because you make it up doesn't make it less real. Things are always in perspective. Remember King Friedrich Wilhelm III and Queen Luise?

The senior cadre leader confronted him. "Why the fuck did you leave formation?"

"Memories—I looted this store in 1938."

"Get your ass back in line."

He hurried to his marching position and joined the song. They passed the Bannführer, who stood on the Melanchthon monument's second step. During the march, Kris slipped into the observation post. The Panzerbüchse squad took positions in the drainage ditch, snipers in the forest, and bike guys along the roads. Zelly went to the map to work out the artillery coordinates and designed a strategy.

Once preparations were complete, he helped Inga peel potatoes and slice carrots. As the stew simmered, they sunned on the Elbe's bank. He took off his shirt to enjoy the warm rays and cool breeze. She slid her hand across his flat tummy, bringing a grin to his face.

Many shirtless boys wrestled in the grass while others bet on the winners. Youthful laughter sounded over the water, not unlike the fun of Scout camping. They ate beside the Elbe.

"May I view the picnic picture again?" Inga asked and smiled when he provided it. "Could we be like this?"

"Aren't we?"

Her smile turned coy. "Only if you lose your shorts."

When the phone rang at Brückenzott, he ran to answer.

Kris reported. "120 strong, accompanied by four trucks pretending to be armor. They're turning south on Elbestrasse."

"Fritz, tell the band to play *Vorwärts*." Soon, the song for that street blared. "Tell me when they clear the intersection near the old city wall." He radioed the first artillery coordinates.

In seconds, the spotter said, "Now."

"Fire, please," Zelly ordered through the radio that connected them to the gunners. Down the phone's circuit, a judge's whistle sounded, declaring casualties.

"Kris, your work is excellent. Are the Panzers moving into the Stadtgraben?"

"Yes."

He transmitted the next numbers to the battery, hoping to attack simultaneously with the Panzerbüchse.

"We're slowing the advance." Kris's voice was full of excitement. When Zelly ordered the big guns to shoot, Kris shouted, "Dead tanks block the roads, but infantry is swarming the swamp, taking our comrades as prisoners."

"Tell me when the enemy reaches the forest." He gave the third target location, aiming for where the road split before entering the woods.

"They're at the trees," Kris said.

"Loose barrage three."

Kris giggled as the casualties increased.

The fourth volley aimed at a bridge crossing a small lake. Zelly radioed those coordinates and waited for the leader's signal to order the firing. Sensing their success, the band played *Fahnenlied*, the HJ banner song. The fifth salvo struck about 500 meters from their Brückenzott position. If the artillery was real, all hell would have broken loose at the forest's edge, but this was only pretend. Soon boys pedaled fast down the road, skidded to a stop, laid over their bikes, and dove into ditches. "They're close behind us."

In just a few minutes, fifteen infantry soldiers emerged from the trees with their helmets raised in surrender. The casualties followed them, and the judges declared the youth's victory. The Bannführer gave a speech, commending the cadre leader's gunnery work. Chocolate milk was distributed from the field kitchen, a welcome treat.

Marching to town, horseplay and high jinks predominated through the ranks while the HJ repeatedly sang *Wir Jungen*. Zelly yelled until he was hoarse, letting Wittenberg realize the boys had accomplished something. Euphoria seized him, like the seconds after catching the winning touchdown pass against Kerrville.

A Kübelwagen, the German equivalent of a Jeep, filled with the referees pulled beside him. "You were key to this triumph. Your spotter idea defined the tactics, and using the band's music for signals was exceptional. We will add a commendation to your file."

Recalling the advice to not stand out, he shrugged as he marched. "Kris was the hero."

"Have you graduated?" A judge asked. When Zelly nodded, the man said, "That makes you eligible for officer's training. Have you considered the Wehrmacht?"

"I'm pledged to the SS."

The man clicked his tongue. "They won't appreciate your talent, as you'll soon discover."

The Kübelwagen's driver glanced at Zelly. "You report in two weeks."

Ready to ask how he knew the schedule, he recognized Stengler behind the wheel.

****

3 March 1941—Wittenberg

Oskar Stengler parked the Kübelwagen at Wittenberg Gymnasium and marched to the office. "Herr Bischoff, please tell him Oskar Stengler is here." As he entered the headmaster's room, the loosely draped trouser leg flowing over the wooden chair's edge reminded him of the man's sacrifice.

"You're here for the transcript of young Zellner, I suppose. He was an exemplary student—among the top in science and quite proficient in sports." Bischoff pushed a folder across the desk.

The agent found the summary topping the sheaf of records. The headmaster continued his assessment. "You'll see his Arbitur scores on the third page. He finished school early for the exchange program. Even then, the needs of the Fatherland outweigh an education. When the HJ calls, the boys go."

Stengler had stopped listening when his eyes landed on the 1938 Italian class. The roster confirmed he was Zellner's teacher. "I don't remember the boy."

"His withdrawal means you had him less than eight weeks," Bischoff said.

"Are any of his other teachers still here?"

Bischoff scanned the list to be sure. "The Reich has called them to other duties. I'm surprised the government even bothers to keep the schools open."

Stengler exited and drove to his next stop, the mayor's house. The door opened as the Kübelwagen parked at the curb. The civilian official rushed to the porch, fawning as soon as he had saluted.

"I'd like to speak with your daughter, Inga."

She appeared at the door, still peeling a potato. "Sir, how may I help you?"

"Did you see the Zellner boy today—he goes by Zelly?"

She blushed and hid a smile behind her knife. "He's a dreamboat, and those eyes."

"Did you recall him from before he went to Italy?"

"Back then, I had little interest in boys, but his pictures of the trip impressed me. Kris already knew him, and another remembered him from a football team—the Junge Adler."

"Did he say or do anything strange while he was with you?"

"Not at all, but with a few more minutes, I would have had him out of his shorts." She caught her father's scowl.

"Thanks, fräulein. If you get him naked, I'd like to know what he says about the scar."

"Naked?" Inga's father shooed her into the house.

As Oskar drove to the Zellner farm, he spotted a rowboat on the far bank of the Elbe's great bend. Pulling to the side of the street, he trained his field glasses on the golden meadow to find three figures kicking a ball. He recognized them from the exercise. Zelly was the tallest, and the other two were Kris and Fritz. Rolf, the Zellner's German Shepherd, had taken the role of goalie. He watched for some time, noticing the close bond between them.

When he pulled into the family's yard, the housewife appeared on the porch. "Did you come to meet him? He's across the river."

"I would prefer to chat with you, Frau Zellner. Just a few more questions."

"Let me roust August from his nap." When she reappeared, she offered him a seat and a glass of water.

August Zellner scowled as he sat on the rocking chair. "Herr officer, what is the issue now?"

"When Frederich returned, did you notice anything different about him?"

"He's two years older, obviously," August said. "Strangely, he has become a hard-working man instead of the starry-eyed boy."

"He's grown up," Freida said. "The other night, he danced with me."

"Did he mention a scar?"

A worried expression crossed August's face. "No, is there something we should know?"

"I'm sure he'll tell you when the time is right. It's nothing important— a minor accident. May I check his bedroom?"

She led him upstairs. "Please ignore the quilting things. I used the room for sewing while he was away."

He took in the armoire quilts, electronic gadgets, and small-sized furniture. Pulling out desk drawers, he found the kid's stash, which included a partial pack of cigarettes and a cardboard box with two condoms and one missing.

Freida blushed as he examined the contraceptives.

"Thank you. I've seen enough." He went back to the Kübelwagen, stood on the seat, and watched the shirtless boys through field glasses. They lined up beside a tree to answer the call of nature.

****

In the golden meadow across the Elbe, Fritz, Kris, and Zelly enjoyed an outing. They'd talked about girls, how Kris caught crabs from Inga and Zelly's naked picnic in Italy. As they played football, Zelly spotted a Kübelwagen on the street. He missed a pass when the vehicle halted at his yard.

"Gestapo at my house," he said.

"That's not my father," Kris said.

Zelly assumed it was Stengler. He tried to keep his mind on the game, but the agent's presence kept him unnerved.

"Time for a piss," Kris said.

"Me, too." Fritz chimed.

Zelly joined the line, remembering to leave his foreskin extended like the other boys. They sprayed urine on an unsuspecting beech tree.

"He's watching us," Kris said. "Shall we give him a show?"

They shook off more vigorously than usual before gathering their stuff and rowing across the river.

On the riverbank, Zelly recognized the spot of the picture of little Frederich playing with the puppy. A sudden panic gripped him and wouldn't ease as terror rose from the water— fear his friends would push him in. Hit him. Drown him. Murder him.

Rationally, he knew the fear wasn't justified. He outweighed and out- muscled the pair besides being four years older. Neither could take him down easily, not even ganging up. He was a strong swimmer, though the Elbe would be damned cold. Still, he couldn't shake the dread.

As they approached the Kübelwagen, Zelly asked, "Herr Stengler, did you have a pleasant chat with my folks?"

Fritz asked, "See anything in your field glasses that interested you?"

Rolf snarled.

Kris asked, "Will you give us a ride to town?"

The officer gave a gruff nod.

Zelly scratched Rolf's ears as Stengler drove away with his friends.

A million questions crowded his brain, not just about Stengler's talk but also about his cover-story family. He headed for the door, prepared to ask some.

He opened the farmhouse door brim-full of queries, but they dissipated when he spotted his aunt's teary cheek and the slump of his uncle's shoulders. "Did he hurt you?"

"No, but any time the Gestapo comes is very unpleasant." She dried her eyes on her sleeve.

German men seldom express emotion, remaining strong through anything. A stoic expression dominated August's face, but he grabbed Zelly in a hug. His uncle's lips strained for his face but could only reach his neck. No man had ever kissed him except Da, and only when the Army staff car took him from home.

August trembled as he broke the smooch. "You must stop such evil."

"I will, Väter, I promise." Zelly's critical questions remained unasked.

CHAPTER 5

Training

16 March 1941—Bergen-Hohne

After two weeks with his family and friends, Zelly took an overnight train to Bergen-Hohne for what Americans would call basic training. When he boarded, the cars were half full, but frequent stops at dozens of villages and cities took it to standing-room-only. By dawn, the young men were packed in so tightly that every breath carried a foul stench.

The multiple thousands of recruits belonged to all services—the Kriegsmarine, Luftwaffe, Heer, and paramilitary organizations like the SS. When Zelly mentioned he had pledged to the SS, the mass of bodies edged away from him in fear—not that he minded. If he had a choice, he would have chosen the Air Force because his dream had always been to fly. But the butcher, baker, and candlestick maker—and conceivably Herr Himmler— had decided for him.

Upon arriving, loudspeakers blared the *Horst Wessel Lied,* a song as precious to the Nazis as the national anthem. They stumbled down the carriage steps as sergeants separated them into zugs, groups of fifty men like an American platoon. Through yelling and manhandling, they formed ten rows of five. Zelly was in position #1 in his group.

Soon, the music stopped, and the speakers commanded, "Candidates, Achtung!" Everyone jumped to attention with their heels clapping together to sound like a bomb detonation.

A mechanized infantry colonel stood on a platform at the headquarters' roof and spoke into a microphone. "Welcome to Wolfstein, 284 square kilometers of forests, rocky hills, and swamps. Before you're finished, you'll have marched, run, dug, defended, maneuvered, and bled into every centimeter." He paused, accenting the mention of blood. "Your first week is physical fitness and close-order drill, then comes marksmanship. Next, you'll learn to dig rifleman pits, build fortifications, and defend them. The final two weeks are live-fire exercises with shells exploding beside you, bullets whizzing over your heads, and bombs dropping in your midst." Then he hit the punch line. "Men, you've arrived at war. What you do and what you grasp will determine whether you survive or go home in a box. Do you understand?"

"Jawohl." They shouted.

A sergeant cycled through Zelly's zug, passing out cloth bags. "Put your valuables in the sack."

He slid in his Leica, the martyr badge, and the things from his pockets.

Returning through the ranks, the man tagged each with the number of their group and the count within it, 48/1 for Zelly. "Place them in the wheelbarrow."

He did, hoping for the return of his camera and pin.

"Strip! Keep only your shoes and papers," the loudspeakers ordered.

Zelly yanked off his clothes quickly, but the guy beside him hesitated.

"Don't be shy, or they'll do it for you."

Naked, they marched through various stations. In the first, a barber buzzed their hair. Following that, a shower of freezing water drenched them as they hurried to scrub with bars of lye soap. In a windowless room, green gas enveloped them, burning in eyes, noses, and throats. Nurses examined their bodies, gave injections, and drew blood. After blood typing, a grizzled war veteran made an oval metal identification tag to hang from a leather strap around the neck. Zelly was O. At the next station, a man grabbed Zelly's left arm, exposing the underside of his muscle, and tattooed the letter.

As they waited outside the quartermaster's hut, a sadistic corporal ordered calisthenics. Naked jumping jacks caused things to flop, producing an erection on the shy boy beside Zelly. He ignored it, but a burly man in the #3 position didn't. "He's got a Ständer."

Embarrassed, the candidate tried to cover with his hands, but the act only called attention.

Someone from the zug asked, "Was he playing with it?"

"Has to be queer if he's getting hard around us guys," another said.

Zelly defended the kid. "Random boners happen."

I'm glad I'm not him.

You're a fool. Remember, don't stand out. How many times can you forget?

When the quartermaster issued athletic clothes, a blanket, and a thin straw-filled mattress, Zelly's bedding stunk of sweat, urine, vomit, and mildew. He carried the bundle to an old barracks, like a log cabin from the *Little House on the Prairie* book. The walls were rough-hewn logs, daubed with mud, and the roof was a canvas tent. A pot-bellied stove at each end of the hut provided a little heat. Double-decker steel bunks with wooden gear trunks under them were the only furniture. Lower beds got chosen fast, so Zelly took an upper and tossed the bedding on the metal straps. When he peeked to learn who had taken the bunk below, he found the shy, boner boy.

After supplying chalk, the sergeant ordered, "Print your last name and initial on your bed and footlocker."

Zelly wrote 'Zellner F' and extended his hand to his bunkmate. "I'm Zelly."

"I'm Peter Unger."

After a five-kilometer run, the group returned to find uniforms and the cloth bag containing their valuables. They set up their bunks and lay awake, struggling to sleep as moonlight from a waning moon filtered through holes in the canvas.

Zelly dozed until muffled cries woke him. A guy in the nearest top bunk was awake, his eyes staring at the tent roof. Zelly rolled to his shoulder and scanned the neighboring lower bed. He found another trainee watching Peter with fear-filled eyes.

****

"Budenzauber," he whispered.

Zelly knew the word to mean jamboree, like Boy Scouts, but it was incongruous with fright. In Fredericksburg, his mother had listened to a German music radio program, *The Budenzauber Boys*. Curious, he leaned over to ask Peter, but he wasn't alone—three others were also in his bunk. One held him in a bear hug while another pinned his feet. The third delivered a flurry of belly punches.

Budenzauber's definition became obvious and outraged Zelly. Jumping from the bed, he planted his knees into the puncher's kidneys—a fighting technique called Defendu. A Brit instructor had taught it at Fort Sam Houston, claiming all British spies mastered it. Its goal was death or incapacitation through pressure points. During hand-to-hand combat training at Fort Sam, Zelly had used the tactics to defeat and kill Bald Bart but got the scar.

Zelly's jump brought a sharp howl of pain from the assailant as he collapsed from the blow and weight. Springing toward the bear-hugger, Zelly stabbed an inverted knife hand at his Adam's apple. Though it wasn't hard enough to kill, the guy's mouth opened to a silent scream. Zelly glared at the third one, holding Peter's feet. "Get off, or you're next."

Sobbing loudly, Peter curled into a tight ball and spewed vomit on his attackers.

They scrambled to square up on Zelly. "Fuck you," one spat.

Every guy in the barracks was on an elbow to watch.

"You die," a froggy voice threatened.

The goons surrounded Zelly in a fighting triangle. The burly boy charged, swinging a roundhouse blow aimed at his eye. Zelly snatched the fist in midair, twisted it, and dove through the bed frame. As he landed on Peter's bunk, he wrenched the arm around a steel post. It snapped, leaving the recruit howling in pain from a broken arm.

As Zelly stood, the uninjured assailant closed. He slammed Zelly against the bunk rails and launched into a flurry of belly punches. Zelly stomped his heel above the guy's instep, crushing the foot. As his chin came down to view the damage, Zelly landed a palm strike to the bridge of his nose. He flopped backwards to the floor, hitting his head as blood spewed.

The sergeant rushed through the door with his shrill whistle sounding. "Achtung!" Forty-six recruits leaped from their beds and braced. Zelly came to attention in the triangle of attackers, standing in their blood.

"What's happening here?" the NCO shouted.

The recruit with the injured throat swung a round-house punch as Zelly stood, seemingly defenseless. He had put all his power and weight behind the hook. When Zelly ducked, the strike hit a steel bedpost, and the man crumpled to the floor. Zelly stepped to the side and resumed his ramrod posture.

"He broke my nose," an attacker said.

"And my arm," the burly one cried.

"Ow, my hand. You saw what he did."

"What they claim is true, I must admit," Zelly said.

The sergeant chose a nearby observer. "What did you see?"

"A budenzauber. Them against that one until he stopped it." He pointed a finger at each person involved.

"Boner boy needed a lesson. It was only some fun," the burly guy said.

"The injured go to the hospital," the NCO ordered. After they left, he stepped to Zelly. "The lieutenant will deal with this tomorrow."

As the candidates climbed into their bunks, Peter said, "Zelly, thank you."

"Where did you learn to fight like that?" someone asked from across the room.

Zelly's sleep was restless and full of nightmares.

He dreamed he was little Frederich Zellner, skinny dipping in the Elbe. A gang of five teenagers in HJ uniforms joined him in the water. At first, having playmates was fantastic, but soon, the older boys turned mean by hitting and kicking him.

One pushed him underwater. Another kneed his belly, knocking the air out of him. Unable to breathe, he fought to the water's surface. They dunked him again, but this time, a foot forced him to the river bottom and held him there. As he panicked, rocks fell around him. A boulder dropped on his head. As blackness came, he could hear the teens giggling. "Budenzauber!"

Zelly woke in a cold sweat, remembering the eerie moment with Kris and Fritz on the riverbank. He recalled the doppelgänger who resembled him on the wall of pictures and the white cross near the barn.

Is this how you died?

Did someone save you and send you to America...to become me?

****

17 March 1941—Wolfstein

At breakfast the next morning, the sergeant took recruits, one at a time, to meet the lieutenant. When each returned, they stole a furtive glance at Zelly before finishing their meal. He surmised he was the topic of the discussions.

Finally. the last summons came. Zelly entered a small office containing a metal desk, chair, and filing cabinet with a second door beyond it.

"Candidate Zellner reporting as ordered."

"What is your version of the night's events?" the officer asked.

"Three guys ganged up on the recruit in the bunk beneath mine. They called it a Budenzauber, but I think they were bullying him. Two held him down while another pounded on him. When I came to his aid, they turned on me."

"Why help him? None of the others did."

"I believe I should defend a comrade from my zug."

"Were you friendly before?"

"No, I met Peter yesterday."

The exasperated lieutenant wrote a note. "Some candidates are weak. Stronger ones toughen them up to improve their soldiering."

"Was that the purpose of the Budenzauber?"

The officer smiled, thinking Zelly understood.

"Sir, I would protect any member of my group. Even the three thugs who went to the hospital if they were in danger. Isn't that my duty?"

He sighed. "Where did you learn your fighting technique?"

Zelly realized he'd need to invent another lie.

I can't say I learned Defendu in San Antonio, Texas, taught by a British spy.

It would be the truth—when you killed Bald Bart and got the groin scar.

I've lied too many times about that event already.

Can't you come up with one more?

"Really, it's not a method, only knowledge of science and anatomy. Bodies have weak points, and I strike at them, often using the opponent's momentum against him. Once at summer camp in Halle, a bully tried to Budenzauber me, and he paid."

The officer made a loud harrumph and regarded Zelly with a curious stare. His next question shifted directions. "Why are you unusual?"

The query perplexed Zelly. "I'm not. Every soldier should defend his friends."

He knuckle-tapped a folder. "Your SS record has a black band. Usually, the stripe calls out a troublesome lout who needs discipline and straightening out. These documents tell the story of your whole life. They came from HJ headquarters in Berlin and the Wittenberg town hall and gymnasium."

Zelly's jaw dropped, and his mind raced. *Is my cover blown? Is everything exposed?* The silence became burdensome, but fear kept him silent.

"When I asked for your file, I got more than I bargained for—a visitor." The lieutenant opened an interconnecting door. The colonel entered, followed by a Gestapo agent with a Cheshire grin.

Zelly's heart crashed into his stomach. "Herr Stengler, I'm surprised."

He spoke in English. "I've taken an interest in you, boy. In ten years, I've never seen an English book in Germany. Or found a Wittenberg student who speaks the language."

Zelly observed the colonel keeping up with the agent's words. "If speaking the language is a crime, I suspect the colonel is also guilty."

The base commander nodded. "But that's not the issue, Herr Stengler. Why does the candidate's folder have a black band? And why, when we made a customary phone call, does a Gestapo officer arrive with a complete set of files in hand?"

"Someone of great importance has taken an interest in young Zellner." Stengler lifted his briefcase to the desk, opened it, and withdrew the *Morgenpost* picture. "Dancing with a Reich Marshall's wife may explain it, or maybe he's a swing kid who needs some indoctrination and discipline."

Zelly looked sheepish. "When Frau Göring asked to dance, should I have disappointed her?"

The Colonel's gaze lingered on the agent. "By graduating from gymnasium, Zellner is qualified for officers' school. What's he doing here?"

Zelly tried to smile. "I'm sorry I broke an arm, nose, and fist on my first night. I'm here for training, like the rest. What I did last night might be wrong, so I'll accept punishment for my misdeed."

The lieutenant chuckled. "You accomplished something I've never seen. In only a few minutes, you earned the trust and respect of forty-six men. They corroborated your story and asked for you as their barrack chief. Your file will have another commendation and a recommendation for the officer's school."

"Congratulations, corporal." He pinned chevrons to Zelly's sleeve.

Herr Stengler put his nose in Zelly's face. "You still stink of rotten fish, but I'll figure you out."

Zelly finished breakfast and his cold cup of coffee.

No matter where I go, Stengler turns up.

He suspects you. Once, a lion had a taste of human meat...

Can't be that bad, or I'd already be under arrest. Does he know about Himmler?

Or is it from the picture he kept and his fascination with your scar?

****

After the candidate left the office, Oskar Stengler glowered at the training officers. "An advancement in rank?"

"Well warranted," the lieutenant responded.

"When you inquired, I assembled his records and drove all night to bring them, but not for a commendation and a promotion. The boy has lied to me and refused a direct order. There are too many curious things about him, like English and swing dancing. I used to be a teacher, and his transcript puts him in my class, but I don't remember him. He is a project of mine."

"But he is currently my work-in-process," the colonel said. "The documents you provided show an exemplary young man who I will train, as expected. While I would like a better explanation of the black band, I don't see your concerns reflected in the documentation."

The lieutenant grinned. "I find nothing abnormal about him. Instead, I see leadership potential and may have him teach the hand-to-hand combat course."

Oskar placed his business card on the desk. "If you become suspicious, please contact me."

Stengler collected the records and made an about-face. His scar twitched with irritation as he marched from the office. Though exhausted and in need of rest before heading back to Berlin, he considered taking quarters for the night, but too much adrenaline coursed through his system. The drive south to Hanover allowed his pique to dissipate. Exhausted, he gave up the car keys at the motor pool and bought a train ticket for Berlin. The regional whistled for departure within minutes of his boarding. He napped as it left the station.

About an hour later, he woke at Braunschweig to change to an intercity. A dream clung to him—Zellner's scar. The answer I seek is in Italy. He lied because the Italian Bannführer ordered him to avoid a diplomatic incident. That's a story I can check.

****

18 March 1941—Gestapo Headquarters

Oskar found an empty desk and summoned a junior clerk. "Find me the name and contact for the officer leading the Italian exchange program."

Before he could unpack to unpack Zellner's records from his valise, she delivered a piece of paper. He requested a telephone connection to the provided number.

A man answered. "Heil Hitler. This is Karl Stoppel, Bannführer at the consulate in Rome."

"I'm Gestapo agent Oskar Stengler from Berlin."

"Hello, Herr Stengler. What may I do for you?"

"I'm inquiring about Frederich Zellner. Youth exchange to a family in Naples for two years."

"I recall him. Are you calling about the incident?"

Oskar's eyes lit up. "Of course, I've been told it could have caused diplomatic tensions."

"Very true. Having the Italian navy open fire on a German was problematic, I'll tell you. It required plenty of work to keep things hushed and out of the newspapers."

Shocked, Stengler paused for minutes because he expected a scuffle with a Jew at Garibaldi's statue and not a naval attack. He recovered his demeanor. "What happened?"

"A patrol boat was on routine submarine surveillance out of Naples. They received a radio report of a surfaced British sub off the island of Ischia very late at night. Upon arriving at the spot, they encountered a drifting trawler and fired across the bow. They didn't realize the vessel was attempting to recover the Zellner boy and his Italian host from the water after they fell overboard. Our shot came close to Zellner, causing him temporary hearing loss. We didn't know he was German until they discovered a pin with a swastika on his jacket."

The martyr's badge, Oskar thought. "I expected a story about a murdered Jew near the train station."

Stoppel chuckled. "Since when would a dead Jew cause diplomatic issues?"

"So, you know about that situation?"

"I do, and it was nothing."

"Even with Zellner's injury?"

"What wound? He was fine."

"What happened in the altercation?" Oskar asked.

"During the Panzer parade through Naples, a Jewish man took exception to the German's youth uniform. Police intervened to break up a brief scuffle. The man was charged with affray and fined."

Disbelief struck Oskar. "Back to the trawler incident. Who owned the boat?"

"Head of Vincente Testanuevo's family, Primo."

"Ever find the sub?"

"No, but the sighting came from a consistently accurate source."

"Thanks," Stengler said. The phone call gave him lots to consider. His suspicious nature and Gestapo training wouldn't allow him to consider the boy and the submarine as a coincidence. Were those Italians passing on information to the enemy or maybe smuggling for the resistance?

He clicked the telephone hook to draw the operator's attention. "I'd like to speak to the commander of the Italian anti-submarine forces stationed in Naples. I do not have a name or number, but when you have him on the line, ring me back."

While he waited, he read Zellner's file with fresh eyes. He put away any prejudging from his meeting with the boy in Brenner. As he reconsidered, he saw what others recognized—an accomplished kid with a ton of commendations. By the time he finished reading, the call hadn't come through. He wanted another look at the snapshots from the Zellner family's parlor, so he took the film to the darkroom for processing.

Finally, the phone rang. "I have Tenente Mateo Casalegno for you."

A series of clicks and beeps came over the line before the lieutenant spoke. "I am at your service, sir."

"What can you tell me about the German boy who fell overboard from a trawler, and a patrol boat nearly killed him."

"I was the officer commanding the boat, and am sorry for the incident, but I had no way of knowing he was aboard."

"Tenente, this is not recrimination, but I need more about the event."

"To prepare for your call, I pulled the logbook and reread my entry. We use the Castle Aragonese on Ischia as a submarine lookout to protect Naples Bay. On January 25, 1941, the spotter reported sighting a periscope. Dispatch sent my crew to the site. Minutes later, I received notice of a conning tower breaking the surface. We arrived with sirens howling and illuminated our searchlight. The fishing trawler tried to pull away, so we fired our deck gun across the bow. They launched a distress flare, and we spotted two figures in the water. After rescuing both, one said, 'Nicht schiessen,' hinting he was German. He seemed to have lost his hearing. We put them in the engine room under blankets for warmth and gave them dry clothes as we towed their boat to shore."

"Any sign of the sub?"

"No, sir, and we stopped looking when the situation became a rescue. Our C.O. figured the spotter saw the trawler and mistook it. The fishermen claimed mechanical trouble had kept them out late."

"How did the boys fall into the water?"

"The German boy said our siren and light scared him, and he fell overboard. His Italian friend jumped in to save him."

"Did anything make you doubt the story?"

"We searched the vessel and found no contraband. Primo, the captain, explained it all to a judge who accepted the tale as he told it."

Stengler sighed as he thought. Two youths in the ocean would make a convenient reason to not pursue a submarine, wouldn't it?

CHAPTER 6

War Becomes Real

5 April 1941—Event at Wolfstein

During the third week of training, after digging thousands of rifleman pits and sleeping in them, Zelly's group made their way to the primary camp and hit the showers. Soon after, the colonel visited their barracks and announced, "Congratulations, Zug 48. You are currently in first place and have earned a reward: an elite movie night. Be in the mess hall at 19:30."

"Sir, what's the title?" Zelly asked.

"*Uber Alles in der Welt*, a new flick starring Paul Hartmann. My son is a Luftwaffe pilot who flew in the film, and he will join you. We'll have chocolates, popcorn, and drinks." The men cheered.

Privately, the colonel said, "Zelly, please come to dinner at my house before the show."

"Sir, an honor."

He spotted the colonel's house perched on a well-tended lawn. When he knocked, a man a year or two older than him answered. Service colors on his collar and pips on his shoulder boards pegged him as a Luftwaffe Oberleutnant. Zelly saluted.

The officer ignored the gesture and raked an arm around his shoulders. "I've heard so much about you, Zelly. I'm Ernst." He was tall, muscular, blond, and had steely eyes that sparkled from his tanned face—a golden boy in Luftwaffe blue.

Zelly's eyes lingered on the pilot's wings. "I've always wanted to fly." He recalled the '35 San Antonio Air Show when he was twelve, and Amelia Earhart had let him sit on her lap. Together, they had taxied to the runway, roared the engine, and shot skyward like a brace of quail. She had vanished in the Pacific—rumors claimed she was spying on the Japs. She was the reason he was in Germany, his driving force for saying yes to recruitment as a spy.

In the parlor, the colonel filled three fancy glasses with a dark amber drink, handing one to his son and one to Zelly. He raised his glass. "Once, cognac was a delicacy, but now it's a resource of the Reich."

When Zelly took a sip and shuddered, Ernst's laugh brought a blush to Zelly's cheeks. "Ah, a virgin."

"My son flies He-111s for the 3rd Airforce out of Melun Villaroche, southeast of Paris. He's my source for the finer things in life."

Ernst's arm still draped Zelly's shoulders. "I understand you speak English, so prepare for a decadent evening of utter corruption."

Zelly matched his mischievous grin. "Sounds fun."

They carried the drinks to another room, where Ernst wound up a Victrola and put on a record. The speaker blared Duke Ellington's *It Don't Mean a Thing If It Ain't Got That Swing*. Banned music surprised Zelly, but Ernst swayed with the beat and pulled him into the rhythm. "You like, don't you?"

"Yes." Zelly closed his eyes and pictured the scene—speaking English, listening to forbidden songs, a young officer swaying him like an older brother, a snifter in hand. He expected Stengler to destroy the moment.

The door did open, making him shudder in fear, but an SS squad didn't enter. Instead, a tall, shapely brunette in a burgundy dress entered. "I love this song." Her English was perfect.

"Mom, this is Zelly, one of Dad's trainees, and he needs a dance."

"May I?" She swung him to Duke's doo-wop beat.

As they danced, Ernst played *Take the A Train* and *Mood Indigo*.

"Zelly, you're skillful," she said.

"You speak English well."

"I should as I'm American."

He almost shit his trousers to keep from saying, 'I am, too.'

She spotted his surprise. "I was a student at Vassar while my husband served as an attaché in Washington. We met at a New York mixer and fell in love, with Ernst being born before his posting ended. Despite the Third Reich, I've given him a penchant for Western culture."

The fly-boy refilled Zelly's snifter. "I warned you about corruption, but those songs revealed your secret. Väter, your star trainee, is a swing kid."

"Not surprising, as I have a picture of him swinging out with Frau Göring at a Berlin party. He's a man of unique abilities."

"Ernst, a dance, please?" his mother asked.

Zelly sipped cognac and kept the records playing with Basie's *Swingin' the Blues*.

The Colonel tapped his son's shoulder, cutting in. "Ernst, you know which song."

He played Al Jolson's *April Showers* and said, "This is the one that made me. Can you imagine them making love to this?"

Ernst smiled while his parents shared a kiss.

They moved to the dining room, where two servants provided dinner. In Texas, Zelly had visited families who had hired help, some of them black and descended from slaves. As he studied their drab dresses, a yellow, six- pointed star caught his attention with the word 'Jude.'

After the meal, Ernst drove them to the movie. Zelly's group was already present, enjoying plates of cookies and chocolate, things highly rationed. They sat in reserved seats as the room darkened and the silver screen lit.

The film opened in 1939 when Britain and France declared war on Germany. A German journalist in Paris got arrested. On a London stage, a similar fate met a Tyrolean yodeling troupe. A British destroyer sunk the *Elmshorn* and imprisoned her sailors. A Luftwaffe officer addressed his pilots on the flight line. Ernst pointed. "That's me." The crew piled into a Heinkel. "My plane, and I'm flying it." Over Poland, antiaircraft fire brought down the bomber.

Fortune shifted. The reporters and singers escaped imprisonment. A U- boat sank the Royal Navy ship and rescued the mariners. A Dornier 17 swooped in to rescue the downed aircrew. Everyone returned home, motivated by their love of the Fatherland.

When the movie ended, the group rose and sang *Deutschland über Alles* with the credits. The song stirred Zelly, and he saw the pride in his men's faces. Ernst's posture was splendid, back ramrod straight, voice deep and pure, muscles primed for action.

Ernst hugged him, bringing goosebumps to Zelly's skin. "You feel it, too. I can tell."

Born in America to a German parent. He came home, like the characters in the show. I have, too. We are bound by a common language and culture.

Zelly, the cultural ties making you tingle aren't real. I choose 'the rocket's red glare,' not 'Germany above all in the world.'

****

6 April 1941—Spy Work at Wolfstein

Zelly dragged himself out of his bunk with a colossal headache and immediately regretted the cognac. Overnight, a cold front passed, bringing torrential rain. The schedule called for regimental field maneuvers and learning blitzkrieg, but the weather postponed it. The guys played Scherwenzel—a betting game much like poker that uses four cards with jacks wild. Back in Texas, Zelly remembered teaching a strip version to Betty Jean, his prom date.

Today's the day, he recalled, April 6th, the start of the blitz against Greece. He stole a radio from the sergeant's mess so his zug could listen.

Despite the headache, he grew curious about the forces his group would soon fight in live fire training. Around noon, the weather slightly improved, and Zelly resolved to spy. He slung the Leica over his neck and donned a trench coat. He stepped into the drizzle and trotted to the forest.

Hearing some engine noise, he followed the sound to a dozen parked Panzer IIIs in a clearing. He recognized them from newsreels of the German advance in France, but these differed. The turret was larger, and its gun had a longer barrel, probably 75-millimeter.

He snapped pictures.

A few Wehrmacht armored-division soldiers scurried about the tank park, starting engines and giving them ten minutes at idle before shutting them down. Zelly selected a vehicle on the clearing's edge and darted in for close-ups. The armor was thin at the rear, where exposed spare fuel cans rode.

He stayed hidden and waited until the engine roared to life. When the worker exited, leaving the top hatch open, Zelly scrambled inside. He took snapshots of the controls, ammunition storage, viewports, and such. As he climbed out, he spotted a windsock high in the distance. He adjusted the camera and zoomed the lens to photograph the airfield. His desire to fly made him pause just a moment too long.

"What are you doing?" a trooper growled.

Zelly spun toward the voice and found a man climbing onto the shield above the tracks. Judging the soldier hadn't seen his face, he flashed the Leica to blind the man and scrambled down the opposite side. His boots squished in mud as he pushed for traction to sprint to the trees.

"Stop him!"

The pursuit was swift. A Wehrmacht sergeant leaped from behind a neighboring Panzer, blocking Zelly. Reacting instinctively, Zelly dodged with the best American football moves and landed a solid, stiff arm on the guy's chin. Voices told him more pursuers had arrived to join the chase. He cornered the Panzer's front and dove beneath its sloping armor. Digging in the mire, he squeezed under the axle. Wiggling past the drive shaft, he spotted the sergeant's boots going toward the woods.

The bottom hatch wasn't tightly shut, so Zelly pushed the metal plate inside and opened a portal. He shimmied through and closed the trapdoor without tightening it. Crossing through the Panzer, he found an escape exit on the side, away from the men. Squirming through like an earthworm, he came out between the wheels that drove the treads. With the chasers headed for the trees, he sprinted to the airstrip using broken-field running.

Twenty Junkers Ju-87 dive bombers lined the taxiway. A close approach proved impossible because guards patrolled the area, and the tower was manned. He ducked into a drainage ditch and cleaned mud from the camera.

The sight of the aircraft brought him joy. He snapped pictures of the planes' gull wings, three-bladed propellers, wing-based machine gun ports, and empty ordnance racks. As he dreamed of flying one, a rain slicker flapping in the breeze startled him. Caught, he rolled to the chilly water and peered into a hooded face.

"Impressive, aren't they?" his sergeant asked.

"I like airplanes."

"Tomorrow, you'll hear the Jericho Trumpets on the Stukas. When they scream, soldiers piss their trousers. What did you think of the Panzers?"

"You've been watching me scout the opposition?" He chuckled with surprise. "They are more intimidating than in the newsreels, mighty and invulnerable. No wonder we'll conquer the world."

The NCO offered a hand to lift him from the muck. "You're rather different from the meatheads back in the barrack."

Zelly expected him to confiscate the camera. "I took some pictures."

"I did, too, when we flanked the Maginot Line and roared through Belgium."

"So, I'm not on report?"

"Hit the showers. Maneuvering class is in thirty minutes."

After marching his group to the classroom, they stood at attention while the mechanics looked for the guy they had chased. When they couldn't identify him, his sergeant winked.

The lesson taught the basics of blitzkrieg, mixing the concepts of massed attack, encroach and encircle, and coordinated signals. Two situations received emphasis—infantry preceding armor and vice versa. The instruction ended with an important warning. "The easiest way to die is to stop in front of a Panzer."

Striding down the aisle, the colonel said, "Tomorrow, your maneuvers are live-fire. Make no mistakes."

****

7 April 1941—Live Fire

The next day, they marched to the exercise grounds—a gigantic, pockmarked field. Grass and soil rolled away from a network of cement trenches spider-webbing between a domed brick building and a concrete structure shaped like a submarine. The fortifications sat on the highest point, with an expanse of dirt sloping away into the forest. Craters left by bombs or artillery shells from previous exercises provided the only cover. The odor of explosives lingered along with yesterday's mud and rainwater. Clouds made everything gray.

The group stopped at one edge, formed battle ranks, and marched twenty steps forward. Peter was at Zelly's side. "This is like the Maginot Line near where I live."

The conversation became futile when the LVI Panzer Corps arrived, shaking the ground. Zelly's eyes jostled in their sockets, and his teeth chattered. The sergeant positioned his troops to follow the vehicles, fanning out about ten yards beyond the fenders.

"Shoot the infantry you encounter, and yell if you spot anti-tank weapons."

The Panzers moved in a pincer movement against the submarine building. Zelly trotted after one vehicle and popped sideways to fire at soldiers manning portholes in the cement sausage. He pretended the field was Greece, and they were the 2nd Army.

Soon, Stukas appeared overhead, diving like Texas seagulls to pounce on food along a beach. Their shriek was ear-splitting, making Zelly understand the bit about pissed trousers. Falling bombs made the earth rain as hard as the storm. The group jogged on quaking soil as everything around them rattled, vibrated, and exploded.

Shouldering his rifle, he pulled the Leica from a pocket. He shot pictures of the swarming metal gulls and the line of tanks leading them. When Peter warned him, he pocketed the camera. Panzers downshifted as they powered up the embankment. Armor plates in the tracks grabbed the dirt and threw it toward the trainees, who ran to keep up.

The Panzer ahead of Zelly lifted its barrel skyward and climbed a berm. Its cannon rotated and fired—a jarring 'whomp' that knocked it back a foot. Acrid smoke burned Zelly's nose, mixing with the stink of diesel fumes, oil, and grease. An immense hole appeared in the cement structure as the Panzer's machine gun poured rounds through the gap.

"Grenades to the flanks," the sergeant gestured. The wings of the formation tossed their explosives at enemy trenches.

A 'move out' command sent them scrambling over the next small hill. Zelly slid down into a pool of rainwater. Some tumbled in the knee-deep puddle of mud.

Their Panzer climbed a rise. As it struggled, the squad shoved on its rear as it shifted and built power. As the tracks took traction, the vehicle stuttered and jerked before it lumbered over the rim and belly-flopped to the ground.

'Infantry to the sides,' the sergeant signed.

Leveling their guns, they aimed at men swarming from the fortifications like Texas fire ants around a threatened mound. Zelly's tank curled behind the submarine structure. The turret's cannon pivoted toward the fort's door and blasted a hole.

"Mop up," the NCO called.

Peter and Zelly sprinted through the obliterated door, taking prisoners. Others joined, fanning out to check every room until shouts of "Clear" echoed. Across the field, another zug had cleared the brick building. A siren blew, ending the exercise.

The Stukas flew away, the armor withdrew, and masons and construction workers repaired the buildings. As the sergeant gathered the group, Zelly leaned against a concrete wall and lit a cigarette to calm his nerves. Peter approached with wet trousers to bum a smoke and endured Zelly's teasing. Nearby ordnance exploded. When Zelly ducked in surprise, his piss flowed and gave Peter a chuckle.

****

8 April 1941—A Training Death

In the morning, they returned to the same field. The bombs and Panzer shell holes remained, yet the structures looked as if untouched. Yesterday's smells flooded through Zelly's lungs, including the stench of urine. He promised himself he wouldn't do it again.

The sergeant waved at the open area and explained the exercise. "There's a minefield up to the structures and anti-tank weapons in the windows. Use the craters for firing pits, as there are no mines in them. This time, we lead—and whatever you do, don't let the Panzers catch you."

The massive vehicles lumbered in a v-formation behind the soldiers. Without a pause, they rushed forward like race cars, getting the solid green flag. Zelly's group sprinted ahead, moving from crater to shell hole. When a bullet whizzed near his ear, he took cover and spotted a Panzerbüchse. He quickly took aim and fired. Engine noise wasn't close, so he snapped a picture of the Panzer line.

Peter jumped into his pit. "You might do better filming for newsreels than soldiering."

When a tank approached, a machine gunner in the brick building fired tracers across their location. Zelly sighted the man and pulled his trigger as Peter scrambled ahead to the next cavity.

They leapfrogged each other over thirty yards and ended up in a massive crater. Zelly spotted a Panzerbüchse barrel protruding from a window and aimed. When a face appeared, he fired. His shot brought return fire. Rounds peppered the lip of their hole. Swiveling, Zelly located the shooter in the cement submarine and blasted him. Diesel engine noise filled his ears, and he spun to locate the Panzer. Its front armor panel towered overhead as the treads pawed at the air.

"Peter, out!"

The armored monster teetered at the edge.

Peter clawed up the crater's side, but the mud slid him to the bottom. The tank dropped directly over him. He screamed, "Grab my hand." Zelly extended his arm, but his fingers never found a grip. Peter's hand disappeared. Metal covered every angle of Zelly's vision as the armor's underbelly obscured the sky. He crouched to avoid being crushed as the Panzer cannon fired. Crumbled soil cascaded around him, and death seemed seconds away.

He spotted an open hatch—the same one he had shimmied through to escape the mechanics. As he stretched to reach it, a spent shell casing dropped through, still smoking, and bounced away.

He grabbed the hatch's side and pulled himself upward. Water sprayed from the hole. Pushing against the shifting earth, he jumped and grabbed the steel lip. Someone snatched his wrist and hauled him inside. A dangling penis came into view—the water's source.

"We have a visitor," the tanker reported.

Zelly collapsed on the floor plates, astonished at his dumb luck. When the siren blew to end the exercise, and the tank stopped, the driver shouted from the turret. "I have one of yours."

As friendly hands helped, the sergeant asked, "Is Peter with you?"

"No."

Zelly dug in the mud where Peter had been, and his zug came to help. They yelled for Peter, but no answer came. Others joined the search, and they found a lifeless hand. Scraping away, the earth exposed a severed arm. His friend was dead, mangled and crushed beneath the Panzer.

Because of Peter's death, the group had a somber dinner. Zelly blamed himself. Previously, combat was something for the future—unseen, distant, and not yet relevant. But the day made the reality of war obvious.

The radio reported that five hundred bombers from France had raided Ireland, with Belfast as the primary target. Zelly had friends there—Fergus and Meg, who lived at a short distance from the city. He had met them during a brief stop-over when he stayed in their home. They might be as dead as Peter. Ernst would have flown in the strike force. One friend is killing others.

That night, he lay in his bunk and remembered four months ago.

****

30 December 1940 to 5 January 1941— Belfast, Northern Ireland

The *HMS Salisbury* delivered Zelly and Vinny to Belfast.

An officer caught them topside. "You're off here. On the 5th, you'll catch the *Rochester* for the ride to Gibraltar. Then, a sub will sneak you through the Mediterranean."

Wrapped in pea coats against the frigid weather, Zelly and Vinny queued on the gangway with the sailors. Knowing nothing about the town, Zelly asked, "Where're you going?"

"The bars at High and Skipper Street for a brew with the birds."

They followed the Royal Navy men to a pub named A Pint of Plain. The bar offered a bevy of dames and plenty of the black stuff—Guinness Extra Stout. They took a table between the stage and a roaring fireplace. The beer arrived with a creamy head, and ladies took interest before they wiped the foam from their lips.

Two college-aged broads with big smiles wandered over. "Do you fellows want company?" Her long, bright-red hair was in a ponytail tied by a black velvet ribbon. A friend, a raven-haired beauty in finger curls, eyed Vinny. They took the spare chairs.

"Have a girlfriend?" The redhead asked. Zelly answered with a headshake while noticing the freckles splashed across her nose. She rested her hand on his hip and said, "If you want one, I'm available."

He grinned—this's my lucky night.

"Sweetie, buy us drinks?" Vinny's girl asked.

Zelly had won some Brit money from *Salisbury*'s crew shooting craps, so he agreed.

When the bartender brought pints of Guinness with shots of Old Bushmills for chasers, he said, "That'll be two quid."

Zelly didn't understand British pounds, so he fished a cash wad from a pocket, including some American greenbacks, and dropped it beside the beer.

As the barkeep extracted the right amount, the ginger gal slipped her hand from hip to groin. "You're a Yank merchant seaman?" If he had missed her double entendre, her tugging on his erection cleared the meaning. "What's your name?"

"Zelly, it's my nickname."

"I'm Meg, short for Margaret." Her breasts filled his vision as she straddled his lap. Freckles fell into her cleavage like strawberries. He buried his face to kiss them.

"Meg, leave him be," a male voice said.

When Zelly glanced beyond Meg's bosom, his eyes found a boy— younger, with orange hair and more dappled than her. "Hey!" He prepared to pound the lad's teeth down his throat.

Unaffected by Zelly's bluster, he pulled a chair from the neighboring table to join them. "I'm sorry for my sister. I bet you were plannin' on a quick fuck, but you'll be gettin' the trollop-wallop. By mornin', she'll have you broke, naked, freezin', and frustrated as hell." His lilting laugh sounded Irish tenor. "When they snare a Brit sailor, I don't mind if they embarrass him twenty ways to Sunday, but your money is American."

"Fergus, you're spoilin' my evenin'," Meg said. "Don't you have to sing?"

"Zelly, I got invited to a New Year's Eve dance," Vinny said, winking at his girl.

"You'd both be welcome," Fergus said. "First, stay and listen to my songs. There's no better entertainment in town."

"Where can we find a room?" Vinny asked.

"The likes of you won't fit at The Merchant. The Mermaid's cheap if you can stand the fleas, rats, and venereal diseases." Meg curled her nose in disgust.

An arpeggio came from a piano, and a booming voice said, "And now, the song-styling of our own Fergus McAuley."

"I've got a spare bed, so you can bunk with me." Fergus darted to the platform, buoyed by applause from the packed pub. "This song's for Zelly, my new friend." He sang like an angel.

In a neat little town they call Belfast,
Apprentice to trade, I was bound.
Many an hour's sweet happiness
Have I spent in that dear little town.
A sad misfortune came ov'r me,
Which caused me to stray from the land.
Far away from my friends and relations,
Betrayed by a black velvet band.
Her eyes shone like diamonds.
I thought her the queen of the land,
And her hair hung over her shoulder
Tied up with a black velvet band.

His singing was exquisite, but Zelly caught the trollop-wallop joke and reference to Meg's hair ribbon. Fergus crooned the song as he wandered the bar with the audience joining the chorus. As applause thundered, Fergus made his way back to the stage.

"For my next song, I've changed the words a little from the ones you'd recognize. I dedicate this version to my older brother, who enlisted in the 8th Belfast in 1939. He didn't return with the boats from Dunkirk. Danny, where'er you are, this'n's for you."

I wish I was in bonnie Belfast, where life waits at rainbow's end

I would swim over the deepest ocean just to see her again.

But the sea is wide, and I cannot get over, nor have I wings to fly

I wish I had a friendly boatman to ferry me to Ma's mince pie.

I close my eyes and remember the fields of green and gold

Where I could walk in sunlit meadows with my brother so bold.

But the sea is wide, and I cannot get over, nor have I wings to fly

So I'll just dream of bonnie Belfast, and the day I said goodbye.

Tears poured from his eyes while he sang and from many in the crowd. When the song ended, he launched into his next tune with, "Come on and get those Irish eyes a-smilin'."

When the set finished, he came to the table and sent the bartender for leek and potato soup and soda bread. "I hope you fellas are hungry 'cause I ordered for you, too. First, tell me what you Yanks are doin' in Belfast?"

On such a freezing day, the steam hovered over the bowl, and melted butter split the loaf.

Zelly started an answer, "We're headed to—"

"Eagle Squadron," Vinny interrupted. "Americans flying with the Royal Air Force."

"Since Danny went missin' I have no intention of joinin' up," Fergus said.

Meg stole a slice and dipped it in Fergus's soup. "I'm sorry for teasin' you."

Zelly blushed. "I kind of liked it, especially since you're so beautiful." She pecked his cheek.

Fergus made a face. "You're the first Yanks I've met. Tell me about America after my set?"

"We still need a place to crash, so let's try The Mermaid." Vinny stood.

"I thought we decided you would share Fergus's giant bedroom," Meg said.

"We couldn't impose," Vinny said.

"I insist." Fergus rose.

Meg took Zelly's arm. "You can be my date for the New Year's Eve dance tomorrow." A loose grin was his answer.

"After I finish, I'll give you a lift." Fergus took the stage and sang patriotic songs, ending with *There'll Always be an England.* His voice soared above the audience, like a Spitfire high in the sky, and brought them to their feet. When finished, he bowed and disappeared. Meg led Zelly and Vinny to an old jalopy parked behind the pub.

"What a piece of shit," Vinny complained about the car.

"Beg pardon. I built this fine vehicle from scratch and scrap. Insult her, and she'll nary carry you."

"You put the steering wheel on the wrong side," Vinny advised, making them laugh.

It was a two-seater, so Vinny and Zelly scrambled to the truck bed. Meg covered them with a blanket. "This'll keep you warm to Knockbreda, a few kilometers." She offered a bottle of Tullamore Dew.

Zelly torqued the cap and downed a swig of smooth Irish whiskey with a faint cherry flavor.

Meg watched his Adam's apple bob as he swallowed. "Not good liars, are you? You're not joining the Eagle Squadron—too young, but I'll find your secrets."

As they rumbled away, Fergus sang *Belle of Belfast City,* and Zelly joined in. On the chorus, even a Brooklyn Italian knew the words.

The jalopy bumped and bounced to a two-story farmhouse. They tip- toed upstairs. Fergus lit a lantern, revealing two massive feather beds. "That one was Danny's." Vinny yawned, flopped on it, and snored.

Fergus and Zelly tucked into his bed and shared the whiskey. "Will you teach me the beautiful song you dedicated to Danny?" Zelly asked. As he did, Zelly memorized it.

The next morning, Meg opened the curtains to flood them with sunlight. Spotting the empty bottle on the nightstand, she shrieked, "I'd have liked some. Hurry! We have chores to do before we set up for the dance."

They walked to Knockbreda and climbed the Parish Church's stone steps. Zelly helped band members unload their instruments and position everything on the bandstand. Meg arranged refreshments—enough cakes and cookies to consume the entire village's sugar ration. Fergus and Vinny moved pews to create space for dancing while ladies hung handmade decorations.

With preparations finished, they hiked home. Fergus's mother had water warming on the stove and a washtub near the fire. "Boys upstairs," she shooed, leaving Meg for the first bath.

"I hope you don't mind," Fergus said, "but we'll share the basin."

Twenty minutes later, the guys' turn came. After they stripped and started washing, Meg stuck her head around the doorjamb. "Rub-a-dub-dub, three men in a tub."

"Ma, Meg's lookin'," Fergus complained.

"I've seen it before," she said while gazing at Zelly.

Fergus insisted Vinny and Zelly wear clothes from Danny's armoire. They rode the jalopy to the church and found it packed with people dancing to the booming music.

Meg led Zelly to the floor. "Can you reel?"

He took his place in the male line and held hands with the others. She mirrored his position on the girls' side. They moved in sync and apart in tiny steps and circled in both directions. It reminded him of a Texas square dance.

In the next tune, the band raced with a faster beat. Meg jumped and stepped with her arms at her sides. "*Geese in the Bog*—a jig—move your feet and try to keep up." He failed, but valiantly.

When the music slowed, Fergus sang a ballad about the wind blowing down the glen and shaking fields of barley. The rector wasn't pleased, scurrying about to stop him.

Meg whispered. "That comes from the rebellion and is illegal to sing." She yanked Zelly on stage, forming a buffer around her brother as the tension thickened. When the anthem finished, she silenced the rector's protests by saying, "Fergus, do *Irish Rose*." As everyone joined an old favorite, the stress drained.

When Fergus finished, he winked at Zelly. "I want you to meet a friend from America. I've heard him sing, so do you fancy a tune?"

Singing for an audience made Zelly's nerves catch, and sweat poured, but he had a thought. You're already in a performance far more fearful than this one. So, he said, "We have roses in Texas, too. This one's about the flower from San Antonio." The fiddler smiled knowingly. As he crooned, the nave filled with couples doing a passable swing. On the instrumental bridge, he gave Meg a twirl.

Fergus called for an encore.

Only one song came to Zelly's mind. "On this one, clap along. You'll understand quickly." He belted out *Deep in the Heart of Texas*. He felt bittersweet, wondering if he would ever make it home again.

Meg tugged him outside to a cemetery stone bench where the cold air fogged their breath. When she leaned toward him, he ventured a tender kiss. She responded with passion while a shooting star crossed the inky sky.

"I made a wish," she said. "That you'd take me to America."

"I'm not going there. Not for a long time, perhaps never."

Moonlight filtered through trees, revealing the sorrow in her eyes. "Why not?"

He tried another smooch, but she turned. "Wars create waves, and they push me around out of my control. I'm like a piece of driftwood, never knowing where I'll land—like I never expected to be here."

"How can war make you go anywhere—America isn't in it."

"One day, I was home, and a wave flung me to Belfast. I'm glad it did… to meet you… but the next one is scary."

"Jump ship and stay here with me. We can have children and run a farm, or you can take me with you."

Zelly sighed, recalling how he hated the idea of farming six months ago. But with Meg, the proposal had an enticing charm. "The ideas are tempting but impossible."

She went back to the dance and avoided him, but several other danceable girls kept him busy.

When the band struck up a ballad, Fergus took him outside. They sat on a high stone wall beside the church steps and smoked. Moonlight glistened in Fergus's eyes. "Take me with you?"

"I'm not going to America."

"Anywhere's better'n here."

"I'm sure of one thing, Fergus. In a year or two, you won't be in Knockbreda. You'll fly a Spitfire over the Channel or hunt U-boats in the Atlantic or fight in France."

"I'm not like Danny. Bugger the King, I say, and I won't lift a finger for the likes of 'im. If I'm your friend, you'll tell me true."

The earnestness on Fergus's face made Zelly unable to lie, but Meg saved him from making a response when she called, "Fergus, they want *Danny Boy*."

"I'll cry," he said, reluctantly following her inside.

When Zelly walked in, he found Fergus standing at the piano. The band played a slow, mournful and slow. Fergus grimaced and shut his eyes. His tenor voice held the audience spellbound. Though his tears flowed, he never missed a note or word. He finished with, "Danny, I love you and miss you."

"Midnight," someone shouted. The crowd formed a ring, hands joined, singing *Auld Lang Syne*. The combo raced into a lilting jig with people leaping, twirling, and shouting, "Happy New Year."

After the party, they undressed in Fergus's bedroom and climbed into the beds.

"I'm wishin' we'd saved the Dew for tonight, "Fergus said. "After *Danny Boy*, I could use some whiskey-enhanced forgettin'."

New Year's Day was frigid. They stayed close to the stove, playing Twenty-Five at the kitchen table and listening to Sandy MacPherson's organ on BBC. The news was drearier than the music—the Luftwaffe blitz dropped incendiary bombs that set London burning, according to a report by American correspondent Ernie Pyle.

When darkness came, Meg and Zelly snuggled on the couch near the fireplace, sharing their warmth under a blanket and watching the glowing coals. Meg's mouth was more interesting than radio reports of explosions. As she straddled him, kissing and rubbing, he felt something for the first time. He ached for her, but this was more than lust, something like forever.

I think I'm in love.

Don't tease her. Like Amelia Earhart, you may never return from this perilous mission.

He left Meg and went to bed.

The next morning, they saddled horses and rode pastures to check pregnant ewes.

"Zelly won't tell me where you're bound, but I'm sure it ain't the Eagle Squadron," Fergus said. "I've been doing some figurin'. The other night, Zelly was talkin' in his sleep…in German. America isn't at war yet, but I think that won't last long. I'm bettin' you two are headin' for Germany to spy."

Vinny stiffened, as icy as the air. "No, we aren't going there."

Zelly's emotions boiled. He didn't want to betray Fergus's trust, any secrets, or his relationship with Meg. He broke an unbearable silence. "You're right." His words floated like a dirigible.

At the barn, Vinny said, "Zelly and I will take care of the horses."

When Fergus and Meg went into the house, Vinny exploded. "How fucking stupid! Couldn't you keep your mouth shut?" He slammed down a saddle and broke a sawhorse. Seizing Zelly's coat lapels, he backed him into a stall. "You've killed us—maybe not today, but soon."

Zelly slumped. "I'm sorry."

He pushed Zelly against the barn's rough wall. "I've had enough of your fucking mistakes. They have consequences for me, too." His breath made puffs of vapor that hung in the air like the accusation.

"They'll never tell," Zelly said.

"After Dunkirk, blitzkrieg will come to these islands." Vinny's left hand found Zelly's throat and held him up. "The Nazis will capture him, either here or wherever he goes. They'll torture him, and he'll squeal like a pig."

Zelly couldn't breathe as Vinny's grip choked him. A lightheaded dizziness came over him. The scarlet color of Vinny's face was all he could see.

"He'll finger us. How long before the Gestapo catches us and murders us?" Vinny balled his right hand into a fist and clobbered Zelly's cheek.

Icy fingers of pain shot through Zelly as he plummeted to the floor. Board splinters and sharp nails gouged through his pea coat. "I'll make him promise not to tell."

His eye swelled shut, and his head hit hard metal.

As oblivion claimed him, he heard Vinny say, "Oh, the anvil."

Later, Zelly woke and screamed.

"Shush." Mrs. McAuley said.

Ice pressed against his injuries, but he didn't feel cold, thanks to the blazing fire beside him. His back stung from iodine dabs. He tried to sit at the hearth to tell them he'd slipped and fallen, but Vinny was already apologizing.

By the morning of January 5th, Zelly had recovered. A blackened eye and a lump on his head were the only remaining signs of injury.

Meg slid into his bed and kissed him awake. "I have an Irish blessing for you. I pray God will grant you courage and strength, stealth and wisdom, and patience and perseverance. And I'll provide a reason to survive and return." This kiss was French, and the passion was delicious. "Goodbye, Zelly, go fuck up the Germans."

"Bye, Meg." In that second, he realized he was in love.

One truthful moment while living a lie is fulfilling.

Vinny was right. You made another mistake. Likely a fatal one.

After breakfast, Fergus drove them to the dock in the jalopy.

"Please, tell no one where we're going or what we plan to do," Zelly said.

"I never will. Your secret's safe."

As they climbed *HMS Rochester*'s gangway, Vinny took his arm. "Zelly, I'm sorry. I forgot the mission is about you and not me. I wasn't a friend."

"Don't think about it, buddy." Zelly embraced his shoulders and wondered how long it would be until Vinny let him down again.

****

Before sleep took him, Zelly bent to check Peter's bunk. It was something he had done since that first night at Wolfstein. Only tonight, Peter was missing. There wasn't even enough of him left to bury.

CHAPTER 7

Graduation and Leave

20 April 1941—Wolfstein

Graduation day began with breakfast and a news-reel of the Belfast bombing. Goebbels had ensured the narration would stir awe, boasting 203,000 tons of high explosive bombs and 800 incendiary canisters. The film made Zelly's stomach twist with worry for Meg and Fergus. But when the reel included an interview with Ernst, one of the bomber pilots, he felt proud. The contradictory emotions scared him. After the movie, they showered, shaved, and donned freshly laundered uniforms for the ceremony.

One side of the rectangular parade grounds held bleachers filled with dignitaries, friends, and parents and a stage covered in red and black bunting. The band played *Deutschland Erwache, Germany Awake*—the traditional song was for Hitler's birthday and graduation. Banner bearers began the march, carrying flags from all parts of the Reich. Behind them came Zug 48, and Zelly threw a smart salute as they passed in review. In groups, over a thousand candidates followed.

An ancient, white-whiskered general, whose uniform sported ribbons and awards of every kind, returned the honors. He gave a brief speech that ended with, "Never make the mistake of asking what is good for you… only ask what serves the people."

As the band played the *Horst Wessel Lied,* the colonel stepped to the podium. "Raise the Schwurhand and repeat after me." Zelly expected the traditional arm raise, but his men raised their right hand with the index and middle finger pointed towards the sky, and the others curled but not in a fist. The similarity to the Cub Scout sign caught Zelly by surprise.

Thousands of voices repeated the colonel's words in unison. "I swear to God this holy oath, that I shall render unconditional obedience to the Leader of the German Reich and people, Adolf Hitler, supreme commander of the armed forces, and that as a brave soldier, I shall at all times be prepared to give my life for this oath."

The new soldiers returned to their barracks to change into the uniforms of their services. Most of Zelly's fifty wore fighting outfits for armor, artillery, or infantry. Zelly donned the gray-green garments of the Allgemeine-SS. When the guys teased him about becoming a paper and pencil pusher, he pointed out the stripe on his sleeve. The rank of Sturmman came from his service as a zug leader.

When the group was called to the mess hall, the colonel read a name from a clipboard. Then, the graduate marched forward to collect an envelope with orders for his next assignment. Zelly watched his guys scattered to the mighty Reich's four winds. He wondered why he wasn't summoned. His men shot him worried glances at the oversight. They left for the trains, exchanging handshakes, hugs, and backslaps as they said goodbye.

Only the commandant and Zelly remained. "Your zug heads for war— the Balkans, France, Poland, and Libya, but not you." He handed Zelly a sealed white packet bearing the stamp of the Reichsführer-SS. "As I learned on that first night, you're unique, black-banded. Someone has expectations for you, and I wish you the best of luck."

Zelly opened his mail to discover a promotion to sergeant, paperwork for almost two months of leave, and a train ticket to Berlin. Behind those was another ticket to Heeresversuchsanstalt Peenemünde for July 18th. He translated the compound noun—Army Research Center Peenemünde.

At the train station's window, he asked, "Where's Peenemünde?"

"It's on the Baltic and a pleasant vacation spot. My family enjoyed a summer on Rügen, a nearby island."

In the ten minutes before departure, Zelly telegraphed Vinny of his arrival.

****

As he stepped from the carriage, Zelly spotted Vinny's huge grin. "Any ideas about a place called Peenemünde?"

"I'll ask around, but we have some things to do."

They took an S-bahn to Kochstrasse and climbed to street level, where Vinny led Zelly to a building. "One of Albert Speer's buildings—labor district headquarters." He pointed to an eagle statue hovering eight stories up on the golden-brown structure, making Zelly crane his neck to see.

In the building's portico, Vinny pulled a shiny key from his pocket. "Yours to the apartment, in case you need it. Slide it behind the dedication plaque to a ledge where it will hold—magnetized."

Zelly whispered, covered by noisy traffic. "I took some pictures I'd like sent to Uncle August; can you develop and deliver them?"

Vinny recognized their code from Camp Ritchie and nodded. "Let's grab a bite to eat."

They entered an old building, a historic palace now serving as a restaurant, and took a table near the kitchen in the courtyard. The banging of pots and pans and shouts of orders kept their whispered conversation private. "Let's check what you remember of the codes."

They had developed the skills during a stay in Maryland, where Zelly learned spy craft. He remembered everything but played along the test. "We communicate through protocols and metaphors in ordinary communications, like letters and postcards, so our messages pass censorship and go unnoticed."

"Like what?"

"Uncle August is Uncle Sam."

"What does 'Dear Frederich' mean?"

"Things are terrible, and 'Dear Zelly' means everything's fine—same with 'Dear Vincente' or 'Dear Vinny.'"

"If I say I'm great?"

"You aren't, but I'm fine, means you are. So, Vinny, are you a great friend or a fine one?"

"Asshole."

"I don't recall a code for that," Zelly said.

"So, about the research?"

"Family relationships describe the job, using the first names of the pioneering scientist."

"Radio detection and ranging?"

"I'll mention an Uncle Heinrich for Heinrich Hertz. Every relationship implies a metaphor."

"To write about Jews?" he asked.

"I'll talk about Cousin Carl or Bob."

"How about the most important one?"

"Zähle or zählen, which means to count. If that word appears anywhere, we string the capitalized letters from Italian or German to form a hidden English message. All the other sentences must make some sense and sound like a regular letter."

"You Germans capitalize nearly everything," Vinny complained.

As they ate, Vinny talked about his embassy work, mostly business or culture, but with a few military things. Zelly's attention lingered on the map of the new Germany hanging on the wall beside the requisite picture of Hitler. It stretched from Norway and occupied France to Reichsgau Wartheland, which was once Poland. Zelly found the Ostsee, known in America as the Baltic, and traced the coast to Peenemünde, north of Berlin. "It's here."

When Vinny came for a look, Zelly dropped a film canister in his pocket.

"What's that?"

"Some pictures of gulls and turtles for the butcher. You know he loves wildlife."

"But you weren't near the seashore." Vinny's eyes sparkled as he deciphered the metaphor. "Was it too much risk?"

"Nearly cost my life," Zelly exaggerated.

****

22 April 1941—Berlin

As Vinny dressed for embassy work, Zelly tinkled on the apartment's piano keys. The cornflowers were gone, replaced by the last of the tulips Zelly had clipped surreptitiously in a nearby park.

"Tonight, let's celebrate your graduation and promotion. You won't want to miss this club, so wear your fancy new uniform. At 18:00, meet at the café nearest the traffic light on Potsdamer Platz."

"Can you be more specific?" He imagined the square would have many lights.

"Ask for the oldest one in Germany if you need help."

That evening, Zelly showed up as scheduled and sipped ersatz coffee in the shop as he watched the antique signal direct the flow of cars. Being at war had made certain changes. Coffee couldn't get through the British blockade, so they ground acorns as a substitute. The flavor wasn't terrible.

Vinny took a seat. "Your package is in Lisbon. The city is a global nest of spies." Vinny leaned closer. "I'm not sure the butcher will be happy, though. The risk was too great for wildlife snapshots."

Zelly groaned. "I thought you had planned a celebration at a club, not a dressing down over a cup of fake joe."

"Haus Vaterland is across the plaza."

Zelly read the massive building's sign, 'Germany's largest pleasure palace offering cheap recreation travel.'

"The place is a world fair of restaurants and bars—eat in Vienna, drink in Turkey, and dance in Spain. They have a cinema."

For a Tuesday night, the building teemed with customers as they climbed stairs and entered a club through swinging doors. The walls were murals of prairie vistas with Indians and buffalo. A black man dressed in boots and chaps did lariat tricks. "Welcome to Wild West Bar, y'all."

Zelly rolled his eyes. As they grabbed a table, a guitar struck up a Gene Autry tune, and the crowd chorused *Du bist mein Sonnenschein.* The strong beer reminded him of Texas.

When the musician played another tune, the audience chanted and clapped to a familiar beat. The words weren't German, and Zelly struggled to understand. "What's that music?"

Vinny's eyes sparkled. "You sang it for Meg."

Zelly's brain flipped, allowing *Deep in the Heart of Texas* to emerge from memory.

After another beer, they ate in the Grinzing, a Viennese café, finishing the meal with a Sacher torte, chocolate cake with a hint of apricot.

On the walk to the apartment, Zelly snapped a bootlace and bought a replacement. Upon arrival, Vinny switched on the radio and dialed Funk- Stunde Berlin. *Der Marsch* from the Luftwaffe Musik Korps played as Zelly removed the broken shoelace.

Vinny whispered, "Kill me with the garrote like I taught you."

Zelly wound the new shoestring through his fingers and snapped it around Vinny's neck. He twisted, tightening the knot, and lifted his friend off his feet. "I never thought I'd do this to you."

As Vinny's face shaded blue, Zelly released him.

While the military music continued marching, they tucked into the sway-backed bed, and the mattress rolled them into a center pile.

"Tell me what's happening in the world?"

Vinnie rattled off the news. "Yugoslavia surrendered. Vichy France withdrew from the League of Nations. The Greek Prime Minister committed suicide. British Commandos landed at Bardia in North Africa and destroyed an artillery battery and supply dump."

"And back home?"

"The debut of a new comic called *Captain America*."

"I bet my buddy Jimmy has already read it."

"Charles Lindberg and his America First gang are still pressing for non- intervention."

"Too late because I'm already here. Vinny, if his group wins and the U.S. avoids war, what happens to me?"

****

28 April 1941—A Run and a Date

As Vinny dressed for work, Zelly donned his sports shorts and athletic shirt. "I'm running the Tiergarten since we have a warm spring day. Apple and chestnut trees are in bloom, and the meadows are full of yellow dandelions and the fragrance of lilac."

"The Maypole went up last night, and swastikas are blooming like the lily of the valley," Vinny said. "Shall we meet for lunch at Goethe's statue?"

Zelly nodded and considered his fate.

If the America Firsters win and there isn't a war, will I have to stay German forever?

The mission was a gamble, and you knew it.

As Zelly stepped onto the sidewalk, his neck hairs arise, and a sense of uneasiness caught him. He blamed it on his thoughts until he scanned his surroundings and spotted a Daimler Maybach with a man in a black fedora leaning on the vehicle. Stretching his hamstrings against the building's stones, Zelly studied him through peripheral vision. The guy pretended to be disinterested.

While Zelly jogged, the man entered his car, and it followed in the morning traffic. He wondered whether Reichsführer Himmler wanted another chat or Stengler had returned to haunt him. Attempting to lose the tail, he forced his way through a revolving door. The local rumor claimed the place was the inspiration for the 1929 novel *Menschen im Hotel,* which became the 1932 Greta Garbo film *Grand Hotel.* Zelly recalled the movie's opening line, 'People coming, going. Nothing ever happens.' After lingering several minutes in the lobby, he left through a side door and found the Daimler waiting at the curb.

He shot a glance through the rear window, only to discover a newspaper blocking his view. When he started a quick sprint, the car's engine roared to life. A block later, he turned toward Unter den Linden, hoping the broad boulevard's heavy traffic would impede the pursuit. Racing through Pariser Platz and under Brandenburg Gate, he headed for the Tiergarten, where the car couldn't follow.

Thousands of blooming crocuses greeted him. The park was even more beautiful than he had imagined on that frozen day. He glanced back to find the Maybach at the curb. Stengler doffed his fedora and smiled.

Zelly's stomach soured—*what the fuck does he want?*

Continuing the run, he followed Bremer Weg, a wooded trail among fields of verdant grass where picnickers relaxed and retrievers fetched sticks thrown by well-trained boys. The Tiergarten was full of walking, playing, or cycling people, but the black hat lingered in the near distance. Zelly left the path, running across the grassy glades where dandelions waved in the breeze, but Stengler knew shortcuts that kept him close.

Why doesn't he come directly? Stengler's lurking was frightening.

He attempted to escape through the children's playground at Luiseninsel. As he crossed a bridge, memories flooded back of confronting Vinny on this very spot. As he rested on a bench, a bumblebee buzzed by, and the sound of distant woodpeckers reached his ears. Stengler wasn't in sight.

Nothing has changed since I was here. All the lies linger.

You've found more strange things. A German Shepherd showered you with affection. A family you've never seen treated you like a long-lost son. People in Wittenberg accepted you as a friend. It's like you've always been here.

Is this my authentic life, and America is fiction? This story goes beyond what I've grasped. Someday, I must know the whole tale.

A click and whir disturbed his reverie. His eyes followed the noise and located Stengler's black fedora in the tree shadows. Beneath the brim, a small rectangle partly covered his face with a round glint in the center—a lens on a tiny camera.

Zelly sprinted to a bunch of boys who played football—not the American kind. "Can I play?"

"Join my team. Take off your shirt, and we're going that way," a boy said.

He stripped it off, relishing the warmth of the sun on his skin. He remained with the game for a long time, hoping the Gestapo agent would grow bored. Soon, glances away from the field failed to find the fedora. Tired, he grabbed his top but remained bare-chested. He walked beside a creek and shortly reached the lake and bench where Vinny denied lying. Stengler occupied the seat.

"I wondered when you'd stop lurking," Zelly said.

"You're not much of a football player." Stengler stood. "Let's walk. I have a few questions." He headed Zelly towards a gap in a hedge of roses. "I spoke to Bannführer Stoppel in Italy about your incident. You'll be happy to know the Jew is still alive. He avoided a broken back and being stabbed by your dagger. Why lie to me?"

With a shrug, Zelly said, "I wanted to appear tough and never figured you'd research it."

"Go in there." He flicked his hand at the hedgerow's break.

Zelly entered a circular rose garden in full bud with a few petals peeking for the sun.

"I also spoke with the commander of an Italian patrol boat who fished you and your comrade out of Naples Bay. That seems to be the incident close to causing diplomatic problems. I understand you couldn't hear for a bit." Stengler's breath stunk of apricot snuff.

He nodded. "Their cannon shot frightened me. Since then, I've had worse experiences."

"Why were you in the sea?"

"I was sitting on the gunwale when Primo reversed the propellers, and I tumbled over."

Stengler drew his Walther special, the favored gun of undercover cops and the Gestapo.

"If you plan to shoot, the park has lots of witnesses. The noise will draw a crowd."

"Drop your shorts," Stengler ordered, and Zelly complied, leaving him bare from head to sock. Stengler kneeled to examine the scar. "When will you tell me the truth about this? That patrol boat was searching for a submarine spotted where you fell into the drink. Such facts make me suspicious."

As Stengler moved to grab his pocket, Zelly launched a bronco kick. He could have struck 10 times harder but feared injuring the Gestapo officer. Stengler fell on his back, getting the wind knocked out of him. The gun tumbled from his fingers and over the grass.

"So, you want a picture?" Zelly pulled the tiny Minox camera from Stengler's tunic and took four shots of his groin. "Now, you have your evidence or something for your masturbation fantasies." He placed the photographic equipment and weapon on the man's chest. After raising his shorts, he sprinted through the rose hedge. On the horizon, he spotted the tall Siegessäule, the victory column commemorating past Prussian conquests, and set a personal speed record in reaching it.

The avenue around the monument buzzed with cars in the roundabout and pedestrians in business suits, uniforms, and elegant dresses. They reminded him he'd run off without his shirt, but no one seemed to notice. Craning his neck to glimpse the golden monument on the top, he merged with the strolling crowd. Several black fedoras perched on their heads, but not Stengler's.

An hour before noon, he found a map pinpointing Goethe's statue and reached it in thirty minutes. Goethe stood in marble, wearing academic-style robes and holding a scroll. Surrounding him were representations of three muses—poetry, drama, and science—accompanied by naked boys. One, he recognized as Eros, the Greek love god, because of his arrow. In America, he'd be Cupid, the flying baby of romance. This representation showed him as a near teen, still prepubescent and rather under-endowed.

When Vinny arrived, Zelly told him about encountering Stengler.

"Kicking a Gestapo agent is never wise," Vinny advised.

"Do you think he's queer?"

"What matters is that he's a tenacious detective, investigating everything."

"I should have said you ripped my scrotum in a wild, passionate night of sex."

"That he might have believed."

"I'm thirsty for a beer."

They strolled to a biergarten on the park's edge, overlooking a lake. Zelly ate schnitzel with potato salad and cranberries and drank three steins of Hefeweizen.

As they left the table, Vinny asked, "Want some feminine company tonight? Ambra has a friend, an American who works as a secretary for some big shot at Ford, and I've arranged a double date. Her name is Nancy, and she's a lithe blonde. Can you summon some English after not remembering *Deep in the Heart of Texas?*"

"I'm game."

At the flat, Zelly's athletic shirt hanging from the doorknob, where Stengler had left it. After a shower, he picked out one of Vinny's diplomatic suits from the closet. When he reached Brandenburg Gate, he spotted Stengler's black fedora near a pillar. Soon, Vinny and Ambra arrived, bringing a blonde from the American Embassy.

"This is Zelly," Vinny introduced. "He's a German soldier on leave, and we've been friends for years. He speaks English and would enjoy some practice tonight."

"I'm Nancy, and would you mind if I let down my hair?"

His heart skipped when it cascaded around her shoulders.

"Should I call you Herr Zelly?" she asked.

"There's no need to be formal."

"A refreshing change from all the Herring and Heiling."

He offered his arm. "Where are we going, Vinny?"

"I'm tired of schnitzel and sausages," Ambra said. "Why don't we have some Italian cuisine?"

"I have the perfect spot," Vinny responded.

As Vinny led, Zelly opened the conversation. "Nancy, how much time have you spent in Berlin?"

"Since early January, how about you?"

"I arrived yesterday—on leave after training. I'll go to a post on the Baltic coast soon."

"Are you part of the blitz-shits?" she asked.

"I'll work in science."

"What branch of service?"

He considered lying but didn't. "I'm a sergeant in the SS."

She stiffened and stepped away as revulsion covered her face. His hopes for a pleasant evening evaporated.

The foursome caught a U-2 train to Wittenbergplatz. Two cars back, Stengler slipped aboard.

Vinny led them to Die Taverne, where the clientele fit into three groups—uniformed Germans with their wives or dates, fancy-suited embassy personnel, and journalists in threadbare suits with an ear to every conversation.

"Germany has a uniform for everything," Nancy mumbled.

The head waiter recognized Vinny and offered them a splendid booth for four. Stengler, however, took a nearby table without waiting to be seated. The lighting was dim, and the ambiance was romantic. Conversations around them entirely avoided war.

Nancy's steely eyes stabbed like daggers. "So, sergeant, what do you think of Jews?"

Zelly shrugged. "I think very little about them. I understand the claim is they hurt the country, but none have wronged me."

Stengler nearly unbalanced his chair as he leaned to listen.

As the server brought wine and took orders, Zelly said, "Please excuse me."

He stepped to Stengler's table and said, "Thanks for returning my shirt, but there's no need to lurk, bark commands, or sneak around. If you want to see me naked, just ask. Aren't we part of the same organization? Shouldn't we be comrades in arms?"

The Cheshire cat grin made the scar near Stengler's ear twitch. "Perhaps if you didn't lie. I heard you say a Jew had never wronged you—I would consider a ripped scrotum as a wrong. Liars cover something up. What are you hiding? And why are you with an American?"

"I'm practicing English, despite your distaste for the language." Zelly returned to his table.

Nancy was waiting for his arrival. "You must hate Jews— everyone understands the Nazis do. Don't you read *Der Stürmer*?"

"I don't subscribe."

"Don't you realize what Germany is doing to them?"

Zelly rose again. "Ladies, I've enjoyed your company and hope you have a wonderful evening. Vinny, I'll meet you at the apartment." He clicked his heels, shot his hand in the air, and left with a "Heil Hitler."

When Zelly reached Die Taverne's exit, he caught sight of the eyes of a journalist watching him from the portico.

****

28 April 1941—Jockey Bar

Outside the restaurant, Zelly sniffed the journalist's intoxication as the man laughed.

"Woman problems?" he asked in English.

"Are there other kinds?" Zelly responded.

The newsman opened his valise, revealing a bottle of Jack Daniels. "How about a drink if we go somewhere safe?" When Zelly nodded, the man grabbed his elbow. "Hurry before your Gestapo friend catches us."

Despite inebriation, the man took a quick corner and led Zelly through an alley to a well-hidden joint. They ducked inside. The speakeasy was jiving to smooth and warm jazz harmonies.

"What is this place?" Zelly grinned as Big Willy's 7-piece band played *It Don't Mean a Thing*. A mixed crowd danced, segregated by sex. "I love the music."

"Welcome to Jockey Bar." The journalist took a table, poured two fingers into a tumbler, and slid it across the table. "Jockey for the American underwear, not horse racing, and that's Willy Berking on the trombone."

After downing the whiskey, he smiled wistfully and wobbled his glass, asking for more.

"Strange conversation you had with your bird." The newspaperman refilled Zelly's drink. "Quite a spirited woman, right?"

"That was Nancy, a blind date organized by my Italian friend. She was an obnoxious weasel. It started hopeful; went horrible fast." Zelly downed his drink. "Does Jack have a couple more fingers?"

A blonde with long hair curled at the shoulders sang *Bei Mir Bist Du Schön* as she performed an erotic dance.

"I'm Herschel." The man refilled the tumbler and watched Zelly's eyes as they lost focus.

"Fuck, I'm getting drunk." He bounced in time with the song.

Herschel leaned close. "What about Germany's treatment of Jews?"

He shrugged and gulped the liquor. "I know nothing about it." Zelly swayed with the music as he sipped. "Say, is the dancer a female impersonator? I see a bulge."

"Why, I think you're correct. What do you know of the war?"

"I haven't been in it. I'm on leave after training, but I'll leave for the Baltic soon." As he burped, he stood and turned to catch the end of the show.

The performer dropped her dress, leaving him wearing only bulging Jockey briefs.

"I was right," Zelly said.

The band played *Shout and Feel It.* Many from the audience came forward to jive as same-sex couples.

Herschel rounded the table and touched Zelly's shoulder. "Would you like to dance?"

He reacted with horror, spilling his drink and overturning his chair.

"Gestapo!" Someone shouted.

Instantly, the dancers switched partners, merging the sexes, and changed to a foxtrot. The musicians transformed the music into *Das ist Berlin.* While Zelly scrambled to upright his seat, he recognized Stengler.

"He keeps ruining my evening," Zelly pointed.

The journalist rushed through a door, taking his bottle and valise with him.

Stengler's eyes met Zelly's. He drew his pistol and fired a shot into the wall behind the bandstand. "This place is closed!"

The panicked crowd rushed to escape. In the bedlam, Zelly followed through the door Herschel had used. Beyond, he found a filthy toilet room with an open window. He realized his drunkenness as he struggled through the obstacle. Down the block, the reporter paused and motioned to him— around the corner and in. Zelly followed the directions, ending in an upstairs club that was smaller but just as jumping as Jockey Bar.

"I was hoping for a talk," Herschel said when Zelly joined him.

"Weren't we? Until you asked me to dance."

He pulled a glass from his valise and poured Zelly a drink. "I figured you as queer with your fascination at the bulge. It wasn't real, you know."

"You're sure?"

"Doing my due diligence, I investigated."

"This place won't be any safer than the other one. That Gestapo officer is following me, and he'll find me here, too."

A lady who looked like Lotte Lenya sang *Mack the Knife* in its original German.

"Another impersonator, as Lotte's long gone to America," the correspondent said.

"I love the tune." Zelly joined in and sipped Gentleman Jack. "I'm new to Berlin. How do I get to Wittenbergplatz station?"

"I'll take you."

With the whiskey bottle empty, the man led Zelly through the late-night streets and left him at the platform for a U-2 train. While waiting, he sang the song buzzing in his head, the prologue from *The Threepenny Opera.*

His stomach revolted from nearly a complete bottle of Jack. He spotted a trash can on the platform's edge and sprinted toward it. Unfortunately, he couldn't keep up with the urgency and vomited on a man standing nearby. After three purges on the bystander's trousers, he rose to make an apology. His eyes locked with Stengler.

"How could you allow yourself to get so drunk?" the officer asked.

Zelly took the questions literally. "I haven't eaten since lunch, but you already know from tailing me all day."

"You shouldn't spend time with foreign journalists or in places like that," Stengler scolded.

"Sorry," Zelly said as the next upchuck struck.

When the U-2 train arrived, Stengler helped him board. When it made a jerky start, Zelly's heave splattered his suit and Stengler's shoes. By the time they reached his stop, Zelly sang the song at the top of his lungs, and in English.

Stengler got him to the building and up the stairs. "Someday, your taste for illegal music will be the end of you."

****

29 April 1941—The Morning After

Zelly woke in the apartment, curled under a blanket beside the piano, naked, hungover, and hungry. He found the clothes he'd worn last evening wet in the tub but didn't remember taking them off. The empty bedroom still smelled of Ambra's perfume and the lingering odor of sex. Angry and depressed, he headed for food at Café Kranzler on the corner of Friedrichstrasse and Unter den Linden. He chose a balcony table overlooking the street and ordered strong coffee and an assortment of French breads and fruit preserves.

As the meal assuaged his headache, he inspected people, paying particular attention to men in black fedoras, but Stengler wasn't among them. He grinned as he remembered spewing vomit on the agent.

Why did he follow me all day?

He's lurking until you make a big mistake, like singing banned songs in English.

Did he walk my drunken ass up the stairs?

And probably undressed you.

Over the railing, he spotted Vinny strolling across the avenue. "Vinny, I'm up here." In minutes, he joined him at the table.

"Buddy, I'm sorry about last night. I was too shit-faced drunk and interrupted your fuck."

"We got right back to it. Did Ambra's moans and shouts keep you up? And why did Stengler bring you home?"

Zelly shrugged. "He dogged me all day, but I hope he didn't put me to bed."

"Ambra and I did it, and a warning—she's seen your goods."

"If she did, I'm surprised she went back to screwing you." Zelly used the German slang word 'bumsen.'

Vinny grinned and thought of the English lingo—'bum' for 'butt.' "I remember when Stengler stole the skinny-dipping picture. He wants your bum, sen?" He filched a pastry from the basket.

After paying the check, they walked Unter den Linden to the Spreekanal and stopped on the bridge. Vinny verified they were alone. "I have news— Uncle August has your pictures."

"What did he say?"

"That you shouldn't have sent them. They weren't worth the risk. Don't you think the Brits or French hadn't provided it?"

Zelly's head bowed in disappointment. "But I'm supposed to spy."

"Still, the butcher learned some valuable facts," Vinny offered. "The updated turrets, bigger guns, weak armor in the rear, and gas cans on the bumper. The Brits never mentioned those important details."

"So, I'm not a total bust?"

"Have patience. When you're on the Baltic, you'll discover things Churchill doesn't know."

****

1 May 1941—*Hilf Mit!*

Oskar Stengler ate breakfast at another Café, Kranzler on Kurfürstendamm in the Charlottenburg district of Berlin. Thirty minutes later, he was in a lawyer's office to complete the purchase of a beach bungalow in Zinnowitz on the Baltic. Neither he nor his wife had visited the house, but the picture revealed shoreline colors, high gables, and gingerbread trim. She had fallen in love with it sight unseen.

The restaurant's radio droned on about the siege of Tobruk—Rommel's Afrika Korps were trying to wrest the port from British hands, but he paid little attention. His mind focused on some film he'd left for development at the Gestapo darkroom. Pictures of Zellner's scar and the photo wall at the house in Wittenberg. He hoped the complete file and images would bring the guy into sharper focus. Within a few days, he would report to Peenemünde and a new job, head of the base's security office. Soon after that, the Zellner kid would arrive.

In minutes, they finished the property transaction because the SS had contributed most of the purchasing funds. He strolled north on Ku'Damm to Zoo station and hopped a U-2 train to Potsdamer Platz. After a short walk, he stepped to the photo processing counter to get his images. The quality of the Minox's snapshots surprised him, even the ones he had asked to be enlarged. Clutching the packet, he went to headquarters and spread the pages across a desktop. He examined each one with a magnifying glass.

The man at a neighboring table chuckled at the groin pictures Zelly had self-shot. "Are you adding to your collection of penises, Stengler?"

"I'm perfecting a new torture." Oskar selected two shots and took them to the basement. He chose one of the medical professionals who ensured interrogation subjects could endure more pain. "Doctor, what can you deduce about this scar?"

He hummed as he examined. "The youth had a scrotal injury—a tear rather than a cut by a blade. The suturing is fine, done by a skillful surgeon. I'd guess about a year old."

Oskar pulled the skinny-dipping image from his shirt pocket. "Same boy, but I can't see the blemish. What do you think?"

He put on glasses with a surgical loupe. "It's not there, so this is earlier."

When Stengler returned to his desk, a fellow Gestapo agent hovered there. The man tapped a picture. "Oskar, I've seen this guy in a party magazine several years ago, as I recall. It's a youth-oriented publication from the HJ, so I would figure *Jungen: Euhr Welt* or *Die Junge Kameradschaft*."

"Thanks for the tip. I'll ask at a bookstore." With the print in hand, he took a brisk walk down Unter den Linden. At the store, he placed the image on the counter. "Do you recognize this?"

The man studied it for an instant. "It was the cover of *Hilf Mit!* a few years back. I've got the issue if you want it." He disappeared into the shelves and brought a thin, newsprint-style magazine. "Number six of 1938, a publication for teachers."

Instantly, Oskar recognized the two photos matched and decided to purchase the booklet. While I taught, I got these magazines monthly. As he flipped through, he discovered a call for entries to an essay contest, which he had used as a writing assignment.

Three years ago, Zellner would have been fifteen—around the time he joined my class. Still, I don't remember him, but everything seems fine. So, why does my intuition sound an alarm every time I see him?

CHAPTER 8

Peenemünde

18 June 1941—To Peenemünde

After six weeks without a glimpse of Stengler, Zelly hoped he was gone for good. Vinny accompanied him to Stettin station, where they said their goodbyes. The ticket promised a 90-minute ride to Eberswalde, followed by a train change for the last leg to Wolgast. He shared a compartment with a nurse whose clacking knitting needles made him nervous and repeated switches to the sidings to let priorities pass grated at him.

"Sister, this was supposed to be an express, but I'm 30 minutes late for a connection."

The needlework stopped for a brief shrug. "Something significant is happening in the East."

He hoped a conversation would settle his fretfulness. "Where are you going?"

"Danzig, to a hospital. You?"

"Wolgast for duty."

"North," she said in surprise. "I figured you were joining a more eastern unit."

Priority freight trains and nurses headed east with soldiers already posted. Hitler's planning blitzkrieg against the Soviet Union.

No wonder so many of your training group are headed to Poland.

After missing the connection by over an hour, he flashed his SS orders at the ticket window. Without glancing at his papers, the clerk pointed to track three. "Board before it leaves in ten minutes."

Zelly hurried to the train—third-class cars filled with rows of benches already packed with passengers. He chose one with two zones. In front, a gaggle of young women, probably secretaries and file clerks, chatted in lively clusters. Men occupied the rear, discussing engineering issues. A single row of Wehrmacht uniforms separated the sections. He worked his way to it as the engine whistled, made steam, and chugged into motion. A plain-clothed Gestapo agent circulated through the carriage, checking ID.

When he finished, he stepped beside Zelly. "Excuse me, but I think you took my seat."

Zelly jumped up, recoiling in surprise when he recognized Stengler.

"Ah, English book boy, your papers, please."

Unbuttoning his pocket to retrieve the documents. Zelly concluded meeting Stengler wasn't a chance encounter. "Is everyone aboard heading to Heeresversuchsanstalt Peenemünde?"

"Like you, they're going to a new job, but they know little more. Loose comments like that are dangerous when espionage is all around."

Zelly suppressed a grin at how correct Stengler was—a spy was listening. He handed over his documentation and orders.

"Your assignment is in guidance. No wonder you over-think."

The train swayed, bouncing them together, and Stengler grabbed him. "I said I'd uncover your secrets. You're Sicherheitsdienst, aren't you? That explains the black band on your file."

Zelly's face remained impassive—that was the intelligence agency of the SS, spying for the Reichsführer and a sister organization to Stengler's Gestapo.

I suppose I am, but Himmler never said so.

And your documents don't hint at it.

They squished into the single-seat space.

"I never had the chance to thank you for taking me home that drunken night," Zelly said.

"If you obey my orders, perhaps we can be comrades."

A fear-filled apprehension coursed through Zelly.

How can I work for America with him trailing me?

Obviously, he has a new job, too, and it might be you.

****

18 June 1941—Army Research Center

The carriage grew quiet as the third-class train slowed, nearing Wolgast. The station's little red brick building housed another commuter train waiting on a second track. Tables lined the wooden platform, manned by clerks to process passengers. The car door opened, and Wehrmacht soldiers, armed with machine guns, entered to distribute a paper.

"This is your security agreement." Stengler's voice boomed through the car. "To work here, you'll sign it and guarantee it with your life. If you can't agree, you'll go back to where you came from. After signing, hand your documents and this paper to the nearest guard and disembark. When you hear your name, go to the table for clearance. After that, board the other train."

Zelly read the pledge and realized he was set to commit a series of major violations as required for his job to both Himmler and Uncle Sam. Since Stengler had figured out one, Zelly hoped he would never uncover the other.

It wasn't long before a clerk called Zelly. The worker verified his identity and matched his orders against a clip-boarded list.

"I'm your roommate, Wilhelm Dotzel, but my friends call me Helmut." He reminded Zelly of Edward G. Robinson in *Kid Galahad*—nearly six inches shorter and heavyset, round face, chubby cheeks and deep lines outlining his mouth. As his thick lips talked, his eyebrows bounced beneath his combat helmet.

"I'm Zelly."

He pinned a golden stick pin to Zelly's pocket beside the martyr's badge and handed him a colored card. "In Peenemünde, you must always wear this tinnie and carry the passcard. Every functional unit has a color, and you're yellow for guidance. To screen you, I'll need you to open your luggage and empty your pockets."

The handful of stuff he carried wasn't of interest, including the lockpick. As the sergeant flipped through the suitcase, he smirked at the nasty Italian magazines. When he found the electronic parts, Helmut reached for his whistle. "Sorry, but I have to do this." The whistle's shrill note caused the dogs to bark. When the machine guns arrived, Zelly raised his arms in surrender.

****

The commotion caused Stengler to intervene. "Sergeant, bring his belongings inside, and I'll screen him."

The small station was one room with stairs leading to a partial second- floor office. Stengler took Zelly to a table and stood opposite while Helmut delivered luggage and left.

"Herr Stengler, they are the same electronics you examined at Brenner.

Why paw them again?"

When Helmut exited, Stengler said, "An excuse to talk privately. Wonder why I'm here?"

"I figure Himmler made me your special assignment. Are you responsible for the black band?"

"That came when the Reichsführer chose you as Sicherheitsdienst. When I asked about you, he offered me the job as your courier. You'll write the reports, and I'll deliver them. Clear?"

"Jawohl. May I ask why you inquired about me?"

"I don't remember you from the gymnasium, but all the records show you were in my class. Your skinny-dipping picture proved your scar stories were lies. I enjoy solving mysteries." His grin turned jack-o'-lantern evil. "Let's straighten something out— you work for me, and I hold your fate in my hand."

Boots pounded as a colonel descended the stairs. "What's taking so long?"

Stengler held up the cloth bag. "Sir, he's smuggling electronics."

The senior officer sighed. "Stengler, you're new, but the crime of concern is stealing parts—going out, not coming in."

****

Zelly tossed his things into his suitcase and rushed to the train. Helmut had saved him a seat. As the locomotive left the station, they passed through a gate and crossed a small bridge.

"Welcome to Usedom Island," Helmut said and turned into a tour guide. "The Luftwaffe has a site on the west side, and the Army owns the east. So, we only meet the fly boys in Karlshagen, that town over there."

They emerged from a pine forest and rode along the village. A road to the right led to a beautiful beach. On the left, Helmut pointed to barracks arrayed in a horseshoe around a common yard. "That's your new home, an old Strength Through Joy camp. Only us two in the room with a shared bathroom and lounge for a dozen guys."

They got off at the next stop near a sports field where a football game was in progress. Over lunch in the soldiers' mess, they shared life stories. Helmut was a year and four months older and came from Hamburg, where his father worked in the port. His job was guarding the perimeter and prisoners. Zelly explained the martyr's badge, but Helmut couldn't believe a mother would abandon her child.

After the meal, Helmut led them to their building and room. Zelly put his suitcase on the unoccupied bed. As Zelly unpacked the necessaries, Helmut asked, "May I read one of your nasty magazines?"

"They're in Italian." Zelly tossed him one.

"I'm more interested in the pictures." He flipped pages.

Zelly tacked two items on the wall above his headboard, the *Hilf Mit!* magazine and the *Morgenpost* picture, and stowed his gear in the locker. His luggage went beneath the rack.

Helmut introduced him around the barracks, and showed him the shared bathroom and radio lounge.

In the afternoon, Helmut stood guard duty. Zelly donned his athletic outfit for a run to scope out the facility. Like movie spies always do, he drew a map upon his return. The action was contrary to the security agreement he had signed only hours ago. He hid the sheet in the Italian magazine Helmut had perused and put it behind the suitcase's false bottom.

****

19 June 1941—First Day at Work

The next day, Zelly put on his uniform and boarded the commuter train that traveled the length of the base. One passenger's yellow tinnie matched his, so he followed him to a building, one of many scattered throughout the forest. At the first desk, he presented his orders to a mid-twenties guy. "Heil Hitler."

"Welcome to Flight Mechanics, Ballistics, Guidance, and Control. I'm Max from Mechanics. What uni?"

"Do you mean unit?"

"No, what university? Most here are from Darmstadt, next is Dresden. I'm from the Institute for Oscillation Research in Berlin."

"The SS took me after graduation." Zelly wondered if he was the dumbest one on the island.

Max checked the clipboard. "You'll work with Hirschler in guidance and control. Tomorrow, no uniform nor salute, as they don't mix well with science. Come along for the grand tour."

He waved toward a dozen men discussing math on a chalkboard. "The center one is the head boss, Dr. Ernst Steinhoff. He's a director, thirty-two, Darmstadt doctorate, and holds a world glider record."

They walked to another section. "This is your area. The man drawing angles and calculating trigonometry is Helmut Hölzer, your department chief—Darmstadt and worked at Berlin's Telefunken, so he loves radio shit." Next, they paused beside a guy wielding a smoking soldering iron. "Doctor Otto Hirschler, this is Frederich Zellner, your new man."

"Please, sir, call me Zelly."

"Well, are you ready to work?"

"Very much so."

"Then fetch me black coffee."

Zelly found a coffeepot and delivered a cup to Herr Hirschler. He wandered the building, poking his nose into people's activities with a smile and an offer to deliver coffee. When he returned with the drink, they took a minute to talk about their job.

He learned Peenemünde was constructing rockets—although everyone called them Aggregate. The place had a language all to itself, with everything coded by a euphemism. The new vocabulary was daunting to master, but he mapped his technical knowledge with German metaphors. Soon, he could tell a Tisch launch platform from an Intra fire extinguisher. He found the work exciting, more than he could have hoped for.

A fresh engineering graduate assigned him math and physics problems. The first was easy—a boy throwing a rock. He had to calculate its trajectory and the forces acting on it. Correct answers brought increasingly hard questions involving more massive stones, faster throws, and longer distances. In short order, he went beyond his semester of calculus but puzzled out solutions.

After he calculated the force required to throw a thousand-kilogram stone 500 kilometers, the grad said, "Welcome to ballistic rocks. Now, vary the parameters. Would a crosswind change your answer? Does a hot or cold day matter?"

He learned small conditional variances might alter the course and determine whether a rocket reached the target or failed. Things like wind, propellant load, and fuel burn rate proved critical.

The tutor pointed out a too-long trajectory. "A mistake in range." Then he showed examples where the projectile missed left or right. "An error in cross-range."

Zelly drew a set of concentric circles on the plot. "Then, this is the circle of probable error, distributed on a bell curve."

"It usually takes rookies weeks to discover that," the man grinned with delight.

After work, Helmut caught him on the train. "Help me at Wolgast to process more workers?"

"What do I do?"

"Check ID and take their security agreements. Very simple."

Hours later, he had stamped so many clearances he grew sleepy. A brown-haired girl with a beautiful smile and rosy cheeks brought him to his senses. Her scarlet dress, cinched with a black sash at the waist, defined her curvaceous figure. Beneath its hem, shapely legs descended to heels. She handed him her papers and pledge. He forced his eyes away from the folds over her breasts to her shy expression.

He memorized her name, Gertrud Ehle, and her birth date, January 17, 1926. "You are seventeen, five months, and two days."

She cast down her eyes in embarrassment. "Is that too young?"

Her ID picture showed a bashful girl. To overcome her reticence, he said, "I'm only eighteen."

She blushed and averted her eyes.

Returning her documents, he grinned and checked her arrangements. "Fräulein Ehle, your work is at the production factory, and you'll stay in the women's dorm on Strandstrasse."

The man behind her thrust his papers forward.

Zelly took a chance, ignoring him, and offered, "Miss, would you like me to show you to your building? It's near the train stop."

"I'm sure other girls will go that way." She stepped away.

The man waved his agreement in Zelly's face. "I'm waiting."

Zelly let his eyes follow Trudl's every step and hip wiggle.

She stopped, turned, and smiled—as beautiful as a spring sunrise, full of hope and promise.

Before the next man could scold him, he stamped him in.

Later, in the carriage, he tried for a seat beside her but couldn't. When she disembarked, he scampered out with her. "Fräulein, this way." He gallantly led several women headed for the dorm.

Returning to his building, he slipped into the shared toilet where Helmut sat on the throne, still wearing his helmet. While one hand masturbated furiously, the other grasped an Italian magazine—the one with the leopard.

"I've discovered you got your nickname from your perpetual cover."

Helmut glanced up, but his hand never slowed. "Hope you don't mind.

I borrowed this."

"No problem," Zelly said, except he'd tucked the map inside the cover of that publication.

"The guys in training pestered me when I wore it in the shower."

"No one's shooting for a thousand miles." Discreetly, Zelly tried to determine if his map was still within the pages without appearing to gaze at Helmut's other activity. "What picture struck your fancy?"

Helmut turned the page toward Zelly.

Instantly, he knew it was gone. He forced a chuckle, but the missing paper brought a panic. "You're stroking to a condom advertisement about gonorrhea?"

"Tripper? Ever caught it?"

"No."

"An older Hamburg Blitzmädel broke me in, and I pissed burning needles for days."

"How old were you?"

"Fifteen." He shot Zelly a curious expression. "Does that mean no sex?" Zelly's blush told him the answer. "Wait until the guys know you're still a virgin."

"Did you find a map inside the cover?"

"Yes. You forgot your security pledge."

Zelly's heart dropped to his toes. "Where is it?"

"I reported it to the Gestapo."

****

20 June 1941—The Map

Sleep was impossible as Zelly stewed over the map in Stengler's hands. *He holds my fate in his grubby fingers,* he thought. *Any minute, he'll burst through the door with soldiers and rifles.* To break the spell, he walked along the beach as a crescent moon dipped below the horizon. No other lights disturbed the blanket of stars or the inky blackness of the Baltic Sea.

I drew it despite the agreement.

He's bouncing in excitement over what he'll do to you.

I can't change it.

You make a lot of mistakes.

Soon, the sky lightened as dawn approached. When it was bright enough for safety, he swam in the brisk water, which helped clear his head. When the sun rose from the ocean, he marveled at the beauty. He faced the day with courage and went to work.

He spotted the new girl, Gertrud, waiting at the train platform and joined her. "Fräulein, I'm Frederich Zellner, but to friends I'm Zelly."

"I remember." She flashed a shy smile. "Call me Trudl, my dad's nickname for me."

She reminded him of Bette Davis in *Jezebel* with gorgeous eyes and a coquette hairstyle. His fingers longed to uncurl it. He stepped behind her and sang.

"I love *Lili Marleen*," she said.

He learned the song about a year ago, part of Bob and Carl's tutorial on Nazi culture, but never figured he'd use it to charm a girl. "Would you like to go on a date?" Her answer was a shy nod.

At work, he reviewed yesterday's calculations until Otto Hirschler, his boss, interrupted. "Come on to the guidance team staff meeting in Karlshagen." Zelly followed him to a restaurant and chose an unoccupied chair by the door.

Dr. Steinhoff announced the agenda and introduced new employees, including Zelly. Section heads delivered reports thick with Peenemünde- speak, making his brain whirl to understand. As the lectures continued, he learned of the years invested in the project. A gentleman entered and sat beside him. Some waved the man to a reserved seat in front, but he remained.

The division functioned with three competing teams, pursuing distinct solutions in a contest. As Zelly listened, he gleaned their approaches. One system required five gyroscopes, tons of gears, and launched down a ramp. Another method used two gyroscopes with hydraulics to launch vertically but needed a complicated 45° pitch-over maneuver to head for the target. The third had four gyroscopes and electric motors to steer, like a pilot-less airplane.

He examined drawings of rockets, code-named A-3 and A-5 (A for Aggregat), and viewed films of test launches, both successes and failures. Each group trumpeted its solution as ideal for a new

A-4, capable of hitting London, and the future A-9/A-10, a two-stage rocket.

The gentleman beside him asked, "If you could choose the system most likely to succeed, which one is best?"

Zelly thought he was being tested with another theoretical problem. "None, sir."

The questioner's eyebrows rose, as did the volume of his voice. "Why so?"

The staff fell silent, and all eyes turned to the room's rear. Sweat beaded on Zelly's brow as he worked to tamp down his nervousness. "Each has necessary features but, alone, is insufficient for success. I would suggest that a mixture of the approaches is required."

Concern crossed the man's face. "Tell me more."

Perspiration drenched Zelly. "They all use the same principle, detecting deviation by gyroscopes and steering to correct it, but that will lead to over- control. Momentum will push the rocket beyond zero and require additional correction. Oscillations inject inaccuracy into the aim, conceivably compromising stability and definitely enlarging the circle of probable error."

A system champion challenged him. "A-3 and A-5 haven't exhibited such behavior."

Zelly shrugged. "Maybe the flights were too short. Were you trying to hit a target?"

The gentleman asked, "Son, in which department do you work?"

"Zelly is in my group," Hirschler said with trepidation.

The man touched Zelly's shoulder. "Perfect—then you and Otto develop the right mixture."

"Jawohl, Mein Herr," he barked as the man left the room.

The boss hurried to the chair beside Zelly. "Didn't you recognize Dr. Wernher von Braun?"

"Shit." Zelly crumbled. He lingered after the staff departed to study the poster of a future two-stage rocket, the A-9/A-10. His stomach soured when its name, Amerika, made its target obvious.

They're designing this missile to attack the United States. You must stop them.

The butcher predicted I'd find a mission, and this is it.

With your map in Gestapo hands, you're dead from the get-go. Then, who'll save America?

****

Stengler stared at the two men who had stormed his office. Major Stegmaier, the base commandant, was in a fit of anger, but Dr. von Braun relaxed in the wooden guest chair.

"This boy has been here two days and has already violated his pledge." Stegmaier pounded the map on his desk.

"I intend to take action, but how serious should we be?" Oskar asked.

"Very. He could be a British spy or part of the resistance!"

The doctor looked dubious. "I met Herr Zellner in today's staff meeting, and he made the most insightful observation I've heard in months."

"Protecting the facility is my concern, not yours," Stegmaier said.

"Without my program, the installation wouldn't exist," von Braun argued. "It seems premature to conclude his act was nefarious. Since he's very new here, why not ask him why he drew it?"

"He has lied to me before," Stengler said.

"The agreement specifies death for violators," the commander reminded.

"Are you proposing a public hanging as an example to all?" von Braun asked. "He may have other valuable ideas. I'd hate to miss out on them."

"His file is full of commendations, but he has always made me suspicious," Stengler said.

"I noted a recent recommendation for the officer's school," the doctor pointed out.

Stegmaier's furrowed brows and squinting eyes showed skepticism. "So, you recommend leniency?"

Von Braun nodded. "He holds a yellow tinnie and has access to every location on base. He heard more secrets in today's staff meeting than either of you know."

"It's my job to handle such things," Stengler said.

The commandant considered the idea. "Dr. von Braun, are you comfortable letting the Gestapo take care of this?"

"Only if we see the boy together. Our joint presence will signify the importance, but remember, dead men no longer offer insights."

The major sighed. "I'll send for him."

"Let's visit him in his quarters," Stengler said. "The intrusion into his space sends a message."

****

Zelly's workday ended after the staff meeting. He headed back to his room and wrote Vinny a postcard, recalling a joke he'd once played on Uncle Robert—Robert Goddard was the code for a job in rocketry. He stuck the card in the mailbox near a train platform where Trudl waited.

"Was your invitation for tonight?" she asked. "My roommate is Greta, another new gal, and she'd like a date, too."

"Mine is Helmut, and I'll bet he'll be willing."

"Meet on the beach outside the dorm," she said.

When Zelly entered the barracks, he found Helmut lounging near the radio. "Would you like to spend the evening with a lady?"

Helmut's helmet nodded enthusiastically. "After a shower. Are you angry at me for turning in the map?"

"It was a breach of trust and friendship. If you have something against me, I'd rather you talk to me first, before the Gestapo. The consequences are unknown so far, but you might get a new roommate soon."

"It was my duty." He undressed.

"I don't believe searching through my private stuff is part of a Wehrmacht sergeant's job!"

"Sorry." Helmut headed for the shower, naked except for his helmet.

As they dressed, Zelly suggested, "The dames will like you better without it."

"They will realize its sensibility."

They strolled Strandstrasse to the beautiful beach. Silver sand sparkled in the sun, and blue waters lapped against it as the girls came from the dorm. Greta was striking, about two years older than Trudl, with blonde hair in a ponytail. After a wolf whistle, Helmut dropped to a knee, took her hand, and kissed it.

"The gesture would be much more gallant without the gear," Zelly said.

"You should wear yours." Helmut used 'du,' the familiar form of 'you,' meaning he'd accepted Zelly as a friend. Whether the friendship was mutual was yet to be determined.

They took the ladies to the Karlshagen Gasthaus, where the hefeweizen was refreshing, and the schnitzel and fried potato wedges were superb.

"Mittsommernacht is coming when the sun hangs until early morning," Greta said.

"Greta, will you jump the bonfire with me?" Helmut asked.

"Trudl, will you—?"

"I thought you'd never ask."

After a wonderful evening, they separated as couples on the walk. Trudl and Zelly shared a kiss in a stand of alder trees. At the dorm, the guys reconnected. When Helmut opened their door, three men occupied their room. Zelly groaned, popped to attention, and barked, "Heil Hitler."

The sight of an officer holding the map made Zelly sweat rivers. When Stengler waved Helmut away, he disappeared into the lounge.

Zelly's heart raced as he stepped forward to face the inquisition. The beat was faster than when on a long-distance run. Stengler's Cheshire cat grin revealed his glee, while Dr. von Braun's eyebrows arched with curiosity.

Stengler said, "You've met Dr. von Braun, and this is Major Stegmaier, base commandant."

Zelly tried to repress his panic with a Prussian bow as Stengler closed the door for privacy.

"After only two days here, you've already committed a significant violation of your agreement," Stegmaier said.

"I'm sorry," Zelly said, "but this place is so confusing. Half the buildings hide in the forest. I had to follow someone to find my workplace and the staff meeting. I sketched it to help me navigate."

"There are reasons for the security restrictions," the major said.

"I understand. In electronics, I work so much better with a schematic of a circuit."

A corner of von Braun's mouth curled upward at the comparison.

"We intend rules to be followed," the Gestapo agent said.

The doctor appraised Stengler with some amusement. "You are also new. Not every mind works in the same fashion. I often draw when I'm wrestling with a difficult concept." Von Braun turned his scrutiny on Zelly. "I find it hard to believe this young man is engaged in espionage."

Zelly stared at Stengler. Was this the time to speak of Himmler's assignment?

Stengler kept him silent with a waving finger.

"Of course, the base is your area of responsibility, and security is yours, Herr Stengler, but I think a warning would suffice."

The commandant wadded the map, tossed it in the trash, and reclaimed the pledge. "Consider yourself warned."

"Jawohl," Zelly barked. "I'm sorry, sir."

When the commander and doctor departed, Stengler lingered and pointed to the *Hilf Mit!* magazine tacked above Zelly's headboard. "When and where was that taken?"

"Summer camp when I was fifteen. Should I have told them we're spying for Herr Himmler?"

The agent flinched at the suggestion. "That must remain secret. The commandant wanted to hang you as an example, so you owe me your life. Obey the regulations and give me a full report of the staff meeting." Stengler poked Zelly's chest with a finger hard. "Remember, I own you from your cowlick to your toenails. Anything I ask of you, you will provide. Clear?"

Zelly nodded.

Stengler kneeled on the bed to scrutinize the picture. "Cover boy, I'll research this." He scribbled something in his notebook. As he left the room, he said, "The more I learn about you, the worse you stink."

As Helmut readied for the night, he asked, "Only a warning?"

Zelly nodded. "Please be a bit more considerate?" He used 'du,' as Helmut had.

I guess I have a buddy and a girlfriend.

They are your enemies, not your friends—never forget it.

CHAPTER 9

Extra Work

21 June 1941—Toilet Cleaners and Threats

When Zelly woke, Helmut was on his bunk, leaning on an elbow. "I didn't know if you would survive yesterday, but golden tinnie wearers must enjoy extra privileges."

"Just remember that before you report me again."

He shrugged. "It would be even safer if you didn't violate the security protocols."

As they dressed in uniform, Zelly planned on how to prevent discovering his activities to Helmut.

The labor shortage in Peenemünde resulted in many soldiers having extra duties. Zelly's assignment was guarding Polish janitors as they cleaned toilets. The job allowed him to take a Mauser pistol from the armory to show his authority. His men wore a 'P' for Poland on their shirts and spoke German. Despite measly pay, their work was thorough and completed by noon. Zelly rewarded them with cigarette breaks, and they thanked him. There was no reason for the handgun. The duty provided an opportunity to enjoy a pristine shitter. The chore became a Saturday ritual.

After a mess hall lunch, Zelly dressed for a run and wandered to the beach near the gals' dorm, hoping Trudl was there.

She walked to him. "Are you interested in me? You are so handsome, with eyes like a deep blue lake, well-developed muscles, and a killer smile. A wink and all girls would have formed a line."

"From the first second when I spotted you in processing."

Her shyness struck. "I've never had a boyfriend and don't know what to do."

He stretched on the sand, and she sat beside him.

"We could kiss, or I could run my fingers through your curls… and do other things, too." He hoped his grin and raised eyebrows would inspire interest.

"Not now, because I have a shift as an antiaircraft helper."

"That's better than supervising the cleaning of toilets, my part-time job."

Her eyes explored the muscles revealed by his athletic shirt. "Perhaps we'll have time for those activities after jumping the fire tomorrow?"

As she walked away, he inspected her sway.

I'm sure she likes me.

Would she, if she knew you're an American?

He ran around the island, covering a full fifteen kilometers. While Helmut conducted tours of the perimeter, he used the private time to re-draw a map. Rocket test pads, the many buildings, and the Luftwaffe airfield took their places. He added a fenced area to the north, a spot that intrigued him. With the drawing complete, he needed a hiding place.

Don't forget, Helmut has whistled at you twice.

As he searched, his eyes found the *Hilf Mit!* magazine tacked to the wall. The publication hadn't attracted Helmut's interest.

After tucking the page inside the booklet, the change in thickness wasn't noticeable.

He dropped the pistol on the bed, took a shower, and lounged on his rack in only a towel. After drifting off for a nap, he woke to see Stengler hovering over him.

****

Through his office window, Oskar Stengler spotted Zellner exercising. Curious, he crossed the base to the Luftwaffe field and watched the sergeant on the return leg from circumnavigating the island. Returning to his desk, he checked the guard schedule to ensure Zellner's roommate, Wilhelm Dotzel, would be out. Sleep noises greeted him in the room.

Stepping quietly inside, he saw Zellner asleep and covered only slightly by a towel. The boy was beautiful, a perfect specimen of Aryan bloodlines. Oskar felt his blood warm as he studied the napping body. A Mauser pistol rested beside the youth's knee.

He slid the weapon to the side and tugged away the cloth, waking Zellner instantly. His face showed his shock, and his hand searched for the gun. "It's time for your scar examination. I would have asked, but didn't want to wake you."

"You saw it months ago," Zellner said, covering himself with his hands.

Oskar moved faster, pushing Zelly's arms aside to see the blemish. "It's healing fine and almost all white. I can't believe you let a Jew do this."

He pulled out a snapshot from the park. "I had a physician examine this, and he concluded your injury was a year old—not from 1938. Tell me the truth."

"I already admitted it happened when Panzers arrived in Naples."

"According to Army command, that was six months ago—on February 7, 1941, which means I've uncovered another lie. The doctor said the suturing is professional. Do you remember who treated you?"

"Someone at the hospital. I was in too much discomfort to care."

"Now, that interests me. Was the pain exquisite?" Oskar rolled the right testicle between his thumb and two fingers.

"Horrible, but please stop touching me."

Oskar's eyebrows peaked as he thumped the ball twice. "Gestapo officers are torture experts. I've jolted penises with electricity and crushed testicles, but I've never seen one outside the sack. How did it look?"

"White and bloody, as it dangled from the cord."

Stengler licked his lips. "Suffering can be a strange thing. It starts as terrible but can suddenly turn beautiful—from horror to ecstasy." He stroked Zelly's cock.

The touch repulsed the boy. "Look, I'm not queer."

"Nor am I. You've inspired a new idea for making a man talk. What if I slice open his scrotum? Let the subject view the raw orb for the first time. Hold the knife to the ligature, where I can sever it or sew it in place with ragged stitches for another session."

The youth rolled, trying to escape, but Oskar grabbed the right testicle in a death grip and squeezed. "Don't move!"

A mournful cry came from Zellner's lips. As he stilled, Oskar released the hold.

"I love wails like that," Stengler chortled. "Here's a lesson in interrogation for a new SS Sergeant. It isn't pain that makes one confess, and it's anticipation. Right now, you're lying there, worried about what I'll do next. You would tell me anything to make me go away. In your dark cell, you hear the faint sound of boots coming. They get louder right outside the door. It edges open. I reveal the carpet knife which will rip your sack. You'll talk so fast as the familiar ache rises from your balls."

"Are you threatening me with torture?"

Stengler's laugh was gleeful. "As you have pointed out, the Gestapo and SS are part of the same organization. One day, you might try these techniques. Remember, the key is anticipation. The victim will tell me everything I want—and so will you when the time comes."

Wild panic filled the kid's eyes.

Oskar squeezed Zellner's dick with a tight grip. "I know you're a virgin, so this appendage seems unnecessary. My knife could slice it off completely or just hack away at it for hours. Let me show you I'm discovering every one of your secrets." Stengler rolled him onto his belly. "Look at the magazine over your headboard."

Zelly complied.

"Do you see the tiny print under the picture? It credits the photographer, Kurt Baltschun, and I've researched him. He achieved fame in 1934 when his photos of a ship sinking appeared in a French newspaper. I plan to look him up."

Oskar took the pistol and laid it across the boy's butt. "You owe me a report covering the staff meeting."

"Haven't had time because I guarded Polish toilet cleaners." Zellner's voice quivered.

"This afternoon." Stengler marched from the room.

****

As Stengler's footfalls echoed in the hallway, Zelly shivered like in the dead of winter.

At first, the beat of his heel grew quieter, and then the volume increased like he was returning. Zelly's throat tightened, and his testicles shriveled into his body. He shook uncontrollably, and when the door squeaked open, he couldn't breathe.

He heard Helmut's laugh. "What a greeting! Your asshole winked at me, and it's armed."

Zelly rolled from the bed and put on underwear. "Seconds ago, the Gestapo was here to terrorize me. Did you tell him I'm a virgin?"

Helmut blushed. "Sorry, but I guess he overheard. Me and the guys were talking, and I said I hoped you'd get lucky with Trudl on Mittsommernacht… Dinner at the biergarten?"

"I have too much work to do." Zelly tucked the Mauser under his mattress. As soon as Helmut left, he started the report but found concentration difficult. He recognized Stengler's threat and how well it had succeeded.

How can you put him off balance?

Himmler called me 'Sohn der Bewegung,' referencing my father's martyrdom.

Grinning, Zelly made a fresh start, addressing it to Onkel Heinrich. He detailed the staff meeting and his conversation with von Braun. He gave full details of the three systems, the need to mix, and the rocket plans he'd seen. Also, he wrote about not liking Stengler but didn't say why. Adding a PostScript, he asked to meet on his next leave in Berlin.

Can you trust Stengler to deliver it?

Who knows?

He grabbed his camera and took a picture of each page in case Stengler betrayed him.

If he threatens me again, I'll shoot him.

How do you explain a dead Gestapo agent in your bedroom?

I'll come up with some lie.

It will need to be a lot better than your recent ones.

****

22 June 1941—Mittsommer

On the morning of the summer solstice, Helmut pulled Zelly from the bed. "Something massive is happening. Come listen."

Zelly slipped into his trousers and joined the others around the radio. Hitler's voice boomed as he announced Blitzkrieg against the Soviet Union. He remembered the train delays and the knitting nurse's remarks about something to the east.

While his transfixed barracks mates listened, Zelly thought. In the Great War, fighting two fronts proved impossible for Germany. How can Hitler afford another enemy? He had captured Paris in six weeks, covering 400 kilometers, but Moscow is four times that far. At the same pace, reaching the city will take until December—well into a Russian winter, a lesson Napoleon made obvious years ago. Our rockets can't help—they aren't ready for battle yet.

On his morning exercise, Zelly discreetly snapped pictures with his Leica of the places on his map—another violation of the security agreement.

When he entered his room, Trudl stood outside with her arms crossed on the windowsill. He opened the window.

"Tonight, we jump the fire," she said.

"I'm looking forward to it—only a little more work for today."

"I can't wait," she said, breathless from examining his physique.

"Me, too."

As she walked away, he admired her curves.

Helmut returned not long after. "Trudl said Herr Hitler is fetching her a Cossack groom from Russia because you're too shy to make the first move."

They lingered by the radio throughout the afternoon, listening to the news. The Luftwaffe had taken down sixty Russian bombers at Pinsk. General Hoepner's Panzers roared across the Memel River into the Lithuanian Soviet Socialist Republic. The Lithuanians rebelled against the Soviets and embraced the arrival of the army. Zelly wondered how many of his training mates were in the attack. Since most went to Poland, he expected they were engaged.

As evening approached, Helmut announced, "Time for the torchlight procession."

They joined the men's line, and the girls came along to choose partners. Greta stopped beside Helmut, and Trudl took Zelly's hand. Beneath blazing torches, they marched to the beach, singing songs. Circling the woodpile, they tossed their firebrands to ignite the fire.

The flames erupted, and smoke curled upward. The sand shimmered with a brilliant coral color. Trudl's grin gleamed as she tugged at his hand. "Let's be the first to jump." They trotted to the center and leaped with the smoke parting around their bodies. Firelight danced in her eyes. "Now, we're cleansed of all tonight's sins."

He kissed her in anticipation. "Good, because I planned a long list."

A young couple jumped after them and ran off into the forest. Trudl giggled and yanked Zelly toward a tight circle of beech trees. He hollowed out a sand pit between roots, lined it with leaves, and found pine boughs to cover them. In the nest, he stretched out, and she snuggled against him. As they smooched, he arranged branches to cover them.

When he unbuttoned his shirt, she put her ear on his chest. "Your heart beats fast."

He thought of Helmut's comment about making the first move. So, he trailed kisses over her neck and opened her blouse to flow them to her breasts.

Her fingers explored the hair beneath his belly button. "These are blond, but how about lower?"

He unbuttoned his slacks. "Why don't you check?" As her hand scouted the bulge of his erection, he trembled.

Snap—a stick broke under some weight. She stiffened with fear, and they peered into the shadowy forest. Though it was about eleven o'clock in the evening, the woods were still lit in dusky gray, interrupted by inky shadows.

Not spotting anything dangerous, she slipped down his trousers to reveal his boxers. "Tonight is when witches appear and cast spells. I'm Frau Holle and have put my hex on you."

Bob and Carl hadn't warned him of German witchcraft.

As she parted his fly, he spotted the interloper in a cigarette glow beneath a tall pine tree. "Gestapo!"

She crossed her arms and pushed away. "What would they want?"

"Pleasant evening," Stengler said.

Zelly climbed from the nest, trying to restore his clothes but failing. "It was."

Trudl scrambled up, furiously buttoning her blouse.

With a laugh, Stengler adjusted his erection. "You made me so horny, I'd like to join the fun."

"Go home to your wife," Zelly said.

"I will, but I'm craving an appetizer."

When Trudl gasped, Zelly assumed he intended to rape her. The thought was as repugnant as killing the baby at Brenner. "Trudl, run!"

She sprinted toward the bonfire.

"Well, I guess you volunteered, didn't you, boy?" Stengler chortled.

****

In the gloaming, Oskar appraised the youth—hands in fists, ready to fight. "Before you attack with those fancy techniques you used in training, I'm armed." As he approached, he removed a glove from one hand and tweaked Zelly's nipple. "You're smart enough to realize you have no choices here."

"I'll report you."

Oskar's other hand circled Zelly's waist and slipped inside the boy's loose trousers. He squeezed a glute. "That's not a threat. My Gestapo friends will handle the investigation. It's my word against yours—an officer versus a sergeant. Who will they believe?" The gloved hand parted Zelly's butt cheeks.

"I'll tell the Reichsführer."

"He's far away, and my finger is on the mark." Oskar's digit found his puckered hole.

"Don't," Zellner begged.

"I can enjoy your sweet ass anytime," Oskar laughed. "But tonight, I have an appetite for the bird." He turned and sprinted after Trudl.

****

Zelly took a minute to arrange his clothes before giving chase. The delay caused him to lose track of Stengler in the deepening shadows. When he reached the beach, the fire was nothing but wet coals, and nobody lingered. He searched along the forest edge, interrupting the lovemaking of several couples, but couldn't find Trudl or Stengler.

He ran the short distance to her dorm. "Is Trudl here?"

"She hasn't come home," the matron said. "Wasn't she with you?"

In the room, he woke Helmut mid-snore. "Seen Trudl?"

He yawned. "No, and you'll stay a virgin forever if you scare them away."

Zelly found Stengler's office dark and locked. In Karlshagen, the gasthaus was closed. He went back to the nest in case she came back. As exhaustion set in, he slept in the leaves and sand.

****

When Oskar didn't catch Trudl at the beach or bonfire, he figured she had a place to hide—somewhere she was familiar with but unknown to most. He knew her secondary role was as an antiaircraft helper, and the flak guns command central was near the island's northern tip.

During his brief stay on base, he had never visited the Starplatz but decided it was time for an inspection. He moved through the Luftwaffe section and headed north on the peripheral road around the airfield and runway. A wooden tower loomed above the trees. He climbed the stairs first and then a ladder. He heard breathing as he neared the pinnacle.

Pushing through the floor's trapdoor, he said, "That's quite a climb."

When Trudl recognized him, she blanched and screamed.

He sat cross-legged over the trapdoor to block the only exit.

She cringed and searched for an escape, finally realizing the only way out was to throw herself over the railing.

"What can you tell me about Frederich Zellner?"

"I have little to tell. In my short time here, we've dated. Why is he in trouble?"

"He broke his security pledge and drew a map."

"Then why haven't you arrested him? And what does it have to do with me?"

Oskar gazed into the star-filled heavens as he changed strategies. "You may not know this, but I find you alluring. I'd have loved for you to jump the fire with me.

The revelation astonished her. "But you're married."

"That doesn't change my attractions. Soon, you'll be 18 and have a duty to bear children for the Fatherland. I would love to father your child."

"I was hoping Zelly might, but you interrupted us. He's so tall and blond, a perfect man."

"True, but the Lebensborn program specifies an officer, and he's only a sergeant. My blood is pure. Do you find me attractive? He can never provide for you and a baby, especially if he violates security. I'm a very skillful lover and have already fathered two strong Aryan boys. I would be a better choice for you."

"But your wife."

"Isn't involved in this situation. Greta told me you are eleven days past your period, so you'll be fertile. Fulfill your obligation to the Führer and let me father a baby for you to love. Come sit beside me."

She moved to close the gap between her and escape. "I'm really not interested."

"Additional information might help your decision. Authorities in Jena have arrested your parents, and I can make the charges go away."

"It must be a mistake, as they're staunch party members."

He put his arm around her shoulders. "Still, sometimes these things can take years to settle." She turned cold. When he kissed her, she responded without passion. "But I can handle it quickly if you want me to."

"If I do it, will you leave Zelly alone?"

"If you lift your skirt and lower your panties, you'll never have me bother him again."

She hurried to comply. "It's my first time, so please don't hurt."

He spread her legs and kneeled between them to open his trousers and fish out his penis. Hoping she would marvel, he wagged it around, but it seemed to repulse her. She managed a nod as he spit into his hand and stroked himself to hardness. His chortle sounded demonic when he aimed and prodded. He pressed harder, causing her to gasp with pain, which he relished. Suddenly, he felt a small wetness—a virgin, and it drove him into a frenzy.

He lifted her hips from the floor, deeply impaling her. She screamed, but he quickly throttled the noise with a gloved hand. His deep strokes and furious rhythm pushed the wind from her lungs. She panicked from lack of air, but there was little she could do.

Oskar wondered if she was thinking of the Zellner kid.

A rising moon shimmered from the tears on her cheeks. He moved his hand, allowing her to catch a breath before he stifled it with a kiss. He bit her lips as the animal in him erupted. After ripping open her top, his bites found her nipples. With every thrust, he groaned and grunted. Soon, he stiffened, shuddered, and withdrew, wiping himself on the hem of her skirt.

As he restored his trousers, she scooted to the far railing. "That was more like rape!"

He found her words hilarious and answered with a demonic laugh. Pulling a notebook from a shirt pocket, he asked, "Would you like to report the crime, fräulein? Tell me, didn't you want it as much as I?"

In the starlight, he saw hope drain from her eyes. "I can teach you to be a masterful lover in trade for you spying on Herr Zellner and telling me of anything suspicious he does."

"You promised to leave him alone!"

He ignored her protest. "I have to straighten out the matter for your parents."

****

23 June 1941—Spy Sortie

As dawn broke, Zelly crawled from the forest nest with sand, pine sap, and leaves covering him. He dashed into the ocean to remove the detritus and showered at his barracks. Dressed in uniform, he took his report to the Gestapo office, hoping to learn of Trudl's whereabouts.

He saluted and passed the papers. Concern crossed Stengler's face as he read the document's opening line, but wonderment replaced it when he continued. "Fantastic reports like this will earn me a promotion."

Without a smile, Zelly asked, "Where is Trudl, and what did you do to her?"

Stengler's chortle mocked his questions. "She'll show up today."

Zelly seethed at the sound, sure the agent had done something despicable.

Stengler studied him like a cat with a captive mouse. "Is the Reichsführer your uncle?"

Zelly stormed from the office and slammed the door.

He spotted Trudl at the train stop. As he approached, he scanned for visible injuries but found none. "Last night, I searched for you for a long time. Where did you go?"

"I hid in a flak tower."

"I thought Stenger might have followed you."

She flinched at Stengler's mention and when Zelly touched her. As the train stopped, she asked, "Why is Stengler after you?"

"He's one of my bosses and thinks I lied to him."

As she boarded, she sat with a friend, leaving him by himself.

That evening, Zelly lingered in the forest near the Gestapo office. When Stengler left, he used his lockpick to gain access. Trudl's file was on the blotter. A quick scan told him she and her family were perfect National Socialists.

Below her folder, he found his. He flipped through pages inserted by the Jewish conspiracy until he came across a fact circled in red. The document was a transcript of his Wittenberg schooling. The highlighted information chilled him.

Stengler was my Italian teacher.

No wonder he latched onto you like a snapping turtle.

On the blotter's edge was a biography of Himmler, open to the chapter on his early life.

Stengler realizes Himmler isn't my uncle. He'll suspect another lie.

****

28 June 1941—Fence

On Saturday, Zelly was to oversee the toilet cleaning in one of the large dormitories. The Polish janitors worked diligently and created no issues for him. He enjoyed a shiny pot as they labored. As he sat, he wondered about the fenced area he had discovered on a run. "Do you know what's inside the fence up north?"

"Construction spot," one said. "I work there on weekdays."

"What's your name?" Though he treated the workers well, he'd never asked their names.

"I'm Boryslaw, sir."

"You can call me Zelly."

The Pole reacted like he pulled a gun. "But you're German."

"I'm also human."

A mischievous grin crossed his face. "Those don't go together."

"Are you a runner?"

The question paralyzed the worker with fear. "What do you mean?"

"You know, exercise?"

Boryslaw relaxed. "I thought you meant escaping from camp."

Zelly hadn't made that connection, so he smiled to soften the perception. "I love to run for exercise, and nobody will accompany me. I'd like you to show me that fenced area."

Boryslaw's head shake rejected the idea. "We would both catch trouble."

"I would consider it a favor. Maybe I can repay it."

As Zelly walked him to the stockade, Boryslaw said, "I'll jog with you this evening."

A few hours before sunset, Zelly slipped into his athletic clothes and hid the Leica under his shirt. After checking out Boryslaw, they began their exercise.

The Pole laughed at the bobbing bulge. "You can't hide a camera that large."

When they reached the area, Zelly asked, "What're you building?"

"Rocket launching pad—Test Stand VII."

Boryslaw moved along the fence until they reached a cut in the wire. He dropped to the ground, parted the mesh, and crawled beneath. After Zelly followed, they crouched and ran through the sandy forest until emerging in a clearing circled by an earthen berm and a dry, shallow moat. At one focus of the concrete oval, a towering gantry stood. Railroad ties laddered through a valley in the hill, waiting for rails. Wooden forms outlined a blast deflector tunnel ready for cement. A bunker-like control building and a vast hangar were under construction beyond. Zelly whistled in disbelief and took pictures.

"Isn't that a security violation?" Boryslaw's stare was incredulous.

"Not my first one."

"You aren't like most SS."

"Thanks. I'm not."

"In other times, we might be friends."

"Who needs other circumstances?"

After returning Boryslaw to his camp, Zelly thought.

The film is more indicting than the map.

I'm doing my job—spying. Both of my uncles will enjoy these images.

CHAPTER 10

An Officer

4 July 1941—Promotion

The picture calendar on the barracks wall stirred a wave of homesickness Zelly. The feeling didn't stem from the image of a Tyrolean sheep flock. It came from the first day that wasn't crossed out—July 4th, a day mattered only in America.

He fondly remembered past Independence Days—marching with Scouts in the morning parade, picnicking by the river, devouring watermelons, playing baseball, and stealing cold bottles of beer from the Kiwanis.

At his workstation, he found three letters marked up by censors. The note from the Reichsführer was handwritten on personal stationery. 'My Dear Nephew, I enjoyed your report. You're adjusting to the job well. Plan to spend an evening when you return to Berlin.'

Vinny's letter came in an embassy envelope. It talked about his job and casually mentioned Uncle August's pride in Zelly's position.

The third correspondence came from Aunt Freida in Wittenberg, saying Uncle August wasn't doing well. She had requested help from the labor district.

As he finished reading, Doctor Hirschler said, "Zelly, I need your mixing device poster now." The boss's order returned his mind to finishing the schematic. In the distance, a radio announced glorious victories, with Riga surrendering and blitzkrieg capturing Minsk and nearing Kiev. When the time for the Friday staff meeting came, he took the drawing.

Dr. Steinhoff began with a lecture about seeing things through fresh eyes. He singled out Zelly by name, pointing to how his innovative perspective had found a solution to a challenging problem. With Zelly's sketch, he talked through the points where the Siemens system's gyroscopes and hydraulic control mixed with Kreiselgeräte's servo motors and steerage vanes. He praised adding an accelerometer to manage pitch-over. Then he asked Zelly to stand.

Major Gerhard Stegmaier, the base commandant, took a deep breath and read from a paper. "By personal order of the Reichsführer-SS, Sergeant Frederick Zellner is promoted to the rank of Untersturmführer, effective immediately."

Dr. von Braun gave him a collar patch with three silver pips and the shoulder boards of a second lieutenant. "Your ideas and insight have been invaluable. I recommended your promotion, though we'll lose you for officer training."

Stunned, Zelly sank in his chair as the audience applauded. Von Braun's recommendation might have played a role, but Zelly realized his spy report was the catalyst.

I'm the first Texas farm boy Himmler's ever commissioned.

You're the only and last.

According to tradition, he celebrated at the biergarten by buying drinks for thirsty friends, Trudl, and the girls.

When Stengler arrived and sat beside him, the group drifted away. "Congratulations, Lieutenant, Berlin loved your dispatch.

But Himmler isn't your uncle. He has two brothers, Gebhard and Ernst, and neither is your father."

Zelly managed an aloofness. "I assume you read his letter, so why write 'dear nephew?'"

"I'll find out."

"Here's a theory for you to consider. In the early days, party members were tight-knit, like a family. I've heard my mother was quite a tramp. Who knows whose sperm fertilized me, maybe Gebhard, Ernst, or even Himmler himself?" The comment stunned Stengler, so Zelly pounced to further destabilize him. "You were a fucking terrible Italian teacher. I learned more in a day in Italy than all my time with you. Even then, I hated you."

Surprise blossomed in the officer's eyes. "I don't recall you, and I remember every student."

Zelly's lips pursed in distaste. "At first, I didn't know you either, but unpleasant memories soon surfaced when you talked of torture."

"I'm sure you aren't what you seem, Herr Zellner."

Zelly let his voice carry to the crowd. "Herr Stengler, why do you carry a naked picture of me in your tunic pocket?"

Instantly, Stengler reddened and retreated from the club.

Trudl returned to the table, taking the seat Stengler vacated. "I'm sorry, but I must end our relationship."

Surprised, Zelly had only questions. "Why? Is it Stengler? Did something happen, Mittsommernacht?"

"I think it is better if I stay single until I'm eighteen," she said, but he knew the answer wasn't truthful.

Zelly ordered a fresh bottle of schnapps and refilled his friend's glasses before polishing it off. After a short, 14-day affair,

Trudl had ended it. Sad but not devastated, Zelly grew curious about her reasons.

****

5 and 6 July 1941—A New Uniform

As usual for a Saturday, Zelly went through the breakfast line, looking forward to kolaches, a Czech pastry. Eating them always took him thousands of miles away into fond memories. Weekend breakfasts on the farm always had them, and Ma made his favorite, apricot. These weren't as tasty, but he took a dozen for the toilet cleaners to celebrate the promotion. With Stengler's breath on his neck, Helmut turning him in, and Trudl dumping him, he felt the Poles were his only friends.

As they gathered at the work camp, he gave Boryslaw the sack. "I'm celebrating my advancement."

He peered inside. "They'll think we stole them."

"I'm just showing my appreciation. If you eat them here, no one will know."

They exchanged a glance, ate the rolls, and completed their jobs in record time.

When Zelly returned to his room, Helmut was in swim trunks and the ever-present helmet. "Boys on the beach afternoon."

They joined the soldiers, scientists, and engineers frolicking in the surf. They swam, wrestled in the sand, and played football. After scoring on a breakaway, Zelly left the strand to prepare his second report. In it, he thanked Onkel Heinrich for the officer's rank and reminded him of his dislike for Stengler. He shot pictures of the pages.

Next, he answered Vinny's letter, telling him about the promotion and other friendly things. In a PostScript, he mentioned not liking a Gestapo officer who turned out to be his Italian teacher and suggested Vinny tell the problem to the man who bought the new HJ uniform in Berlin. Also, he wrote to his family.

A file clerk handed over Stengler's address in Zinnowitz, and comrades pinpointed the location near the corner of Dannweg on Möwenstrasse— twelve blocks from the railway station.

On Sunday morning, Zelly dressed as a soldier and took the train to town. He posted the letters there, getting a different censor than Stengler.

On Dannweg, he passed a house with a sign advertising photography. A knock brought the proprietor. "My apologies for disturbing your Sunday, sir, but I have a film roll to be developed. Can I leave it for tomorrow?" The canister contained the launch pad shots and others.

The shopkeeper agreed, and Zelly continued to Stengler's house, a beach bungalow in shoreline colors with high gables and gingerbread trim. On the seaward side, the paint had cracked and peeled. When he climbed the steps and knocked, no one answered.

A neighbor approached the fence. "They're at the youth gathering. Were they expecting you?"

"No. We work together, and I was in town and stopped. Two boys, right?"

"Little Heini is DJ, and Max commands the Streifendienst."

Moments later, a car braked at the house. The chauffeur assisted a leggy blonde out from the auto with two uniformed HJ behind.

"Heil Hitler," Zelly saluted. "Frau, pleased to meet you. I'm Frederich Zellner, a colleague of your husband at Peenemünde."

She offered her gloved hand. "He won't be home for an hour. Would you join us for lunch?"

"Delighted to." He shook hands with the oldest child. "You're Max. How was patrol?"

"We stand strong for hometown and the Fatherland."

"No doubt through your fine efforts."

The younger boy came beside him. "We marched for hours. When we passed the Catholic Church, we sang the *Fahnenlied* so loud."

"Heini, I love that song—the reason I joined the HJ."

"You know my name, too?"

"Your father is proud of you and speaks of you often."

Heini's grin spread.

Lunch had ended by the time Stengler arrived. He found Zelly on the parlor settee with his one son at each elbow. His wife perched in the rocking chair, laughing at Zelly's jokes.

Stengler's face progressed from surprised to ashen. "Why are you here?"

Zelly shot to attention. "Heil Hitler, I have a report." He removed his tunic and untied the tie.

"What're you doing?"

"Getting the document. For secrecy, I hid it beneath clothes." He shrugged off his shirt and undershirt. Bare-chested, he handed him the papers.

"Check out his muscles," Heini said.

Zelly flexed and grinned at Heini before turning to Stengler. "Perhaps you'd like me to remove the trousers, too."

The Frau's eyes narrowed.

Ignoring her, Zelly unbuckled his belt and unbuttoned them.

Shock crossed Stengler's face. "My wife—"

"She's raising boys, so there's nothing new to see here." He stepped out of the slacks.

Stengler thought fast. "My old uniform. Honey, they promoted him to lieutenant. He'll never find SS officer attire at Peenemünde. I promised to give him an old one. Will you please fetch it?"

Zelly winked when Heini flashed his physique.

The boy circled Zelly's upper arm with his fingers. "Max, his muscles are bigger than yours."

The older brother couldn't resist the challenge. In an instant, he was shirtless and comparing. Zelly gave him the victory.

"How about mine?" Heini was bare-chested, too.

Stengler was thunderstruck. When his wife returned, lots of male skin showed in her parlor. She handed Zelly the officer's trousers, and he stepped in.

"I never thought I'd earn the stripe." Zelly admired the ribbon flowing down each leg and donned his undershirt and shirt.

Max moved Zelly's pin to the tunic. "I've never met a martyr."

"One doesn't meet martyrs—they're dead. My father was an early National Socialist."

Heini stood on the settee to tie Zelly's tie. "You look awesome."

"I must go. Thank you for the uniform and the hospitality."

As he left the house, Stengler followed. On the porch, he slammed Zelly against the siding, his forearm choking. "How dare you?"

Zelly didn't struggle.

The agent choked tighter. "And such a vulgar demonstration."

"Like the one your children are watching through the window?"

Stengler glimpsed their faces behind the glass and relaxed his grip. "You'll pay for this."

"You're jealous of my promotion and seem to misunderstand our relationship. I'm the star, like Paul Hartmann, and you're just Courier #1 in the credits. Still, you have delightful boys, and I love spending time with them." Zelly kept his voice jovial, but the threat beneath the friendliness was unmissable.

When he disembarked in Peenemünde, Trudl waved from the line queued to travel in the other direction. He crossed over to her and admired her stunning sundress. "A day with the gals on a sunny Zinnowitz beach?"

"You might as well know. The Gestapo agent and I are having an affair."

"Stengler? Why?"

She dropped to a whisper. "I might be pregnant."

Filled with a dozen emotions, but mostly anger, he spun away.

I guess Vinny was right. I can't love them and leave them.

You've known her for only fifteen days. You're American. How else could it end?

But Stengler? Why would she want him? What happened Mittsommernacht?

****

Oskar Stengler opened the door to his house and popped in his head. "I'm going for a walk."

As he strolled toward the strand, he struggled to understand why he had an erection. The sexual energy of his encounter with Zellner was palpable. The near nakedness exposed to his spouse and boys had produced the reaction. He'd always kept his lovers apart from his wife and family. Something made him want to take Zelly with them as an audience. He felt thankful for the upcoming tryst with Trudl, their fourth, not counting the flak tower.

He rented a room at the Strandhotel and crossed the street to the promenade. Over a cup of coffee, he enjoyed the view of sand, sea, and the famous pier with people strolling in their Sunday finest. In minutes, she arrived and ordered a cola-flavored Fanta. Smiling, she reached for Oskar's hand. "I think I might be pregnant."

Panic consumed him as blood rushed from his penis. "So soon? How can you tell?"

"Well, it's only a feeling, but Greta says a woman often knows."

"You told her about us?"

"No, silly, she thinks the baby is Zelly's."

"Have you found anything for me?"

"He's taking lots of pictures of places around the base and of the documents he writes."

"Where can he get them developed? If he uses the base's photo lab, they'll report it."

"I followed him this morning when he came to your house. He dropped off the film at a house near yours—on Dannweg. The building has a sign advertising photography."

"I know the place." Stengler stiffened. "Did he spot you?"

"While he visited you, I took the train back. When he disembarked in Peenemünde, he saw me boarding. We talked for a minute, and he thinks I came for a beach day with the girls."

Oskar relaxed. "Good."

"Have you spoken to your wife as you promised?"

"Not yet, but have some patience."

"I'm trying, but it's hard." She finished her Fanta with a slurp.

"Ready for the room?"

"I was hoping to do it near the waves." She giggled.

"And leave my bare butt bouncing in the dunes?"

She shot him a coquettish expression. "A little danger would be nice, and I don't mind getting spotted. Besides, it's my choice—a reward for telling you about Zelly's photography."

****

7 July 1941—New Extra Duty

The promotion brought a new set of odd jobs. Zelly became a defective parts delivery boy instead of managing janitors. Peenemünde's machine shop couldn't manufacture every part of rockets—factories elsewhere made many pieces. Getting them correct was a challenge. No one had seen a rocket, let alone built components for one.

Wooden crates held the defectives, each with a cardboard tag containing instructions on how to remedy the flaw. He trucked them to the train in Zinnowitz, but nobody told him he had to load the boxes.

He moved them as he had hay bales on the farm and thought that guarding toilet cleaners was easier. A voice called. "Zelly, is that you? Do you need a hand?"

He looked up to spot Max and a group of HJ boys approaching. "I'd love some help."

Their shirts came off. Young muscles lifted, carried, and stacked. In minutes, they finished.

"Thanks. May I reward you with a beer?"

"Hell, yes," They climbed into Zelly's truck, and Max directed him to a beach-side tavern. He parked in the sand near the Baltic's waves and bought a case. By law, all were old enough to drink but not in uniform. Their chests stayed bare as daggers popped the bottle caps.

They had questions about a soldier's life, and he shared stories from his training. He told them how his roommate Helmut had earned his nickname, and they laughed. With sun, sea, and suds mixing, they discarded the rest of their clothes and skinny-dipped.

As they tanned naked on the sand, a boy said, "Max says you have a martyr's badge."

"My father died trying to help the Führer escape prison." He pointed it out on his uniform and became their instant hero.

Soon, Max announced, "Time for a piss." They lined up beside him, and Zelly joined.

"Zelly, what are you doing?" a boy asked.

Shit, I retracted my foreskin.

You forgot one of your first lessons and in front of the son of the Gestapo officer who hates you. Think fast.

"If sand gets inside the skin, this cleans it." Zelly grinned. "And when your girlfriend sucks on it, she won't gag on your piss."

The line of guys peeled back their foreskins, making themselves look like Jews. With empty bladders, they dressed and piled into the truck. He drove them home.

God, I hope he doesn't tell his father.

One more fucking mistake. How many will it take to get you hung?

****

18 July 1941—The Mixing Device

A week later, at the Friday staff meeting, a joint committee made up of the three competing teams presented the outcome of Zelly's idea. Though he served with the group, higher-level thinkers had advanced his simple solution by several iterations.

The chairman spoke. "The plans contain a new level of abstraction. Now, a matrix of relays maintains tighter control, eliminating the over- steerage Herr Zellner described." He removed a covering over the poster, which now had an overlay.

A Siemens engineer rose. "I've studied Konrad Zuse's designs, and you've created a mechanical computer."

"Unlike his Z-machine, this isn't programmable but dedicated to the Aggregat," the chair said.

The three competing groups were now one. Dornberger grinned when Dr. von Braun gave Zelly a military salute.

In the report for Onkel Heinrich, Zelly bragged about his role to the extent decorum allowed.

I'm proud of what I achieved. Why not brag?

Because you've empowered the Germans to kill thousands, you shouldn't have suggested it.

I'm fitting in, being an ardent Nazi.

You did more than fit in. You couldn't stomp a baby but enabled rockets to destroy London.

The solution was obvious. One of those exalted minds would have discovered it.

The teams would have kept fighting. Your idea unified them.

Our rocket will fly.

Whose? You and the fucking Germans. You've gone off the rails— batshit crazy.

Not in the slightest, Fred. I'm smart. I'll be an engineer someday.

****

21 July 1941—A Favor

To get assistance with the next defects trip, Zelly drove the truck to the Polish work camp and requested for the same crew he'd worked with before. The officer in charge asked no questions and called them to the gate.

"I need you to help me load a truckload of parts onto a train in Zinnowitz. It's a chore I do many Mondays, and I hope you'll assist."

Boryslaw studied the other two. After a few minutes, they agreed and climbed into the truck's cab—four men made for a tight squeeze.

"Boryslaw, I'd like to know all your names."

The Pole introduced Arek, the suspicious one, and Radzim, who was young, quiet, and strong.

On the station platform, they quickly transferred the crates as they chatted in Polish. Zelly understood almost nothing. They worked so well that he asked for another favor. "Let's paint a Gestapo officer's house."

Radzim waved a finger around his ear to show the idea's craziness while Boryslaw groaned.

"The guy is on my back, and I'm hoping if I do something for him, he'll cut some slack."

They exchanged telling glances and argued until Boryslaw ended the discussion. "We help."

Zelly bought supplies at the hardware store and drove to Stengler's house. After he found two ladders hanging in the garage, he began painting. When Max and Heini discovered what was happening, they and dozens of their friends pitched in. Boryslaw taught them how to mask the trim. When finished, the job delighted Frau Stengler.

Zelly pulled Max aside. "Can I trust you to deliver this your father? It's part of our work together."

Max's smile bloomed like a rose, and he tucked the sealed envelope under his shirt.

On the return drive, Zelly asked the Poles, "Willing to unload for me on future trips?"

Boryslaw agreed. "Soon, we may need to ask favors of you."

"Any time." He thought of cigarette breaks and kolaches, but deep down, he knew it would be something more.

****

28 July 1941—The Waterworks

While Zelly worked at his desk in guidance, the radio announced the Luftwaffe bombing of the Kremlin in Moscow. A cheer sounded throughout the building.

The mail arrived. He opened the official envelope from the SS Main Office to find travel orders to officer training at Wewelsburg Castle. The train ticket was for tomorrow and provided a brief leave in Berlin before.

Vinny's letter mentioned meeting the Reichsführer-SS at a diplomatic function. He'd expressed gratitude for Zelly's promotion and concern over Stengler. Also, he wrote about planning Mussolini's visit to meet Hitler in Russia.

Aunt Freida's note complained that the labor service sent two immature girls as farm help because the boys were all away fighting. She feared harvest time would be too much for August.

With defective parts waiting on the truck, Zelly signed for his Polish crew at the stockade. The load was light, so he relaxed as they transferred the crates. At their camp, he held Boryslaw back. "I need a place to hide things for a few weeks."

Boryslaw's eyes revealed suspicion.

"Stuff I can't leave in the barrack while I'm gone—you know, personal items. Would the fenced construction area have a suitable location?"

He nodded. "Also, I want to show you something."

"Exercise after dinner?"

Helmut went drinking with friends, and Zelly packed for the trip to officer school. Then he loaded papers, film canisters, and the map into a wax-permeated ammo pouch. After stuffing it in his running shorts, he checked Boryslaw from the laborers' camp.

"Let me take you to some places you haven't visited," the Pole said. Heading off in an unusual direction, he took Zelly to a wind tunnel and rocket fuel plant.

Zelly pulled out the map and added those locations.

Boryslaw watched with growing curiosity. "I know the perfect hiding place at the launch pad."

They came from the north and wiggled beneath the chain-link barrier. Boryslaw led to the waterworks and a wide pipe planned to fill the moat. He unscrewed the cap. "No water until the first test fire, and that's still months away."

Zelly slid in his items and replaced the plug.

While squirming under the fence, a blinding spotlight hit them with. Zelly saw a Kübelwagen bristling with machine guns and raised his arms to surrender. Boryslaw's were already overhead. A Wehrmacht sergeant rushed them. "Identification papers."

When Zelly showed his gold tinnie, the NCO reported it to the wagen, and Stengler stepped into the light. "What in the hell are you doing here…and with a foreigner?"

"This is Boryslaw. He said he works on construction here, and I asked him to show me."

Gestapo pointed to the six-inch high letters on the sign—Verboten.

"Does it apply to gold tinnies?"

Stengler spat in frustration.

Two soldiers stayed to repair the fence, and Zelly and Boryslaw took their seats. The vehicle returned Boryslaw to the foreign labor compound. En route to the barracks, Stengler lectured, "An SS officer should avoid fraternizing with Polish workers."

"I'm sorry, sir, but I felt seeing the new launch pad was vital for my job."

Stengler seemed to accept the explanation and drove away.

Zelly had sand inside his shorts, so he undressed and showered. A few minutes later, he had the temperature adjusted and relaxed in the warmth. As he lathered, he heard the door squeak and glanced up to find Stengler. The man's eyes roved over him.

Stengler positioned a wooden bench by the door and stepped across the tiles to the shower. "I caught you in a prohibited area with a foreign worker, another violation of security rules." He turned off the hot faucet, leaving Zelly in an icy flow. When Zelly stepped from the stream, he pushed him under.

"Look, I never hear about construction progress at staff meetings.

Himmler needs to know."

The officer closed the cold handle and fully opened the hot one, turning the water scalding.

Zelly wanted to move but refused to show weakness. The heat became unbearable. "My work for Himmler requires violating restrictions. You know that!"

Stengler balanced the temperature. "Acknowledge how much I own you, or I'll scald you."

"You own nothing about me. I work for Himmler, not you."

Stengler drew his Walther pistol. "For being in a secret installation with a Polish worker, I could shoot you now. Instead, I order you to stroke your dick like you did at the gymnasium."

"I won't give you the satisfaction."

"So, you willingly disobey a superior officer's order for the second time? This is for your benefit. I want to know if you suffered testicular damage in that altercation."

"It works fine." Zelly tried playing with it, but circumstances inhibited an erection.

Stengler's laugh was demonic. "Doesn't seem that way."

"Why would you care?"

"Trudl is pregnant. I need to be certain you are not the father."

Zelly's failure to perform was humiliating. "We never got that far."

Stengler chuckled, kicked away the bench, and left.

****

29 July 1941—Berlin

Zelly's train arrived at Berlin's Stettiner Station during the busiest part of Tuesday's evening. Beneath the glass dome, people rushed over the crowded platform to and from trains, trams, and buses. He made his way to the exit, planning to walk a short distance to the underground.

Vinny caught him in a hug. "I've planned a fabulous night."

"How did you learn I was coming?"

"The Nazi with glasses."

They crossed Friedrichstrasse Bridge and settled into a riverside restaurant beside the Spree. Nearby fishing boats' diesel engines roared, bringing the catch to the harbor and providing some cover for their conversation. Over schnitzel, potato wedges, and steins of beer, they shared stories.

Vinny started a story about Ambra, but a swarm of SS soldiers with machine guns left it incomplete. He flashed his diplomatic passport.

The plain-clothed Gestapo agent ignored it. "Your friend will come with us."

As they led Zelly away, Vinny called, "Our plans will keep, so meet me at the apartment."

He found himself at SS headquarters once again. This time, the captors marched him to the basement and a cement room furnished with a table and two chairs. He sat in one chair, wondering why he had avoided handcuffs. He estimated an hour had passed when the door opened.

"Stengler? How did you make it here?" he asked.

"Airplane. There was an explosion." The agent's expression was grave as he studied Zelly's reaction.

"The rockets? Trudl? Helmut?"

"Wrong guesses—the train carrying your defective parts."

"Where?"

"Eberswalde."

"Collateral damage?"

"Took out the tracks. Tell me everything about loading in Zinnowitz." "I used Polish laborers, the same janitors I supervised—Boryslaw, Arek, and Radzim. I signed them out at the work camp, so it's on record. As usual, I verified the packing list, checked the crate seals, and observed as they loaded. When they finished, I confirmed the count, and nothing was out of the ordinary."

Did Boryslaw kick something under a pallet, maybe a grenade or bomb?

Don't mention it.

"Boryslaw? The one with you in the restricted area?"

He gave a curt nod. "Are they suspects?"

"They're being interrogated in Peenemünde. We'll see if the statements match."

"You can't believe I did it." Zelly sighed. "Why would I blow up defective parts?"

"You wouldn't. That's why you're not in chains."

"I don't like your methods—making me jerk off in the shower and fucking my girl on Mittsommernacht."

"She told you?"

"About your affair, but I didn't know the other until just now. Do you want me to stop using the Poles?" Zelly stood, assuming he was free to go.

"If they did it, they'll try again. I'll catch them." He walked to the door and quickly spun toward Zelly. "What photographs did you have developed in Zinnowitz?"

"Pictures of the base and launch pad construction for Himmler."

He pinned Zelly against the stone wall. "Enough of the shit about you and Onkel Heinrich. I was in his outer office when he called you a son of the movement. I've understood your metaphor all along. He may be near, but my bullet will kill you before he can save you."

Zelly chucked him off his chest. "While we're being completely clear, I've had enough of your security violations. You know why I am doing them. I've also had enough of your threats and sexual deviances." He marched through the door and upstairs, leaving Stengler in the room. He cleared the building without attracting further attention and strolled to Vinny's.

Vinny was in bed, listening to the Wagnerian Valkyries ride. Zelly undressed and slipped in. The sway-back mattress rolled them together. With faces inches apart, the music masked their whispers.

"What was that about?" Vinny asked.

"Gestapo. A train I loaded blew up in Eberswalde."

"You on the hook?"

"No, but my Polish workers are."

"Were they involved?"

"I'm suspicious they're in the resistance." Zelly sighed. "What's happening back home."

"Joltin' Joe's ran a 56-consecutive-game hitting streak, and Teddy Ballgame is batting .406. *Citizen Kane* is on the inside track for the Academy Award. The Andrews Sisters' hit is *Boogie Woogie Bugle Boy*." He sang a few bars as the Valkyries wailed.

Vinny soon fell into quiet snoring, but Zelly remained awake, his mind retracing the events of loading the train. Its fate was becoming more obvious. Boryslaw had kicked something under the pallet.

CHAPTER 11

Secrets

31 July 1941—To Wewelsburg

To reach officer training, Zelly took an express from Berlin's central station to Hanover, then switched to the Bielefeld regional. In Hanover, he waited almost 90 minutes for a local to Paderborn. He was still sixty kilometers from Wewelsburg and had no idea how to traverse the distance. The sleepy ticket agent offered no help.

Outside the building, a fancy Mercedes idled at the curb. Zelly spotted the license plate, SS-1. When the chauffeur opened the rear door, he slipped into a seat beside Heinrich Himmler.

The Reichsführer's eyes rose from his last report. "Nephew, your work is factual, insightful, and well-written. I wish all my spies performed so well."

"Thank you, sir. I'll always do my best."

"You believe in the rockets, don't you?" Himmler asked as the driver put the car in gear.

"I'm sure they'll fly. The enemy can't shoot them down, and they'll strike without warning."

"How accurate?"

"Before the mixing device, they'd reach England, but now they'll reliably hit London. As guidance improves, they'll knock the King off his chamber pot."

"When?"

"Six months. The launchpad will be ready at the year's end, but getting precision parts is hard. Would you like some pictures?" He opened his suitcase, fished in what Stengler had called the secret compartment, and provided photographs.

En route to Wewelsburg, Himmler analyzed the photos. He asked a few questions about the launch site which Zelly answered. "Nephew, can I count on more reports and images like these?"

"Jawohl."

Overhead, airplanes flew low as they prepared for a nearby landing. The Reichsführer swiveled in his seat as worry lines crossed his forehead. "Tell me about your problems with Stengler."

"Sir, I don't wish to be indelicate."

Himmler frowned. "Your work is too important to jeopardize, so tell me."

"He threatened me with torture… and forced me to masturbate at gunpoint. He's a sexual sadist."

"In the Gestapo, that's an admired trait." Himmler's eyes clouded. "He's been curious about you since Brenner Pass and asked for the job."

"I lied about my scar, but he has the truth now. He listened as I told you in your office."

Himmler's lip curled as he took delight in his games. "I've arranged for a new courier."

"Thank you."

He dismissed Zelly's thanks with a wave of his hand like he had millions of couriers waiting for work. The car curved through a sparse forest of beech, maple, and ash on a steep, chalky limestone slope that descended to a river. After crossing a small bridge, the chauffeur downshifted to climb a cliff towards a stone castle.

"When a Norwegian named Sev visits Peenemünde, I expect you to show him every hospitality," Himmler said.

They parked on a hill beside a barn-like structure, and the chauffeur opened Zelly's door. As he stood, he said, "I expected our destination to be the towers I spotted from the stream."

"This is the Ottenshof, our officer's club, and we're overdue for dinner." The driver led Zelly through the heavy timber doors.

Above them, a rustic wagon wheel of log spokes and glass decorated the entrance. The place was awash with SS as cadets lined long center tables. Booths with six to eight junior officers surrounded them on the ground floor and balcony.

The chauffeur pointed to the basement door, and Zelly went down. He entered a room of whitewashed plaster, including the massive beehive fireplace. The ranking elite sat in an arch facing the hearth. Two front-row chairs were vacant, and Zelly chose one.

"Achtung!" Everyone jumped to attention. Hundreds of stomping boots sounded like artillery shells. Himmler slipped downstairs, offered the Hitler greeting, and took the remaining empty seat.

After the meal, they trooped upstairs for Himmler's speech, marking the students' graduation and commissioning. When he finished, he raised a beer stein for a toast. The audience rose with their drinks lifted to shoulder level. He said, "Struggle is the father of all things, and as you join the Kampf, seek only one thing...."

"Sieg Heil," the crowd responded and drank.

Zelly carried his beer into the garden's twilight, where songbirds serenaded him and two lupine sprigs decorated his table like Texas bluebonnets. He felt the presence of someone watching him, he thought, and the instinctual alert led his eyes to a shadow lurking behind the garden door and connected to visible feet. Leaving his drink, he walked beyond the door, quickly glimpsing a cadet uniform. He continued into the shadows and rounded the corner as if for a piss. Instead, he flattened himself against the rear wall and waited a few seconds for the student to follow.

He flicked his cigarette lighter to examine the cadet's face. "Who are you?"

The boy's smile was disarming. "I'm Kurt, your courier assigned by the Reichsführer."

"You could have introduced yourself at my table."

"I've never met a Sicherheitsdienst and wanted a glimpse first."

"Now that you've had one, let's drink beer together."

As they drank, the fresh graduate told the story of his eighteen years on a farm in Minderlittgen, a tiny Rhineland town. He listed a dozen nearby places, but Zelly recognized none.

"What inspired you to join the SS?" Kurt asked.

"My father was a martyr, so the organization seemed like my destiny.

You?"

"I hated the Frogs who held the territory since the Treaty of Versailles because they made me speak French. When the glorious German army returned on March 7, 1936, I was first in line to sign up for the Hitler Youth. The party and Schutzstaffel came as soon as I was old enough."

Zelly yawned. "I'm dead tired. What do I have to do for a room around here?"

"Follow me—we're sharing." They walked a cobblestone road, crested a hill, crossed an arched bridge, and entered the stronghold's gate. Wewelsburg Castle was triangular, with a massive north tower and two smaller towers to the southeast and southwest. Timber doors took them to the west wing's school dormitory. Zelly's suitcase waited on the bed beside Kurt's while almost eighty beds sat empty.

"A new class isn't starting?"

"You misunderstand—since you first met Herr Himmler, you've been an officer. Your uniform is a disguise."

"Why didn't you come to Peenemünde instead of me coming here?"

"The Reichsführer wanted us to bond as friends before we venture under Stengler's thumb."

"Have you met the man?" he asked, but Kurt shook his head.

****

1 August 1941—The Perfect Aryan

The next morning, Zelly dressed for running as Kurt rose from his bed. "Jump in your athletic gear and follow me if you can." He scrambled into clothes, and they rushed to the courtyard. Zelly ran where they had walked last night while Kurt lagged. At the Ottenshof, Zelly slowed for him to catch up. "If I pick the way outbound, you remember how to return."

"How far?" Kurt's breath was heavy.

"Five kilometers."

The boy groaned as they rounded the Biergarten's corner, and Zelly curled northward. He crossed the Alme River on a bridge and jogged along fishing paths. The castle sat high on the hill above, a spectacular sight as it glittered in the sun. As Kurt struggled behind, Zelly relaxed the pace south of town and forded the stream on stepping stones. Sitting on the bank, he allowed Kurt to join him.

Kurt gulped for air. "One… question… what was the issue with your first Gestapo courier?"

"At gunpoint, he made me jerk off."

"God, how awful." Disgust crossed his face.

"It started when I lied about a scar I have in my groin. I showed it to him and inspired his lustful thoughts. See?" He slid his leg hole aside to reveal the mark.

Kurt whistled. "Must be quite a tale, and I'd love to hear it sometime. You do not need to lie to me because I can keep your secrets—all of them. Can I ask something about this Baltic place? Are there cute girls?"

"It's a military base, so the ratio of cocks to pussies is very unfavorable, but I had a girlfriend for two weeks before she tossed me over for my Gestapo courier."

"Ouch, I can tell that scar is still fresh."

Zelly winked. "You lead now."

"Getting back isn't far because the river meandered in nearly a circle, and the castle is only a few blocks away." Kurt led through a series of steep switch-back streets to the castle's approach.

"Shower?" Zelly suggested. While Kurt grabbed towels and soap, he started the water. "No one ever told me I was a Sicherheitsdienst or even an officer."

Kurt popped a salute. "You're a captain in the intelligence service, department D, industry and power."

"I outrank you?" Zelly asked in surprise.

Kurt shrugged under a lather. "Being your courier is my primary job, but not the only one. I'll run the radio detection truck. Here's something for you to consider, though. What Stengler did— Himmler may have ordered him to do it."

"What?" Shampoo ran into Zelly's mouth, and he spat it out. "Why?"

"He has something on everyone—me, you, Stengler—and he uses it to manipulate us."

"What's he got on you?"

"It's about my sister." Kurt shampooed. "I might tell you when you share the scar story."

"What's he got on me?"

Kurt grinned but didn't answer. They dried, dressed in uniform, and ate breakfast.

"Time for your tour." Kurt led the way to the imposing North Tower. In the Säulenhalle, a domed crypt full of pillars with a black sun embedded in the marble floor, Kurt spoke of Teutonic Knights. "We are the modern incarnation of these Germanic warriors, minus the religious crusading." Throughout the castle, they examined relics from days of chivalry—swords, pikes, shields, banners, and sets of armor. Kurt told every artifact's story, pointing out the knight's heraldry and how the SS regalia replicated it. The tour ended at a doctor's office. "Let's check if you're a Jew."

The man measured Zelly's body, noting the length of his legs and arms and the ratio of his torso to his height. Calipers gauged the distance between ears and eyes and the shape of his face and head. Then he compared a series of glass eyes to Zelly's and matched a set of hair snips to his locks. "You're a perfect Aryan."

While grinning widely, Zelly laughed on the inside. Not bad for an American.

"You're just like me." Kurt swelled with pride.

The doctor explained the wrongs Jews had perpetrated on society and the scientific principles of racial superiority. How Aryans, like Zelly and Kurt, were better than the Slavs, Gypsies, and Negros.

Over the course of week, Zelly listened to lessons on the history of the glorious Volk and how Hitler summoned Germany from the depths of despair after the Great War to rise like a phoenix. Kurt taught Zelly the runes, symbols, and ciphers of old, including the swastika.

Zelly visited the original death's head that bound SS officers to their brotherhood, represented by the rings worn by the few and the collar tabs on his uniform. In another room, a model of Albert Speer's imposing Germania, planned as the capital after Hitler ruled the world.

Zelly took it all in and worried such an outcome might come far too soon. After the week, he was ready to do anything necessary to halt it.

****

8 August 1941—Gustav Siegfried Eins

When Zelly and Kurt arrived in Peenemünde, North Sea storms brought frosty rain. The base didn't have room for another bachelor officer, so the command added a third bed to the existing room. Helmut grumbled about bunking with two officers but didn't request a change. Kurt took a desk in Stengler's office, and Zelly resumed his guidance job.

After work, Kurt caught Zelly leaving the train. "I need your help at the motor pool." He led to a panel truck with silver antennas bobbing from the roof. "Fucking thing won't function. Since you were in Signals-HJ, I'm hoping you can fix it."

Zelly tightened the cables and located two defective parts, which he replaced from the stash in his bag. When he flipped on the power, the system hummed to life.

"Your reward, if you want to, is a ride-along."

"Sure." This could prove useful, Zelly thought.

Kurt parked at the tip of the Luftwaffe runway and listened through headphones. "No illegal transmissions on the island." He switched the sound to the speakers for Zelly. "Local traffic is uninteresting, so shall we try Rostock's air defense frequency?" They heard a voice directing antiaircraft fire toward a small group of Russian planes. Fighters scrambled but found no enemy.

In search of excitement, Kurt tried every point of the compass for other signals. He gave up with a shrug, and a sheepish grin crossed his face. "Want to try the British?"

Zelly's shocked expression came with a laugh. "Really?"

"You've never done something against the law?"

"I danced swing with Emmy Göring at a party. Does that count?"

"So nasty," Kurt teased. He dialed the BBC, where a commentator reported on a speech by Churchill announcing an Atlantic Charter between Britain and America. "If they join the war, they'll regret it."

"Maybe they'll come in on our side. How would an American do on the castle doctor's hair and eyeball test?"

"Aren't they mostly Jews? Shall I find some music? Gustav Siegfried Eins? GS-1 pretends to be Germans broadcasting subversive propaganda to the Brits, but it's truly the opposite." His expression was like a mischievous boy being caught in the act as he dialed the illegal station.

Zelly recognized the sounds of Glenn Miller's band as Ray Eberle sang *The White Cliffs of Dover.* "Do you understand English?"

When Kurt expressed surprise, Zelly crooned hastily translated lyrics. "Hope we don't get discovered."

"Catching is my job."

"So, you'll keep some secrets?"

"Every fucking one."

****

11 August 1941—The Underground

While Zelly was away, no one had done the defective parts run, so today's truck was filled with crates. He signed out the three Poles and brought the Mauser pistol just in case the gamble he planned went sour. The men were willing to help, almost happy to be requested.

While driving, he said. "I understand the Gestapo met with you."

"They accused us of sabotage," Boryslaw said.

"We didn't do it," Arek said.

"Torture?" he asked.

Heads shook.

Zelly mustered courage and gripped his weapon between his left leg and the door. "I saw Boryslaw kick something beneath a pallet—a grenade or bomb, most likely."

They stared at him like he was *The Son of Frankenstein.*

"And you didn't tell the authorities?" Arek asked.

"They claimed you corroborated our story," Boryslaw said.

"I did and omitted any mention of your stunt." The silence was thick with fear.

Boryslaw spotted the pistol. "Are you planning to arrest us?"

Radzim whistled at the foolishness, and Arek expelled his breath.

"Perhaps we're not on opposite sides. I've guessed you're with the resistance or Polish underground—"

"Fuck." Arek stretched the word for many seconds.

"Impossible," Radzim said.

Zelly braked, stopping at the roadside. As he scanned their faces, he hoped he hadn't misread them. "This may come as a surprise, but I'm an American spy."

The truck cab was like a coffin—air gone, breathing unfeasible. After a long minute, Arek exhaled. "Holy shit."

Shellshocked, Boryslaw studied him before responding. "I graduated from the Massachusetts Institute of Technology in the class of 1936."

Zelly switched to English, which was like a foreign language. "I am Fred Brown from Texas, and my mission is to stop the rockets."

"You've found the Polish Underground," Boryslaw said, "and stopping them is also our job. I'm a captain in the Polish army, captured during the invasion in 1939. Nazis thought a degree in civil engineering would be worthwhile here."

Zelly chuckled as the clock gear metaphor swirled in his mind. "To clean bathrooms?"

"It was a grenade," Boryslaw admitted. "I've hoped to recruit you to get us inside info."

"Blowing up defective equipment does nothing to stop the rockets."

"We would hit ammunition trains but have no access to the timetables," Boryslaw explained.

"I might provide some better targets."

Boryslaw expected to bargain. "What do you want in trade?"

"First, leave my shipments alone. Second, one day, I'll have something for you to take to a friend in Berlin."

Arek laughed. "Wrong direction, but we can get things to London."

On the way back, Zelly felt empty, drained, and hollow—as if stomach acid had scalded his insides.

You played all your cards. Was that wise?

I can't accomplish anything without help. I need partners.

The Poles might report you.

If they do, I can easily finger them.

In deep thought, he walked the beach until Greta surprised him. "Hi, Zelly, this is Katchen." She introduced a blonde. "She's a nurse and wants to meet your new guy."

"Right, Kurt is an SS officer, and I can introduce you." He led them to the horseshoe common area outside the barrack and returned with Kurt. "Kurt, this is Greta, Helmut's girl, and her friend Katchen."

Kurt's grin stretched. "Fräulein, a pleasure."

"When Helmut gets off guard duty, we're going to *Happiness Is the Main Thing* at the cinema. Would you like to accompany Katchen?"

"I'd love to." Kurt turned on the charm. "Is it a comedy or romance?"

Katchen winked. "A bit of both."

Zelly edged away, realizing he'd be the fifth wheel.

"You come, too," Greta insisted.

He was uncomfortable going without a date but went anyway. The Stengler family also attended the picture. During intermission, Max and Heini teased Zelly for going stag.

As the house lights dimmed, calling everyone back to their seats, the agent button-holed him. "Your photographer friend will no longer develop your photographs."

"That might disappoint Himmler. When he gave me a ride in Paderborn, he acted impressed at the ones I showed him."

"You rode in Himmler's car?"

"Mercedes with the license plate SS-1. Onkel Heinrich treats me well."

"You won't smirk when I tell you about a visit with Kurt Baltschun. He took lots of pictures of youth at the Elbe River summer camps, HJ and BDM activities, and simple photos of life. Several are in a book *Pimpfe im Lager*. But he didn't recognize the image of you on the cover of that magazine, and he didn't take any at Army Signals School in Halle."

****

20 August 1941—Gestapo Skills

To prepare for the meeting for von Braun, Steinhoff, and Dornberger's with Führer, the guidance team made illustrative props. Zelly's contribution was a set of model rockets. Steinhoff knew of Zelly's interest in flying. When they departed from the airfield, he invited Zelly to the flight line and watched as they boarded the four-engine Focke-Wulf 200 Condor. When the mighty engines rumbled, his stomach shook, and his skin goose-bumped. The plane dragged its tail down the runway, balancing like a prima donna on tip-toe, before lifting it into the air. Enraptured, Zelly watched until the dot disappeared in the sky.

At the mess hall, he sat with Kurt. "You know the shy girl who is friends with Greta and Katchen? That's Trudl, who was my girl for a few weeks before taking up with Stengler. Can you use your investigative skills to learn why she dumped me?"

"I owe you for fixing the radio truck, but do you truly desire to know?" At Zelly's nod, he said, "Tell me your version of the story."

"We jumped the fire together on Mittsommernacht, and I made a nest in the woods, anticipating sex. She was into it, but Stengler interrupted. Fearing he might rape her, I told her to run. The next morning, she said she'd hidden in a flak tower. After that, everything changed. I suspect Stengler found her and…who knows?"

"Greta is the gossip master, so may I ask her? The big question is, do you want her back?"

Zelly shrugged his response. However, if she chose Stengler willingly, he would consider her spoiled meat.

****

After work, Oskar remained in the office, waiting for a phone call. When the handset jingled, he answered.

"This is the editor-in-chief of the National Socialist Teachers' Association. We have completed the *Hilf Mit!* archives search. We couldn't locate either the original or negative used for the issue you asked about."

"I'm still unsure what you are implying."

"After a complete audit, we have those items for every image—all except the one you asked about. We have published hundreds of Kurt Baltschun's photographs, and every file is complete and also has a photographer contract and record of payment. Not this one."

"Any speculations—?"

"Without the original and negative, we would have had nothing to publish. I suppose someone could have removed them without replacing them. Even if the image was damaged in printing, I would still expect the contract and payment."

"I spoke personally with Herr Baltschun, and he claimed he didn't remember taking it."

"Photographers recall every one of their shots. Perhaps this one came from another source." Oskar leaned back in his chair and wondered why everything about Zellner seemed so fishy.

****

21 August 1941—Sev

As Zelly desk-checked the circuits for the mixing device, Max from flight mechanics interrupted. "A Dresden Tech student named Sev wants to meet you."

Zelly spotted a dark-haired man with a black mustache, neatly trimmed to fit over his mouth. He guessed the age of the man to be two years older. "You're Norwegian, right? I've been expecting you. How about lunch?" They went to Karlshagen's biergarten and chatted over wurst and beer.

"How long have you been here?" Sev asked.

"A few months." Zelly read the disappointment on his face.

"They promised a senior scientist."

He acted nonchalant. "What level are your studies at Tech?"

"First year."

Zelly feigned disgust. "So, you don't have a degree, either."

"Touché. We'll manage."

"Everything in Germany has ears, so let's go someplace private," Zelly suggested.

"Where?"

"Do you swim? The Gestapo can't bug the beach."

"I didn't bring trunks."

"I never realized Norwegians were such prudes." After Zelly settled the bill, they strolled Strandstrasse toward the sea.

"We aren't afraid of a skinny dip." Sev had his clothes off in seconds, and Zelly did, too.

"If we were hounds sniffing each other's butts, here's what I would smell on yours. You're Himmler's henchman, spying on the rockets and pretending to be SS. Really, you're in the intelligence branch, know English, and dance swing."

"My job is writing reports for Himmler, and my sniff says you speak English, too."

Sev smiled and nodded. "My dad was an engineer in New York City. I'll return when this shitty war ends."

Zelly darted to the water. "I hope to go one day. How can I help?"

"Can your missiles carry our bombs?"

"Give me details so I can do the math."

"More formidable than anything ever and bigger than the toys you calculated."

"Atom-smashing ones?"

Sev's jaw dropped at the guess. "How do you know about that?"

Zelly ignored the question. "Here's the rest of what I sniff. You've seen life in America and came from a free Norway before the invasion. In Germany, you discovered two major engineering projects and think, if you can amass enough information, future benefits may come your way. You baited Himmler, and he bites to send you here, but he's not sure you aren't a spy. He sent you to me, putting my ass in jeopardy for anything you learn."

Sev nodded. "Pretty astute, but he said we should share freely."

"Well, we're already beyond the 'I'll show you mine if you show me yours' moment." Zelly grinned. "To talk technical, we'll need space for math and note-taking."

"I have a hotel in Zinnowitz."

"I bet the Gestapo booked it for you, didn't they? The chance of someone listening is too high. I have an SS colleague with a house in town, and his wife will permit us to visit."

They dried, dressed, and took the train. When they reached Stengler's steps, Max hugged Zelly, full of questions. "What was Wewelsburg like? Did you stay in the castle? Was the Reichsführer present? Did you learn any secrets?"

"Yes, to all four, but the matter can wait for a different time. We need someplace private. Will your mother allow us to use the parlor?"

Max nodded. "You met Himmler?"

"He gave me a ride from the station."

Heini was awestruck. "You rode in his limousine?" He ran into the house, yelling, "Mama, Zelly was in Herr Himmler's car. He wants to use the drawing room."

She ushered the men to the room, shooed the boys away, and closed the pocket door.

"What's the secret to the atom-smashing bomb?" Zelly asked.

"Heavy water and Norway has plenty."

"Do you get fat if you drink too much of it?"

Sev laughed. "Don't pretend you're stupid."

They spent seven hours together while Zelly relayed rocketry progress and Sev shared the details of mighty new bombs. Zelly found their conversation chilling—the crux of victory in the war. He remembered Professor Koehler's words, "The side with the smartest scientists and the craftiest engineers wins." When the meeting ended, he had dozens of pages of notes.

With rockets and atom-smashing weapons, Germany will be victorious.

You must send this data to the baker now.

****

25 August 1941—Nothing More

The truck's cab was silent on this defective parts trip. Zelly understood the Polish workers' secrets, and they knew his. Turning knowledge into something valuable hadn't yet happened, but he planned to change the situation. "Are you ready for something I promised you?"

"Desperate," Arek admitted.

"On Thursday the 28th at 11 PM, a train will leave Stettin heading for Auschwitz. The route takes it through Wronke and Posen. It will carry several of Poland's political and war prisoners, besides many undesirables. Interested?"

"Not for a bombing, but perhaps we can rescue a few important people," Boryslaw said.

"I know the area," Arek said. "The Warta River bridge would be a perfect intercept location."

"The timetable calls for arrival in Wronke at 2:02 AM," Zelly said. "Promise one thing—do whatever you wish, but nothing can point to Peenemünde."

While the workers carted the parts, he relaxed on a platform bench until someone called his name. He expected Max and his friends, but a man in a dapper Italian suit arrived. "What the fuck, Vinny? Why are you here?"

"I'm waiting for the train to visit you." He gripped Zelly in a bear hug. "Il Duce's visiting the Führer. Once I tucked them in and the foreplay started, my work ended."

Zelly chuckled. "Unfortunately, they won't let you on base."

"The trip was Himmler's suggestion. I have a super-secret pass."

Zelly examined the signatures of Hitler, Himmler, and Field Marshal von Brauchitsch on the document Vinny flashed.

For the ride, Vinny took the cab, and the Poles rode in the truck bed. Engine noise flooding the vehicle masked the conversation.

"How long can you stay?" Zelly asked.

"A week while they tour the Russian Front."

"Maybe the war will be over by then. Novgorod fell today, and it's only 160 kilometers from Leningrad. Soon, the Panzers will cut the rail line to Moscow."

"You believe Goebbels's radio shit?" Vinny asked. "It's pouring rain, bogging Blitzkrieg in the mud. Mussolini is here because Hitler wants more help from Italy, so no quick victory."

"That bad?"

With a penetrating gaze, Vinny changed the subject. "Let's talk about you—cover intact?"

Zelly thumbed toward the truck bed. "They're Polish Underground trying to stop rockets, and I told them."

Vinny didn't mask his disgust or disappointment. "You compromised yourself? I've feared that ever since Belfast. Though your missions intersect, it doesn't make you friends."

"Understood, but I'm trusting they'll keep secrets secure."

"What actions are they taking? What if they're discovered?"

"Sabotage, but I'm not helping. Still, I'm connected to them. I've kept copies of my reports to Himmler and have pictures of everything. Can you get things to my uncle?"

Vinny shook his head. "I'm not safe because the Germans have pegged me as an Italian spy. Anything about this base that I carry would get you killed."

"That isn't all," Zelly admitted. "I met a Norwegian guy working on the atom-smashing bomb, and we shared lots of information. He knows nothing about me but might make a lucky guess."

Vinny grinned. "That stuff I could easily move. It's exactly what Mussolini's spy would do. Is your work hidden?"

"The bomb notes are recent and in my barracks. The bulk of my work is in a drainpipe at the launching pad." He didn't mention that the Poles knew the stash's location.

Vinny's super-secret base pass got him a gold tinnie. They went to the Karlshagen biergarten and joined Helmut, Greta, Kurt, Katchen, and Trudl. Vinny noticed a game of dancing eyes between Trudl and Zelly. She couldn't take her eyes off him, but they never connected.

Helmut grinned. "Trudl, have you seen Zelly's Italy photograph—a skinny-dipping picnic? Well, Vinny is the other naked guy."

"What?" Trudl blushed.

"You haven't shown me," Kurt said.

"Or us," the other gals feigned hurt.

Vinny told the story. "It was a wonderful summer afternoon by the river near Naples. We ate, swam, and talked."

Helmut's face was lecherous. "Did you get some?"

"I did, but not Zelly. He's a virgin unless something happened here."

"Did you intend to embarrass me?" Zelly pretended harakiri.

"Why didn't you mention it in Wewelsburg?" Kurt asked. "The SS had a brothel, and I could've set you up."

"I won't do it with some old cow," Zelly retorted. "I'm not the only one, am I?"

"My first time was in the DJ," Kurt said.

"Same here," Helmut said, "and Kurt and I can vouch for Greta and Katchen."

All eyes fell on Trudl.

"Not me," she said.

Kurt pulled Reichsmarks from his pocket. "Comrades, toss in to get our buddy laid?"

"Assholes!" Zelly left for a meeting in the Officers' Club.

****

Helmut Hölzer and Otto Hirschler had arranged a private room to celebrate Hitler's approval of rockets and provision of more funds. When Zelly arrived, the mood was glum. Hirschler turned up his palms. "No luck. We get nothing more."

"At least Hitler liked the movies of A-5 launches," Hölzer said.

"Did he view my models?" Having der Führer appraise one's work didn't happen often.

"He played with them, clearly excited by rocketry, but still no funding priority," Hölzer sighed. "This rocket will fly. Isn't that the important thing?"

"We'll launch this year," Hirschler said, "but we're too little and too late. Blitzkrieg will soon take Leningrad and Moscow. When the rich Caucasus oil is ours, what use will rockets be?"

Zelly drained his beer stein. "England and America."

"Hitler thinks the Brits will make peace, and the United States won't care who owns Europe," Hölzer said.

"Churchill will never reconcile with Germany," Zelly said.

Hölzer leaned in. "Do you think Hess turned traitor when he flew to Scotland with a secret armistice proposal? Everyone thought it wise to end the Western front before moving east."

"They were uninterested and put him in prison," Hirschler said.

"U-boats and Rommel in Libya may have changed things," Hölzer said.

"So, who will der Führer fly over the channel next? Göring?" Zelly asked.

"Spectacular idea," Hirschler said.

When Zelly returned to the barrack, he found his friends pouring over the Italy album that Helmut had removed from his suitcase.

Kurt flashed the naked picture. "With those tits, how could you stay a virgin?"

****

30 August 1941—Proof

To avoid adding another bed to the room, Helmut slept in the radio lounge during Vinny's visit. Zelly woke Vinny for an exercise run to help him understand the base since he wouldn't take the reports to D.C. He checked out Boryslaw from the labor camp, and the three of them jogged along the shore between trees and sea.

"Boryslaw, my friend Vinny understands my secret. It's fine to talk freely."

"Then thank you for the tip on the train. The resistance intercepted it at Wronke Bridge, and we recovered several important politicians. In return, the underground sent a package of information to you. Follow me." He led them from well-traveled paths into the deep forest, where he paused. Extracting a burlap pouch from his shorts, he revealed photographs and papers.

"What's this?" Vinny asked.

"Proof the Germans murder Jews in Russia like they did in Poland. The first four pictures come from Vilna in Lithuania—a killing spot called Ponary. They march them ten or twenty at a time, naked, to a pit, line them up, and shoot. Women and children, too. The bodies fall like stacked firewood; then, they cover them with lime and repeat the process. When they fill the hole, bulldozers close it."

"Who took these snapshots?" Zelly asked.

"The Germans send them home like postcards. Here are more images from Lvov in Ukraine."

The first illustrated German soldiers surrounding a woman who they forced to undress on a town street. In the second, she ran naked along a stone wall, like she was escaping. The third has her arched abnormally near a pile of corpses. In the final one, her lifeless body lay atop the heap.

"Are they Jews?" Vinny asked.

"Check the circumcisions on the men."

Zelly stepped away and threw up in the sand. His sickness came from his thoughts, not the pictures.

You can't stomach everything the Nazis do, can you?

Major Donovan ordered me to fit in, and I think I am.

Don't overdo it and turn into a Stengler.

Boryslaw unfolded pages of written text for Vinny. "Testimonials in Russian telling what is happening. You must send them to America so the world will understand what Germany does."

Vinny refolded and wrapped the bundle. "A diplomatic pouch through Lisbon might work. Mussolini loves Hitler's handiwork." He focused a puzzled gaze on Boryslaw. "If you are underground, why not London?"

The Pole smiled. "Already there, but the time has come for your country to act."

****

1 September 1941—Suspicions

Monday was sunny and warm, though the deciduous trees were coloring for fall. The broken parts trip involved only a single crate, so Vinny assisted the box's transfer instead of the Poles. Zelly was melancholy over his friend's 3 PM departure on a train to Görlitz. They lingered at the station for as long as they could before saying their goodbyes.

"Are you carrying your important deliveries?"

"Yes, the baker and candlestick maker will appreciate them."

"Wish you'd take my work."

"You'll manage."

In silence, they hugged on the platform. Vinny climbed the steps to the carriage and helped a lady with her luggage. Zelly watched without a smile and waved as the locomotive gained speed.

At the motor pool, he found Kurt tinkering with the radio detection van's engine. "Stengler summoned us," Kurt said, wiping his hands and leading Zelly to the office.

****

Oskar Stengler waited impatiently for Kurt and Zelly. The papers in his hand had upset him greatly—Peenemünde was linked to a major action by the Polish underground. The report warranted investigation, even though he considered it unlikely. When the two entered and saluted, he began the briefing. "Some days ago, criminals attacked a train in West Prussia, about three hours out of Stettin. Our Danzig detachment captured two resistance fighters. One claimed the raid's coordination came from here."

Both Zellner and Kurt appeared bewildered, and Kurt said, "Impossible. We're two hundred kilometers west of the action and never receive notification of trains that far away."

"We did this one." Oskar handed Kurt another paper that warned Peenemünde of a shipment delay for incoming parts because of the Stettin train's schedule. "It was in my office, and someone had to find it and pass on the information."

"Only you and I have access, and I haven't read the notice before," Kurt said.

"People come and go—people with issues, brought in for questioning, the cleaning crew. I have my suspicions."

Zellner swallowed hard. "Remember that bombed train? Are the resistance here?"

"I hadn't considered that link, but we must be watchful and diligent and share reports of suspicious activities."

"Jawohl," Kurt and Zellner said together and headed for the door.

Stengler held up a hand. "Zellner, please remain, as I'd like a word with you."

He stopped and pivoted. "Sir?"

Oskar got in his face with their noses almost touching. "I spoke with the publisher of *Hilf Mit!* They do not have the original or negative of your cover picture. However, their files are complete for every other image. How do you explain the fact?"

"I don't, sir, and I'm as curious as you. Thanks for sharing the results of your investigations."

As Zellner stepped out of the room, Oskar caught the scent of the boy's sweat over the smell of apricot snuff. Though frustrated by finding nothing, Oskar vowed to continue his inquisition.

CHAPTER 12

War Arrives

2 October 1941—Zählen

As Zelly and Helmut walked from the barracks to the train stop, a thick fog clung to the pine trees at a temperature hovering slightly above freezing. Drops of icy mist splashed Zelly's face. Glad his job kept him warm indoors, Zelly realized Helmut faced a day of walking the perimeter of the Polish camp.

"It will snow soon," Helmet said as they split up for trains in opposite directions.

Once aboard, Zelly huddled around a cabin heater and lifted his shirttails to let the steam waft against his skin. A letter from Vinny was waiting on his desk. Upon opening it, Vinny's mix of German and Italian words made sense but didn't. Each sentence referred to things and people Zelly didn't recognize. The note ended with, 'I count the days until you return to Berlin.' For a second, the line reminded him of his leave in early December, then the word zählen caught him short—the Camp Ritchie code.

Scanning the page, he arranged the capitalized letters to make a message: BMB DOCS AND PCS DLIVRD. He grinned with pride at his spy craft. Doctor Otto and Professor Koehler had received Boryslaw's documents that Vinny had carried.

For a moment, he felt successful, but Hirschler brought another change for the mixing device's logic. He spent the day puzzling out how to include it—every new idea had the potential to jeopardize things somewhere else. When he solved the issues, most of the team was gone.

Kurt was in their room. "Have you learned anything about Trudl?" Zelly asked.

"Nothing unusual in Stengler's files for her, and her work evaluations are perfect. Checking further, I discovered Stengler reported her parents as Jewish sympathizers. They were in custody at Jena for a few days based on his tip, but without witnesses or evidence, the authorities released them."

"She would sacrifice everything to protect them." Zelly wondered if Stengler blackmailed her into the relationship. "What does Greta say?"

"That Trudl didn't lie about not being a virgin, and your guess was correct. She's having an affair with Stengler, who got her pregnant. Some quack doctor aborted it with ergot, a poison."

"Was it rape?"

"Not technically. Greta said she wanted it, but I figure it's part of his sexual sadism. Why don't you talk to Trudl?"

"I would feel bad if he did it to force her into manipulating me. He's been after me since catching me in some lies."

"I've read your complete folder and found nothing damaging. Sure, you lied about the scar but eventually told the truth." Kurt pointed to the magazine tacked over Zelly's bed. "Why is he fascinated with that picture?"

Zelly shrugged. "The publishers can't locate the original, and the photographer doesn't recall taking it."

"Is their incompetence your problem?" Kurt asked.

"There's more. Stengler was my gymnasium teacher, but I don't remember him."

"I wondered why he had your school file. Hell, I've forgotten teachers on purpose."

"He won't—"

The door opened, and a barracks mate popped in. "Hitler is on the radio."

They went to the lounge and listened to Der Führer. "Tremendous events are now unfolding on the eastern front. We have launched a large-scale operation that will lead to the final elimination of the enemy in the east." He promised victory in days.

Instead, war news turned as gloomy as the weather. The mist coalesced into raindrops and poured from a dark gray sky. Vinny was right about blitzkrieg being bogged in mud. The conquest of Russia was late, and winter came early. Zelly drew hope from the reversal of fortune, but everyone else clung to Hitler's promise of triumph.

****

14 November 1941—The Pipe

When the staff meeting ended, Zelly wrote a report while surrounded by the stove's warmth. Beyond the window, it was colder and wetter than ever in Texas, where storms lasted a few hours and not months. He had several reports to add to the stash in the pipe. The unyielding, freezing rain would ensure privacy but also chill him to the bone. He donned layers and a thick parka.

He regretted his decision when the wind lashed the raindrops through his clothes. As he lumbered on, mud clung to his boots, making them heavier with each step. The deserted beach led to the forest, and under the trees, the deluge relented somewhat. Someone had re-opened the fence hole, and he attributed it to the Poles.

In the gloom, the launch pad was monstrous and frightening. Its gantry and block house scraped the low black clouds. Icy water filled the moat, spilling over the berm like a flooding dam. He located the pipe and unscrewed the cap.

It was empty. He reached deep, but his ammo pouch was gone. In a panic, he tried nearby pipes in case his memory had failed. Nothing. Losing his work hit him like a Stuka's bomb. He screamed in fury. Did Stengler find it? Have the Poles betrayed me? Either way, he was as good as dead. The loss left him with nothing to help save America. Two horrible years were wasted, accomplishing nothing as a spy except for aiding Himmler.

****

24 November 1941—Lockpicking

For ten days, as life continued in Peenemünde, worry and dread consumed Zelly. He re-checked the pipe, hoping he'd made a mistake, but it remained empty. If the documents had turned up, that would have been more frightening, so he hoped the torrent washed them away. When Kurt gave him a haughty look, he felt sure the Gestapo had pegged him. Stengler was aloof, which convinced Zelly he had the material.

Kurt's not your friend, despite listening to illegal radio together. He'd finger you to save himself.

Why haven't they arrested me? The papers match what Himmler has, so there's no doubt I'm the culprit.

Maybe they enjoy watching you stew.

I'm going to find out if they have them or not.

When the storm brought early darkness, he waited thirty minutes after the Gestapo office went dark. He used a blade at the stoop to scrape his boots and washed them in a nearby pool.

He extracted his lockpick from under many layers of clothes. After his previous experience, the door wasn't a challenge. Inside, he removed his footwear and parka, shaking the excess water outside, and locked the door. In the cloak alcove, he stripped to underwear and socks and hung his soaked outfit on pegs. Adrenaline from practicing his spy craft flooded his veins.

The Gestapo office door delayed him only a second. Inside, Stengler's possessions dominated the room. Kurt's desk was away from a wall, only enough for him to slide into a chair. After drawing the blackout curtains over the single window, Zelly removed the flashlight Kurt kept in a drawer and turned it on.

Kurt's desktop sported a small picture of his sister and Zelly's last report in a corner basket. At Stengler's workspace, he splashed the light over the papers on the blotter and rifled through the drawers. He expected his lost material would be recent and on top. But every paper, document, or folder was a normal priority. His file was no longer there, but he found it in Stengler's cabinet. The pages hadn't changed from when he scanned it before. The office had nothing concerning any documents from pipes, so he exhaled in relief, finally feeling safe.

Voices came from the hallway, and a key slid into the door's lock.

Zelly crawled into the leg hole of Kurt's desk and doused the light. His knees and chin met as he folded into the small space. He worked to keep his breath silent as someone stepped into the room.

****

Oskar Stengler held the door. "Come in, darling. I thought I left the blackout curtain open." He flipped on the lights.

"With the rain, this will be so much cozier than the flak tower or the beach," Trudl said. "Why don't you stoke the fire while I hang our cloaks on the doorknob?"

The metal grating on the pot-bellied stove squeaked as Oskar tossed several coal chunks inside and added paper wads as kindling. As he blew into the flames, things ignited from the previous coals. "If you'll slip out of the dress, we can make each other toasty."

"What about the after-dinner digestif you promised?"

Oskar pulled a bottle from a file cabinet drawer. "I've been saving this 1899 Terrantez Madeira for a noteworthy occasion—twenty-two years in oak casks and bottled in 1936. You'll find subtle touches of caramel and chocolate fudge. Interested?"

"Mmmm," she purred.

"We must finish it because it's too expensive to waste. Promise?"

The cork popped, landed on the floor, and rolled under Kurt's desk. The bottle's lip chimed against a glass as he poured.

She sipped the drink and felt the rush of intoxicating deliciousness. "This is delightful." She kicked off her shoes.

"I want to make love to you."

"I know you're disappointed about losing the baby, but I was too young to be a mother. My body was unprepared."

"I would enjoy making another."

Trudl shook her head. "Currently, sex hurts, but the doctor says it will get better soon."

"But I need it now. See how ready I am."

****

The cork wheeled between Zelly's feet and stopped its motion when it nestled against his crotch. He heard liquid being poured. To take his mind off cramping legs, he pretended to savor the caramel flavor. It worked for only minutes until the pain made him yearn for a stretch, but he couldn't risk it.

He recognized bright red toenails when they appeared under the desk's modesty panel.

She hasn't told Stengler of the abortion.

She's making it seem like a miscarriage.

The metal of a buckle scraped the wood before the belt tumbled to curl on the floor. Stengler's voice was gruff. "Take care of this."

"No," she protested.

Zelly was ready to spring from hiding and save her.

I can't stop him.

You'll end up in chains if you try.

The sleeve of a party dress dangled over the pencil drawer. The floral print seemed Hawaiian. His legs tightened painfully, and he rubbed the knots in his calves. Though his muscles cramped, the fear of discovery made him hold an uncomfortable posture.

He heard Stengler's grunt as he entered her. The toes of the man's shoes poked his butt, and the hiding place lurched. She muffled a cry. Stengler's knees pounded the modesty panel in rhythm with his strokes. The pushes jarred Zelly's kidneys, and he needed a piss.

This isn't making love because there's no tenderness in his thrusts, Zelly thought.

She squealed and cried like it was torture, but the oaf nearly silenced them. Zelly pictured Stengler's hand gagging her. His legs cramped terribly, so he tried to massage them.

If I had my pistol, I'd kill him—but not instantly.

You should shoot off his pecker and then....

The bravado in his brain was futile. There was no way he could save her without compromising himself.

The motion and friction got more violent, and the furniture rocked. Her cries continued unabated. He tossed the cork to the room's center, hoping to distract them, but they ignored it. The desk careened a dozen centimeters, scooting him with it.

Stengler gasped, and she screamed around the gag. The wine bottle tumbled into Kurt's chair, landing with a chime. Trudl's hand appeared inches from Zelly's nose to retrieve the container.

"Perhaps you'd like that, too," Stengler said.

The desk's legs screeched as they scooted over the wooden floor. Her shriek jumped an octave.

Did he shove it into her? Zelly couldn't fathom Stengler's sadism.

The flagon fell, shattered into dozens of glass shards. Liquid streamed along a crevice in the floor, wetting the seat of Zelly's underwear.

She moved, taking her painted toenails out of Zelly's sight. Her light footsteps sounded like the wind as they slipped out the door. Stengler chortled and staggered to the door. Zelly peered around the pedestal to catch Stengler buttoning his pants. In a minute, the lights flickered off, and keys jangled as the Gestapo agent went away.

Zelly was alone and perfectly safe. He climbed from hiding, stretching muscles to return life to them. As the mess hall dinner rose in his stomach, he used the flashlight to navigate through bottle shards. He vomited in the trash can, then dropped his wine-soaked underwear above the pool of vomit.

He sat in Stengler's chair, gulping deep breaths.

That was the most disgusting thing I've ever witnessed.

Don't you realize you created this by getting involved with her? The torture is your fault.

He retreated to the cloakroom, dressed in his water-logged clothes, and entered the icy rain.

If the Gestapo doesn't have my stuff, who does?

Obviously, the Poles betrayed you.

He trudged to the workers' compound. Helmut was on guard duty and grumbled at a request to fetch Boryslaw. When the Pole appeared, Zelly walked him away from the guardhouse, each on opposite sides of barbed wire.

A hood obscured Boryslaw's face. "Hard winter."

Zelly had no patience for small talk. "I went to the pipe, and everything has vanished."

"I didn't want it discovered." The words came in puffs of breath. "While stuck in plumbing, it accomplished nothing."

Panic pounded Zelly. "What did you do with it?" Betrayal stabbed like a knife. He grabbed the fence with his gloves. "Return it, now."

"We burned it in the stove for some warmth. Except for the map." The Pole pulled the dirty paper from a pocket. "The Union of Armed Struggle, the new name for the resistance, sent a report to London using your stuff."

Zelly choked on tears of frustration. "I needed it in Washington." He snatched the sketch and pocketed it, the only thing remaining from almost two years of work. "All my work gone to ashes."

"They'll forward it."

Defeated, Zelly turned away. "You've exposed me because the work required an inside source."

"We summarized everything and cited an anti-Nazi Austrian sergeant. We covered for you."

The gears of espionage spun in Zelly's mind as he realized he was spying for Poland now.

"Did the packet about Jews reach America?"

"Yes. The Brits won't believe you. No Austrian sergeant has access to the technical details. What if you made errors? They'll either think it's science fiction or that the Germans hoaxed you with disinformation." As Boryslaw disappeared into the rain, Zelly called. "You played me like a symphony and left my mission in tatters."

Soon, you'll be on the far side of the barbed wire.

Vinny was right. I make too many mistakes and trusting them might be the fatal one.

****

25 November 1941—Clues

Stengler and Kurt simultaneously arrived at the Gestapo building. While Stengler unlocked the door, Kurt brushed a light dusting of snow from his trench coat. They hung their wraps in the cloakroom and opened the office.

"Something reeks," Kurt said. His boots crunched on glass shards, and his nose led him to a pile of vomit in the dustbin, not quite frozen. "Someone was here last night."

"Clean that out," Stengler ordered as he turned away because of the guilt on his face.

As Kurt hauled the can outside, he dropped the boxers at the door. After emptying the wastebasket, he sluiced it with water from a spigot. When he returned, he examined the underwear and found a wine stain.

Stengler was sweeping the floor. "We had a break-in."

"I'd say it was a party with wine. The culprit left a frozen shoe print where some spilled." As he kneeled to investigate, he spotted a few black drops. "This's serious; that's blood."

Oskar rifled through his papers to ensure they were undisturbed.

Kurt's desk had been pushed nearly to the wall. He had to restore its position before he could sit. Rolling some paper into the typewriter, he typed and read his notes aloud. "The smell of wine. A broken bottle of a fine vintage of Madeira—could it be the one Herr Stengler keeps hidden in his file cabinet? I detect perfume, Trudl Ehle's fragrance. A frozen shoe print in some wine. I believe it matches Herr Stengler's boots. Sir, I've deduced the culprit."

"We were here, but that sickness in the trash wasn't mine or hers."

Kurt banged out another line. "An eyewitness says that the vomit did not belong to Fräulein Trudl or Herr Stengler."

"Will you stop typing? Forget this ever happened."

"Look, I have no concern over who you fuck." He plucked the paper from the typewriter, wadded it, and tossed it to the can. "But the blood concerns me."

Stengler's cat-like grin emerged above his shrug. "I took her in the ass and with the bottle. Injuries happen."

Kurt shrugged and took Zelly's recent report. "I'll send this on its way. You square away your mess." At the door, he picked up the boxers and carried them to the trash receptacle near the mailroom, laughing all the way.

****

That evening, Kurt and Zelly did some repairs on the radio truck. The fuel line occupied Kurt's efforts while Zelly used tubes from his bag to fix a radio problem.

"Did you hear someone broke into the Gestapo office?" Kurt asked.

"Really? The resistance or saboteurs? Remember what happened at Wronke? Were any train schedules out?"

"Evidence included spilled liquor, a broken bottle, a well-preserved footprint, and the scent of Trudl's perfume. Though I found a few drops of blood, my conclusion was one of Stengler's sexual dalliances. I expect you already know all about it."

Zelly came to the fender beside Kurt. "What made you think I know?"

Kurt stopped working. "Vomit in the trash can and a pair of men's undershorts. The boxers had a Hugo Boss RZM mark and your name on the waistband."

Zelly looked sheepish as he moved to let Kurt slam down the hood. "Does Stengler know?"

"Your secret is safe with me if you explain."

"I was there, hiding in the kneehole of your desk. It was gross, more like torture. Some wine got on my shorts, and I think he shoved the bottle inside her. It sickened me."

"You've explained everything except the most important one. Why you were in my office?"

Zelly found Kurt's smile threatening.

"I spotted Stengler and Trudl together last night and decided on a stakeout. When the office was unlocked, I went in, assuming they would return. Trudl said some things that confirm my research. She was pregnant with his kid and got an abortion. I heard her say that sex was painful, but he impaled her anyway."

"Stenler claimed to have done her in the butt and with the bottle. So, here's the critical question—Do you want her back?" Kurt asked.

With eyes big at the news, Zelly shook his head.

****

27 November 1941—Christstollen

As Zelly showered, he speculated about Thanksgiving in Fredericksburg, Texas. Though Lincoln started the federal holiday, President Roosevelt moved the date during the Depression to maximize Christmas shopping and stimulate the economy. It left Texans confused about what day to celebrate, but he figured this was the right Thursday. He recalled Ma's turkey, the gathering of relatives, pumpkin and pecan pie, and an afternoon of football on the radio.

How are the Aggies doing?

I could have—should have—been one.

Who won the World Series? How many homers for Joltin' Joe?

I'm so far from home.

In Peenemünde, no one would care about the holiday. Heavy snow fell, coating the ground, piling on the roof, and sagging pine branches. Then, a blizzard descended on the base with a vengeance. In guidance, everyone tried to assuage the gloomy weather with jokes.

Max, from flight mechanics, said, "When we fly, Hanna Reitsch should be the pilot."

"No cockpit," Hirschler said.

"Perhaps if we strap it between her legs," Zelly offered.

"You do that," Hirschler said.

While the crew laughed, Zelly drew a cartoon—the rocket with Hanna riding it, reins in her hands, and an orgasmic grin covering her face. Hirschler tacked the drawing to his office door.

The mail brought a package and a disheartening letter from Wittenberg. With no manpower to help on his uncle's farm, much of his crop spoiled in the field, and party officials scolded him for missing his quota. The stress led to a heart attack. Aunt Freida wrote he was recovering but not the man he used to be.

"What's in your parcel?" One of a half dozen anxious guidance workers asked.

Zelly cut the strings and peeled the brown paper to uncover Christstollen—Christmas fruitcake, an old German tradition. When knives, plates, and forks appeared, he sliced the delightful ring of almonds, raisins, dried fruit, and marzipan. Then he re-wrapped the rest for his friends.

On the train, he sat beside Kurt. "I'll have Christmas cake in the radio lounge, bring Katchen and Greta. I'm sure Helmut will be there."

The five friends enjoyed the sweet as they listened to *Es war ein Edelweiss,* a song about a little star-shaped flower growing in the Alps and binding the hearts of a man and his girl with luck and sunshine. Zelly watched Kurt and Katchen cuddle and Greta feeding Helmut small bites like in a harem.

I'm alone, the fifth wheel.

Probably the best position for a spy.

With two pieces of Christstollen left, he wrapped them separately and passed one to Katchen. "Would you give this to Trudl?" He intended it as a peace offering, nothing more, and saved the last piece for Vinny. Checking the date on his train ticket for leave in Berlin, he found it was for December 8th.

****

7 December 1941—The BBC

Well after dark, Kurt parked the radio truck beside the liquid oxygen plant, which would soon fuel the rockets. After Zelly deployed the antennas, they huddled together for warmth from the glowing electronic equipment. Kurt dialed an illegal station, the British Broadcasting Corporation. The speakers popped to life with the chimes of Big Ben's bells.

> Here's the news, and this is Alvar Lidell reading it. Japan's long- threatened aggression in the Far East began tonight with air attacks on the United States naval bases in the Pacific. Fresh reports are coming in every minute. The latest facts on the situation are these.
>
> Messages from Tokyo say that Japan has announced a formal declaration of war against the United States and Britain. The Japanese air raids were made on the Hawaiian Islands and the Philippines. Observers report that an American battleship has been hit and that several Japanese bombers have been shot down. A naval action is in progress off Honolulu…

The news crushed Zelly like an artillery shell. Like the butcher predicted, war had come to America, but from across the globe. A Saint Nicholas Day present. Zelly's Lutheran family celebrated the day instead of Dec. 25th. As a child, he put out his boots for presents.

If Jimmy hasn't enlisted, he will tomorrow.

You should be in line with him, not play-acting in Germany.

A flood of memories struck Zelly.

Sophomore year in high school, he played football with Andy at tight end. He had joined the Navy and was on the battleship *Oklahoma*. Was it the one hit? Teddy, named Theodore after the first Roosevelt, had been in his Scout troop and was flying off the *Enterprise*—presumably in the battle near Honolulu.

Fuck the Japs, and damn the Brits for their lack of details.

What can you do about it from Germany?

The mission.

But what have you accomplished? You've lost a full year of reports by trusting the Poles.

Zelly wiped his eyes to keep Kurt from spotting tears.

****

8 December 1941—Berlin

On the train to Berlin, Zelly wore sadness and depression like a uniform badge. Wounded men filled the carriage with distant stares from hopeless eyes and shell-shocked faces. They wore tattered uniforms, but he knew America's Pacific bases would have the same war-torn tableau.

Being the only able-bodied person on the trip, he felt their glares like daggers and read their thoughts. Where are your bandages? Why were you spared? Coward!

When Vinny met him at Stettin Station, he instantly recognized the changes that had overcome his friend. Vinny's eyes darted with suspicion, and his muscles remained primed for action. No jokes came at the greeting, only a brief nod of his head.

"Not glad to see me?"

"I'm being followed, and they bugged the apartment."

Zelly hugged him and clapped his back. "What happened?"

"War." His eyes pointed to a man dressed in a trench coat and reading *Völkischer Beobachter*. "My tail follows me everywhere."

"Gestapo. I can smell them."

As they walked south, the street was quiet, and Berlin was like a silent movie. They went to a beerhouse and ordered Weissbier, but the agent sat nearby almost instantly.

Zelly strode to the man and shoved his SS documentation between his eyes and the newspaper. "Excuse me, but I'm Frederich Zellner, and I'll be spending a few days with Vinny Testanuevo. I would appreciate some privacy. Herr Himmler is aware I'm here, so please check with the Reichsführer if you need clarification." As the man scurried away, Zelly returned to the table. "I've bought us about ten minutes." They crammed many conversations into a short time.

****

9 December 1941—Scribbles

Zelly lounged in Vinny's sitting room until he finished work. They'd planned a day of Christmas shopping, but the news left them too glum. Vinny shook the drizzle from his coat and handed Zelly two printed papers from his pocket. The first extended the Tri-Partite Pact so that Germany agreed to declare war on the U.S.A. The second was the text of a diplomatic note from Reich Minister for Foreign Affairs Joachim von Ribbentrop to the American Chargé d'affaires, breaking relations and making the conflict official.

Vinny found a pen and scribbled in the margins: Italy said madness. So did Ribbentrop.

Zelly wrote: Japanese?

Ecstatic. Churchill, too, I'll bet.

The Poles sent my rocket info to London. Have Uncle request it.

Vinny burned the papers in the sink.

As they turned to ashes, Zelly warmed the last piece of Christstollen on the hot plate. "What can I do to help?"

"Be the solution instead of the problem."

CHAPTER 13

Bonzai

22 February 1942—Peenemünde

For two weeks, intense snowstorms battered Peenemünde without halting the work. Zelly found the cold unbearable to venture from the heat unless his job demanded it. On this Sunday morning, temperatures were well below freezing, too cold for snow to fall. Only one thing was worth rejoicing—today was his 19th birthday.

Helmut and Kurt hadn't returned to the barracks over the night. He visualized them tucked under covers with Greta and Katchen, languishing in the afterglow. After Trudl with Stengler, he decided being single was better.

The blond peach fuzz on his cheeks was too much to ignore. So, he dug out the straight razor and peppermint soap Vinny had given him last year. After finishing the shave with only two nicks, he surrounded himself with steamy water in the shower while he remembered that day.

****

"Buon compleanno," Vinny and Turtle, his cousin, called when Zelly woke. After he dressed, Vinny looped a rope around his neck, dangling a sign: 'Baciami. Sono diciotto anni oggi.' The lettering said, 'Kiss Me. Eighteen years old today.'

Primo, Vinny's uncle, laughed as he handed Zelly ten Lire. "We're out of eggs. Buy a dozen at the market?"

He headed out, and every girl he passed demanded a kiss. With the purchase complete, he garnered many more kisses on his way home. Starry- eyed, he returned for breakfast to learn the errand was only a practical joke.

At 4:30, neighbors streamed into the house. The girls he had kissed brought their families, and dozens of Primo's friends and relatives arrived. Primo put glasses full of Fiano di Avellino wine in their hands. "A toast to our young friend. Cento di questi giorni."

Searching for an elegant reply, he came up with, "If I should have one hundred of these days, none will be as memorable as this one." The crystal clinked.

They sat him on a chair and carried it around, depositing him beside a round cake. "Here are the eggs you purchased this morning," Primo said.

"Not all." Turtle broke one on his head in the German tradition.

A band played, and the guests danced into the evening's chill. He walked a brown-haired girl home with Turtle between them and Gracia, Primo's wife, and the girl's mother two steps behind.

As he readied for bed, Vinny handed him a wrapped package. It was a straight razor and some peppermint-scented shaving soap. "I don't shave."

Tugging at Zelly's wispy chin hairs, he predicted, "You will soon."

****

Once he had finished with the shower and barbering, Zelly went back to his room and looked up at the magazine cover attached above his headboard. Even after trying to solve its mystery for a year, he marveled at his scoutmaster's photograph being published in a Nazi magazine.

He wondered about the story of Kurt Baltschun, the credited photographer. Was he in the international conspiracy of Jews and complicit in publishing it? Could he have been the scoutmaster who took the snapshot—a German spy in America? He remembered the circumstances of the picture on his 15th birthday.

****

The Boy Scout troop was dog-tired and sweat-drenched when they reached the Blanco River. Water gurgled over rocks about thigh deep, and the boys lost not an instant in getting wet. With the hardest section of the hike behind them, they would follow downstream to Wimberley and El Rancho Cima, an expansive mountain ranch where scouts were always welcome.

Cooled and refreshed, they set camp and tossed hobo packets, a favorite, in the fire. The foil contained hamburger and potato chunks with some onion and bell pepper.

When they finished the meal, the scoutmaster called, "Fred, put on a fresh shirt for a picture."

He realized the dirtiness. "No spare."

The man pulled one from his backpack, and Zelly shrugged it on. "You're Eagle now." He handed him a black neckerchief with the bird embroidered on the back and a new whittled slide. He looped it around his neck in Scout fashion and added a wool jacket for the cool evening.

The man positioned him in profile, facing the setting sun and staring into the distance. Zelly drew his comb from a back pocket and dragged his bangs down a little over one eye. The scoutmaster stepped back to frame the shot. "That's the cover of your Court of Honor program."

Teddy, who might now fly off the *Enterprise*, joked, "Girls will wet their panties over you."

The troop sang *Happy Birthday* and lifted a Dutch oven from the coals. The peach cobbler's aroma made Fred's mouth water. An adult leader brought out ice cream he'd trucked in from Wimberley. With vanilla scoops on the cobbler, the celebration was heavenly.

****

Another birthday came to mind—his 17th, three months before high school graduation and the spy stuff's beginning. He had spent the night with Jimmy, playing penny-ante poker.

"Hey, there's a war picture at the Stagecoach—catch the movie?" Jimmy asked.

"Sure. They're a favorite."

They ducked out the dormer window, climbed down the rose trellis, and thumbed a ride to town. For a quarter each, they got tickets and a bag of popcorn. *The Fighting 69th* lit up the screen.

"They're an all-Irish regiment from New York," Jimmy said. "I saw the preview last week."

Jerry Plunkett, played by James Cagney, was a blundering fool of a soldier, and his commander, a major, wanted to court-martial …. Zelly's blood curdled as he recalled the major's nickname—Wild Bill Donovan. He was the butcher with the baker and candlestick maker. A recollection of those three at the airstrip in San Antonio came to mind. An Army-painted DC-3 cargo plane sat on the tarmac. The officer offered a handshake. "I hope we meet again someday, should fate allow. I won't lie to you. Returning is doubtful. Yet, I'll pray for you every day."

As he shook Zelly's hand, he whispered, "When the end comes, these words will bring you home. Say, 'I work for Wild Bill,' that's your pass phrase." When Zelly forced a smile, the man came to attention and saluted Zelly.

Don't you wonder if that works without ruby slippers.

Shit. I just realized my butcher is the same guy as in the movie.

****

Kurt and Helmut came in and interrupted his remembrances. "Let's go, or you'll miss your party."

Friends and coworkers filled the officers' club, where Greta and Katchen met him with a kiss. Trudl came, much to his surprise, but she remained aloof. Everyone sang the birthday song and enjoyed the cake. Kurt poured a sweet Riesling, and they toasted his birth.

Hölzer pulled him to a table where a small box rested. "Without you, the mixing device wouldn't have happened. The mechanical computer you built is tremendous."

"It was the entire team." Zelly opened the present to find gold cuff links of the rocket from Dr. von Braun.

Kurt passed him another gift, a three-inch round silver medallion on a chain. One side had a swastika, SS runes, and the motto—My Honor is Loyalty. The other contained the inscription, 'Presented on his nineteenth birthday to my nephew by Heinrich Himmler.'

As the party ended, Trudl tried to sneak away, but Zelly took her elbow and pulled her aside. "Trudl, will you tell me why we broke up?"

Her eyes misted as she drew a deep breath. "He found me in a flak tower. He had arrested my parents to force me to spy on you, but I had little to tell him. I said you wrote reports and took photographs that violated your security agreement. He demanded more."

"I had Kurt check. Your family is fine, released unharmed."

Tears formed. "Imagine their embarrassment. They were pillars of the community and party."

"I'm so sorry you got caught up in my problems."

"I was so naïve, and he said it was my duty to make babies for the Fatherland."

"With Stengler, wasn't it terrible?"

"Not always, but it's over now. He doesn't want me anymore. Bye, Zelly." She walked away.

You're as deceitful as he is, using her for your own pleasure. You aren't German. Consider how much the truth about you would embarrass her family.

I could use a girlfriend. All my friends have one.

Do your duty and let her have children for Hitler. The rockets are so close, and you haven't warned America.

Kurt came to his side. "It's your birthday, and your face looks like you've eaten a lemon."

"I feel like a failure."

****

25 February 1942—The First Rocket, Ever

Word spread that the Assembly team had finished the first A-4. Each part was custom-made across Germany and assembled in the fabrication hall. It was placed on a unique trailer capable of raising it vertically. A twelve-ton half-track towed it three kilometers to Test Stand VII while newsreel cameras recorded. The launch pad inside the fence was ready for its delivery.

The rocket's checkered paint captivated Zelly, and he marched proudly behind. Excited for it to fly, he dreaded the thousands it would kill. He carried the Leica beneath his shirt, balanced on his belt buckle. An unfastened button exposed the lens. He snapped the shutter.

Soon, Stengler joined the march by falling in step beside Zelly. "Your belly is rather large."

"Are you arresting me for taking pictures?" Zelly asked.

"Himmler appreciated your previous ones and he'll like these, too, though I admire your subterfuge. You need a miniature camera like my Minox. I'd like to discuss the findings from the Warta River bridge investigation with you tonight."

"We're planning on the cinema to see *Comrades*."

"I'll catch you there."

Behind the parade, the massive doors of the fabrication building closed, and the crew started construction of another missile.

****

When the six friends arrived for the movie, they seated themselves in couples, leaving Trudl with Zelly. The newsreel featured Japanese footage of the Pearl Harbor attack, which killed Zelly's interest.

That's Oklahoma upside-down, and Andy was on her.

He's dead. Nobody could survive that. How can you view this?

I must.

The images wrenched his gut. With tears rolling down his cheeks, he worried that wiping them might attract attention.

As the victorious pilots landed on their carriers, crews shouted, "Bonzai!" The theatergoers jumped to their feet and roared with their allies. Trudl was among the first and loudest.

With a wet face, he stood and yelled. While mourning a friend, he celebrated the people who'd murdered him and attacked his country. At that moment, he felt like a failure and a traitor.

Trudl noticed. "Zelly, why are you crying?"

"I'm happy at sitting with you again." It was the first idea he came up with, and he instantly regretted speaking.

****

When the movie ended, Oskar Stengler caught them in the lobby. "I need to chat with Zellner so the rest of you run along."

"We're going for drinks in Karlshagen," Helmut said.

"Trudl, will you join us?" Kurt asked.

Zellner's eyes followed them out the door before he asked, "What about the attack?"

"As the preliminary report claimed, the tip for the resistance came from here. During the interrogation, several perpetrators reported the planning came from our Polish workers. It confirms we have a cell here."

"On that, I concur. It fits with my suspicions about the train bombing. But how would they access the schedules?"

"Security of their compound is lax, so they may have ways in and out. I plan to double the guard. I'm hoping you have some ideas about which prisoners are likely involved."

"Me?"

"The log sheets record you using their labor more than anyone else, and you were in a restricted area with one." Zelly blanched, and Stengler noticed. "Your workers trust you. Making a simple inquiry might gather valuable information."

"Sure. I'll inform you if I discover anything, but I doubt we have the planner here."

"They just don't seem smart enough," Oskar said.

****

Zelly went to bed with Bonzai's shouts haunting his sleep.

After your lies, who would believe you?

I had to cover myself. Tears showed my genuine emotions.

What relationship can you build on something so false? If you love her, tell the truth.

Impossible. I'd have no chance of survival.

She was honest with you and told you about Stengler.

Why would she have sex with him and not me?

He slid his hand under the mattress and gripped the Mauser pistol.

If you're planning to shoot yourself, just do it. Bonzai. Harakiri. That's what Japs do.

*I'm an American—hot dogs, apple pie, and **real** football.*

You fool, I'm the American.

You're the pretender.

Traitor. Will you turn in Boryslaw and the guys?

More precisely, will they report me?

Zelly's mind held two people, and the argument was incessant. Each questioned his sanity, and both were right. Though the gun would silence the voices, a good scout does his duty to God and his country.

****

18 March 1942—The Korsett

The spectacular rocket sat on the launch pad, ready for a test fire. A clamp called the Korsett in Peenemünde-speak fastened it to the gantry like a steel girdle. The guidance team could pivot the assembly, checking for how controls responded. They wanted to know whether the graphite steering vanes would withstand the exhaust's heat.

Water flooded the moat as Zelly's secret pipe got used.

Dr. Walter Thiel's crew scrutinized monitors for fuel injector performance and thrust measurements. Everyone in Zelly's group was eager for the all-important pitch-over maneuver.

Tons of cold hydrogen peroxide and methanol hydrazine flowed into the rocket. Loudspeakers echoed mission control's voice, reciting the procedures and counting down to the ignition. Excitement grew as crews cinched access panels, his co-workers spun the gyroscopes, and the electrical umbilical fell away.

Condensation beaded on the rocket's skin, sweating down its sides.

When the engine lit, flames and smoke filled the berm. The command voice switched, counting up rather than down. "One." The assembly trembled as the thrust built. "Two." It tugged upward, wanting to fly despite being restrained by the Korsett. "Three." The missile slipped, sitting back on the pad like a tired puppy. "Four." The metal cylinder shrunk as it crumpled into itself like wadded paper. "Five." An enormous fireball erupted. Zelly thought of Boryslaw's sabotage.

Curses came over the speakers while ground crews surged to fight the fire. The dejected design teams gathered to diagnose the failure.

"Not enough power," Max suggested.

"The gauge showed plenty," one of Dr. Thiel's crew defended. "This is guidance's problem."

After listening to the bickering, Zelly said, "Herr Hölzer, it fell out of the clamp."

An airframe guy said, "We made everything to measure."

"What if cold fuel caused some shrinkage?" Hölzer asked.

The possibility stunned everyone. A Korsett engineer flipped out blueprints to study the fit. "You're right."

When Zelly left the blockhouse, crews had extinguished the fires. Blackened wreckage littered the pad, and Polish workers cleaned it, Boryslaw, Arek, and Radzim among them. As Zelly boarded the train, he nodded a greeting, and Boryslaw returned a wink.

On the route, Trudl caught him. "I worried about you when I saw the huge fireball."

"I was at a safe distance and careful of the risks." Failure rankled him more than he wanted to admit, especially when Boryslaw's gesture spoke volumes.

The rocket will fly. I'm getting close....

...to killing thousands of people.

What can I do? My job is making the miracle of rocketry happen.

Wrong. Your goal is helping America, not Germany.

"I'm glad we're friends again," Trudl said, disturbing his thoughts.

****

23 March 1942—Exorcizing a Demon

Number 4002, the second completed A-4, was outfitted with a newly designed Korsett. At ignition, the oval berm filled with flame and smoke, and Dr. Thiel's engineers cheered its thrust. With perfect timing, the assembly executed pitch-over, rotating like a clock's minute hand. Guidance wiggled the girdle, and the mixing device, servomotors, and steering vanes corrected. After fifty-eight seconds, the engine sputtered to silence when it exhausted the fuel. The launch team hurried to the officer's club for a celebration.

It wants to fly, and I want it to soar so high.

Your mission is to stop it. By helping, you betray your country and yourself.

But I'm caught in the dream of space flight and thrilled to have a role.

You're guilty of treason.

I could make it fail.

Forget sabotage—the Gestapo would trace it to you. Leave that to Boryslaw.

My orders were to become a trusted and irreproachable Nazi.

Congratu-fucking-lations.

As Zelly left the party in the early evening, Trudl intercepted him. "I have something spectacular planned." She led him to a wooden tower, hovering above the trees near the island's tip around Test Stand VII.

He looked up the stairs. "Quite a climb." Once he made it up, the view from the platform amazed him. Tiny workers swarmed the launch pad far below. To the east, the Baltic's blue-green water stretched to infinity. In the north, a spit of land from Rugen Island pointed like a finger to a boat at anchor.

"This is Command Central, where we control all the antiaircraft guns, even the flak ship." Her voice dripped with pride. "Look west."

As he did, a bevy of activity caught his eye at the Luftwaffe field. Beyond, pastel clouds floated in front of an orange sun as it dipped behind the tall masts of Lubmin's sailboat harbor.

"Isn't it beautiful?" she asked.

"One day, my rocket will go to space. With today's success, we won't have to wait long."

"I have a surprise," she said with a giggle. Opening the locker, she pulled out a red-and-white checkered tablecloth, champagne in a bucket of ice, and cans of smoked salmon. She spread a picnic on the wooden floor, and they enjoyed every bite.

After the meal, he sprawled on the cloth, peering into the heavens. The aurora borealis lit up the northern sky with green and fingers of gold, making the moon's crescent seem pale.

"How beautiful." She surprised him by unbuttoning his shirt and laying her head on his belly. "On Mittsommernacht, I think my blouse was open, too." She pulled it over her shoulders and off. When she lowered her head to his body, she faced his feet and touched the bulge in his trousers. "Do you know I saw it once? You were skinny dipping with another guy near my dorm."

"That was Sev, a Norwegian."

"You were more handsome, and this was spectacular." She groped him.

Physically, he was very excited, but his emotions felt revulsion. "Are we heading toward sex because I don't want any discomfort?"

She flinched and turned to see his face. "Why would you say that?"

"I've heard you've said it's painful."

"Who told you that?"

"You know guys talk. I really don't want to do it in your butt like Stengler."

She burst into tears and scampered down the ladder two rungs at a time, leaving the picnic supplies and her blouse behind. While buttoning his shirt, his ardor vanished.

Why did you hurt her so cruelly?

I was exorcizing a demon.

****

28 March 1942—Lübeck

As Kurt and Zelly rode in the radio truck, the night was clear and cold. The waxing moon was bright, and a light frost covered the ground. They stopped at a beach on the island's northwest corner, between the forest and the airfield's clearing. Zelly deployed the antennas, and Kurt powered the equipment and tuned Rostock's weaponry control. "It's a perfect night for a bombing."

"Danish radar tracking over two hundred Brit bombers," he reported, removing his headphones and switching to the speakers.

Rostock deployed fighters to Kiel, expecting an attack on the massive shipyard and submarine pens, but the Brits chose another target—Lübeck, a medieval city of culture and history. Forty-two minutes before midnight, bombs fell only 240 kilometers west.

Kurt switched to the city's civil defense frequencies. The attack's first wave dropped blockbusters, ripping off roofs and blowing apart structures. Incendiaries followed, setting everything ablaze.

"I hate this constant destruction. Some music, please?" Zelly asked.

"Soon, your rockets will do the blasting." Kurt spun the dial to an illegal station, and *Don't Sit Under the Apple Tree with Anyone Else but Me* burst from the speakers. "An English song?"

"American." Zelly relished the harmonized feminine voices and translated the lyrics for Kurt.

As his head bobbed in the rhythm, Kurt said, "I'm thinking of Katchen."

The comment shocked Zelly back to reality, because his mind was on Meg McAuley in Belfast. "I think Trudl will end any friendship with me. I hinted about what she and Stengler did in your office."

"You badly need a lesson in charm."

****

27 April 1942—Shangri-La

The room was still dark when Kurt undressed and collapsed on his mattress. "Rostock, once again, for the fourth night in a row."

Helmut repositioned his helmet. "That's only 140 kilometers away. Will they bomb here?"

"To them, this place doesn't exist," Kurt said.

Can't be true, Zelly thought. Information from an anti-Nazi Austrian sergeant should have alerted London to Peenemünde's existence and value.

Who'd ever believe in rockets? Your work was science fiction. Dumbed down by the Poles.

I must send it to Washington.

Too little, too late.

"You got a new message from Vinny that I censored last evening," Kurt mumbled, half asleep.

When Zelly arrived at guidance, the letter was on his desk. He skimmed it and found surprising news—America had attacked Japan. Since Germany wasn't involved, Kurt left much of it uncensored, and Zelly dug into the details. Eighteen American bombers had hit Tokyo and other cities. The planes were army, not navy. Though the Japs caught and executed some pilots, a few made it to China.

"What are you grinning about?" Hölzer asked. When Zelly shared some by reading aloud, Hölzer pulled out a map and drew a circle around Tokyo. "Here's the probable aircraft range, so the planes must have launched from China."

The next section quoted a speech by Roosevelt saying the attack had come from Shangri-La. As the guidance team searched for the city, Zelly suppressed a laugh, knowing that it was a fictional place in Tibet and the setting of *Lost Horizon.* Germany had banned James Hilton's utopian fantasy.

After work, Kurt, Katchen, and Zelly went to the cinema for *Love is Duty-Free*, a romantic comedy. Trudl was also in the audience, glaring at Zelly.

The newsreel showed the bells of Lübeck's St. Mary's Church. They'd fallen from the bell tower and melted on the stone floor. The image burned in Zelly's heart.

After the movie, Katchen invited Trudl to join them at the Karlshagen Biergarten. "Trudl, lighten up. Your stare could have killed him twice already. What happened?"

Trudl stared into her stein while Zelly choked and coughed.

As Kurt took a sip, a mischievous grin came over his face. "Trudl, what happened on the flak platform? Zelly unable to perform?" He waggled an index finger to emphasize limpness.

Katchen elbowed his midsection. "Manners, Kurt, you don't ask questions like that."

Trudl answered, anyway. "I made a mistake with Stengler, and somehow Zelly learned the details. I doubt we can even be friends."

Kurt glared at Zelly, who looked away to avoid eye contact. Kurt's smile became roguish. "If Katchen is willing, I'm up for a three-way."

Katchen howled in exasperation and clamped a hand over his mouth, but his eyes still grinned.

Zelly changed the subject. "Those melted bells in the newsreel were haunting. Why would the Brits destroy such a cultural site?"

"Comrade, you're not weaseling out of this," Kurt said. "We've all got baggage from previous relationships, except you— you're still a virgin."

A matronly waitress delivered their food. "Schatzi, if you need relief, I can give you a toss." The lady reached into Zelly's lap for a grope.

He blushed while his friends roared with amusement.

****

15 May 1942—*USS Enterprize*

A letter from Vinny came, and Zelly's work colleagues wanted him to share it aloud.

"The Japanese had a glorious victory in the South Pacific near New Guinea, a place called the Solomon Islands. Where in the hell is that?"

Hölzer pointed to a world map hanging on the wall. "Bougainville, in the North Solomons, was German territory before the Great War."

Zelly continued reading. "In the battle, Japan sunk two American aircraft carriers, the *Lexington* and *Yorktown*, and reported continuing attacks on the *Enterprize*."

"Bonzai!" someone yelled.

Zelly puzzled over Vinny's misspelling of *Enterprise*. Must be purposeful. A clue?

Later, he met Kurt and Helmut at the mess hall. "Got a letter from Vinny today."

"What's the news?" Helmut asked.

"In the South Pacific, the Japs had a victory at the Marshall Islands."

"Solomons," Kurt corrected, "remember, I've read everyone's mail."

As they left the building, Zelly pointed out a single British Spitfire circling overhead. "Kurt, do you still think they won't recognize anything here?"

"With the runway, they'll figure a fighter base. The forest hides the rest."

"I hope so." Helmut tightened the chin strap of his helmet.

"They can't miss the oval launching pad," Zelly said.

Kurt dismissed the worry with a wrist flick. "A football field."

Ahead, they spotted Katchen, Greta, and Trudl as the girls laughed at some joke.

"Trudl likes you," Helmut said. "Please stop your self-flagellation because the bed squeaks."

"But Stengler…"

"What she did was to protect you. Since that night, she's rejected him. Doesn't she deserve a second chance?" Kurt's appeal soothed Zelly's emotional sore.

****

13 June 1942—Failure

After almost a month, the A-4 was ready for flight, and Zelly's colleagues in guidance were on edge with anxiety. Dornberger had invited several Berlin dignitaries for a spectacular program, amplifying everyone's fear of a fiasco. Albert Speer, General Fromm, Admiral Witzell, and Field Marshal Milch came to the island.

The event started at the airfield, where the VIPs viewed three Me-163 Komets take off, fly in formation, and glide to a landing. They were an experimental Luftwaffe plane, nicknamed the Gnat for all their whine and bother. Still, they competed for needed resources.

A missile waited for their arrival at Test Stand VII. Everyone from scientist to file clerk turned out for the launch. Convenient viewing places filled fast, so latecomers climbed trees near the beach. Zelly's spot was on bleachers installed on the guidance building's roof.

When the command for ignition came over speakers, the engine sparked, spewing flame and smoke through the blast deflector. The rocket hovered on a reddish-yellow ball of fire, fighting against gravity, and won the battle at 11:52 AM. Lifting from the pad, it crested the dunes and ascended above the treetops. It sounded like rolling thunder and obliterated the cheers.

The fuselage's checkered paint showed a strange twist. "Something's not right," Zelly said.

"Might correct at pitch-over," Hölzer speculated, but the maneuver made the oscillations worse. As it disappeared into clouds, the rumbles turned to a screaming howl, like a dive-bombing Stuka.

"Here it comes, falling with no tail fins," Hirschler said, pointing as it plummeted and tumbled into the Baltic, less than a kilometer away. The explosion geysered water high into the sky.

"A washout," Hölzer muttered.

Unimpressed, the dignitaries left. In the debriefing, the pitch change caught the blame and disheartened Zelly.

Von Braun tried to cheer them up. "No such thing as a complete failure because each bit of data makes the next step more certain."

A letter arrived from Vinny, but Zelly tucked it into his pocket while analyzing the problem. Answers remained elusive. They dismissed his observation of twisting until gyroscope information confirmed the increasingly rapid rotations.

"When did the tail fins go?" Hirschler asked. They had no answer.

Zelly was dead tired when he left work, but a boat unloading debris at the beach caught his attention. When he approached, he spotted a rocket fin. "Where did you find it?"

"Not far out in the surf," Boryslaw said with a broad grin.

Zelly grew certain of the Polish sabotage effort. At the officers' club, he sat at Kurt's table and placed Vinny's letter beside his beer. "I'm too exhausted to read it. Tell me what's in it."

Kurt shrugged. "The Japanese rule the Pacific after sinking the last two American carriers, *Enterprise* and *Hornet,* at Midway."

Zelly unfolded the page to check Vinny's spelling—*Enterprise* with a 'z.' Another clue?

****

16 August 1942—Frozen Lightning

The day was bright and cloudless as the next A-4 stood poised on the launch pad. Expectations were high but also desperate as Berlin dignitaries came to judge rocketry's future.

Zelly invited Kurt to view from the guidance building's roof. When ignition brought it to life, they shared a grin as the fiery roar dominated sight and sound. Zelly's breath caught when the flight count reached three, and he held it as the missile zoomed skyward. The checkered paint was stable and straight, but something broke off the nose and plummeted into the forest. Despite his groan, the missile leaped upward, undisturbed by a missing part.

Zelly made a wish for success, wanting the technical marvel to astonish the world. In the same thought, dread arrived as he considered the many deaths it would cause.

Twenty seconds later, a loud cannon shot swept over everyone.

Zelly scanned the sky for a rain of falling debris.

His glum face brought a smile from Hirschler. "Speed of sound. Von Braun said there'd be a boom."

"Look at the frozen lightning," Kurt said of the jagged condensation trailing it.

After five more clock ticks, another explosion echoed. Zelly looked at Hirschler, wondering if this was another expected event, but disappointment washed over his face as small pieces of rocket fell.

Discouraged, the guidance team hurried down the roof hatch to overcome another defect. Over the radio, the dignitaries complained about the waste of their time.

"What fell from the nose at launch?" Max asked.

Hirschler examined telemetry. "Electric failed at T plus 4. We're absolved. Not our fault."

Someone channeled the boss, "Not a complete failure because the data will help us succeed."

"It flew," Zelly argued, "and I'd call that successful."

Hirschler smiled. "It was faster than anything ever before. Our Frau needs a bit more foreplay."

As he left work, the broad grin on Boryslaw's face angered him.

Fuck sabotage. I want success.

At least the Pole is accomplishing his mission while you're not.

****

11 to 13 September 1942

The Brits preferred to bomb during the nights with bright moons when targets were easiest to find. Zelly often accompanied Kurt on these occasions, when German cities shook and crumbled to dust. Eavesdropping on the events by radio became an obsession, bringing trepidation at the huge, unnecessary loss of life and joy as the potential defeat of Germany neared.

He knew the raids were revenge for Germany's devastation of England. If the bombing hadn't subdued the English, the Nazis were as unlikely to succumb to it. An allied victory would require more than tons of bombs. Still, he developed a fresh perspective on the war from listening.

After midnight on Friday, September 11th and under a brilliant, waning gibbous moon, five hundred Royal Air Force bombers attacked Düsseldorf and Neuss, cities on opposite banks of the Rhine River. Kurt and Zelly knew the number from radar intercepts and the BBC. The next day, German radio's mid-day reports claimed 2,417 houses destroyed, 148 civilians killed, and 33 aircraft shot down.

Zelly did the math—seven percent losses. England can't afford the ratios. In ten or twelve raids, British air power will vanish.

Brit radio painted a different picture—380 acres of destruction, thirty war material factories out of commission, and the central railway station damaged.

On Sunday, September 13th, five hundred Wellingtons struck Bremen on the Weser River near the North Sea. Goebbels reported six schools and two hospitals hit and 21 downed planes.

Helmut said, "We have as many cities as they do airplanes."

"How can they send 500 every night?" Zelly asked. "Goebbels must be lying."

Helmut shot him a scornful glance for the defeatist talk. Shortly, Helmet dressed and left.

****

In the Gestapo office, Kurt's eyes rose from Zelly's latest paper. "He thinks the beast will fly."

"They're getting close, and Himmler is relying on it to win the war," Stengler said.

Kurt opened the door at a knock. "Helmut, why are you here?"

He stepped to Stengler's desk. "My duty requires me to report my roommate's defeatist talk."

"Me?" Kurt asked in surprise.

Helmut kept his eyes on Oskar. "Herr Zellner."

"What did he say?" Kurt asked, not wanting to be excluded from the conversation.

"Perhaps you should wait in the cloakroom." Stengler dismissed Kurt.

When the door closed behind Kurt, Oskar's grin broke through. "Tell me what he said."

"He called Herr Goebbels a liar."

Oskar worked to contain his smile. "What was the context?"

"We listened to a radio report of Bremen's bombing, and Zelly said, 'How can they send 500 every night? Goebbels must be lying.'"

Oskar nodded with the utmost seriousness. "Is that all?"

"Isn't that enough?"

"Certainly, and I've noted it, but have you witnessed anything else? As I recall, you brought me the map when he first came to base."

Helmut's chest puffed. "There are many strange things— always writing, taking pictures, and trying to hide those activities from me. He goes with Kurt in the truck to listen during enemy bombing raids."

****

At the officers' club, Zelly sat down with Arthur Rudolph, an engine specialist overseeing the fabrication works. After several drinks, Rudolph said, "I worked in Bremen, and I'll tell you something. The English aren't targeting factories. They picked sections of the city known to burn— neighborhoods of wooden apartments with lots of people and no basements for shelters."

"But they kill so few, only seventy last night," Zelly said.

"You believe the numbers? How do they count the dead? These districts would blaze like a crematorium, leaving nothing but ashes and bones. Do they weigh the ash and divide it by six pounds per person or lay out each skeleton's 206 parts? Could Goebbels even do the math?"

Rudolph's analysis made the atmosphere gloomy. To liven the mood, Zelly drew a cartoon showing King George sitting on a palace chamber pot. Inspired by Helmut, His Royal Highness did his toileting while wearing his crown. His face had a horror-filled expression as the rocket penetrated the roof. On its fin, Zelly wrote 'For Bremen.'

"Can I keep it?" Rudolph asked.

Kurt caught Zelly in the horseshoe outside the barracks. "Helmut reported you to the Gestapo for Wehrkraftzersetzung. The penalty for sedition is prison or execution."

"Shit, he gave Stengler exactly what he needs to put me away."

CHAPTER 14

Splashdown

3 October 1942—Outer Space

For weeks, Zelly waited for questioning or torture by the Gestapo, but Stengler never called him. Stengler was right—the anticipation might be worse than the pain.

For the launch of Aggregat #4004, Zelly monitored from a television set, another marvelous invention. The crawler lifted it to the gantry. Next to the checkered paint, someone had added a cartoon on the fin patterned after his Hanna Reitsch drawing, made a year earlier and still hanging at Hirschler's office. The artist depicted an A-4 crossing behind the crescent moon. A gal wearing only black stockings sat on the moon's edge near the caption—Frau im Mond.

Control held the countdown, delaying for Albert Speer's arrival because he was the only VIP to come. Zelly spotted Dornberger and Colonel Zassen waiting on the measurement house roof and Wernher von Braun standing on top of assembly works. At 4 PM, the general grew tired of the delay and ordered things to proceed.

The rocket thundered off the pad, stable and straight. Pitch-over execution was flawless, and the sonic boom rolled over the audience.

"Twenty-two seconds," the loudspeaker said. It was out there, somewhere, traveling fast and being chased by frozen lightning. On the count of fifty-eight, the speaker announced, "End of engine burn."

Hirschler tracked the missile on the scope and announced the telemetry after splashdown. "Altitude: ninety kilometers, speed: 5,000 kilometers an hour, and range: 200."

Dornberger and Zassen hugged and danced while Peenemünde cheered. In a Messerschmitt 110, Dr. Steinhoff buzzed overhead and waggled his wings before speeding away to locate the splash point. Everyone smiled, anticipating Steinhoff's radio call. He'd filled the rocket's nose with bags of dye and soon reported through the static, "The Baltic has a bright-green stain 4K off target."

Hirschler slapped Zelly's shoulder. "Should have aimed for Georgie's chamber pot."

Zelly drew another cartoon featuring Winston Churchill puffing on an A-4 instead of a cigar.

Hölzer asked him to put it on a poster board. "You're invited to Dornberger's epic party in the officers' club, and bring your art."

Excited by success, Albert Speer attended. "I viewed your launch while landing—wondrous and spectacular."

Dornberger gave a speech that ended with, "Today, and for the first time, we have invaded outer space."

The bartender filled glasses with fine champagne. When Dr. Steinhoff returned, still in his flight gear, the crowd toasted him. "Outer space."

Hölzer and Hirschler presented Speer with mementos—a rocket model and Zelly's poster of Churchill.

"Who's the artist?" Speer asked, and Kurt pushed Zelly to the stage. "Will you autograph it?"

"I'm happy to meet you again, sir," Zelly said as he signed. "When I was in the HJ at Halle's signals school, you commended me for electronics. Your letter may have brought me to Peenemünde."

Speer tousled Zelly's hair with a smile before gazing around the platform. "I'd like to think I contributed to this spectacular effort. Tell me, has the lad lived up to my recommendation?"

"His idea led to the mixing device," Dr. von Braun said.

"Without it, we wouldn't have been so close," Steinhoff said.

"Remember, I discovered him."

As the party ended, Zelly felt like continuing the celebration. He grabbed a bottle of Asbach Uralt Brandy and another sweet wine from behind the bar.

He found Kurt in the room. "We flew—as smooth as satin and as perfect as a sunset. I have libations."

"Katchen and I are heading to the beach, Trudl too. Come along?"

Zelly shrugged with liquor in each hand.

Kurt loaded blankets and firewood into the truck before driving to the girl's dorm. "Are you up for a difficult conversation with Trudl?"

"I suppose so."

Trudl brought a fruit cake she had baked from apples her parents had sent from Jena.

Kurt selected a coastal spot north of Test Stand VII. He parked perpendicular to the surf. The guys built two sand-pit fires, one on each flank of the truck. While Trudl sliced the dessert, Zelly mixed cocktails of red peach wine and brandy. Katchen and Kurt settled on the driver's side to enjoy the cake, and Trudl and Zelly stretched a blanket near the other fire and sat.

"I'll start with the burning question. How do you know so much about Stengler and me?"

"Kurt told me about the bottle and blood on the office floor. Through personal experience, I know Stengler is a sexual sadist. I took some wild guesses."

"You weren't wrong. We haven't been together since then."

"Kurt also informed me of the baby and the poison you used to abort it. I'm sorry."

"I hope he said Stengler's relationship was a trap. The Gestapo wanted me to tell him what you were doing so he could arrest you."

"I understand. If there is any person in the world I hate, it would be Stengler."

"Does it rub off on me?"

Zelly took a deep gulp of the cocktail. "Rationally, I know it shouldn't, but I'm still angry."

She forked a cake piece and held it in front of her mouth. "I haven't changed. I'm still the same girl as when I arrived."

She's being honest with you. Why not do the same?

I can't, and you know it.

Kurt popped around the truck, naked. "We're going skinny dipping.

Coming?"

"It's October," Trudl shrieked.

Zelly chuckled. "You'll freeze off your balls."

With a grin, Kurt said, "Katchen knows how to warm them."

Trudl shivered. "Do you want to cuddle underneath the stars?"

Zelly wrapped her in a blanket, spooning against her back. "We can be friends, but I don't know about a romantic relationship."

"Good enough for now," she said.

He noticed Kurt had tuned to Radio Belgrade, an approved frequency. The song was *J'attendrai* by Rina Ketty, a French love song with the title of 'I Will Wait.'

****

Oskar Stengler answered the phone in the Gestapo office. A voice said, "Please hold for Reichsführer-SS Heinrich Himmler."

Himmler's tenor crackled over the line several minutes later. "Though protocol won't allow me to express it directly, I want you to pass this message to my little spy—congratulations on the rocket's success."

"Jawohl," Oskar barked. "May we discuss another issue concerning Zellner? His roommate has accused him of sedition."

"The courier?"

"A Wehrmacht sergeant named Wilhelm Dotzel."

"Tell me the details," Himmler sighed.

"When they listened to radio reports of a recent bombing, Zellner was quoted as saying, 'How can they send 500 every night? Goebbels must be lying.'"

Himmler guffawed. "What does a propaganda minister do but lie? Oskar, you're wise enough to understand unless you're holding something back."

"How should I handle the matter?"

"Buy him a drink, deliver my commendation, and offer a casual warning. I'll visit Peenemünde soon."

When the line went dead, Oskar wondered why the Reichsführer was coming.

****

28 October 1942—Brawl

The Luftwaffe had an experimental missile project called Kirschkern, a cherry pit in the vernacular. The vehicle was like an airplane with a rocket engine mounted on the tail. As the fly-boys celebrated an outstanding test with cherry schnapps at the Karlshagen beer hall, Kurt, Helmut, and Zelly arrived. As usual, the Luftwaffe and the rocketry guys separated themselves by an invisible line.

"Kirschkern has wings, and rockets have fins," Max spoke loudly to be heard across the line.

"But it has a rocket motor," a flight officer said.

Max laughed. "You'd shove a tailpipe up a chicken's ass and call it an automobile." He caught a punch in the mouth. Instantly, the division vanished, and an inter-service brawl began.

Helmut decked the flight lieutenant, stole his liquor bottle, and ducked under a table.

Kurt pulled his pistol and fired into the ceiling, bringing an end to the fight. When he shouted, "Gestapo," the magic word sent everyone scurrying away.

As the three roommates made their way to the barracks, Helmut proudly showed off his stolen schnapps. They shared it around the room until Helmut dropped into a drunken snore.

"Zelly, let's shower," Kurt suggested. With water running to mask his words, he said, "Your last report impressed the Reichsführer. He's planning to visit and wants to meet with you."

"Shit! Is this about Helmut reporting me for defeatist talk?"

Kurt shrugged. "That I don't know, but I'm to keep it low-key. I'll be his driver and slip you into the car at some point."

"When?" Zelly asked with a shudder.

"Since Heydrich's assassination, they haven't made Himmler's schedule public." As the showerhead sprayed, he said, "So you know, Himmler knows you're into swing and listen to illegal radio."

"He's known about my music tastes for a long time. Putting the sedition report together with illegal listening will get me hung. You promised to keep secrets."

As Kurt's head shook, drops sprinkled from his hair. "This may shock you. **He** told **me** to use the tunes to bait you into it."

Zelly's knees buckled, and he fell on his butt. "You tricked me?"

"Himmler plays both of us like a violin."

"So, tell me about what he holds over you."

Kurt moved to the basin and lathered to shave. "Remember how I hated having to learn French in Minderlittgen? Well, my sister was the opposite. When I joined HJ, she went to the resistance. The SS required me to report on her activities and supply her with false information. Without her knowledge, I put her in the predicament of being a double agent. Since I'm here, she has a boyfriend doing the same thing."

"Why don't they arrest her?" Zelly soaped his face with his peppermint soap.

"They trust her, although she passes them disinformation. Should I not follow my orders, they'll convince her friends she's a collaborator. I feel guilty for putting her in that situation, but what choice do any of us have?"

As Zelly tried to sleep, his mind raced with Himmler's deviousness.

Soon, your rockets will kill Americans—like the Japs did at Pearl Harbor.

I've got to complete my mission.

Which one? The time to choose is now.

I want them to succeed and to help America win the war.

Right. The headline—Texas Boy Scout invents rockets to give Hitler a monumental victory. Where will your statue stand, in the Tiergarten or on the Capitol steps?

****

1 November 1942—Algiers

On Sunday, Kurt and Zelly tucked into the radio truck and parked close to the airfield. They eavesdropped on the tower frequency to give Zelly some Kirschkern data for his reports. When the action ended, Kurt dialed the BBC, and unexpected news poured from the speakers. American troops of the 34th Infantry Division had taken Algiers.

The situation dumbfounded Zelly as he considered it. Kurt laughed at his gaping mouth. "You'll catch a bug."

Hitler's Thousand-Year Reich is two thousand miles from the end.

And when the United States Army arrives on this island, they'll shoot you like a Nazi pig.

****

2 November 1942—Explosion

Rockets #4005 and #4006 had abject failures, and the Zinnowitz run had lots of defective parts. The Poles didn't act interested in talking, which increased Zelly's suspicions. Finally, he pushed, "Boryslaw, how's sabotage?"

The answer was a grin and a thumb pointing to the stacked crates in the truck bed.

"Consider this. We know rocket science is correct. Soon, when things fail, they'll search for saboteurs and tighten quality control. Eventually, every failure will bring a massive investigation and unrelenting scrutiny."

The Pole sighed. "We know. We couldn't stop the rockets, only slow the project."

"I have news. Americans have landed in Algeria."

"And the Soviets have forced a Nazi retreat. German diesel engines don't turn over at forty below, and the Volga River is thick with ice, so only Russians can cross it."

While the Poles moved crates, Zelly shopped for Christmas presents. The stores had little stock, and what was available was high-priced damaged goods. In a porcelain shop, he found a beautiful figurine—a woman playing the piano for her passionate lover. A small chip made the price reasonable.

As he debated buying it, a familiar voice said, "These days, what doesn't have a defect?"

He glanced to find Frau Stengler nearby. "For my aunt in Wittenberg.

What do you think?"

She ensured Meissen's mark of blue crossed swords was on the base. "She'll treasure it."

As the clerk wrapped his gift, Zelly asked, "How are the boys?"

"Max is in the Wehrmacht's 6th Army at the front in Stalingrad. Heinz is tall and skinny and prefers his formal name now."

When the cashier handed him the present, he said, "Good day, Frau Stengler." At the railroad platform, he found the train had departed, and the Polish workers lounged as they waited. He trucked them to their camp and checked the truck at the motor pool. As he walked away, a Kübelwagen approached with Kurt driving and Stengler riding beside him.

"Climb in," Kurt called. "An explosion in Züssow took out your train, and an ammunition freight headed in the opposite direction."

Stengler appraised the surprise on Zelly's face, wondering if it was genuine. "What happened at the loading in Zinnowitz?"

"There was nothing out of the ordinary, all duly documented. I used the same three Poles." Then, Zelly lied. "Like always, I supervised everything and double-checked the boxes against the packing list." He wondered if Stengler's wife would mention his shopping to her husband.

"This attack was more sophisticated than earlier," Stengler said. "Someone had to figure out the timing for both trains, and that's advanced math, similar to rocket trajectories."

Zelly caught the hint and recalled Helmut's accusation.

Kurt said, "We had no notification of the ammunition freight, so I wonder how anyone learned about it. We're on our way to inspect the scene."

"That's great. I might solve the case from the wood's distribution," Zelly said. "Railway cars are hardwood—ash, beech, and oak while our crates are soft pine. If the softwood is on the outskirts of the blast, we're at fault. If it's only scattered around one track, the ammo started the explosion."

"How do you conclude that?" Stengler probed.

"Ballistics—those high-order math trajectories."

When they arrived at Züssow, things weren't so simple as the pinewood station had also exploded. The resulting fire had burned through town, killing people and igniting secondary blasts. In the massive rubble field, woods of both types had mingled as they flamed.

While Stengler interviewed witnesses with the criminal police, Zelly and Kurt walked the service road beside the tracks. When they reached the furthest piece of lumber, Zelly examined it. "Kurt, our fault. I can make out the Peenemünde brand mark." When they returned to Stengler at the Kübelwagen, Zelly reported, "Our parts are on the outskirts."

Stengler nodded. "The witness stories are consistent. Multiple detonations with our train followed by a series of blasts on the other."

Kurt drove to the southeast when leaving Züssow and crossed onto the island over the Zecheriner bridge.

"Why are we detouring?" Zelly asked.

Stengler answered with a disturbing grin. "I want to question your Polish workers away from the base. I had them taken to Swinemünde, the largest town in the area."

****

Oskar Stengler directed Kurt to park at a brick building bearing the Nazi eagle. Across the harbor, he spotted a round lighthouse powered by windmill vanes, a novelty to him. A visit there might be a great outing for the boys, he thought. When he entered the lobby, a sergeant greeted him with a Heil Hitler and grabbed a keyring.

The jangling keys led him, Kurt, and Zellner through a hall of cells. Once these small cubicles had held the enemies of the Prussian Duke of Pomerania, but now mostly captured resistance members. Oskar had selected the site because the prisoners could easily communicate through the bars and around the brick walls. Of course, a Gestapo agent fluent in Polish had listened since the detainees arrived.

The group stopped at an office where Stengler asked the listener, "Anything?"

"They have wondered why they're here and concluded another explosion has happened. However, I suspect they're smart enough to know I was eavesdropping."

Oskar tapped Zellner's chest with his index finger. "You, first." He watched the boy walk to the cell, expecting incrimination in the first few seconds.

When Zellner stepped into the cage, Boryslaw switched from Polish to German. "Thank heavens! Why are we here?"

"The train we loaded this morning exploded. Our defective parts were the last, so they're the logical starting place. Tell me what you remember, and I'll see if it fits with my memory."

"We stacked eighteen sealed crates; none were different from usual," Radzim said.

"The lids and seals showed no sign of opening or tampering," Arek said.

"And you matched each one to the manifest," Boryslaw said.

Zelly relaxed, knowing Boryslaw had just supported the lie.

"Could someone have hidden an explosive inside the crates?" Boryslaw asked.

"Are you suggesting we have an active underground on base?" Zelly asked.

Stengler chose the moment to intervene with his cat-like grin focused on Boryslaw. "That theory might connect to the Warta River attack. What do you know of resistance activities?"

"Nothing, sir, I merely offered the possibility."

"One that seems chillingly accurate."

Arek said, "The boxcar was nearly full, and the train had at least another dozen freight cars. It wasn't us."

Stengler stared at Zelly. "Why don't you and Kurt return? I'll catch a ride after I finish the interrogation."

****

After returning to Peenemünde, Zelly and Kurt waited for an hour in the Gestapo office for Stengler. When he arrived, Kurt asked, "What did you learn?"

"They're not smart enough to pull this off—too much math."

I'm sure the time, rate, and distance problem was well within Boryslaw's engineering degree.

But Stengler can't grasp it because he can't see beyond the Poles being a subhuman species.

"What do I put in the report?" Kurt asked, poised at the typewriter.

Stengler dictated, "A saboteur placed a time bomb in one or more crates. Calculating the timing between that point and the train's arrival in Züssow would require some major work. We'll search for the traitors here, starting with those who have significant computation abilities." As he finished, he glared at Zelly.

"Don't jump too quickly on that theory," Zelly warned. "Detonation by remote control is also possible. Someone near the station could have had the trigger device. Züssow's criminal police should investigate."

"So, I'm looking for a genius in both math and radio like you." Stengler's gaze became a stare.

"To a language teacher, I suspect most of the people here look like geniuses in mathematics and electronics." Zelly shrugged and pointed at Kurt. "Even him."

As Stengler growled in frustration, Zelly and Kurt hurried to the barracks. "Thanks for fingering me, buddy," Kurt said sarcastically.

"About time he glared at you some."

Demand that the Poles end the sabotage before you're implicated.

They won't stop. This is their battlefield.

So, scram—grab Vinny and run. Just don't die here.

Fred, you're the one who wanted a life of adventure. Better than milking cows, you thought.

Vinny does his own thing with the dead Jews and atom-smashing bombs but won't help me.

And Stengler hasn't talked to you about the defeatist attitude.

Nor have I completed my mission.

Have you even begun?

****

28 November 1942—Something Fell

With the temperature nearing freezing, the passengers on the commuter train huddled near the stoves instead of sitting in the seats. Zelly was in his usual spot when Greta pushed through the crowd. "I'm glad you're back to friendship with Trudl. She likes you a lot."

"Hey, would you and Helmut like to see a launch? Rocket #4007 is on the pad."

Later, they climbed to the rooftop bleachers. Greta's eyes followed the missile's shape. "Do men ever design something that doesn't resemble a penis?"

Helmut stared at the vapor cloud filling the television—condensation from the liquid fuel. "To me, it looks like a dragon."

At ignition, the beast belched fire and exhaust. In the pitch-over, it wiggled back and forth like an ice skater shifting blades. Zelly gasped as the missile cartwheeled and exploded.

"Fuck," Hirschler said. "Boys, this one is on us."

Greta pointed to a spot in the sky. "I saw something fall off there."

"It sparkled in the haze," Helmut agreed.

Zelly leaned through the hatch and called, "Did radar show anything falling?"

An operator responded. "A small object at T+27, which I tracked to the ground near the beach."

The guidance crew hurried to the sea as fishing boats prowled the waters. Germans, arrayed in marching ranks, scoured the sand while Polish workers waded through the icy surf.

"Something here," Arek said, pulling a meter of steering vane from the water.

Zelly took it from him and noticed deep gouges and scrapes pockmarking the metal. He understood that the failure was sabotage but avoided the word. To withstand exhaust heat, the vanes required a specific steel at a particular thickness. This one had burned through—either the wrong alloy or poor milling. He passed the defective part to Hirschler and pointed out the aberration. While his boss examined the flaw, Zelly watched the Polish workers march to their camp. Boryslaw's subtle smile made Zelly seethe.

Why are you angry? He's doing his mission. Far better than you.

The resistance is larger than I ever suspected. No Poles work in fabrication, only Germans.

They've recruited help. You are only a patsy in their scheme.

The train bombings already point to them.

And to me. Stengler is more than suspicious.

You'll be one of his torture victims unless you do something quickly.

****

10 to 12 December 1942—Kill Them

Zelly arranged a Thursday off duty to listen to the Luftwaffe's flight test of Kirschkern with Kurt. "Cherry-pit" soared away from its launching ramp and created a sonic boom.

At the success, Zelly groaned. "With two rockets seeking funding, the competition for resources will be ferocious."

"Himmler's viewing from the runway," Kurt said.

"Shit. Is this his visit? Will he stay long enough to see our launch on the twelfth?"

Kurt said, "I have something else for you, but we'll be dead if you breathe a word."

Zelly held one earphone to his ear.

Soviet forces surrounded and cut off Stalingrad. Hitler has ordered the Luftwaffe to fly in supplies. Reports show they manage about 65 tons a day. German soldiers will find it hard to survive the winter and fight their way out of the pocket with the cargo they delivered. The Russians claim to have intercepted cargoes, including vodka, summer uniforms, black pepper, marjoram, right-footed boots, and, finally, millions of condoms.

Zelly's eyes grew large. "Even Goebbels couldn't make up a lie like that."

The next day, Zelly joined his crew to discuss the possibility of adding radio guidance. By shooting two thin beams, one for direction and the other for altitude, the rocket could steer to follow the rays.

A shout of "Achtung" disturbed the gathering. The men rose for Reichsführer-SS Heinrich Himmler, General Dornberger, Dr. Wernher von Braun, Dr. Steinhoff, and Kurt. When Himmler recognized Zelly, he gave a subtle nod.

"Managing a launch every few weeks is impressive, but faster production is imperative," Himmler said.

Dornberger complained of the need for more trained workers, and Von Braun asked for higher-quality parts.

"None of that will matter until you ferret out the saboteurs and eliminate them. Kill everyone under suspicion." Himmler's words chilled Zelly. The man issued the order without passion, effectively ordering Zelly's execution.

When Kurt tapped Zelly's shoulder, he followed his friend outside and slid into the car. "Reichsführer, I hope you enjoyed the tour," he said.

"All based on your outstanding work, nephew." Himmler cleaned his spectacles.

"Rocket Nine is ready for launch tomorrow. Will you be staying?"

"No, but I've wondered about number eight?"

"I didn't report it, sir, because it wasn't a real launch. They shot it from a train."

"And how did it go?" The Reichsführer asked as his eyes sparkled beneath arched eyebrows.

"Perfect."

"That was the most important one. A locomotive can haul them to battle anywhere."

Zelly then realized something he'd missed earlier—a missile launched from Italy could reach the U.S. forces in Algeria. With American lives already at risk, he decided it was time to act.

Himmler poked an index finger against Zelly's chest. "I have an additional mission for you—identify the saboteurs and kill them."

"Jawohl, Mein Reichsführer."

"Please, no more defeatist talk. Your rockets will win the war." He patted Zelly's knee.

On December 12th, rocket #4009 failed dismally. Four seconds after the ignition, it exploded on the launching pad. The cause was a fuel leak— sabotage.

I'm glad Himmler didn't stay to view it.

He expects you to eliminate the traitors. Rat out the Poles? Turn the Mauser on yourself?

I'll find a way.

That man is a shrewd weasel and maybe has already pegged you. Stengler will chortle with glee.

****

24 December 1942—A Christmas Song

Since Christstollen hadn't arrived this year, Zelly assumed things were tough for his uncle and aunt. The three roommates and their girls had Christmas Eve dinner at a Karlshagen restaurant.

Zelly was affable to Trudl, and she repaid him with smiles. The meal was less than plentiful and included a noteworthy announcement from Radio Berlin.

"This is Stalingrad, the front on the Volga." Then, soldiers' voices sang *Silent Night*.

Kurt and Zelly exchanged glances, recognizing another of Goebbels's lies. For more than a month, Russians had the city surrounded. Without food or ammunition and living in below-freezing temperatures, the men couldn't be singing.

"That makes this the best Christmas." Helmut wiped a tear.

Zelly had no holiday spirit because Himmler wanted him to catch the saboteurs.

Will you expose the Poles? They're responsible for the trains and many failures here.

We have the same goal—stopping the rockets.

But you make the dastardly machines better.

My orders were… be a good little Nazi….

You've done that far too fucking well.

As the evening ended, Kurt said, "I'm not supposed to tell you, but you can expect a visit from Stengler. They found a radio-control device in the wreckage at Züssow, proving your theory. His first thought was your stash of electronics, and he asked Himmler for permission to interrogate you ruthlessly."

CHAPTER 15

Sabotage

7 January 1943—Gallows

The first launch of the new year, rocket #4010, made a massive fireball. As Zelly powered down guidance equipment, Stengler and Kurt met with Arthur Rudolph, in charge of manufacturing. His specialists quickly identified the point of failure: a sabotaged fuel line.

Stegmaier, the commandant, was furious and ordered the arrest of the five workers who had assembled the piping and two who had provided quality control. Seven nooses hung from the gallows erected on the football field.

With the ground frozen and a frigid wind whipping the tails of their coats, every employee in fabrication and assembly stood to witness the event. Though attendance was not required for the guidance team, Zelly went with Kurt. Helmut was a guard marching the criminals to the platform. Ropes circled the necks of Germans, not foreigners.

Stegmaier pronounced the sentence not for those about to die but for those gathered to observe. Everyone shivered as much from his threats as the temperature. "The punishment for sabotage or treasonous acts is death." When the trap doors opened, the bodies dangled and twitched.

"In this frigid weather, the corpses will hang until the spring thaw," Kurt said.

Later in the barracks, Zelly wrote a report describing the radio- controlled self-destruct logic he had added to the mixing device. The goal was to protect friendly forces from an aberrant missile. He included a brief paragraph about the execution, hoping Himmler would think subversiveness had ended. When finished, he handed the pages to Kurt.

As Kurt read, he chuckled, "Your rockets blow themselves up well enough already," Then he passed Zelly an opened letter from Himmler. The note was curt and accusing. "I'm disappointed you haven't found the saboteurs as I directed."

****

25 January 1943—Crimes

By the next launch, many changes had taken place in Peenemünde. Parts suppliers had set up shop in and around the fabrication hall, so Zelly expected fewer trips to Zinnowitz. Also, a stringent quality control program included fines for poor workmanship or defects.

Rocket #4011's flight spun so fast that its checkered markings blended to gray. Still, the whirling dervish executed the pitch-over, sent a sonic boom rolling over the island, and flew under power for 65 seconds.

"Over 250 kilometers off target," Hirschler said. "With that accuracy, targeting London might hit Belgium or the coast of France—death by friendly fire."

Zelly spent an hour handling post-launch procedures before heading to the barracks. He found Stengler sitting on Helmut's rack with Kurt on his bed. The sorrowful expression on Kurt's face chilled him to his boots. Electronic stuff from Zelly's bag scattered over his bunk, separated by purpose and type. A wave of dread made Zelly clench his bowels.

The interrogation Kurt warned you about.

They have nothing on me.

Can you be so sure? Maybe the Poles have talked.

****

Oskar Stengler waited for Zellner's reaction.

"I wish you hadn't touched the tubes. They break easily."

The boy showed calmness, but Oskar recognized its fakeness. He gave a deep shrug for show and focused on the tortures he had planned for Zellner. He wanted to teach Kurt, his partner, the exhilaration of inflicting pain.

"Does Himmler know you are doing this?" Zellner asked. "Both of you know my security violations are for his benefit."

Oskar waved his hand in dismissal. "He approved this visit." Turning his menacing glare to Kurt, he said. "Tell your comrade why we're here."

Kurt's brow furrowed. "Suspicion of sabotage, defeatist talk, and listening to illegal radio."

"Himmler agreed to a severe level of ruthlessness." Oskar toyed with the boy. "Stopping the saboteurs is of great importance to him. Lies will bring serious consequences."

****

Zelly's mind struggled to make sense of the confrontation.

Obviously, Kurt was insincere when he promised to keep my secrets. He's become more of a Gestapo agent than a friend.

Helmut and Trudl betrayed you, and now Kurt has. Maybe the Poles have, too.

I shouldn't have trusted anybody, but it's too late now.

When you swing from the gallows, your mission will die with you.

I tried.

But on the wrong things.

Stengler waved over the electronic parts like a magician to make them disappear. "You had more at Brenner, so what happened to them?"

"I fixed Vinny's receiver in Berlin and Kurt's truck—"

"And built a remote detonator for Züssow?" Stengler interrupted.

"The criminal police found it," Kurt said. "What he says is true about fixing my vehicle."

"I didn't make it." Zelly met the Gestapo's gaze with a smile. "Sure, I could build one in a few minutes. The rocket's mixing device follows a similar principle. However, you've missed obvious facts. First, I have no access to explosives to construct a bomb. Second, if I wanted to blow up a train, I wouldn't destroy faulty components. Third, I could make a remote control on the job with materials from guidance."

Stengler erupted in a fit of fury, ripping the blanket off the bed and scattering the electronics over the floor. Many tubes shattered on impact. Zelly responded by stamping on the unbroken ones, destroying them. "There—they are no longer a danger."

"There is still the matter of sabotage," Stengler said.

"I've never been in fabrication hall, so how could I damage fuel lines or steering vanes?" Zelly said in his defense. "However, if I wanted to stop rocketry, I would have them built from the bad parts I truck to Zinnowitz. Or I would turn every rocket into a fireball. Even better, I could target SS headquarters in Berlin or your house."

"Many of your rockets explode. Perhaps you're responsible."

"You'll find that hard to prove, as my bosses praise my work."

"Listening to illegal radio broadcasts is a capital offense," Stengler said, turning his gaze on Kurt. "You blackmailed him to let you listen in the truck."

"Blackmail? How?"

"You refuse to fix it unless he lets you listen."

"Not true, but it's only his word against mine." Zelly collapsed to sit on his bed in reaction to Kurt's accusation.

"In addition, I have the defeatist talk and security violations." Stengler drew his service pistol. "You are under arrest. I'm sure after a bit of torture, you'll confess to everything."

He slumped and lowered his head, admitting defeat. "The accusations have no logic whatsoever. Since the day we met, you've had it in for me." He found the familiar lump in the mattress, made by his Mauser.

Stengler ripped *Hilf Mit!* from the wall above the bed. "At last, I have you where you belong."

In the second Stengler turned his back, Zelly fished out his pistol. Dropping to his knees, he aimed the weapon at the agent's heart.

Surprise crossed Stengler's face as he shifted his police special.

Both guns cocked.

****

Stengler chortled. "The court will consider pulling your gun on me as guilt."

"Put the weapons away," Kurt urged. "Nothing good can come from this."

Neither man moved. Zelly's Mauser centered on Stengler's heart, and Oskar kept his Walther aimed for a belly wound—a slower death compounded by an infection.

The door flew open, banging against the foot of a rack like a cannon shot. Everyone glanced at the door, expecting Helmut's helmet, but the figure who entered was different.

"Herr Doctor, why are you here?" Oskar asked.

"Dr. von Braun, what a surprise," Zelly said.

The man took quick stock of the situation. "Both of you, lower your weapons immediately."

Zelly did.

Oskar didn't budge. "I've arrested him."

"Stengler, I expect you to obey my order. Although I don't wear the uniform often, I am an SS Sturmbannführer and outrank you."

Zelly tossed the Mauser on the bed.

"You're interfering with the arrest of a saboteur and a seditionist," Oscar said.

"Holster your weapon," von Braun demanded.

Oskar complied. "Zellner has admitted he could explode every rocket and build remote-controlled devices like the one used in the Züssow blast."

"Your accusation is foolish. Zelly's work is pivotal for this project—our rockets wouldn't fly without him. Why would he help perfect them only to destroy them?"

"Many things about Herr Zellner make little sense," Oskar said.

"I came here with good news after recently returning from Berlin. The Fuhrer has granted our program priority funding, based upon Himmler's encouragement from Zelly's reports. You will not arrest the most important man on this base."

"That's wonderful, and I'm glad to have helped," Zelly said.

Von Braun stepped between them to diffuse the confrontation. "Herr Stengler, you leave me no choice but to accept your transfer request to the eastern front. Remove yourself from Peenemünde."

Surprised, Oskar said, "I made no such application."

"You will within the next 30 minutes. The Reichsführer will find you another job."

"I have witnesses to his defeatist talk and his radio crimes." Oskar tried to resume control.

Von Braun shrugged in exasperation. "I require three things from you immediately—a salute, leaving this room, and getting off this base."

Oskar saluted and departed with his mind still seething at the interference. He planned his appeal and plotted revenge.

****

Zelly rose and bobbed his head in a Prussian bow. "Herr Doctor, vielen Dank."

Von Braun grinned. "You thought you were Himmler's spy, but what you don't grasp was why he wanted one. I've always kept Himmler up-to- date but knew the authorities would think my reports were self-serving. Any crackpot could send glowing accounts. So, I asked for an independent observer for validation. He selected you, and I couldn't be happier with his choice or your performance."

Zelly connected some facts. "You reported number 8, the train-launched rocket, and I didn't. That's why he knew about it." Zelly's mind was awash with possibilities.

"Damn, that was close," Kurt said as he surveyed the broken electronics on the floor.

"And lucky. I didn't know of his plans to make an arrest. I think he planned to scapegoat you and be the hero for solving sabotage single- handedly." With a wink, von Braun left the room.

Zelly took his pistol and collapsed on the bed. "I should put a bullet in you for reporting me."

"I didn't. He followed us back in the fall and concocted the blackmail story. What I want to know is, would you have killed him?"

"I had a plan to shoot both of you and make it look like you murdered each other."

"So, I'm glad von Braun showed up, too."

****

26 January 1943—Employment Situation

Oskar Stengler was furious. He had planned to appeal to Dornberger, but the general denied the meeting and shuttled him off to the commandant. The major's staff kept him waiting for over three hours, so he paced the outer office. When Gerhard Stegmaier opened the door, Oskar confronted him. "Why was my ask to meet with the general handed off to you?"

Once ushered inside, the two men glared at each other.

"Your employment is a strange situation," Stegmaier said. "You aren't employed by the rocketry project, so Dornberger thought I should handle it as a base management issue."

Oskar huffed at the unfairness. "Since I don't work for von Braun, I'm not obliged to obey."

Gerhard smiled like an old friend. "But you are not on my personnel list, either. Therefore, I can't help you, but I must revoke your base pass. Himmler asked us to use you as a Gestapo agent, so I assume you should consult with him."

"So, I'll appeal to the Reichsführer and explain how von Braun, Dornberger, and you have impeded my arrest of Zellner."

"You might read this communique from Berlin first." He slid an envelope across the desk.

Oskar recognized the Prinz-Albrecht-Strasse address. Inside, he found a train ticket and orders, which he quickly scanned. "How did you get to Himmler so quickly?"

"I wasn't involved."

The rounded shoulders told Oskar of the lie. "I'll telegraph Berlin immediately."

"I believe you'll find facilities at the train station in Zinnowitz." Stegmaier stood and extended his hand.

Oskar ignored the handshake and slammed the door as he left. He considered the new orders. A promotion to major and field command of an Einsatzgruppen in Bialystok wasn't negative at all. He straightened his spine and marched.

I will not let that sneaky little bastard Zellner wound my pride. I'll get revenge, even if it's the last thing I do.

****

February 1943—Too Little, Too Late

On the 3rd of February, guidance failed. Rocket #4012 pitched over too far and flew a flat trajectory. Before the postmortem meeting, Zelly reviewed every scenario and proposed a solution.

"The problem was a malfunctioning gyroscope. We can compensate if we use the mixing device to merge the outputs from two others when one fails." Within an hour, they finished a redesign based on his model. No single failure would ever impede a perfect lift-off.

Kurt and Zelly rode the train to the mess hall. As they passed the fabrication works, heavy equipment crawled over the ground. "What's going on?" Zelly asked.

"Digging bomb shelters," he said.

In the evening, as the roommates lounged at the radio, the somber Adagio movement from Bruckner's *Seventh Symphony* played. As the horns faded to an absolute silence, the announcer spoke with a voice as sepulchral as the music. "Stalingrad has fallen. The 6th Army has fought courageously but has succumbed to vastly superior enemy forces and unfavorable circumstances."

Helmut tumbled from the couch in shock. "It's the biggest army, and they sang for us at Christmas."

Zelly thought about Stengler's son Max—active, youthful, brimmed with Nazi doctrine, more than willing to sacrifice his life to the Führer he idolized. He most likely had.

The next morning, priority funding from Hitler and Himmler's interest transformed Peenemünde. Trains full of fresh workers poured into the base. They weren't scientists and engineers but factory machinists to create an assembly line for rocketry and clerical staff to support the expansion.

On February 17th, the first belch of engine fire ignited #4013's tail. Rising like fireworks, the missile exploded in eighteen seconds, peppering the Baltic with debris.

After the postmortem, Zelly created a packet asking the Allies to bomb Peenemünde. He stayed within the disaffected Austrian sergeant persona but provided technical details requiring an insider from the design team. He included a map, redrawn from his detailed one as a rough sketch. Hoping to preserve life, he X-ed out the housing areas—worker and POW camps and barracks. He added several film rolls containing his recent reports and pictures. When he finished, he hid it in his suitcase.

Kurt suggested dinner and beer in Karlshagen. Near Strandstrasse, construction workers were expanding a prisoner-of-war stockade supervised by the SS, not the Wehrmacht. Kurt pointed it out. "This is Trassenheide, a new concentration camp under Ravensbruck."

Unlike the Polish laborers' enclosure, this one bristled with machine- gun towers.

"There goes the neighborhood," Helmut joked.

The building project grew to 30 wooden barracks surrounded by rows of razor wire. Trains of boxcars brought new prisoners with empty eyes and forlorn faces who stared at people outside the fence. Zelly added the area to his map and marked an X to show it was a housing facility.

On his birthday, February 22nd, Zelly's friends threw an evening party at a fancy restaurant in Karlshagen. Trudl attended, making a table for six.

A troubadour strummed and sang *It Sings, My Old Guitar,* as he wandered to them. "When I sing 'kiss me,' you must kiss your girl."

He played and crooned, "Kiss me, please, please, kiss me."

Kurt locked lips with Katchen. "Your turn, Helmut."

Helmut smooched Greta. "Come on, Zelly."

The friends stared as Trudl pecked first. Zelly didn't mind, much to his surprise.

After dinner, Greta suggested a movie at the base theater— *We Make Music.* Zelly held Trudl's hand as they strolled to the cinema. The film had a little plot and lots of song-and-dance. In one scene, a chorus line of short- skirted girls danced on a piano, bouncing their skirt tails to reveal their bottoms. When Helmut got excited, the group teased him.

After the show, they walked home, pausing under tree boughs for goodnight kisses—even Trudl and Zelly.

A box from Vinny sat on Zelly's bed, along with a birthday card. Inside, he found a navy-colored Japanese robe with a white dragon embroidered across the back. Vinny's note said the present was called a haori, a gift from the delegation in Berlin. Zelly recalled meeting the ambassador, armed with samurai swords, at Fasching. Already in his undershorts, he slipped it on, and it hung to his thighs, much like the skirts in the musical.

"You're stunning in a dress," Kurt teased.

Zelly pranced and sang the crooner's song. When Kurt laughed, he flipped up the haori's tails like the movie's dancing girls, wiggling his underwear-covered ass. "Helmut, are you getting a Ständer?"

As lights-out approached, they climbed into bed. Helmut's bedsprings squeaked while Zelly thought.

I'm glad Stengler is gone. I've done something worthwhile by preparing the request for bombing.

How can you send it to Washington?

I'll do it in the spring when I have a defects shipment with the Poles.

They aren't trustworthy, and you're too little, too late.

But I have a scheme that will impress even you.

****

CHAPTER 16

The Packet and
the Cross

8 March 1943—Iron Cross

Heavy spring rains poured from a dark gray sky, washing away the last traces of winter. The truck carrying defective parts contained crates of engine nozzles because the sabotage pattern had turned predictable. Zelly decided that it was the perfect day for his plan.

He placed a thick envelope on the dash, his request for bombing, and hid the Mauser under the driver's seat, secured by electrical tape.

When he stopped to check out Boryslaw, Arek, and Radzim, Helmut stood on guard duty. "I wish this damn weather would clear. I'm glad you and Trudl are together again. It won't be long before she takes your cherry."

Zelly shrugged. "Fighting a top-heavy truck in this mud will be a struggle."

When the three Poles responded to their summons, they joined him in the cab. He drove from the base on the usual road. At Trassenheide, he turned toward Mölschow.

The workers instantly recognized the misdirection. "Got another stop?" Boryslaw asked.

Zelly handed him the packet. "My request to bomb this place. Can you get this to Americans?"

Boryslaw looked over the papers, map, and film. "Too difficult, but connections to London are quick."

"Will this convince them?"

"Undoubtedly."

Radzim thumbed at the truck bed. "After putting those on the train, we'll start this on its way."

"You're not unloading. This is goodbye."

Surprise covered their faces. "Are you leaving?" Arek asked.

"No, you are."

"This is our job, our post," Arek protested while Radzim whistled.

Zelly drove to the road's edge, masked by forest and farm in all directions, and stopped by a deep ditch partly filled with rainwater. "You can fight for the Home Army somewhere else."

Boryslaw's confusion deepened. "What?"

"If you want to be part of my plan, you'll overpower me and steal the vehicle in a few minutes. Send an engine nozzle from the back with the packet. They'll understand science. Let me live after you pummel me?"

"What?" Radzim's whistle went shrill. "And if we won't?"

Zelly pulled the pistol from under the seat. "I'll arrest you for sabotage.

Shoot you if I must."

Boryslaw sighed. "I see your idea. We don't want to injure you, but we will."

"Make it convincing, and they'll believe because I'm not a soldier. I work with scientists and engineers. Otherwise, they'll figure I helped you escape and execute me." Zelly got out of the cab, and they followed him to the ditch. He pumped three rounds into the embankment and handed the weapon to Radzim. He shook hands with them and stood near the bullet holes. "I wish you luck because my fate and the lives of many allies depend on you. Bloody me."

They waited, unmoving.

"Hurry before someone comes."

"God bless you." Radzim plowed a fist into his belly, curling him into a ball.

"I'll remember your kindness and the kolaches." Arek blackened his eye.

"I'm sorry." Boryslaw struck the pistol's handle against his forehead, opening a gash.

Radzim tackled him to the embankment, and then Arek kicked his side and cracked a rib.

Zelly groaned and rolled into a fetal position as three more kicks caught him. Blood bathed his eyes and kept him from seeing which person delivered them.

Boryslaw said, "My friend, good night."

The gun pounded the back of his head, and wooziness overcame him. The motor started, and the engine headed away as rain pelted him. Mud and gore filled his mouth, and consciousness left.

After an indeterminate amount of time, he woke, feeling disoriented and unable to focus.

"I heard shots," a lady said.

"Prisoners? Gone." He rose to an elbow before the blackness returned.

When awareness arrived, a farm woman held his hand, and people surrounded him—her husband and dozens of soldiers.

"Find the truck," someone ordered, and motors raced away.

"I'm sorry they escaped," Zelly said.

"Rest," Kurt coaxed as he helped lift Zelly to a stretcher.

One removed his boots and rubbed a matchstick over his feet. "Feel that?"

He did and tried to nod, but his head ached too much. They carried him to a van, and the movement made him vomit. A nurse sat with him while a man climbed into the cab and spoke on the radio.

On arrival at the hospital, nurses put a collar around Zelly's neck and cleaned blood from his face. They cut off his clothes and located broken ribs in an expanding bruise. Stitches sealed the scalp wound. When the medical team finished, they wheeled him to a room where Kurt, Helmut, and Trudl waited.

"Some soldier I am. They jumped me." Zelly struggled to chuckle because his side hurt.

Trudl kissed him.

"We found the truck in Wolgast, so they'll be easy to catch," Kurt said. "Hope so," he said, counting on the opposite.

"Do you have a headache?" she asked with concern.

"Pounding."

"If you'd have worn your helmet, it wouldn't have happened," Helmut said.

Soon, the Gestapo, Sicherheitsdienst, and counterintelligence groups arrived to question Zelly. He told a tale of uncovering a ring of saboteurs led by the Poles. When he accused them, they overpowered, beat, and shot at him. He provided their names and claimed they blew up the trains. In a final dramatic scene, he apologized for failing as a soldier.

The ruse worked. No evidence challenged the story. His exemplary record and the testimony from Hölzer and Hirschler of the value of his work proved conclusive. When Dr. von Braun brought a telegraph of well-wishes from the Reichsführer-SS, the text included congratulations for smoking out the saboteurs. The authorities decided his only crime was being too trusting.

When the hospital released him, Kurt walked him home with an arm circling his shoulders. "The culprits are still fugitives, but they found more subversives in fabrication. You were right; those Poles recruited them."

Zelly purposely stumbled as they strode the muddy path beneath a slivered moon and bright stars. "They used me and the defective parts to determine how to break the rockets."

"And explode trains," Kurt said.

"I was their patsy." He showed Kurt a sorrowful face.

"Not at all. You're the hero for breaking up the ring, and Himmler could kiss you. He recommended you for an Iron Cross 2nd class to wear on your button. With security tightened, the ring's collapse was inevitable, so I guess they realized they had to escape."

I'll be the first Texan to win the honor.

Don't let it go to your head.

When the bombers come, I will have completed my mission.

When or if?

****

13 March 1943—Grave News

By the weekend, Zelly was still bothered by headaches and occasional dizziness, but he returned to work. Dr. Steinhoff invited him to the blockhouse, a thick concrete-and-stone building with tunnel windows and an abundance of television screens.

As the crew monitored gauges and instruments, he found a spot to watch both window and screen. Rocket #4018 rested against the gantry because sabotaged engine nozzles had kept #4017 in quality control.

Zelly stood beside the man who performed the countdown. The missile ignited and gathered force, making the floor tremble. It clung to the pad, filling the berm with smoke and flame. "Damn it, fly," the man said, away from the microphone.

"I hope we have good gaskets and flanges," Steinhoff said.

The seals proved perfect as the missile jumped skyward and vanished from view. Fuzzy dots tracked it across the radar scope.

Zelly waited for the critical guidance call at twenty-five seconds and relaxed when he heard, "Pitch-over complete."

At T plus 60, the engine crew announced, "Burnout."

The trail of points continued across the scope for a few minutes before disappearing. "Range of 133 kilometers," the technician said.

Dr. Steinhoff clapped Zelly's back. "Want a plane ride to the splashdown?"

"God, yes."

They hurried to the airfield and parked on the flight line at a twin-tailed aircraft. They climbed the wing, and Zelly dropped into the seat behind the doctor. With the canopy closed, Steinhoff started the engines. A mirror hung in front of them, revealing the pilot's face and Zelly's excitement.

"Fly often?"

"Never, but I've always wanted to. I would have chosen the Flieger-HJ, but codes were very easy for me."

Steinhoff indicated a leather helmet at Zelly's elbow. "Connect it."

Zelly listened to the tower as Steinhoff centered them on the broad swath of asphalt. As he goosed the power, a tingling tremble vibrated Zelly's body. Steinhoff pushed the throttle, released brakes, and they sped over the pavement. The exhilaration Zelly had experienced as a kid riding with Amelia Earhart returned. When they left the ground, he yelped like an excited puppy, and Steinhoff smiled.

They banked on a wingtip and flattened over the launch pad. Steinhoff waggled the wings and talked on the radio to the bunker staff, who provided a heading. As he steered the supplied course, Zelly checked the airspeed gauge and calculated—500 kilometers per hour, ten minutes to the splashdown. At the eleven-minute mark, Zelly spotted the green dye off the nose. "Over there."

They descended and circled while Steinhoff mapped the position. When he turned for home, he asked, "Want to fly?" When the mirror revealed the obvious answer, he said, "Grab the yoke and stay steady."

Zelly followed instructions, and Steinhoff lifted his hands over his shoulders to show him he had the plane.

"A touch right on the stick and push the pedal on that side," Steinhoff directed. "Pull the control a little toward you, and we'll bank into a climbing turn."

Zelly didn't want the flight to stop, ever. With the war far below, he longed to linger in the heavens.

When he returned to guidance, Hirschler took him to the office and handed him a letter from his aunt in Wittenberg. "This is grave news, so sit down to read it." As Zelly did, his boss signed a two-week pass to grieve Uncle August's death.

Zelly packed his suitcase, said goodbye to the gang of friends, and boarded the 3:30 to Berlin on Monday, March 15th.

He thought of visiting Vinny, but something made him hurry onward. It was funny to think of Wittenberg as home, but he did.

Darkness had settled before he arrived, but he remembered the directions to Kris's house. When he knocked, Kris tore through the door and grabbed him in a hug. "Zelly! I'm glad to see you."

"You're not fighting?"

Kris's head dropped. "Dad's keeping me busy here." He borrowed his father's car and drove them to the Zellner farm.

Aunt Freida slept with the farmhouse door unlocked. Zelly curled on little Frederich's short bed while Kris stretched on the floor beside him. Though happy to be home, he wanted a bit of emotional distance and decided not to call her Mutter.

****

16 March 1943—Foreign Symbol

The guys woke to the scent of Aunt Freida's cooking. When they emerged from the dormer, she smiled. "I'm glad you came." Zelly kissed her forehead, but she shrugged away to scramble eggs. "Just like that, his heart gave out after forty years together."

Zelly stepped behind her and hugged her. "I brought a friend."

After breakfast, Kris and Zelly dressed in old clothes for farm work. Much needed doing. "She can't manage by herself," Zelly said while they milked.

"Remember Inga? She married Fritz Kühl, who was the runner to the band in that field exercise. He's a Wehrmacht officer now on the eastern front, and they'll need a place when he returns. They might buy it."

"My aunt won't want to move," Zelly said.

"They might let her stay. Inga's little brother, Dolf, knows farming. He's twelve but strong and can handle everything until Fritz comes home."

Behind the barn, they stripped and washed in the stock tank's cold water.

"I don't see a scar," Kris said. "When Stengler was here, he wanted us to pump you for information about one near your balls."

Zelly exposed the blemish. "Here."

"That's swell, but why would he care?"

"The Schwul is out of my life now. Ordered east."

Kris grimaced at either the homosexual accusation or the trip to the Eastern Front.

They sprinted to the house as the March wind chilled their skin. Wrapped in warm towels, they shared a pot of ersatz coffee and cherry jam on toast. The drink was fake, but the preserves tasted fantastic.

"Aunt Freida, you can't handle everything by yourself, so what will you do?"

She sighed and shrugged.

"What if we sell to someone who will allow you to stay?"

Her eyes watered. "Don't you want the land? The family has owned it for generations."

That surprised Zelly. An American agent shouldn't inherit a German farm. He noticed her painful response and shock. "Do you have room in your heart to share your life with a new person?" The answer was obvious before he asked—she does, and I'm proof.

"First, to visit your uncle's grave. This question, I must ask him."

They loaded into Kris's father's car and drove to the cemetery. Uncle Augustus's tomb was beside his parents on a hilltop overlooking the river bend. Aunt Freida spoke to her departed husband, telling him of the plan.

Zelly wandered until a sudden heaviness took his heart. As it compelled him to stop, an abrupt insight stuck with him. When she arrived at a favorable answer, they went to Inga's house.

Inga acted glad to see Zelly. "Life's been good to you."

He understood what she meant—he'd been lucky. Most guys his age were maimed or in coffins. "Danke, Frau Kühl. I work with scientists far from the front."

"Do you remember Fritz?"

With a nod, he introduced his aunt.

Inga's widowed father stepped forward. "Frau Zellner, I'm sorry for your loss. Your husband was an exceptional man and war hero."

"We have a business proposition for you to consider," Zelly said.

In the parlor, he offered the farm for a ridiculously cheap price on the condition Aunt Freida could stay. Inga was willing, and her father was exuberant. "With this, we won't go hungry," he said.

Zelly caught a hint of defeatism in his voice.

Kris and Zelly moved Aunt Freida's things to the spare bedroom and used a horse-drawn wagon to move Inga and Dolf. As a team of five, they set to work for the spring. The ladies worked in the house while the men tended to the livestock and outbuildings. By nightfall, they were dead tired.

Aunt Freida mulled apple cider, and they sipped and chatted on the porch. "Mutter, walk with me?" Zelly asked, forgetting his desire for distancing.

The quarter moon was bulging over the barn. When aunt and nephew were beyond everyone's hearing, he said, "I have a question."

Based on their route, she deduced his query. "We buried Rolf at the cross."

"Tell me about little Frederich and the crucifix?"

Moonlight made the tears in her eyes glisten. "You know of him?"

"The pictures on the parlor wall and more hidden in his room." He froze in the deep shadow beneath the barn's eves. "This remembers him—small enough that no one would notice. May I move this memorial to the cemetery beside Uncle August's headstone?"

With a gasp and shake of her head, she said, "The Nazis wanted his death kept secret."

"I'll do it by myself, and no one will know. I dreamed some HJ boys killed him as he played in the river, and I presume you never found his body."

"Well, you are of each other." She rose to tiptoe, hugging him for support, and kissed his cheek. "Bless you."

Before thinking, Zelly asked, "Do you mind another question, one more personal?" He fetched a shovel and pushed it into the soft dirt.

When she shook her head, he planned to ask why they helped him—why they provided cover for an American spy. Instead, his soul asked something different, "We're related, aren't we?"

"We promised not to tell, but you've guessed already. Your great- grandfather came here from Austria. Your branch moved to America while three generations of Augusts have worked this land."

"And I sold it."

"The Nazis would have taken the farm years ago had they understood. I'm surprised you haven't discovered it somehow."

In bewilderment, Zelly asked, "What?"

"Frederich bore the mark of Abraham's covenant."

"My family is—" he didn't utter the next word because he couldn't. Another shovel bit the ground beside him. "Let me help," Kris said.

—Jewish. It hit like bombs from a thousand-plane raid.

No wonder Doctor Otto checked me for a circumcision. They knew things I didn't.

Not the first lie you've uncovered.

But this one changes my entire existence. Am I one of the Jews in the international conspiracy?

How many layers of lies are there? How deep are you?

Kris missed Zelly's expression as he lifted some dirt. In fifteen minutes, the little white cross stood beneath the arm of Uncle Augustus's. The irony struck Zelly like the dragon's breath of a rocket at ignition.

Crosses marking Jewish graves! Aunt Freida's life isn't different from mine—a life of deception. She lived with the hatred of Jews and pretended to be a hater. I understand how difficult her life must have been and why she helped.

You are such a dunce—you are the fucking irony!

****

29 March to 14 May 1943—Wunderwaffen

Zelly's return ticket for the base was for March 29th. As he waited on Wittenberg's train platform, a telegraph boy wandered nearby, calling, "Telegram for Frederich Zellner?"

"Here," he said, and the teen thrust a thin paper into his hand. He read, "25 March. #4019—T+60.5 and 268s." The news brought a grin.

A perfect lift-off. My work is fruitful.

No, it's another dreadful irony.

He stopped in Berlin at Vinny's place, but his friend didn't answer. He fished the key from behind the brass plaque at the labor district's headquarters. As he entered the apartment building, the old lady caught him. "Your friend's gone to Oranienburg."

What's there? He wondered. He spent the night in the flat and returned to Peenemünde on March 30th.

As he stepped from the train, Trudl kissed him. "I'm sorry for your uncle, but glad you came back. Katchen said I should enjoy your company and not feel threatened by the past. Can you, too?"

Construction work to enlarge the fabrication hall had turned it into a two-story structure, with the lower part buried in the sand.

"We have a whole production line and places for additional laborers to live below," Trudl explained.

With the departure of the Polish workers, rocket sabotage ended. The next three launches—#4020 on April 14th, #4021 on April 22nd, and #4022 on May 14th—were executed flawlessly. Strong crosswinds caused deviations, but they were corrected using the navigation beams. Now, with the mixing device listening to radio input, the guidance crew had elementary steering ability.

I've improved the rockets by creating the most critical component.

No, you've made them far too stupendous.

Goebbels renamed the projects—Kirschkern was Vengeance-1, and the Aggregat became Vengeance-2. The national liar proclaimed these wonder weapons would quickly bring triumph. Since they competed for resources and priority, General Dornberger arranged a shoot-off. Zelly's emotions ranged from hoping his rocket would win to contemplating the lives it would end.

The packet must be in London by now.

Unless the Poles got caught and killed. And how would a disaffected Austrian sergeant have all the technical details? Soon, your mechanical monster will kill Americans, and their deaths will be your fault.

CHAPTER 17

Shoot-Off

Late May 1943—Mistake

Wednesday, May 26th, was the scheduled day for the contest between the wonder weapons. Both the V-1 and V-2 crews worked tirelessly round the clock in preparation.

Red, white, and black bunting and flags covered the island. Albert Speer came early, along with the minister for war and weapon production. An Army General, the Grand Admiral, and a baton-wielding Field Marshal showed up in dress uniforms. The viewing stand reminded Zelly of Fasching in the Adlon—as many Iron Crosses as any Berlin parade.

From the guidance roof, he viewed #4026 lift off into the noon-time fog. Its bellowing exhaust mixed with the clouds like a flaming comet. When the sonic boom ripped over the dignitaries, they cheered. The celebration grew when the loudspeakers announced the missile splashed down within two kilometers of the target. Gleefully, Hirschler grabbed Zelly and waltzed him around the rooftop.

The VIPs shuttled to the Luftwaffe's side to view the show. When they returned for the afternoon, #4025 waited. The countdown paused for a stiff onshore breeze to blow away the haze.

When visibility was perfect, the V-2 launched to generous applause until mission control's voice said, "Mixing failure causing engine cut out."

Hölzer stuck his head from the roof hatch, glaring at Zelly. "Only 27 kilometers of flight, and this one is on us, boys. We'll never achieve priority."

Crestfallen, Zelly climbed down to seek the failure's cause. The data stream provided the answer—his device had misinterpreted the guide beam as a shut-off command. By the time he discovered the solution, an agitated General Dornberger was at his elbow.

"Sir, I'm sorry the instrumentation made a mistake, but I can fix it." He expected a scathing rebuke.

"You haven't heard? We won! Both V-1s crashed on lift-off while we soared. The score is two to nothing in our favor. You're due at the officers' club to celebrate."

Zelly took Trudl to the celebration, and her hand never left his.

The next morning, the schedule called for another launch. Hölzer ordered the guide beams on, and Zelly flipped the transmitter switches.

Rocket #4024 shot skyward and executed a perfect pitch-over. The flight lasted 248 seconds, and radar tracked it for 138 kilometers, the exact range of the target.

Anxious and pensive, the guidance crew waited for the chase plane's report. When Steinhoff radioed, "Missed," every shoulder slumped at the grim news. After a pause of static, the radio cleared, and he added, "By 32 meters." The collective shout was louder than the rocket's roar because that small distance was still a bullseye.

After work, a British de Havilland Mosquito circled overhead.

"Radar says they viewed the entire event,"

"Soon, we'll aim in their direction," Hirschler winked.

"They'll know about rocketry now and bomb us," Zelly said.

"They'll be curious from witnessing something they've never seen before," Hölzer said.

Zelly smiled at the proof his data had reached London and hoped they would share it with America. Surely, the Mosquito took pictures, and they'll match my reports.

Two days later, the invitation to Dornberger's promotion to Major General read 'Zelly and Fräulein Trudl.' Others considered them a couple, but his emotions remained mixed. Although Stengler was four months gone, Zelly felt his lingering shadow. The image of her and him doing what he'd never done was impossible to vanquish.

At the officers' club, expensive French champagne flowed all evening. In a brief speech, Dornberger thanked a long list of people and included Zelly's name. With his head high and smile unwavering, he danced with his date.

I'm an important rocket scientist. She should want my baby for the Fatherland.

To spawn another Nazi who would grow up to kill Americans.

When he kissed her good night in her dorm's lobby, he was as German as possible.

****

June and July 1943—Cousin Gagel

Sunny June brought six more launches and countless visits by curious British Mosquitoes. For the launch on June 26th, two de Havilland DH-98s circled like hawks.

Kurt shot them a lewd gesture.

"We have antiaircraft guns everywhere, so why don't they shoot?" Helmut wondered.

"If we fire, they'll realize they've found something," Kurt said.

Helmut tightened his helmet's chinstrap. "They'll bomb."

I wonder when the attack will come.

The sooner, the better.

"That's why we have the new shelters," Kurt said. In the executive housing blocks, some were deep and built from cement. In their barracks area, the sand-covered trenches with timber roofs resembled massive dunes.

Kurt brought Zelly a letter from Vinny. "Your Italian friend must be crazy because this makes little sense."

A glance at the opening explained the comment. It read, 'I can count to 10 since we were together.' Recalling the zählen code word, he began to decode. The capitalized words unveiled a message: CUSN GAGEL AWK MSG LISN BBC AT. Though still gibberish, he recognized AWK as radio talk for acknowledgment. So, he sounded out the rest and came up with 'Cousin Gagel acknowledges your message. Listen to BBC at.'

Cousin implies a metaphor.

Who the fuck is Gagel?

The letters of GAGEL came from German nouns except one—the 'L' at the end came from English, the *Lexington*, a new aircraft carrier in the Pacific, so he eliminated it.

The phrase became 'Cousin Gage' and caused a memory of American history. Thomas Gage commanded the British troops at Lexington in the Revolutionary War. He decided the meaning was 'Brits acknowledge your message. Listen to the BBC.' But when? Ten—the number in the beginning?

With the hour difference in time, listening at 10 PM would catch BBC's nine o'clock news.

My documents reached London and brought Mosquitoes to plague Peenemünde. Bombers will soon follow.

You'll be under the bombs, too.

I'll use the radio warning to be prepared.

****

On Monday, the 28th of June, a JU-52 transport aircraft buzzed Peenemunde before turning on the final approach to the airfield. Zelly could read the name 'Otto Kissenberth' lettered on the metal. When Reichsführer Heinrich Himmler stepped from the plane, Peenemünde's band performed *Horst Wessel Lied* and the national anthem on the taxiway.

Dr. von Braun wore his SS uniform, the first time Zelly had ever seen him in it. Braided cords of silver and gold piled high on Dornberger's scarlet shoulder boards.

The dignitaries exchanged salutes and handshakes before walking to the waiting cars. Kurt had driver duty, and Zelly pretended to be a bodyguard despite the muscle entourage. He offered the Reichsführer a handshake. "I hope you had a wonderful flight."

"You're out of uniform," Himmler said.

Zelly gave himself a quick once-over and asked, "Why?"

Himmler pinned a tab with two stripes and the three pips on Zelly's collar. "Congratulations, Obersturmführer."

Two other guests came on the plane—SS-Obergruppenführer Emil Mazuw and Emil Leeb, chief of the army weapons depot. Kurt's vehicle joined the procession of black Mercedes to the officers' club, where the brass discussed things until late morning, with Zelly and Kurt napping on couches.

After breakfast the next day, the dignitaries took seats in the viewing stand. Zelly and Kurt stood behind them, at attention, as the countdown started for #4038 on the gantry. At the ignition, the rocket's roar made Leeb smile. Two hundred meters overhead, the rocket pitched in the wrong direction. Instead of pivoting east over the Baltic, it turned west.

"A run-away, so they'll self-destruct," Zelly said, sheltering Himmler with his body.

Kurt covered Leeb, but Mazuw sprang to his feet and pointed at the misfired missile. Guidance issued the command, blowing up the V-2 and destroying three planes parked near Himmler's.

Dornberger immediately ordered the next A-4 into place, and the tractor tilted it skyward.

"I hope this one doesn't kill us." Amusement sparkled in Himmler's steely eyes.

With #4039 still in quality control, #4040 launched flawlessly. It followed the radio beam for 236 kilometers and splashed down only two from the target.

Despite the first catastrophe, Himmler and Mazuw seemed impressed by the show. They asked for a tour of the fabrication plant and Trassenheide. As they explored, Zelly waited in the car.

At the airfield, Mazuw gave orders to Kurt, "Conditions in the concentration camp must be harsher. There are too many heat stoves."

Meanwhile, Himmler grabbed Zelly's shoulder and pulled him close. "We caught one of your Polish workers—the hulking, strong one."

Radzim. What about Boryslaw and Arek? Zelly thought as he lied, "I'm glad. Where?"

"In Warsaw, where he was helping ghetto Jews in a revolt. That fool still had a rocket engine. He squealed like a stuck pig during interrogation and explained the whole sabotage operation."

Zelly struggled to quiet his panic and was barely successful.

Everything, including about me? Fuck.

If he still had the nozzle, maybe my report wasn't sent.

Could Vinny's secret message be about something different?

The Reichsführer's laugh disturbed Zelly's thoughts. "Imagine if Stengler was right. What if they recruited you for the gang? Then, the mixing device wouldn't exist, and the rockets would fail." His laughter grew into a deep guffaw. "They labored for the man who invented the critical component and never knew."

"I would never…." Zelly expressed his exasperation.

****

During July, Zelly made a practice of accompanying Kurt in the radio truck most evenings. As they listened to BBC's news, he hoped to catch a message. Lots of coded notes came over the broadcast, funny-sounding items unless you were the intended recipient, but nothing came for him.

On the 24th, they switched to air control at 10:30 in time to hear British bombers attacking Hamburg at midnight.

"Helmut's hometown," Zelly said.

For twenty days, Kurt and Zelly monitored the ten o'clock program for nothing. Zelly wondered if London thought he had written science fiction.

****

13 August 1943—Dear Frederich, I'm Great

Mail call brought a letter from Vinny. The salutation was 'Dear Frederich', and the first sentence read ', I'm great,' Zelly's heart skipped some beats. According to the Camp Ritchie code, it meant Vinny was having difficulties, and things were terrible. When Vinny mentioned Uncle Enrico, the metaphor for the atom-smashing bomb, Zelly worried the Gestapo had arrested him as a spy. Vinny wrote of visiting Oranienburg and Gottow and, two weeks later, growing weak from vomiting, diarrhea, and nosebleeds. Though the message was frightening, it ended by saying not to worry.

Still, anxiety consumed him. Vomiting and diarrhea could be almost anything, but nosebleeds and Enrico pointed to radiation sickness. He had read about it in his study at the Rice Institute of Technology in Houston, Texas. My notes from Sev's visit probably caused the butcher to assign Vinny to investigate Germany's atomic project.

That afternoon, a rocket launch missed the target by ten meters. Zelly couldn't enjoy the success because of his unsettled feelings concerning Vinny.

In the evening, Kurt and Zelly double-dated with Katchen and Trudl. After a meal, they rode in the radio truck to a secluded beach. "Girls, you have a choice of a swim or a dance," Zelly said.

"I didn't bring a swimsuit," Trudl said.

"Want to see mine? I was born in it." Kurt joked.

"I'd rather dance," Trudl chose.

Zelly took her in his arms as Kurt tuned to the BBC. The announcer intoned, "For your dancing pleasure, here's Louis Armstrong's *Swinging on Nothing*." English lyrics pouring from the speakers surprised Trudl, though Zelly caught the beat with a rock step in the sand.

Her face filled with disgust, and she froze at the forbidden music. "Black music. Can't you tune Radio Belgrade?"

"But the rhythm is intoxicating," Zelly coaxed.

She removed her shoes and carried them with her as she stormed away. Soon, her shadow disappeared among the bomb-shelter dunes.

"Should I go after her?" Katchen asked.

"No, stay and enjoy a bit of foreign decadence." Kurt danced with her on Tommy Dorsey's *I'm Getting Sentimental Over You* though he didn't understand a word of it.

"Isn't that trombone sweet?" Zelly said. Kurt pulled him into a threesome dance for several tunes.

The broadcast changed as the music stopped and an announcer spoke.

"Some news?" Katchen guessed.

"Zelly can translate," Kurt said.

He did. "The barn door is open, and the cows are coming home."

Katchen giggled. "Do they call that news?"

"The baby cries for its mother's milk," Zelly translated.

"Foolishness," she said.

"Coded messages for the resistance," Kurt said. He glanced toward the truck and spotted a flashing light on a panel. "An illegal transmission." He ran to the headphones and held one earpiece close.

"Can you tell where?" Zelly asked, coming behind.

"Nearby on the island." Kurt gestured for them to climb in. He drove like a maniac through the dunes. Near the liquid oxygen plant, he checked the signal. "It's constant and still sending."

"A British spy vectoring bombers at us?" Katchen speculated.

With two points and vectors, Zelly did the trigonometry in his head. "The launch pad."

Kurt sped over the sand. The truck bounced and swayed like a roller coaster. Katchen tucked her head between her knees while Zelly tried to appear casual. Kurt stopped at the blockhouse, where light came from the windows.

Zelly sprinted inside to find the crew preparing final reports. "Who's transmitting?"

"Wait, guide beam still active," a technician said and flipped the switch.

"Be thankful the Brits weren't riding that signal, or you'd be dead," Zelly scolded.

When he returned to his friends, Kurt had two panels open. "Something broke in the rush."

Zelly located several shattered tubes. "After Stengler's visit, I don't have replacements."

In the morning, Kurt ordered them, but a supply shortage meant they would take weeks to arrive. With a broken truck, Zelly couldn't receive BBC broadcasts, so he cursed his luck.

When he met Trudl on the train, her face telegraphed revulsion, so he stayed distant.

She found American songs abhorrent.

She would find you abhorrent.

****

16 August 1943—Bialystok Ghetto, South-east Prussia

Oskar Stengler listened to the loudspeakers as he waited in his command Kübelwagen on Poleska Street near the Biala River. The disembodied voice announced orders to liquidate the Jews, part of Operation Reinhard and the final solution, the plan since June 1941, when Germany invaded the Soviet Union.

A census of this ghetto established a population of 50,000 in the small 7-by-9 block area. His job was to round them up and screen them. Those fit to work would pack on trains for Majdanek, a KZ south of Lublin. The sick or the weak went to Poniatowa, Blizyn, or Auschwitz camps on their way to death at Birkenau. Children would travel to Theresienstadt as a holding camp until their appointment with the gas chambers. The Gestapo would shoot anyone who remained and burn the buildings to the ground.

Stengler expected little trouble because the Jews were completely accepting of roundups, deportations, and life in KZs. Anyway, they were little more than sheep headed to slaughter. He studied their slow shuffle as they followed Jurowiecka Street toward the waiting cattle cars.

As a group of Jewish kids passed him, his radio crackled to life. "Sir, a disturbance at the corner of Smolna and Poleska— some are trying a breakout."

The Kübelwagen driver spun a U-turn and sped the three blocks to the area. Gunshots sounded as they reached a section of board fence. Around a bend, those attempting to escape had cut the barbed wire. A few fighters came running through the opening, shooting with pistols and tossing Molotov cocktails.

The cadre of German soldiers who ringed the ghetto returned fire. They were mostly auxiliary forces who hadn't expected a challenge, but their superior weaponry soon overcame any bravery.

Stengler's vehicle became a target. A rain of ignited bottles flew over the wooden barrier. The distance was too far for accuracy, but two rolled under the wagon and exploded, setting off the fuel. The car tumbled to its side, spilling him and the radio on the roadway.

He thumbed the microphone button. "I need armored support at Smolna Street. Although we have contained the breakout, we must attack inside."

The reply came, saying, "Panzer is on the way."

When the sounds of a diesel motor reached him, he assembled a handful of the most capable soldiers and met the armor. Command had sent only one tank, an ancient one, but he was determined to make it sufficient.

When the armored driver stopped, Oskar ordered, "Go through the gap in the fence and raze everything to the ground."

When the vehicle drove through the breach, he checked to ensure the procession of children heading to the trains had continued. One of them threw something at him—the object caught the glint of sunlight as it flew. He turned away, but the projectile hit his face from the bridge of his nose to his cheekbone. He closed his eyes as they shattered and spilled liquid over his eyes and face. It burned, so he swiped at it with a sleeve. As he moved his arm away, he found spots where the uniform's material had scorched and dissolved—Acid.

Stengler took a nearby soldier's canteen and poured water over his face to dilute the fluid. The fiery sensation didn't lessen, and the area of discomfort grew as the solution spread. Agony radiated from every facial nerve as he fell.

Someone forced a tablet into his mouth, and he swallowed it. Within minutes, the pain faded, replaced by an intense wave of euphoria. The sounds of the Panzer's gun firing let him relax. When consciousness returned after a stupor, the day's events were elusive to his recall. As his suffering continued, so he screamed for more drugs.

"What medicine?" he asked, finding the euphoric effects welcome.

"Eukodal."

During his nether-worldly sleep, he pieced together the fact that his injuries were bad. Bandages gave him the clue as they masked half his face and covered an eye. He didn't remember what had caused his pain, but he was quick to lay the blame—the Peenemünde smart-ass who got him transferred, and he vowed revenge.

****

17 August 1943—Roundels on Their Wings

Four days later, August 17th was a gorgeous day with cloudless skies and a lingering summer breeze hinting at fall.

On the morning commute, Trudl approached Zelly with a glowing smile. "I'm sorry for storming away from the dancing. How about a picnic?" When Zelly nodded, she said, "Meet me at the dorm at six and wear your trunks."

At the scheduled time, he waited in the small lobby wearing swim shorts and the Japanese haori. She appeared in a pink and purple one-piece and carried a basket. He took the burden, and they walked to the beach. Near a new bomb shelter, she spread a red and white cloth. They ate potato and leek soup and cheddar-cheese-topped toasted rolls. A dozen delicacies from the town bakery were desserts.

They basked in the evening sun. "Zelly, do you think of your future?"

"I want to go to university and become a scientist or engineer."

"Silly, you already are."

"So, what are your plans?"

"A house at the college where my handsome researcher husband teaches and does experiments." She giggled. "With a German Shepherd on the front lawn, playing with two boys."

"Two? What are their names?"

"You can name them."

"How about Kris and Kurt?"

"They are tall, strong, and blond, like their father."

He knew she was flirting but couldn't shake the thought of her tryst with Stengler.

This could be your chance, so don't wreck it.

I could be like Vinny. Do it only for fun.

He played along. "Have I met your husband?"

"I've never introduced you, but he works on the island," her giggle was playful.

"What color is his tinnie?"

"Gold, like your hair."

"If he's in guidance, he's an acquaintance, but does he wear a uniform?"

"Sometimes—he's both an officer and a scientist."

Zelly shot her a jealous expression. "Have you ever kissed him?"

"Yes."

"Well, the next time you kiss him, I'll punch his lips down his throat."

She bussed his cheek and sprinted to splash in the surf. "I'm leaving before the fight."

She's flirting, being coy.

This will be my lucky day, so don't spoil things.

Suit yourself, but remember she carried Stengler's baby.

They swam and played in the water for a long time, talking about life, love, and what lies ahead. At sunset, they returned to the quilt. The evening breeze goose-bumped Trudl, so Zelly wrapped her in his haori and held her against him. "What if war takes away your future?"

"Then I should enjoy it now." Her passionate kiss lingered.

I'm not the person she thinks I am.

If she hated your music, imagine how she'll hate you when she learns the truth.

A full moon rose with elegant grace, and stars flickered to light the night. "Someday, my rocket will go there."

Air raid sirens blared. They gathered the picnic things and scurried into the shelter. Alone, they huddled together and waited, but bombers never came, and the all-clear never sounded. After waiting an hour, they ventured out. Stretching the checkered cloth on the shelter's slope, they relaxed in the moonlight. She tucked her head on his shoulder.

Fred, I'm going for it. It's purely physical, not emotional.

Zelly, do you have to take me?

Don't be a sick voyeur; just go to sleep.

This is my body, my head, my mind—not yours. You're the interloper, only borrowing it.

Seeing his pensive mood, she stroked his nipple until it hardened. To revive him, she dumped a handful of sand on it and abraded.

"Ouch, you've discovered a Gestapo torture," he teased.

She giggled when he slid down her bathing suit top. After pleasuring her breast with his mouth for several minutes, he added a sprinkling of sand and copied Stengler's interrogation voice. "Fräulein, who is your handsome scientist?"

"No, not that infamous torment. Please, sir, I'll tell you anything."

"The gold-tinnie holder's name?"

"Zelly."

He cleaned her skin with his tongue, and she rolled her fingers through the blond hairs beneath his belly button. When she tugged them, she echoed his impersonation. "The Shepherd playing in the yard with Kris and Kurt, what's his name? Quick, Communist spy, or you will suffer."

Only one dog came to him—Beans, his Irish setter in Texas—but that wouldn't work. He remembered the dog from Wittenberg. "We call the mutt Rolf."

She misunderstood him. "Dolf? To honor the Führer?"

"Not at all, but because he had this funny little mustache."

"On a Shepherd?"

"Once he got into some black paint, and it was so cute we kept painting it on."

Airplane noises surrounded them. Dozens of bombers filled the sky, crisscrossing at various altitudes. In the moonlight, Zelly spotted RAF roundels, the blue in red circles, on their wings. "To the shelter," he commanded.

"Why isn't antiaircraft firing? I'm a Flak Helper and must report for duty."

As fast as the planes appeared, they disappeared from overhead. "Guess this wasn't the right place, so you don't have to rush away."

The full moon hung like a golden pendant in a canopy of stars. Beneath it, they spooned on the cloth, and he kept her warm in an embrace. When his erection started, she wiggled against it and slid her hand into his trunks.

Suddenly, the sky turned red. When he jumped up, her hand dragged his trunks to the ankles. Light from overhead flares glistened on his skin in a devil's shine.

"I'm going to the platform," she said.

He jerked up his shorts as they rushed through the forest. Above the pine boughs, the drone of airplane engines made talking impossible. From training, he remembered the bomb's thunderous fury and estimated they were about two kilometers away. "Hurry!"

The southern horizon blazed as they entered her dorm's lobby. The matron directed her panicked girls toward the basement stairs. When she pointed Trudl down, Trudl argued, "I must report to Flak command."

Outside, the explosions grew louder and nearer. A bomb detonated about a hundred meters from the building, spraying sand.

"Trudl, find me in the beach shelter." He ran into the dangerous night and glanced over his shoulder to spot her through a window.

Huge bombs shrieked as they fell like gigantic melons plummeting through the fire-lit sky. A tremendous crack sounded, followed by a deafening explosion that shimmered in yellow. Close, he thought before the concussion lifted him like a rag doll and tossed him to the sand. His back burned, and everything hurt as he struggled to maintain consciousness.

Forcing himself to his knees, he gazed at the dorm. Flames blossomed from the foyer and climbed higher than the tall pines. Hungry for oxygen, red-orange tongues reached from the open window and door. "Trudl," he yelled, but an answer was impossible. Burning pieces of his birthday haori floated down like blazing feathers on the wind.

In the firestorm, more bombs burst around him, flinging sand and igniting pine trees as if they were huge torches. He scrambled to the beach and splashed in the surf. Snaking in the ocean water, he screamed as it brought excruciating pain. Reaching for his back, he found glass shards embedded in the skin and pulled out those he could.

The attack moved north as explosions neared, so he grabbed the tablecloth and rushed into the shelter. He used it like a towel to dry his back, managing to remove much of the remaining splinters despite the suffering. The butt of his trunks had burned away, leaving only the loose tie-string to hold them up. Cold and exhausted, he wrapped in the cloth and curled. He wasn't a brave soldier, and the agony in his back was terrible.

She's gone. Surviving that blast is impossible.

You *caused this by summoning those bombers.*

Now isn't the time for blame.

Don't lament her—she was the enemy, like Stengler.

As bombs pummeled the beach, sand poured between the timbered roofing of his shelter and slipped down the walls. He feared it would bury him alive. The sandstorms propelled him to inch closer to the door, but the explosions made him retreat deeper inside. He lingered like a kid who wanted to play in the snow but wouldn't leave the stove's warmth.

When the battle noise diminished, he emerged. Peenemünde burned with a thick, black smoke hanging like a funeral shroud. Where the cloud thinned, the fire's eerie glow was unsettling. The nearby seashore had yellow embers and white-hot gobs of phosphorous scattered like Easter eggs. The surf hissed as it extinguished them.

Bombers still flew overhead, but the explosions were north of him. They banked away from the island, only a few meters above him. The pilots' faces, lit by firelight, smiled at the destruction.

Don't they know I'm here?

They consider a disaffected Austrian sergeant expendable.

Didn't America tell the Brits I'm here to spy?

You're assuming they remember you—and why should they care? One life for many.

But they're striking the wrong places—the ones I x-ed out on the map.

Smoke and fires told him they'd hit the housing spots, not rocket production or design. "You fucking idiots are missing the most important spots!"

They're hitting your x-es—x marks the spot—dropping bombs on your locations.

So, they want to kill people and not destroy rockets. Murder the brain trust, and the missiles go away.

"Bloody murderers," he accused the faces behind the aircraft canopies. The raid continued north, leaving him in safety, as exhaustion and shock took him—but his mind wouldn't be quiet.

Zelly, you are the murderer. This is war, and the Brits don't care about the people.

They killed Trudl. Why did she have sex with Stengler when she could have had me?

Better that she's dead.

My back hurts as if it's on fire. I'll die, and Himmler will miss his reports.

The butcher, the baker, and the candlestick maker won't shed a tear for you. Your parents will put a little white cross beside the barn to remember you.

They won't have a body to bury.

They would never accept how German you've become or how you've helped the Nazis.

Being a Nazi was my job.

Yeah, but you liked it too much and did it too well.

God, I hurt.

Zelly cried himself to sleep.

At dawn, girls from the dorm found him wrapped in a blood-soaked tablecloth. They summoned stretcher-bearers who took him to a makeshift hospital. On the way, he spotted Greta, "Trudl?"

Her headshake confirmed what he already knew.

Trudl was your enemy and didn't love you, not the real you. You are nothing but a pretend character in a play.

Shut the fuck up.

Kurt was sweaty and covered with soot when he ran across Zelly in the triage canopy erected on the football field. He stroked a dirty hand through his friend's hair. "I heard you're alive, but Trudl and Helmut didn't make it. Bombs obliterated Trassenheide where he had guard duty."

"And how did you survive?"

"I hid under the bed. They missed our barracks, so we still have joy in the camp."

"And Katchen?"

"She's fine and your nurse."

When they moved him to the medical tent, she removed the remaining glass shards, sprinkled his back with sulfa powder, and wrapped him in gauze. "Stay on your stomach because your burns are badly blistered. If you don't develop an infection, you'll be out tomorrow." A hospital orderly placed him face down on a cot.

When Hirschler came to visit, Zelly asked, "How bad was it?"

"Lots of dead, but only one senior scientist—Walter Thiel, whose shelter took a direct hit. Luckily, without the all-clear, most people stayed in their shelters."

"Production and research?"

"Unscathed—fabrication took bombs, but all the equipment still functions. They missed the important places, like the launch pad, guidance, rocket fuel plant, and wind tunnel. Curiously, they spared the Luftwaffe side and the airfield. It is easy to deduce the rockets were the target, but we'll fly again within a month."

"They'll be back, won't they?"

"Dornberger thinks so. He has people painting our buildings to appear like burned-out structures with charred wooden spars—masterpieces. When the enemy snaps damage assessment pictures, Peenemünde will seem destroyed. The scuttlebutt says we move underground."

Zelly tried to grin through the pain. "How can I help?"

"Rest and get better."

Later, when Kurt brought dinner, he wore only a ratty pair of underwear splattered with brown, black, and gray paint. "Are you taking up art?"

"Camouflage masterpieces, but glad your spirits are improving. Don't worry if you hear more explosions because the Brits dropped some timed- detonation explosives to kill fire crews and rescuers. Most buried themselves in the sand, and we've roped them off so people won't go near. When they explode, they make wonderful geysers and leave interesting holes. It generated the idea of detonating our ordnance to fool them into thinking they destroyed us."

After dinner, Zelly was alone with his thoughts.

If camouflage and the craters trick them, rockets may still pummel New York.

All that spy work for nothing and years of life traded for this futile gesture.

He slept until the terrible pain woke him, and he was burning hot. "Help me, I hurt!"

"Shut up and go to sleep," a nearby patient said.

He realized he'd called out in English because he couldn't control himself. The agony, mental anguish, and spiritual forsakenness undermined him, so he cried and screamed.

"Die and get it over," the voice advised.

He waited an eternity for someone to come. When a nurse came, his fever was sky-high, so she removed his bandages and gave him a morphine shot. A doctor arrived with several brawny soldiers. "His wounds are infected. Put him on the train to the hospital in Stettin."

Katchen and Kurt rode with Zelly, and he stayed silent in fear of using English. The drug caused wondrous visions.

His third-grade teacher strolled through his mind. "You're too mischievous and will never amount to anything."

Major Donovan popped in from behind a file cabinet. "Glad you came on the adventure?"

"Mess your diaper?" Bald Bart teased in the boxing ring at Fort Sam Houston.

Stengler said, "Isn't death something to relish?"

"Gott in Himmel," Ma used her favorite expression of surprise.

Uncle August came from the grave. "You are such a disappointment. You were supposed to kill Hitler."

A Gestapo agent handed his Mauser to Ma. "Mrs. Brown, your son was a wonderful Nazi."

"A Nazi?" Ma shot herself in the temple.

Trudl kissed him. "I want to sleep with you."

Stengler took the handgun from Ma's lifeless fingers and killed Trudl. "I have dibs on his ass."

Zelly wrestled the gun from his hands and aimed at Vinny. "Why did you lie?"

"Lie? What lie?"

From *Hilf Mit!*'s cover, he smiled at his scoutmaster. "We boys will triumph every time."

As the man snapped the picture, he grinned. "Tomorrow, the world."

Zelly wanted to pray.

How does a Jew call on God?

I'm not Jewish.

Really?

****

19 August 1943—Stettin

At the hospital, the medics cleaned Zelly's wounds to prevent infection and stitched the deeper cuts. His fever broke near noon thanks to sulfonamide dripping into his veins. By evening, he felt better, as if nothing touched his back.

He went for a dining hall dinner and encountered a man with a strange armband. In a world of swastikas, a cross of red in a white circle stood out. The man spoke foreign German, probably Swiss.

Zelly used Italian to ask about a seat, "Posso prendere questo posto?"

"Naturalmente. Sei Italiano?"

"No, I'm German."

The man extended his hand. "I'm Jakob Dufour of the Swiss Red Cross."

Zelly continued the conversation in Italian. "I'm Zelly, injured in Peenemünde's bombing." He intentionally avoided mentioning the SS. "Do you have any war news?"

Dufour glanced around before whispering, "The American General Patton has taken Sicily."

Zelly pictured him like Jesus marching from heaven.

Jews don't believe in Jesus.

U.S. Army boots are on the same continent as I am. Soon, I'll go home.

But where is that?

****

21 August 1943—Peenemünde's Funeral

Bandaged and hurting but no longer needing hospitalization, Zelly returned to witness the burials and funeral services at Peenemünde. Near the Karlshagen railroad tracks, parallel trenches scarred an area the size of a football field. Between the rows, a Luftwaffe antiaircraft crew stood honor guard.

He joined his guidance team to pay respects as the communal caskets lowered into the ground, including the remains of Trudl and Helmut. Wearing a helmet hadn't helped his friend against a British air raid. Dr. Thiel, his family, and a few others received more specific treatment.

The next day, the base began dispersing to facilities in other locations. Offices and laboratories went into hotels and buildings in Karlshagen or neighboring communities. The wind tunnel and liquid oxygen plant moved to the Alps. The production lines for the rockets transferred to Mittelwerk, an old gypsum mine at Nordhausen. Rocket testing went to a forest near Blizna, Poland, with only a two-month delay to construct the infrastructure.

Zelly went to survey the Austrian Alps for a new development site with Walter Riedel, called Papa, and Godomar Schubert. Papa was the chief rocket designer, and Schubert was an army civil servant. Zelly represented the SS.

At Gmunden, 100 kilometers east of Salzburg, they found a location, code-named Zement, to create the A-10 Amerika. Extensive blasting extended a system of caverns, and slaves made cement pads for the heavy equipment. As the senior SS officer, Zelly's job was the labor supply, so he created a KZ at Ebensee to house them.

CHAPTER 18

Vinny

16 April 1945—Zement

Two years passed while Zelly was in the mountains playing the role of an ardent Nazi. Though he never abused or killed a prisoner, eight thousand souls, mostly Jews, lost their lives under his command. He was part of the organization that murdered them, a responsibility so horrific he blocked it from consciousness. However, he ensured the facility would never become operational by slowing construction schedules, scrambling designs, ignoring orders, and exploiting the scarcity of materials.

Zement was in the Alpenfestung or National Redoubt, a last-ditch effort to preserve Germany as the thousand-year Reich crumbled. Dresden was in ruins. Only the Elbe held Americans back from Berlin, and Red Army tanks idled 100 kilometers from the city. When Dr. von Braun visited in February, he shared his secret plan to surrender to the U.S.

Zelly hoped to avoid Soviet capture. Stories of their tortures were horrific—binding SS officers to fences with live grenades in trouser pockets, driving screws into bones, extracting organs.

He hadn't heard from Vinny since the 'Dear Frederich' letter two years ago. Germany's infrastructure no longer existed, and

Italy surrendered as the people deposed Mussolini. Still, the lack of contact frightened him.

He realized it was time to act and planned to locate Vinny and escape together.

As Riedel prepared to leave work, he said, "Find something to enjoy tonight, eh?"

Zelly grinned, knowing his plans. "I have one more requisition to type, so I won't be long."

With a wistful smile, Papa asked, "Does anything remain to request?"

"Doesn't hurt to try." When Papa departed, Zelly rolled a page of letterhead in the typewriter and invented orders to send himself to Berlin to appeal for additional laborers from Speer and Himmler. Forging Riedel's and Dornberger's signatures, he tucked the paper into his tunic pocket.

He packed only a clean shirt. Anticipating the Russians' reaction if they found him with the silver medal from Himmler, he hid things in a cavity of his room's wall.

Catching the last train from Ebensee to Gmunden, he transferred to a Salzburg local, where he boarded the Berlin Express. In an empty compartment, he put his feet on the opposite bench. Leaning against the painted-over window, he let the rocking motion lull him to sleep.

In the pre-dawn, the door opened in Munich to allow a once-beautiful older woman to enter. "May I share?" As she sat beside him, a closer examination showed her beauty fading. She was more than double his age, and her eyes roved over his frame.

"The pleasure of a lady's company is preferable to a nap."

As the carriage lurched, their knees touched, bringing a sparkle to her eyes. "Does that include an old housewife?" Her smile, laughter, and batted eyes were coquettish. "I'm visiting my sister in Wittenberg, so I'll change at Leipzig. What is your destination?"

"Berlin. I'm from Luther's city and have been told the bombing spared it."

"True, still a beautiful town."

After Nuremberg, they shuttled to a siding so a hospital train could pass. Loudspeakers blared from it, so he opened the window to catch the message—The war is won, and Roosevelt is dead.

While the lady clapped, he remembered meeting the President almost five years ago.

****

25 September 1940—The White House

In the evening, the butcher, Major "Wild Bill" Donovan, navigated the White House like a pro. Vinny and Zelly followed him upstairs, through a grand hall, and to a small dining room where two men sipped martinis.

"Major, I assume this is my Deutschlander boy," Franklin Roosevelt said.

When Donovan gave Zelly a slight push, he felt compelled to speak. "Yes, Mister President, I'm an American of German descent." He wanted to clarify his status as a citizen.

"Dutch ancestors for me, so both of our familial homelands have troubles." He introduced the man with him, "This is Navy Secretary Frank Knox, one of my favorite people, even if he's Republican."

As they shook hands, the President rolled to a sidebar, and Zelly suppressed a gasp—Roosevelt was in a wheelchair.

"I make a mean martini." The President poured unmeasured amounts of liquors, including a dash of absinthe, into a shaker.

After pouring the first, he handed it to the major. "Bill, how're things in Jolly Old England?"

"The blitz is devastating, but the Brits are winning the air war, and Hitler can't risk an invasion."

Roosevelt passed the next glass to Vinny, examining him all over. "You'll make a fine Italian diplomat. Bill, Churchill's asking for more help—strike that, he's begging."

When Zelly's drink appeared, he protested. "Sir, I'm a boy—still seventeen for another five months."

"Hell, I overturned prohibition and can serve anybody I want."

Zelly sipped the dry drink, comparing its taste to siphoning diesel from the tractor. *From the President's hand, I would gulp gasoline with a smile.*

"We're all boys until women grab hold of us, right?" Roosevelt winked. "Come and sit for fried chicken. I'm not supposed to eat it, but since Eleanor's out, I ordered Georgia-style."

Servers brought plates of fine china holding the meat, corn-on-the-cob, and a heap of mashed potatoes covered with gravy. Though a row of silverware surrounded the plate, they ate with their fingers except for the spuds.

When the meal ended, the President wheeled his chair to confront Zelly. Grabbing his wrist and gazing deep into his eyes, Roosevelt made him uncomfortable. "Son, your duty is to our country—you must save American lives."

****

17 April 1945—Mustangs

Emotion from the memory clouded Zelly's eyes as the Berlin Express gently rocked. The housewife studied him with a bemused smile while he thought.

Roosevelt's death won't end the war. The Vice President will dedicate himself to victory.

But you don't even know his name—maybe he's an America Firster who will surrender.

I've been away too fucking long. Over five years, lots will have changed.

Will anyone remember you? Your passphrase won't mean anything if he didn't survive. And, if you get home, will you even recognize the place?

The lady sharing his compartment jarred him from his thoughts. "Have a girlfriend?"

"I was close, but she died in a bombing."

In sympathy, she patted his leg. "My heartfelt condolences."

An hour later, along the Saale River, the express shuttled to a siding to let an armored train proceed. Through the open window, he glimpsed a massive 280-mm Leopold railway gun and jumped up to study it. Wehrmacht soldiers relaxed on the sandbags surrounding it.

A high-pitched whine caught his attention—a flight of P-51 Mustangs lining up to strafe. "American planes incoming," he warned.

One pair closed fast, aimed straight at his carriage as if the pilot planned to fly through the aperture. The aircraft started firing, and machine guns from the other train responded. Tracers arced in each direction.

He pulled the woman to the floor and covered her with his body, expecting pain from bullets any second. They rattled like fireworks in a tin can as they penetrated the metal and shattered wooden splinters off the benches.

She poured kisses on his face. "Thank you." An arm locked around his neck, and a hand kneaded his crotch. She ripped open his trousers, sending buttons flying. Her expertise in where and how to touch was vast.

She's old enough to be my grandmother.

Opening his eyes, he found white breasts filling his vision. A glance downward revealed a mound of hair and bare skin to her garter belts. When she raised a leg to catch his clothes with her toes, his pants and underwear dropped to his boots. Her practiced hand felt delightful as she stroked him.

His brain revolted, but her kisses blocked his words of protest. Trapped by flying bullets and a woman of surprising power, he closed his eyes to pretend.

Her throaty, deep voice sounded like a drill sergeant. "Put it in." She grabbed his butt cheeks and pulled him to her.

It bent, slipped, and wiggled away like an elusive snake.

"Your first time?" Her giggle was guttural as her hand circled it, squeezed, and aimed. She bucked like a rodeo bronco, and he winced at the penetration. In that instant, the Mustangs returned for another strafing run. The sudden slip of his penis into wet velvet made him gasp. She moaned and imprisoned him by locking her legs around him. He thrashed and rocked on his knees, but she wanted more and forced him to her rhythm.

While she groaned and panted, the fighters came for a third pass. Their bullets whizzed and pinged. When she shrieked, Zelly thought one had hit her and searched for blood but found only her smile.

"A Blitzmädel should have done you years ago," she said.

Sensations swirled through him like the attacking planes overhead. He didn't want to pull out, as he hadn't finished, but her grip allowed no movement as she tightened and shuddered.

A second later, she giggled like a schoolgirl. "The conductor's watching at the door."

Zelly jumped to his feet, embarrassed by the dripping juices and his swinging hardness.

The man smirked and averted his eyes. "I'm glad to learn you're fine. The airplanes followed the other train, so the danger has passed."

"Danke, Herr Conductor." She slipped into her dress and pointed to the floor. "Would you give the boy his buttons? They've come loose."

"Perhaps if you loan me your trousers, I can have them sewn."

Zelly kicked them off and handed them to the man. When he tugged up his underwear, his engorgement was still obvious.

April winds blew through the bullet holes, chilling the carriage.

She pulled Zelly beside her and cuddled. "My little bunny, you didn't finish, did you?"

Zelly rebelled at the endearment, thinking it referred to his ineptness.

She caught his expression. "I have something for you as precious as your gift to me."

She slid off her wedding band and pushed it into his shirt pocket. "I can't take your ring."

"He's been dead two years."

"But—but."

"I'd rather a handsome young Aryan have it than a Russian rapist. Save it for your girl."

In Leipzig, the lady changed to the Wittenberg train, and the conductor returned the trousers. Zelly longingly looked down at Dresdener Strasse and wondered if his Aunt Freida was still living. He contained the thoughts by deciding he would never have answers.

In Berlin, bomb damage stopped them short of Anhalter Station. The city was in ruins, with rubble piled everywhere and only a few buildings standing intact. Finding his way to Vinny's apartment was hard, as heaps of fallen bricks and stones buried the avenues he remembered. He honeycombed through small alleyways where once-proud stores and apartments had stood.

Bombs had heavily damaged Kreuzberg, but the key remained at the dead drop behind the labor office plaque. Along the street, nothing remained until he finally reached Vinny's building. It was in a sad shape, with the curved walls of its turret-like corners having collapsed. The sitting room's piano was visible from the street. The structure had been boarded up with a sign declaring it Verboten, forbidden as unsafe, but he had no other place to stay.

When air raid sirens sounded, and people scurried to shelters, he used the time to survey ways to enter. Near the rear, a climbable rubble heap led to a broken second-floor window. He shimmied through and climbed the stairs to discover the key still worked in the lock. Plaster and concrete dust covered everything, making the length of Vinny's absence obvious.

Other than the wall-less turret room, the apartment was usable. Dirt caked the mattress, so he turned it over. In the closet, most of the clothes still occupied hangers, and behind them was a sizeable stash of food cans. The bathroom had a sheet draped over the tub protecting drinkable water beneath. Kitchen bowls, pots, and pans were also filled, too dirty to drink but acceptable for washing. Vinny had prepared well.

The electricity, gas, and water weren't working, but the cabinets contained matches and candles. Lighting one, he looked around while carefully ensuring the glow wouldn't reach the street below. On a small desk, he discovered the letter he had written after he received the 'Dear Frederich' message on August 13, 1943. Vinny had scribbled the beginnings of an answer to it in nearly unreadable handwriting.

Vinny's dead.

You should give up finding him. Go to the Americans like von Braun.

I must know for sure. Maybe he moved in with that girl, or he's staying at the embassy.

Zelly dined on canned cheese and peaches from the hoard. In the gloaming, he slipped out of his uniform and into bed. The glassless window pointed east toward a red-orange horizon colored by the battle glow. Afraid that radiation sickness had taken Vinny, Zelly didn't sleep well. With the signs of combat dangerously close, he knew Berlin had only days until the Russians would swarm in, and he had to be gone before then.

****

18 April 1945—Searching Berlin

The blood-red sun rose, cutting through the brightness of war, providing just enough light to search the flat for clues to Vinny's whereabouts. A small notebook in a pocket of his Italian suit provided notes on the trips to Gottow and Oranienburg. From it, Zelly learned Vinny had investigated the atom- smashing bomb— spying on his own. He wrote about Kurt Diebner, uranium oxide cubes in paraffin, and chain reactions. The information fit with what Sev had shared and Vinny transported.

Back pages held several dozen names and addresses. The only one Zelly recognized was Ambra, Vinny's Fasching date, who lived in Wedding, north of Tiergarten. He planned a visit to the embassy and, if she wasn't there, her apartment.

The devastation had rendered Berlin's transit system unreliable, so walking was the only way around. Rubble blocked many of the streets he remembered and slowed his progress. Berlin was ready for the last battle— rooftop machine guns guarded every corner, and Panzerfausts poked from basement windows.

The Tiergarten was a burned-out mess—the lush park had turned to ash and cinder. Earlier in the war, Berliners had planted vegetable gardens, but only charred tomato vines remained.

The building where Vinny had worked bore a hand-lettered sign: 'Embassy of the Italian Social Republic' on which someone had scrawled 'Closed.' Zelly entered anyway.

A stout German woman eyed his SS uniform as she cleaned. "Geschlossen."

"I'm searching for a friend, Vinny—Vincente Testanuevo, who served here from 1941 to 1943 or so."

She wagged a finger at him. "Is no more. Kaputt, understand?"

"Anybody still around?" he pushed.

"Nein. Verlassen."

On the reception desk, he found a spring-loaded telephone directory. Sliding the arrow to T, he pressed a button, and the device sprung open. Vincente Testanuevo had office 421, so he climbed the staircase. The janitor gave him the evil eye, but he didn't want to run afoul of the SS.

He opened the locked door by breaking the window with a fire extinguisher. A wall calendar showed Lake Como with snow-capped mountains and October 1944. On the 12th was a note in Vinny's handwriting—Rugen. Had he visited the Baltic after I went to Zement?

Desk drawers were empty, but the blotter had doodles, drawings, and notes. One caught Zelly's attention—Luigi Romersa, *Corriere della Sera*. He tore off that section and pocketed it before taking the calendar.

Walking to Ambra's apartment, he crossed the burned and barren Tiergarten—the path where he had run, the spot of Vinny's lies, the rose garden's debris. At the Spree River, SS guards had barricaded the Moltke Bridge while soldiers wired the structure for demolition. His uniform and papers convinced them to let him cross.

He passed abandoned stores of a once-impressive shopping district. Ambra's building was beside Wedding's town hall and was damage-free. He climbed the stairs to the second floor and apartment 2C. Suitcases blocked the open door. He called, "Ambra?"

She stepped around the luggage with a young girl following. The child resembled Vinny. When the child spotted him, fright overcame her, and she hid behind her mother's legs. "We have travel papers," she said, fumbling in her purse.

"Don't you remember me? I'm Vinny's friend and we danced at Fasching in the Adlon."

Her panic curled into a smile. "Sorry, I try to avoid the SS."

"I'm looking for Vinny. Do you know anything that would help?"

"He wasn't well when he returned from Rugen about six months ago. He was weak and bleeding in his mouth, but doctors couldn't help him. One sent him to Oranienburg where scientists might understand his sickness."

Exhausted, Zelly dragged himself back to Vinny's place, where he stripped and plopped on the bed. Late in the night, the puttering of a nearby small engine woke him. He dressed and searched for the sound, tracing it to a flat on the building's far side where a generator nestled in a bathroom. Hidden beneath some trash was a power cord stretching to the next apartment. He listened and heard a muffled radio broadcasting in Russian.

When he knocked, the noise stopped. After waiting a moment, he rapped again. Someone inside whispered, "Go away," in Slavic-accented German.

"Sir, please help me—my friend Vinny lived on this floor. Did you know him?"

The door cracked, and a man gestured with turned-out palms. "Building empty."

Zelly gazed at his face, recognizing a Jewish nose despite a thick white beard and mustache. The man's dark eyes revealed that he also had recognized the SS uniform. Returning to the flat, he wondered if he'd encountered an escaped Russian worker, prisoner-of-war, spy, or an advance party for the impending invasion. He locked the door and barricaded it with a table in case the man grew curious or worse.

****

19 April 1945—Luigi Romersa

When Zelly awoke, the faint puttering of the generator was still audible. From Ambra's reaction to his uniform, he debated what to wear. An SS outfit was a conversation killer, but if the Gestapo caught him in civilian clothes, they'd hang him for desertion.

He chose the Italian suit from Vinny's closet and took two meat tins— bacon with peas and liverwurst cheese. Hoping to establish a relationship, he placed them at the old man's door.

Next, he made his way through the rubble to the Adlon, surprised to see that the hotel was open. Once, it was the center of foreign journalists and diplomats buzzing with gossip, and he hoped it still was. Someone might identify Luigi Romersa or the *Corriere della Sera*. With luck, he might find the man.

In the Adlon's bar, foreigners sat at two round tables, speaking English. At one, he recognized an Italian from Vinny's department. "Didn't you have an embassy job?"

"I used to, but not since the closing. The government has ordered us out of Berlin before sundown. I suspect the city might be New Moscow by then."

"Do you remember Vinny Testanuevo, my friend who worked with you?"

He nodded and leaned close, his breath reeking of liquor. "He was Mussolini's spy and went on a Baltic trip months ago—never returned to work."

Zelly put on a shocked expression.

The man's eyes didn't quite focus. "Say, you're the one who danced with the golden Nazis. I recall your picture in the *Morgenpost*. Fuck you, Nazi." He spat a brown wad on the floor and left.

Zelly tried another approach, "Does anybody know of Luigi Romersa, who wrote for the *Corriere della Sera?*"

"Both him and his newspaper," a man said. "That rat was also a spy, abandoning this sinking ship and scurrying off to Milan."

"What was he spying on?"

"The Germans created a new bomb, and Mussolini sent him to learn about it. He returned from the north with a whopper of a story about an immense explosion killing thousands of KZ inmates."

"Have anything to do with Oranienburg?"

"That's where they manufactured the stuff called Uranverein."

Zelly's thoughts raced as he considered Vinny spying on one wonder weapon while he spied on another. Then, an intriguing connection formed in his mind—rockets in Peenemünde and atom-smashing bombs on nearby Rugen Island. The sum was more than its parts. He remembered solving trajectory problems and Sev's super-sized weapons. We worked complementary angles. The planned Amerika A-10 rocket would have carried an atomic payload. What Dornberger and von Braun had schemed became unmistakable.

Outside, he found the man from the embassy leaning against a lamppost and smoking. "I apologize for losing my temper. Your friend was sick and went to the Curie Poliklinik in Friedrichshain."

Zelly took the lengthy walk to the clinic only to find it closed from bomb damage, but he deduced enough from the name. Marie and Pierre Curie had discovered radiation.

He turned toward Kreuzberg and walked a block before a sight froze him in his tracks. A boy, about twelve, hung from a streetlamp by a clothesline. His eyes had swiveled skyward like a last prayer, and his webbed belt bound his hands behind his back. Shoestrings tied his shoes together. They had removed his Hitler Youth armband to shame him for cowardice or desertion. Beltless, his slacks billowed beneath him to reveal holes dotting his underwear.

Zelly wanted to cut him down, but they had left him as an example and doing so was a crime. The lynch mob probably lurked nearby, waiting for passersby to offer a kindness. He surveyed the surroundings and spotted no one, but any doorway or rubble pile could hide them. Freeing the corpse's hands, he restored some dignity by clinching the trousers with the belt. Then he continued.

Vigilantes confronted him before the block's end. An HJ-Streifendienst challenged, "Why aren't you in battle?"

"Where's your uniform?" A Volkssturm man, old enough to be his grandfather, demanded.

Each had a pistol pointed at him.

He cursed himself for choosing the suit. "I'm an SS officer on orders and with documentation."

"Papers don't mean fuck." The HJ took a forty-five-degree angle, a perfect firing line.

Zelly flashed his SS pay book, but the double lightning bolt on the cover didn't faze them.

"Fucking coward!" The youth cocked his weapon.

Zelly raised his hands and extended his identification documents. When the boy reached for them, he dropped them to scatter in the breeze. The youth's eyes followed them, and Zelly sprang, grabbing the gun with a twist. It discharged. As the teen screamed, his grasp released, and blood seeped from his shoe where he'd blasted his foot.

Zelly spun him, facing the grandfather and covering himself with the teen. Aiming the pistol at the Volkssturm's heart, he said, "Drop it and slide it away."

"Please don't shoot. I have a wife." The old man let his handgun fall.

"Gather my documents," Zelly ordered. When the HJ handed them over, he asked, "Did you lynch that boy?"

"Damned right because he was a coward and cried for his mother."

"You should take care of your foot." Zelly's weapon waved him away. When the youth limped down a side street, Zelly turned to the man. "Go home and destroy your uniform if you want the Russians to spare you."

At Vinny's building, the generator was silent and the door to the Russian's apartment stood open. Bullets and rifle butts had broken the radio beyond repair. The food tins Zelly had provided this morning were empty in a trash pile.

A building sweep caught him.

The next one might catch you.

****

20 April 1945—SS Headquarters

At dawn, Red Army artillery opened fire, targeting Berlin's eastern suburbs. The noise rumbled like thunder, and the concussions made things tremble. Zelly dressed in uniform to visit SS headquarters. The Gestapo kept dossiers on everyone, and he planned to read Vinny's.

The Prinz-Albrecht-Strasse palace had sustained damage but still maintained a flurry of activity. Entrance guards inspected Zelly's papers and asked him to wait for an escort. Soon, an officer appeared. "Captain Zellner, how may I assist?" Since Zelly wore a different rank insignia, he concluded the officer had checked his record.

"I need the file for an Italian diplomat, Vincente Testanuevo, who arrived in Berlin in 1941."

"What's the nature of your inquiry?"

"I've received a tip that he might be a spy."

"Bombing has disorganized things, so finding the records might take a few hours. Can you return this afternoon at two o'clock?"

Zelly nodded and strolled aimlessly north along Wilhelmstrasse until trucks in the Luftwaffe Ministry's courtyard caught his attention. Soldiers were loading them with boxes, so he lingered at the wrought-iron fence. Overhearing their chatter, he learned their destination was Obersalzberg, as the Nazi leaders were abandoning the capital. Next, festivities in the Reich Chancellery's Garden drew him to pause beside a Motor-HJ boy and his motorcycle. "What's the stir?"

"The Führer's birthday celebration. My comrade is getting an Iron Cross for destroying a Russian tank."

"Which guy?"

"The Führer is nearing him. There, Hitler touched his cheek."

"Say, are you available to take me somewhere on your cycle?"

"No, because I have dispatches to deliver today and tomorrow."

"Sunday?"

"Where do you need to go?"

"Oranienburg."

"Gas is hard to find."

"The job's worth 1,000 Reichsmarks."

The boy's face brightened. "Deal."

Zelly gave him the apartment's address and an arrival time.

At two o'clock, he returned to SS headquarters and the officer escort met him. "Your tip was correct—the man was an enemy agent and your friend. Your inquiry was more personal than professional, wasn't it?"

"Both, but I wanted to visit him again."

"Unfortunately, he died on December 12th in a medical facility."

"The Curie Clinic in Friedrichshain?" Zelly asked, and the man nodded.

I'll go to Oranienburg to verify my theory of radiation poisoning.

Who needs verification? Vinny is dead. Let's escape if we still can!

Think about what the Soviets will do to you—us.

****

21 April 1945—The Scar

In the morning's wee hours, the nearby sound of splintering wood startled Zelly awake. In a precious second or two, he grabbed the pistol he'd taken yesterday and shoved it beneath the pillow. Before he could roll to his back, the bedroom door burst open, and three men spilled inside. "This building is Verboten."

As flashlights lit the room, he discovered the intruders were a Gestapo officer, a Wehrmacht sergeant, and an HJ boy. The boy sprung onto the bed, pinning Zelly under the covers.

"Thank God you are officials." He pointed to his uniform tunic draped over the dresser. "You'll find my orders and papers in the breast pocket. This flat belongs to my friend, and he gave me a key. When I arrived last night, the building's back door was open. I didn't see a sign."

Despite the sergeant's machine gun, he knew the Gestapo officer presented the most danger. He appraised the man's face. Burns had melted it, leaving him disfigured. One eye was glass, and his Walther police special wasn't well-aimed.

"Boy, fetch them," the agent ordered.

The youth released his hold and retrieved the papers to read aloud. "Obersturmführer Frederich Zellner of Wittenberg, assigned to Experimental Command Nord and posted at Gmunden. Orders say he's in Berlin to request foreign workers for a rocketry program."

"I served there for a while and knew a Zellner." The officer surveyed the room with his single eyeball. "Is there a martyr's pin on the pocket?"

"Yes, sir," the kid said.

The Gestapo agent tossed away Zelly's covers and painted his body with the flashlight. "Pull off his undershorts."

The sergeant averted his eyes as the youth stripped Zelly. "I have no interest for this." He engaged the machine gun's safety and backed from the room.

With the automatic weapon gone and the boy's pistol still holstered, Zelly's chances improved. His stomach soured as he guessed the officer's identity—Stengler. Again? What are the odds? The Cheshire cat grin was still degenerate and perverted, but the burns made it grotesque.

Stengler fumbled with his trouser pocket and pulled out a well-worn photograph. He handed it to the youth. "He's that one, right?"

The teen grabbed a handful of Zelly's hair to lift his face from the pillow. "Looks like him. What are you planning?"

"Something he agreed to on a Mittsommernacht long ago. Bind him." Stengler kneeled beside the bed, examining Zelly's face with his eye. "I'm going to enjoy this."

The stench of rotten egg, apricot snuff, and unwashed body filled Zelly's breath. "Please, no. I'm not who you think I am."

The kid bound Zelly's wrists with a rope. "Can I watch?"

****

Oskar rose and opened his trousers. "Of course, you can even go second."

"You have the wrong person," the prisoner protested as the teen tied his feet.

"There's a way to be sure. Flip him over and check for a scar in his groin."

Though the captive struggled, the ropes made turning him easy. The HJ boy pawed his organs. "I found it."

"I've waited years for this, and now you're mine! Roll his ass up."

The teen rolled him again.

As the prisoner's butt was exposed, Oskar prepared for action. He pressed his handgun and fist into the mattress beside Zellner's left shoulder and hovered over his target. When his cock brushed a butt cheek, he moaned with anticipation, ready to thrust.

****

As Zelly flipped, he took the pillow and pistol with him. The sway-back bed helped him complete a full turn, and he came up with the weapon pointed at Stengler's belly. He squeezed the trigger.

Stengler's melted face contorted as his mouth gaped. "I'm hit."

Zelly drove his knees into the agent's exposed testicles and pounded the weapon on the chin. As Stengler slumped, he pushed him from the bed, bowling over the kneeling boy. Both tumbled to the floor in a heap.

Zelly jumped off the bed and hopped to the door, keeping his bindings intact. He hid behind the door as it opened. The third man charged in, disengaging the safety.

The kid tried to roll away from Stengler. "Look out," he said.

Zelly fired from the waist with the pillow still shielding his body. The bullet caught the sergeant in the back of his neck. It pinged three times as it ricocheted inside the steel helmet. As the slug crisscrossed the man's brain, he staggered and collapsed.

When the youth scrambled to his feet, Stengler said, "Shoot him."

The boy was slow in reaching for his holstered pistol.

"Move, and you're dead," Zelly said.

The boy froze and wet his shorts.

"Toss your gun and dagger under the bed," Zelly said.

"Shoot," Stengler yelled.

The sniveling kid flung the items beneath the bed. "Please don't hurt me."

"Untie me."

The teen obeyed the order while Stengler pressed his wound.

"Give me your papers," Zelly demanded.

"Find the authorities," Stengler said.

When the HJ obeyed, Zelly memorized the boy's name and address. "Ralf, if I let you go, will you report this?"

"I won't tell—I swear."

Zelly pointed to the door, and Ralf scurried away. Soon, his footfalls no longer pounded on the stairs. The building grew silent.

I couldn't kill him.

You might regret it. Move fast because someone may have heard the shots, or he'll report you.

****

Oskar appraised the situation. Blood and brain poured from the Wehrmacht sergeant's helmet. He watched Zellner drag the body to the sitting room. A grunt reached his ears, followed by the sound of something pounding the rubble three stories below.

He held the bullet hole in his belly, and the bleeding lessened. Breathing came in painful gasps. He tried to slide toward the kid's pistol, but moving was impossible.

Through his good eye, he saw Zellner squat beside him.

"What burned your face and took your eye?"

Oskar detected sympathy in Zellner's voice. "Killing Jews. They ordered me to liquidate the Bialystok ghetto, and a Jewish whelp threw acid on me. All this is your fault for getting me transferred." Blood ran from the corner of his mouth as he spoke.

"You won't live. Belly wounds are the worst because of infection."

"Please get help."

"I'd love to torture you using the things you've threatened to do to me. I could enjoy the look of sheer terror on your face. Do you remember telling me that death was something to relish? Well, I could easily delight in yours."

Stengler made a slight nod and closed his eyes, including the lid over the glass one.

****

Zelly saw the pool of blood flowing across the floorboards. "May I tell you a secret?"

Puzzlement crossed the Gestapo officer's face as he blinked.

Zelly switched to English—confident the old language teacher would understand. "This will hurt you more than any torture."

Stengler grunted.

"I'm an American spy and fooled everybody but not you. You always suspected something from the first day we met at Brenner, and you were right. Remember the patrol boat in Naples? I was on a British submarine that had to crash dive when the Italians arrived. That's why I was swimming. My scar goes back to training in the U.S.—not from a scuffle in Wittenberg or at Garibaldi's statue. The snapshot you've carried in your pocket for years is from a picnic near San Antonio, Texas, and the magazine cover comes from my Boy Scout court of honor back home. An international conspiracy of Jews planted all the documentation you've carefully gathered. In fact, I'm one of them."

Horror filled Stengler's gnarled face. "You're under arrest. The kid will be back soon."

Zelly laughed. "I can't let you live." He dragged the dying man to the sitting room's crumbled wall. He braced himself between the body and the upright piano. His legs propelled Stengler from the ledge. "The launch was spectacular with a perfect pitch-over."

Crumpled and with his trousers around his ankles, Stengler died when he landed in the rubble.

I've killed two men.

More, starting with Bart in training and many Jews at Ebensee.

I had no choice. This is war.

You can't risk another minute here.

Zelly dressed in his SS uniform and retrieved the photo the kid had dropped. He removed all traces of himself from the flat and hid a few days' food and water in a janitorial closet behind rusty paint cans.

He scanned the room. Blood pooled in the bedroom and streaked the floor where he'd dragged the men. The scene perfectly matched a building sweep gone wrong.

He sneaked out of the back door. When he turned the corner, the bodies had attracted a small crowd, including two criminal police.

Sauntering past them, he said, "Good morning, Officers." They glanced at his uniform and showed no interest.

He descended the stairs to Kochstrasse station, where hundreds of people were taking shelter. His SS uniform earned him a bench, though it was quite uncomfortable, and sleep eluded him due to the voices in his head.

CHAPTER 19

Jacques

22 April 1945—Besieged Berlin

Zelly woke at dawn, stretching his cramped muscles from hours on a wooden seat. He made his way through the sleeping masses huddled in the underground. When he emerged at street level, Berlin was eerily quiet. After yesterday's artillery barrage, the silence boded one outcome—a massive attack by the Red Army.

When he returned to Vinny's building, only blood stains remained from the body pile he'd left on the debris. At 8 AM, the noise from a motorcycle engine alerted him to his appointment. The cycle swerved around rubble piles with the ease of a slalom skier.

When it pulled to the curb, he smiled at the driver. "Hungry?"

"Very. I've had nothing for days." The youth removed his helmet.

He led the Motor-HJ boy to the stash in the closet. His eyes bugged at the abundance.

"I'm Jacques, and damned glad to be your friend."

"I'm Zelly."

They shook hands before filling their arms with food. Sitting on the stairs, they opened the tins and gorged.

The Russians launched an artillery barrage. Shells whizzed overhead and pounded central Berlin, a few blocks away. A short round hit the building across the street, the one previously owned by the Jewish family whose portrait Zelly had found chilling.

"We'll be safer away from town," Jacques suggested.

They stowed two days' rations in one of the cycle's saddlebags. The HJ boy already had two bottles of Riesling in the other.

"The wine is from my family's vineyard on the Mosel River." Jacques kick-started the cycle.

Zelly climbed behind and gripped the boy's coat pockets. "That explains your French name, but can I call you Jack?"

They darted away from the curb as a short round blasted the rubble of Vinny's building. The noise made Zelly's ears ring, and the billowing dust brought a cough.

"I like Jack because it sounds American." He steered around huge debris piles and swerved through the overturned trams that blocked intersections. "We'll avoid the artillery by skirting central Berlin."

Once they crossed the Spree in Charlottenburg, the din of war retreated. Jack turned north beside Tegeler Lake into a countryside untouched by combat. The forest was beautiful, and pine trees gave the aroma of Christmas. Tall oaks and ramrod-straight birches were full of opening buds, and hawthorns bloomed for May Day.

Jack stopped near a wildflower patch. White wood anemones and blue star columbine carpeted the ground, and yellow irises stood proudly in the midst. They shared a piss, watering the blooms.

Jack spread his greatcoat like a picnic blanket and opened a wine bottle. "I'm still hungry." Two tins succumbed to his HJ dagger.

Zelly laughed at Jack's speed in shoveling food into his mouth. "How long since you ate?"

"Can't remember. Are we in a hurry?" At Zelly's head shake, Jack took off his tunic and shirt and sprawled in the sunlight. In a soft, pensive voice, he said, "May would be a wonderful month to go home."

"I've been homesick for many years." Zelly stripped to the waist and sprawled beside him.

Jack pulled out a picture and handed it to him.

"Your girlfriend is beautiful."

"Do you have one?" he asked.

"No. Maybe I did. She died in a bombing."

"My deepest condolences. I haven't heard from mine since the Americans took Aachen, like six months ago. I wish I was there."

"Home is far away for me, too."

"How long have you been in the fighting?" Jack asked.

"I joined the war in 1941 but haven't seen combat. I work with the scientists who make the wonder weapons."

Jack laughed. "I wonder where they were when we needed them. I'm sixteen, so this will be over before I serve officially."

Fifteen minutes after resuming the journey, they rounded a bend and found a summer house where the wealthy and influential escaped city life. Passing it, they continued north.

At the Oder-Havel Canal crossing, a roadblock halted them. Armed guards stood behind the crossbar. "Halt! What is your destination?"

"Oranienburg," Zelly said.

A guard studied their uniforms. "Not anymore, sir. The Soviets captured it an hour ago—Sachsenhausen KZ, too. They're executing anyone in an SS uniform."

Jack turned the bike. "I've heard rumors of what they do to the SS."

They retreated to the country house and went up the driveway. Jack stopped at the walkway. "I'll search for gas in the barn and garage. You see if anyone's home."

Zelly knocked and waited, but nobody answered the door. After picking up the lock, he discovered the place was unoccupied. Soon, they sat in the kitchen.

"I found enough fuel to fill the tank, but your destination is obviously impossible. What should we do?" Jack gazed at Zelly's SS uniform. "I'd survive getting caught by the Reds, but you won't."

"Try to reach the American lines?"

Jack's eyes brightened. "I know a route to the Elbe." He pulled out a folded map, grimy with lots of usage. "Tangermünde is about 130 kilometers. There's a bridge, or there used to be. But thanks to that roadblock, we must go back to Rathenow to cross the Havel."

Zelly watched Jack's finger trace the course.

"Will the Americans torture the SS like the Soviets?" Jack asked.

"I'll take my chances."

"Better if we leave in the morning," Jack said.

"There's only one bed."

"We can share."

While Jack started a fire in the fireplace, Zelly searched the closets for something to wear besides his uniform. He found only ladies' summer clothes. When he returned to the hearth, Jack was warming a tin of turkey and another of creamed corn.

With the meal over, they sat and relaxed. Zelly studied Jack's uniform and had an idea.

Jack said he would survive. An HJ boy isn't much of a threat. If I wore his uniform...

How can you accomplish that?

Jack's trousers had a two-inch cuff, the webbed belt had several inches to spare, and the shirt sleeves were too long. It might fit.

Zelly removed his tunic. "I found a shaving kit and would like to lose some scruff."

"Do you mind if I watch?"

He remembered the times when he'd spied on Vinny's daily ritual. "No problem." He prepared the water and soap. Needing to appear as young as possible, he shaved his face, chest, and belly above the belt.

"I've never thought guys shaved there," Jack observed.

How can I get his clothes?

You could tie him up and take them.

I can't risk him escaping or the Russians finding him. It would be best to kill him. I could use the garrote Vinny taught me.

There's been enough killing. He wants to go home, just like you.

Do you remember years ago when I couldn't kill the Jewish baby? Vinny said I was in the SS. Isn't killing Jews what they do?

But you let the boy with Stengler go and the street vigilantes. Let him live.

I'm in the American army. Isn't the purpose of a soldier to kill the enemy? He's one.

No, he's a friend.

With the shaving finished, they extinguished the fire and took the last wine bottle to the bedroom. Zelly stripped to his undershorts and climbed into bed. Shyly, Jack watched.

I've got to get him out of his clothes.

"Don't be shy. Here, I'll turn and look away."

When Jack slipped beneath the covers, Zelly rolled over and spotted the boy's complete uniform draped over the chair. Zelly passed him the bottle. "Take the first swig."

They shared the wine, and Jack drank the most. He started snoring before it was empty, but Zelly remained awake. He touched the boy's back, but the snoring continued unabated. Even a hard poke didn't bother the teen.

Slipping from bed, Zelly gathered his uniform and went outside. He located a burn barrel behind the barn and tossed in his SS uniform. A splash of gasoline and a match started the incineration.

In one armoire, he found a sewing box. He let down the cuffs of Jack's HJ outfit and dressed in it. The mirror's reflection told him he didn't seem sixteen, but he could do no more. He verified the map was in a tunic pocket. Rolling the cycle through the barn door, he mounted and kick-started it. As he rode down the driveway, Jack burst from the house in his boxers.

"Hey, that's my motorcycle!" Jack tried to catch him.

"Thanks for the loan."

It wasn't long before Jack slowed to a walk. "Fuck you," he shouted.

As the nearly full moon rose, Zelly followed the road. Fifteen minutes later, he found the wildflower patch where they had rested. He thought of spending the night there but feared Jack might still be in pursuit.

When the aroma of pine and the spicy almond scent of the hawthorns mixed, he walked the cycle 30 yards into the trees. He fashioned a nest for the night, like he did for Trudl.

Aren't you glad you didn't kill him?

I still might have to. He could walk this far.

In only his underwear?

Or one of the flowery sun dresses.

Let's get some sleep. Tomorrow will be the day we escape or die.

****

23 April 1945—Tegeler Forest

At first light, Zelly traveled south between the lake and the woods toward Berlin. When he reached the Spandau Bridge, the Hitler Youth guards recognized his uniform and waved him through. He headed west and merged with fleeing refugees, dodging pushcarts and wheelbarrows full of prized possessions. The crowd was thick, and he couldn't make any speed. In the countryside, the road became even more crowded, so he drove the motorcycle down the ditch beside farm fences. Puttering by the exodus, he easily found Rathenow.

Five kilometers shy of the Havel River, an HJ boy flagged him, "My bicycle chain has broken, so will you give me a ride to the river?"

"Sure. I'm Jacques," Zelly lied and lashed the bike to the cycle's handlebars. The youth hopped on behind him.

Zelly gave him a tin of saltines from the saddlebag, and the boy talked with a mouthful of crackers. "My unit is the 1st HJ Tank Destroyer Brigade, guarding the bridge with some Norwegian infantry. We're part of Army Group Holste and Wenck's 12th."

"I'm carrying dispatches for the general. Where is he?"

"In Stendal, across the Elbe."

On the riverbank, the boy reclaimed his bicycle and joined his unit for the repair.

The commander examined Zelly with curiosity, checking out his HJ- Motor badge and courier armband.

He handed over Jack's papers. "I have important dispatches for General Wenck, so please don't detain me."

"Do you have news from Berlin?"

"Red artillery pounded the central city and captured Oranienburg and Sachsenhausen yesterday. They'll be here soon." Zelly crossed while engineers set demolition charges on the bridge beneath him.

Thirty kilometers to Tangermünde went fast but brought disappointment. Either German demolitions or allied bombs had destroyed the span. Twisted metal made a long, gravity-defying arch into the Elbe. Though crossing on a cycle was impossible, he spotted people climbing like ants clinging to the remnants.

He retraced his steps to a deserted farmhouse in a grove of spruce, hiding the motorcycle in the barn. Next to the structure was a watering trough with a well and pump. He hollowed out a space beneath the cement base and shoved documentation and paperwork inside.

Taking a chance, he cut the insignia from Jack's uniform. If the Germans caught him before he reached the bridge, they would think it an act of cowardice and lynch him. But to the Americans, the empty shirt would represent surrender and diminish him as a threat. He added his patches, dagger, and pistol to the hole. Packing the gap with dirt, he compressed it with stomps from his boots. The wedding ring was his only remaining possession. He pushed it into his rectum.

In case someone still occupied the house, he climbed into the hayloft for the night.

Fred, your adventure will end in either escape or death tomorrow.

I never imagined exploits like these when I left, Zelly. Too much destruction and death.

CHAPTER 20

To the Americans

24 April 1945—Tangermünde Bridge

In the middle of the night, the owners of the farmhouse in the spruce grove came back. Zelly peeked from the loft at the farmer and his wife, relieved they hadn't found the motorcycle in the barn. But a crowing rooster, clucking chickens, and lowing cows warned discovery wouldn't take long. As the old couple sat for breakfast, he jumped from the hay and trotted to the bridge.

Once there, he blended with the weary Germans trudging toward surrender. Most were civilians, but some were military, and they frowned at his missing patches. He joined the line which snaked through the swampy east bank of the Elbe. As he waded through knee-high water, the twisted steel and timber loomed ahead. The structure resembled a roller coaster soaring into the sky.

When the swamp deepened to his chest, he climbed the arch. Railway trestles, like a stairway to heaven, led him up. Someone had strung a rope as a safety handhold, and he worked his way along it.

At the pinnacle, he reached a section where the bridge hadn't collapsed. Railroad ties provided a simple walk over the deepest section of the gorge. Small plank footbridges spanned random gaps.

The bridge's western side had dropped into a deep V. He descended, heel-to-toe and balancing on each rail with a grip on the lifeline. After reaching the bottom, he climbed upward on corkscrewed railway ties. Over the last distance, he scrambled on hands and knees until an American soldier's hand lifted him.

"I surrender," Zelly said, remembering to speak English.

A sign offered greetings from the 405th Infantry Regiment of the Ozark Division. An officer repeatedly called, "Weapons in the pile," but he had none. When he bypassed the cache, a private gave him a pat-down as well as probing his mouth with a filthy finger. When satisfied, the man sent him to the sorting station. Old men, women, and children could continue on their way. Those in uniform or of military age formed ranks on one side of the road. On the other were boys of the Hitler Youth.

He joined the soldiers, but a sergeant recognized his outfit and ordered him to cross the street.

"I'm American," Zelly said.

"And I'm fucking Betty Grable," the cigar-chewing NCO replied and escorted him across.

Zelly tried his magic passphrase. "I work for Wild Bill."

Tugging the stogie from his mouth, the man said, "I work for Harry Truman, and he's from Missouri, like me."

"I'm from Texas," Zelly said.

"Damn, I didn't know we's fighting them, too." The man bit the stub and kicked Zelly's ass into the youth formation, where he wasn't welcome. Some had witnessed his claim of being American and spotted the removed patches.

Ozark division soldiers marched the HJ boys to waiting trucks. Surrounded by glares of hate and shame, Zelly rode for about three hours on bumpy roads.

****

24 April 1945—Uelzen Detention Camp

Upon reaching the town of Uelzen, the prisoners stopped at a field fenced by barbed wire and guarded by tall towers bristling with machine guns. As an SS Officer, Zelly realized the place had been a satellite camp of Neuengamme's KZ. The camp, originally built for about 100 people, had only standing room for over four thousand.

Troopers prodded them through the gate like herding cattle. Inside the fence, German order ruled. The senior Hitler Youth was a Cadre Leader from Hamburg. He examined the recent arrivals and demanded their names, rank, and hometown. At Zelly's turn, he said, "Frederich Zellner, Scharführer from Wittenberg."

The boy snarled as he noticed the missing insignia of Zelly's uniform. "You're too old for the Hitlerjugend and a stinking coward."

"He claimed to be an American," a new guy announced.

The Cadre Leader's mouth curled in contempt. "Put him in the latrine."

Zelly's spot was at the edge of an open pit overflowing with waste. The stench gagged him, and his boots sank into the piss-soaked ground. Pigsties on his Texas farm reeked less. When boys came to relieve themselves, they jostled him, making a game of trying to tumble him into the muck.

Dinner was a hard biscuit passed hand-to-hand. A mischievous grin split the face of the kid in front of him as he tossed Zelly's roll into the shitty morass. Zelly tried to deny his hunger with memories of Ma's blue-ribbon winners at the Gillespie County fair. Feeling nauseous, he stayed awake all night, fearing a push that would land him in the cesspool. He noticed the guards manning the machine guns wore British uniforms.

I'm out of American control.

Your passphrase won't mean anything, and no one will know of the mission.

Or care about what happens to me.

You'll never make it home or be free.

The voices chirped in his head all night.

****

25 April 1945—The Tattoo

By dawn, the lake of excrement had penetrated Zelly's shoes and soaked his socks. A siren roared before loudspeakers called the prisoners to attention. In perfect high German, the British voice said, "Form a single line. Follow orders and no talking."

Two young goons fetched Zelly and placed him last in the first group. He suspected the leader intended to turn him in to buy favors. Guarded by Tommy guns, they shuffled to a farm wagon. "Shoes off and toss them in." The next stop was at 55-gallon drums with fires burning inside. "Keep your papers, then strip naked and burn your clothes in the barrels."

Undressed, the differences between Zelly and the Cadre Leader were obvious. Zelly was taller, more muscular, and with thicker pubic hair. The others in his dozen seemed puny, except for one guy. He's too old, too, maybe older than me, he thought.

A Tommy gun pointed them toward Brit officers who sat behind tables beneath a canvas canopy. "Hand over your documents and answer all questions truthfully."

Curious about his fate, Zelly watched the mature man ahead of him. He assumed his outcome might match that man's.

For a few moments, a welcome, chilly rain fell from scattered clouds. As it washed over him, Zelly felt cleaner and hoped the stench lessened.

A British officer motioned the older man forward. When he offered his documentation, the SS on his paybook gave him away.

A trooper pushed him to his knees, stopping the process. The line stood immobile as a cloud moved, and the sun spotlighted the scene. Off-duty soldiers came from their tents and sat on a small hill where one strummed a guitar. No one cared about the kneeling man.

"Please," the guy implored in English.

"Check him," the officer said.

The soldier lifted the man's left arm. "Got the tattoo."

Zelly shivered, colder than the rain, because he bore a matching mark given years ago at training. The Brit circled the table, unholstering his Enfield revolver, and pushed the barrel against the back of the guy's head.

"Nicht schiessen," the man cried.

The request didn't stop the gun from cracking and spitting smoke. The man's head exploded an instant before his body slumped. Soldiers dragged it away, leaving blood staining the grass and dirt. In seconds, processing resumed like nothing had happened. It was Zelly's turn.

The officer still held the weapon as he beckoned Zelly to approach. "Papers."

Zelly stood in the gore, answering in English. "Lost in the war."

With a quizzical expression, the officer asked, "You speak English?"

"I'm an American from Fredericksburg, Texas, and I work for Wild Bill."

Surprise filled the Brit's face. He believes me, Zelly thought as relief flooded his body.

Like magic, a superior officer appeared. "Remember in the Ardennes when Nazis smuggled English-speaking soldiers through the lines?"

Zelly's hope vanished when the Brit drew his Enfield. "Check for the tat."

A rifle butt clipped his knees, dropping him just above a pool of gore, still frothy. Someone lifted his left arm and exposed his tattoo.

The dirt won't care if your blood is German or American.

I always realized I might die, but it's unfair this close to the end.

****

25 April 1945—A Song

Clouds cast everything in shadow, except for the bright sunbeam that spotlighted Zelly and his SS blood-group tattoo. The man with the Enfield circled behind him. The Hitler Youth jeered as the weapon's barrel tickled the hairs at the top of his spine.

As death approached, he remembered the family's farm in Fredericksburg, Texas. On the day he left, Ma wrung her hands, and Da stood in the grass, peering down like he'd lost a nickel. Beans, his Irish setter, chased after the Army car as it took him away. Music accompanied his memories, like a movie soundtrack. A guitar played a familiar tune, and a tenor sang with a bright and beautiful voice. He recognized the song and hummed along as words emerged from deep memory. In English, he joined the verse.

> I wish I was in bonnie Belfast, where life waits at rainbow's end
> I would swim over the deepest ocean just to see her again.

It wasn't something a German would sing, even one with mastery of the language.

> But the sea is wide, and I cannot get over, nor have I wings to fly
> I wish I had a friendly boatman to ferry me to Ma's mince pie.

A Brit guard ordered, "Shut up," but the tune had taken his soul, and he couldn't stop singing.

> But the sea is wide, and I cannot get over, nor have I wings to fly
> So I'll just dream of bonnie Belfast and the day I said goodbye.

The soldier drove his rifle butt into the small of Zelly's back, crumpling him and taking the wind from his song. He remembered—from far away and long ago—the words and dedication to a brother named Danny who didn't return from Dunkirk.

"Fergus—the voice of angels!" He shouted as his body writhed with pain and the nearness of death. He peeked through his eyelashes to find boots surrounding him.

The HJ Cadre Unit Leader said, "Shoot him!"

A gun cocked, and Zelly sensed the bullet coming for him.

A soldier squatted beside him. "How do you know me name?"

He forced his eyes open to view the bright orange hair. "Fergus, I'm Zelly. Do you remember New Year's Eve in Knockbreda? How's Meg?"

"Damn, this bloke's a Yank, and I recognize 'im. Can you stand?"

"I think so," Zelly muttered.

Fergus pulled him up and found the tattoo. "Explain this?"

"I went to Germany as an undercover spy."

Fergus put the tattooed arm over his shoulder and walked his friend to the shower. Unsteady, the pall of death hung over Zelly. When his knees gave way, Fergus caught him.

"I never thought I'd meet you again, but I'm so thankful you were here to save me."

"Those waves of fate you talked about have brought us together again."

"I owe you—my life."

"Well, it stinks right now," Fergus said as he started the water spraying. "I have an answer to your earlier question. Meg is a nurse here in Germany."

"I figured she would have married some Royal Marine or Spitfire pilot by now."

"She hasn't been the same since your visit, praying every day that you're safe and will return to her. Today, God answered her prayers."

"She fell for me?" Instantly, enough joy took him so he could endure a delousing. "Can I meet her?"

"I expect you'll have a ton of shit to work through, but I'll arrange things as quickly as I can."

Zelly reached for a striped prison camp uniform ready for the HJ boys— ones previously used by the Jews who'd occupied the KZ.

"Zelly, I'll find you something better to wear. We've been with the Yank's 17th Airborne for a while, and there'll be an American kit somewhere."

"Fergus, please call me Fred, my proper name." Soon, he wore U.S. Army combat fatigues with a golden talon on his sleeve.

Half an hour later, he sat in a colonel's office, enduring the man's stare. "I understand you aren't what you appear. My officer recognizes you from Belfast and swears you're American, but can you prove it?"

"Sir, I doubt I can convince you, but I have a passphrase from five years ago. Does 'I work for Wild Bill' mean anything?"

His head shook. "What's your name?"

"In Germany, I've been Frederich Zellner, Zelly for short, but for my first seventeen years, I was Fred Brown."

"Well, tell me your story, and it better be good."

"I was born in Fredericksburg, Texas. In the summer of '40, I was recruited to be an American spy against the Nazis. I trained in San Antonio with the 23rd Regiment of the 2nd Infantry Division at Fort Sam Houston. For a while, I studied at Rice Institute of Technology in Texas and Camp Ritchie in Maryland. I caught a ride to Nova Scotia on the *USS Claxton,* which became the *HMS Salisbury.* We docked in Belfast for New Year's Eve, where I met Fergus. An Italian named Vinny was with me, but he died in the war. Next, the *Rochester* took us to Gibraltar, and *Rorqual* snuck us to Naples, Italy. From there, the Berlin train took me to my life as a spy."

"2nd Division?" At Fred's nod, he pulled a situation map from his valise and spread it across his desk to locate their symbol. "On the Mulde River near Leipzig." He picked up the telephone. "HQ for the Yank's 2nd Infantry." In a minute, it rang back.

"This is the CO of the British 6th Airborne with three strange questions for you. First, where was your unit in the summer of 1940?"

Fred caught the answer. "Home base at Fort Sam Houston in San Antonio, Texas."

"Second, ever hear of a Fred Brown or Frederich Zellner, who goes by Zelly?"

"No. I wasn't in until 1943 for D-Day—Omaha Beach."

"Third, does the phrase 'I work for Wild Bill' ring a bell?"

"No, should it?"

Cradling the receiver, he glanced at Fred, who shrugged and stared at Fergus, the one keeping him alive. Zelly remembered Vinny's anger when he told Fergus about going to Germany.

"One more thing to check. You mentioned a base in Maryland."

He nodded. "Camp Ritchie—where I learned spy field-craft."

The commander ordered another call. "Ring MI-19 at division."

A soldier answered. "POW interrogation."

"The Yanks have a group of German-speaking Jews they use. What are they called?"

"The Ritchie Boys."

"Any idea why?"

"They trained at Camp Ritchie in Maryland."

"How about an American pass phrase: 'I work for Wild Bill'?"

"William Donovan, head of the Yank's Office of Strategic Services, goes by that nickname. If you have someone using it, I'd say you've found a Yankee spy."

The CO examined him. "Your story checks out so far, but how did you do it? I mean, live with these criminals for five years?"

"I… I was… one of them." The question ripped him apart as he wondered if he should be ashamed of Zelly or proud.

"Did you know about the concentration camps and the killing?"

Zelly nodded. "I helped, but I had to." An agonized sob spun Fred towards the floor. Fergus caught and held him while Zelly cried on his shoulder. "We're so sorry."

The phone rang, and the colonel listened to the end. "That was G2 of the American 9th Army in Brunswick. They want you in Remagen."

"Tomorrow, sir?" Fergus said, touched by Zelly's tears. "For tonight, he needs a friend, an enjoyable meal, and a comfortable bed."

"Lieutenant McAuley, do what's best, but escort him to the Yanks."

Fergus whispered, "Zelly, I've got a bottle of whiskey."

"Tullamore Dew?"

"Jack Daniels. I beat a Yank with a full house, kings over tens."

In Fergus's room, they drank, reminisced, and shared five years of stories. No one mentioned where Zelly would go in the morning or when Fred's fate would be sealed.

Will anyone remember my passphrase?

Will they think you are one of the infiltrating German spies?

Meeting Fergus in Belfast was a stroke of luck, and you thought telling him our mission was a mistake.

****

26 April 1945—The Road to Remagen

As they mounted a Willys Jeep, Fergus stuck a helmet on Fred's head and handed him a flak jacket. His roommate sat behind with a machine gun across his knees. Zelly wondered if it was to protect, guard, or kill him.

Fields full of spring flowers brightened the warm day. They went south to Celle, where a May Pole was being set up in the Schlosspark. Skirting Hannover, they crossed the Weser River on a pontoon bridge near Bad Oeynhausen. In Bielefeld, Fergus chose a restaurant beside the train station for lunch.

"I was here in 1941 and rode in Himmler's car," Zelly said.

Fergus's mouth hung open while the gun carrier said, "You're shitting me."

"He bought me a new uniform so I could dance with Emma Göring, and I called him Uncle."

"You're as Nazi as they come." Fergus's bunkmate threatened. "I should shoot you."

"My orders were to be a good little Nazi and fit in," Fred said.

At Leverkusen, the jeep entered the Rhine's golden meadows and Fergus parked near the IG Farben's factory, which was famous for both Bayer Aspirin and the Zyklon-B gas used in KZs. A spring festival was in full swing, so Fergus bought cool bottles of Riesling and pretzels from a stand. As they rested beneath a shade tree, Zelly noticed the bottle's label matched the ones Jack had shared and wondered if the proprietor was his relative, maybe his father. He raised the wine and toasted, "To the friends we left behind."

Like Jimmy and Vinny.

Kurt, Trudl, Helmut, Kris, and Jack, but not Stengler!

Fergus's roommate spoke next, "Never enough dead Nazis."

He views the world in absolutes—allies and enemies, no in-between.

That doesn't leave room for you.

Or me.

As the jeep traveled south, a realization struck Zelly—returning to Fred's life wouldn't be easy and maybe impossible.

At the Remagen Prisoner-of-War Temporary Enclosure, called Rheinwiesenlager, Fergus got directions to the interrogation center. From that, Zelly guessed what would happen to him. At the building, Thompson's machine guns took aim, and handcuffs snapped around his wrists.

"Best of luck, Fred." Fergus drove away, abandoning him.

The thought of being held prisoner by an American Army was terrifying.

Roosevelt is dead. The butcher, baker, and candlestick maker may have met the same fate. No one to vouch for you.

When they learn what I did for the Germans, will I face a firing squad?

****

26 April 1945—First Questions at Remagen

In the clapboard interrogation hut, guards threw Zelly into a chair across a desk from an Army second lieutenant whose golden bar gleamed in the lamp's light. Though the chains binding the prisoner's hands rattled, the officer didn't gaze up from his papers.

"SS," he said like the initials were the nastiest letters possible. "What branch?" He spoke German as he prepared to take notes.

So far, leading with a claim of American citizenship hadn't worked, so Zelly followed the Geneva Convention protocol. "Frederich Zellner. Either Obersturmführer in the Allgemeine-SS or Captain in the Sicherheitsdienst, department D."

"You're the first Nazi who doesn't know what he was," the questioner muttered in English.

Fred responded in the language. "I have a rather complicated story. My journey began as an American spy in Germany before I became a spy for Himmler. I work for Wild Bill."

Immediately, the lieutenant's eyes went to the prisoner's face, and recognition soon dawned. "Zelly? I'm Bob Silberman. Remember?"

"Bob? You were just a boy."

Bob rounded the desk with a smile. "I never thought we would meet again." Instead of a handshake, he pulled the captive into a hug. Tears of relief flowed from Fred's eyes.

I might go home. Thinking of hope and home brings a terrible sadness.

Death follows you everywhere, like the Grim Reaper.

Fred's knees weakened, and he collapsed in Bob's embrace and bawled on his shoulder. "Bob, I've killed people, working them like slaves and starving them."

"In war, we've all done things—"

"I murdered them, and many were Jews." The cries didn't cease. "I'm Jewish or, at least, Zelly's old-world family was, and maybe Fred, too."

Bob pulled him to his feet, stepping backward and forward. He put his hand over Fred's hair and chanted in a strange language.

Suspicious, Zelly asked in German, "What're you doing?"

"Praying Gehulah, the Amidah's seventh blessing, asking for redemption and deliverance."

"You would pray for Zelly after what he's done?" Fred asked.

"I've prayed for you for five years, so why should I stop when you're delivered? The people you think you've wronged— they're in Heaven, and God has revealed everything to them. They understand why you did things. He has told them you are righteous."

Fred dried his tears. "Where's Carl?"

"He'll be here soon."

Bob had the handcuffs removed and took him to dinner. Fred related his life's journey after Fort Sam Houston, following the driftwood's pathways. Bob shared his training at Camp Ritchie, coming ashore in France the summer after D-day, and the many interrogations since.

After lingering over a cup of real coffee in a comfortable silence like old friends, Bob said, "Tomorrow will be arduous. Uncomfortable questions must have answers, and you'll be under guard for days."

Fred dreaded the events to come, and the uncertain future scared Zelly.

****

27 April 1945—Questions

Thompson machine guns escorted Zelly to Remagen's interrogation room—a table, four chairs, and cameras cabled through the walls. The wall he faced held a mirror, a one-way glass with more observers beyond. And who or how many were viewing on television screens?

Bob and two other officers entered, and an electrical hum filled the room. Zelly stared into a camera lens, waiting nervously. Through the mirror, he spotted a test pattern on a poorly positioned monitor. Instantly, the graphic dissolved to show his face.

The effect was chilling. "Peenemünde had better TVs," Zelly said in German.

Jaws dropped in surprise as a commotion arose in the next room, and doors banged.

"Should we use German or English?" Zelly asked.

"Which is easier?" Bob asked.

"It might be different depending on whether you want to speak with Zelly or Fred. Fred wants to avoid German, but Zelly is fine with either."

When a colonel blustered into the room, he slammed the door and rattled the one-way glass. "You were at Peenemünde? What did you do?"

"I made rockets, eventually called the V-2, while serving on Helmut Hölzer and Otto Hirschler's guidance team." Zelly bragged, "I invented the mixing device for the missiles."

"But I sent the packet that got the British to bomb the place," Fred spoke aloud.

Zelly interrupted, "…that murdered Trudl."

"And I provided the details of the Jewish slaughter and the Nazi atomic program," Fred claimed.

"I did that, not you," Zelly said.

The commotion beyond the mirror became a symphony of sounds and distorted images. Shadow faces appeared in the glass, and papers fluttered like feathers in a birdcage. Doors banged like cannon fire before the interrogation room flooded with men, including a general.

When the cacophony quieted, Fred said, "I'm Fred Brown, born in Texas, and I'll tell you anything you want. I'm American and not a Nazi until Major Donovan sent me to spy in Germany."

"Can you corroborate that?"

"Both Fergus McAuley, who I met in Belfast, and Bob, who trained me at Fort Sam Houston, have recognized me. My passphrase is 'I work for Wild Bill,' and if the major is still around, he should vouch for me."

"True about my part," Bob said.

The general chewed a pencil and perched on the table's edge. "Zelly, tell me the story of Peenemünde."

"First, we'll start with a map," Zelly said in German. When the paper came, he sketched the base from memory and from drawing several maps. For four days, he told his tale with frequent pauses for translation. Many new people came to listen, while others remained constant.

Over time, Fred studied every person who attended.

After what I've done, do we deserve mercy?

****

1 May 1945—Co-pilot

At Remagen, Zelly found himself in a doctor's custody, though the office had no examination table. Instead, it featured a comfortable chair that was angled to highlight the diploma on the clapboard wall—Ph.D., not M.D. The doctor was behind a desk near a window but out of Zelly's view.

"Did you attend the base movie last night?" the man's voice asked.

Fred thought the question was asinine and responded, "I guess the show wasn't for prisoners."

"The flick was *God is My Co-Pilot,* about a guy who flew with the Flying Tigers."

"Never heard of them."

"Robert Scott, the hero, shoots down a Japanese ace named Tokyo Joe despite serious damage to his plane. When he crashes, the Chinese return him, and a doctor grounds him for combat fatigue."

"Is that what I have?" Zelly sniggered.

"Please understand that I have a challenging decision to make."

"Everybody has a job to do," Fred remarked.

"True, so on your mission, who was your co-pilot?"

Zelly's head shot backward. Vinny?

"We were each other's," Fred said.

"Guess so," Zelly said.

"Come on," the doc said. "You're not fooling me, so drop the act because I don't believe I'm talking to two different guys."

Zelly slid his thumb through the middle of his fist and shook it at the man.

"What's that supposed to mean?"

Fred laughed. "It's the German equivalent of flipping you off. Honestly, these years have been very unbelievable, but if it will help, I'm the real one, and he's the impostor."

"Not for the last five years. Fred is the weak one, the pussy boy who won't fight or kill. I've saved his ass many times."

Fred's head swiveled quickly. "You danced with Golden Pheasants, charmed an ancient hausfrau, and loved being German—still do."

The doctor scribbled notes. "I'll try rephrasing—who kept you going during hopeless circumstances?"

Vinny? He wasn't around when things were desperate.

Fergus? But it took like forever.

Trick question? Is he asking if I believe in God?

God hasn't been in Germany for years.

Only one name came to mind, so Zelly said it. "Himmler, for promoting me."

"Himmler, for protecting me from the Gestapo," Fred echoed.

The doctor choked. Fred spun, thinking the man had swallowed a piece of horehound candy from his desk jar, but the man fired another query. "Are you more German or American?"

"Wasn't I supposed to be German?" Zelly asked.

"Though he kept trying to shut me in a box, I'm American and wouldn't go."

Fred said, "I murdered Stengler, giving him what he deserved."

An astonished expression covered the doctor's face, and he pressed. "Choose one or the other."

"What's the point?" Zelly realized the question hurt, and he didn't want to think about it.

"Seventeen years attest to the fact I'm American, and that's way more time than when you were a German." Fred wondered if the doctor was toying with them like a kitten with a mouse.

"Those were simpler times," Zelly chuckled. "I was proud when we boys won at Wittenberg and when the rocket flew! Like Ernst, I'm both American and German."

"I was a boy when I went to Germany," Fred said.

"We became a man there, together," Zelly said.

He's ripping our souls and minds apart.

We are like the shards of Ma's coffee cup in 1940 when the butcher, baker, and candlestick maker took us from home.

This office is stifling.

Let's scat.

"Will you excuse me? I like to run when I need to think." Fred sprung from the chair.

"Sit down!" the doctor commanded.

"I'm gone," Zelly bolted out the door.

"Stop him!" The doctor called the military policemen.

Guards drew their weapons. "Halt, or we'll shoot."

While the idea of bullets in his back didn't threaten Zelly, the thought offered Fred a strange sense of relief.

"Go ahead," Zelly challenged.

"Please do," Fred said.

After Ebensee, I deserve punishment.

Not for fulfilling the mission.

Zelly cornered a building, sprinting through a common area outside a mess hall. Whistles blew, calling more people to join the chase. He plowed through a chow line, sending trays of food flying. Jumping on the serving tables, he scanned for an exit. Soon, the pursuit seemed overwhelming as a mass of soldiers joined the race.

I love the exhilaration of running, like in the Tiergarten or around the island.

Like when I scored the touchdown against Kerrville.

Yeah, just like then.

Hands grabbed at Fred, but he juked and twisted away like from the safety at the ten-yard line. He spun a corner, and his eyes landed on the beautiful Rhine River.

It's wide, but not as much as the sea in Fergus's song.

I can swim—don't need wings to fly.

Zelly crested a small hill and found a long, barbed-wire fence at the top. Between the barrier and the water, the Rheinwiesenlager imprisoned a million Germans. Zelly spotted them—half-dressed, sunburned, and gaunt from starvation. While the vision propelled him with renewed vigor, the sight stunned Fred.

Zelly threw himself at the twisted cable and climbed despite the barbs tugging at his skin. He lifted each foot to the next strand, but Fred saw the blood on his hands and grimaced in pain.

People grabbed at Zelly's boots, trying to pull him from the fence. He kicked and continued scaling, ripping the prongs away when they snagged his clothes. Grasping the top wire, he pulled up with all his strength, like a chin-up over a bar. Fred pushed against the wire as Zelly swung over and jumped toward the prisoners.

Someone caught him with a grip on his shoulder. He glanced at the hand to spot a swastika ring circling a finger—the death's head, the symbol of the SS. He relaxed in the man's arms.

Fred, I'm home.

Fred felt surrounded by roaring cheers.

Like the touchdown against Kerrville. Are Ma and Da's voices in the crowd?

Zelly stood, bloody and torn, to confront the pursuit. Gun barrels pointed at him from weapons of all kinds.

"Back away," guards ordered. They fired warning shots from the tower.

U.S. soldiers rushed through the gate and toward him while prisoners scattered. The guard towers cocked their machine guns in case a riot ensued.

Out of breath, the doctor arrived. "Let's talk."

Fred sat in protest. "How can you treat them like this, putting them in a disgusting camp? I'm ashamed to be American."

A song emerged from Zelly, and he belted it out.

> Deutschland, Deutschland über alles,
> Über alles in der Welt,

The Germans joined the singing—their voices rising in the most massive and defiant chorus. A guard held his arm while the doctor injected him. Though he fell silent and slumped to the grass, the chorale continued—a million prisoners belting out their national anthem.

Surrounded by Germans, Zelly's heart sang as blackness overtook him. In American hands, Fred felt closer to home than he had in five years as the medicine took him to sleep.

Fred and Zelly grew content within each other while colorful ribbons braided them together like a Maypole in the Tiergarten.

****

2 May 1945—Another Mission

In the morning's psychiatric session, the psychologist tossed Fred a newspaper and said, "Read the front page."

The paper was *Stars and Stripes*, and its headline read, 'Hitler Dead. Fuhrer fell at Command Post, German Radio Says. Doenitz at Helm, Vows War Will Continue.'

"Why won't they surrender since it's obvious they lost?" the doctor asked.

"Would you give up only to go to a Rheinwiesenlager?" Fred asked.

The doctor's shrug showed he didn't care. "They did worse to Jews."

"Ever been to an Indian reservation to see how compassionate America has been to its minorities?"

"It's different."

"What a lame-ass justification," Zelly challenged.

"My question still stands—are you German or American?"

"Both," Zelly said.

"Neither," Fred said.

"Why does the choice trouble you so much?"

"Write what you fucking want in your damned report," Zelly spat.

Tears streamed from Fred's eyes as he tried to reason. "At Fort Sam Houston, Dr. Otto said to 'lock Fred away in a box in your heart and be Zelly. When the time comes, set Fred free and lock Zelly away forever.'"

"Who's locked away?"

They shrugged together. "We couldn't implement the advice."

Later, at the mess hall, a general caught them. "Son, America needs you."

"Yes, sir," Zelly said.

"How can I help?" Fred asked.

"A group of scientists in the Austrian Alps want to surrender. If their story is true, they'd be a grand prize because they claim to have invented the V-2. Can you identify them?"

"If they are telling the truth, they'll recognize me, too," Zelly said.

The general pulled a nearby lieutenant. In no time, they had traded clothes, and the briefing proceeded. "My staff car will take you to a C-47 waiting in Cologne. We'll have captured Innsbruck's airport by the time you reach the city. Transport will take you forty miles into the Tyrol Mountains by morning."

I'd enjoy meeting old friends and raising a glass of hefeweizen.

They'll spot you despite the American outfit, and I doubt they'll want to share a drink. Like Amelia Earhart, we must help America. That's what we set out to do.

CHAPTER 21

A Job

3 May 1945—Tyrol Mountains

The surrendering German scientists passed through Fern Pass, a route the Nazis had named Adolf Hitler, and spent the night negotiating surrender. Fred traveled in an Army Studebaker, posing as a brigadier general's aide- de-camp. As they drove through the Gurglbach River Valley, he searched for a glimpse of Zugspitze, the highest peak in Germany, but clouds obscured his view. They parked beside a meadow of daffodils.

A team of greeters met the Germans in the afternoon rain. Though Zelly stayed at the crowd's rear, he recognized many friends. Wernher von Braun had broken his left arm, and his cast and sling were a mockery of the Hitler salute. With him was his brother Magnus, who worked at Mittlelwerk supervising gyroscope production, and Dornberger who was smoking.

Otto Hirschler and Helmut Hölzer, Zelly's Peenemünde bosses, were in the group. He remembered Hirschler visiting him in the hospital and Hölzer giving him credit for the mixing device and enjoying his cartoon sketches. As Dr. Ernst Steinhoff surrendered, Zelly recalled flying in his plane.

Some others he knew only casually, like Konrad Dannenberg, who had taken over after Dr. Thiel died in the bombing. Herbert Axster always had corrected his Italian mistakes, and Hans Lindenberg was Dornberger's chief- of-staff. Bernhard Tessmann architected the plans for Zement, ones Zelly had ensured remained uncompleted.

Fred was glad the Germans wanted to surrender, while Zelly wished to shake hands and swap stories in the biergarten.

The general collared him. "Well?"

"The V-2 masterminds—the whole guidance brain trust and a number from propulsion," Zelly reported.

"This'll earn a second star."

"Only for a promotion—what a cavalier attitude," Fred said.

"What will happen to them? The same as with me?" Zelly asked.

"They'll make rockets for America."

"Why? The war is almost over."

"For outer space."

****

4 May 1945—Remagen

The next day, Fred stood in the office of Brigadier General Edwin Sibert, commanding G2 of the Twelfth Army's intelligence service, as he said, "Good work yesterday."

"Send me home to Texas?" Fred asked.

"Impossible." He slid a thin manila folder across the deck.

Fred hesitated when he saw the red stamp. 'Eyes Only.'

"Go ahead, read it."

Zelly opened the psychological evaluation, which was fast reading. 'A dissociative and multiple personality disorder, possibly schizophrenia. Allegiances are still in doubt because the subject talked to himself and mixed pronouns—we might mean the Americans or the Germans.' The recommendation was 'indefinite detention.'

"Sir, do you plan to lock me up or send me to a death camp?" Zelly asked.

Gathering his wits, Fred chose a different tactic. "Sir, are you the same as before the war?"

Sibert sighed. "I've seen and done things that will stay with me forever, but I've performed the job as best I could."

"So, have I—if you deserve to go home, so do I."

The general tapped the report in answer.

Despite the discouraging setback, Zelly pressed on, "When you joined the U.S. Army, you took an oath, right?" When Sibert nodded, Fred said, "I did, too."

Zelly caught the drift of Fred's strategy. "But the Army placed a swastika under my palm and ordered me to take this second pledge—'In the presence of this blood banner, which represents our Führer, I swear to devote all my energies and my strength to the savior of our country, Adolf Hitler. I am willing and ready to give up my life for him, so help me God.'"

Fred resumed the appeal. "If my pronouns are mixed or my allegiances are divided, what caused it? If I suffer from a dissociative personality disorder, it seems the U.S. Army bears the fault."

"I followed my orders and did my duty as best I could—the same as you," Zelly said.

"But I remember which oath I took first and have been true to it—and I still am," Fred said.

Sibert shredded the folder and paper. "I agree, and so does William Donovan, but we want you to stay in Germany a little longer. Lieutenant Frederick Brown, I'm offering you a job with the Office of Strategic Services, America's new spy organization. You'll go home soon, but there are some other jobs for you first."

When Sibert extended his hand, Fred and Zelly shook it.

****

7 May 1945—War's End in Europe

After Reveille, a loudspeaker announced, "It's over!" A grand cheer arose around the flagpole, and Fred joined it. The news was nearly unbelievable because the war had dominated life for years. Remembering a time before was almost impossible for Fred. When the German POWs heard the translation, they let out shouts. Everyone wanted to go home.

I was away longer than anyone—over five years.

What will we find in Texas and the U.S.A.? I've changed in so many ways.

Fred had breakfast with Bob and Carl Gettler, the boys from Wittenberg who had taught him German culture. They had arrived last night. Scuttlebutt swirled through the installation—who would transfer to the Pacific to beat Japan?

Enterprising soldiers organized a camp show titled Wonderful Follies to celebrate the victory and circulated a sign-up sheet. Carl put himself down to join a skit and added Fred Brown as a singer.

"Asshole, what should I sing?" Fred asked.

"An idea will come to you, like everything does, including this message from HQ."

Fred opened the telegraph to find orders promoting him to the rank of First Lieutenant, backdated to 18 August 1943, the day after Peenemünde's bombing.

Bob pinned the silver bars to Fred's collar. "Congratulations."

****

12 May 1945—Camp Show

Wonderful Follies packed the theater. The show was a comedy lampooning Germany with raunchy, ribald humor and minor talent, like vaudeville.

Carl's skit featured Herr Schicklgruber. The name meant nothing to Fred or Zelly, but they immediately recognized the Hitler caricature—a short man with a piece of black Kent comb stuck to his upper lip. He arrived for a surprise inspection of the Chancellery Guard, eight GIs, dressed in only underwear. The guy with the fake mustache blustered and goose-stepped around the stage, asking, "Wo ist Mein Juder?"

At every squad member, he performed the Nazi salute to comic effect, a slap to the face or a finger up the nose, before he dropped the man's undershorts. When he didn't find what he searched for, he said, "Juder nicht hier."

The last guardian was Carl, and Hitler discovered a circumcision, recoiling in horror. The audience erupted in laughter, but Schicklgruber was more interested in a rolled paper that tumbled from Carl's shorts. He unrolled the page, showing a signed picture of Judy Garland. "Hier ist Meine Juder."

As Zelly's turn came, he stepped on stage, still not sure what to do. Only German music filled his mind, so he leaned to the keyboard player. "Know *Lili Marleen*?" The piano struck the opening notes, and Zelly began to sang. Surprisingly, many GIs joined in, despite the song being in German. When Fred repeated the song in English, the entire audience sang along. At the end, the listeners shouted for an encore, so he performed *The White Cliffs of Dover.*

"*Home for Christmas!*" The pianist struck up the number, but neither Fred nor Zelly recognized the tune. The crowd belted out the lyrics with longing while Fred wished the words would come true.

****

23 May 1945—An Interesting Chap

Around midnight, a ferocious knocking brought Fred to the door.

Fergus said, "General Sibert has approved another task for you, so hurry and dress."

Fred followed the Irishman to a Jeep. "Where are we going?"

"Lüneburg, Bremervörde, or Barnstedt—I'll check where he is when we arrive."

"Who's he?"

"His documents say he's Heinrich Hitzinger. He wore an eyepatch, but according to our medic, it was purely for show. During the interrogation, he blustered about and claimed to be Himmler. You knew the bloke, so you tell us if he's Hitzinger or Himmler."

The idea of meeting the man, again, was terrifying. "Can't you compare him to pictures or newsreels?"

I'll recognize him, and he'll remember me.

Himmler's steely eyes will glare with betrayal and anger.

And dredge memories I prefer to avoid.

"Command asked for certainty," Fergus said.

Fred was pensive, focusing on the headlights flashing off the trees after years of blackouts to keep from dreading the encounter.

After a while, Fergus interrupted his thoughts. "Someone else wants to greet you."

"Who?" Zelly asked.

"Meg."

"I'd love that," Fred said.

"All arranged for after the identification."

They drove through the night toward things both feared and exciting.

****

24 May 1945—Lüneburg

Just after dawn, they arrived at the headquarters of the British Second Army. Fergus made a phone call and returned to the Jeep with news. "We're in the right place, but he chewed a cyanide pill last night."

Zelly was relieved at not having to meet Himmler's eyes.

Fergus stopped at a suburban house, and they entered the parlor. The room's plush furniture surrounded a bare floor and a body beneath a gray blanket. A general hovered as a doctor slid down the wool to reveal a face.

It was instantly recognizable, with closed eyes behind the familiar glasses. Putty-colored cheeks were puffy and dark with stubble, and the lips were blue and swollen from the poison. An ugly bruise marked the corner of his mouth, and dried blood streaked to his neck. He seemed less a regal Reichsführer and more of a chicken farmer.

When Zelly remained quiet, the Brit grew impatient and jerked the cover to expose the entire corpse. "Is he, or isn't he?"

Someone had put an army shirt on the body but hadn't given it the dignity of trousers. Zelly recalled the boy he had found lynched in Berlin, and Fred felt sick. "This is Himmler."

Fergus saw a green cast on Fred's face and pulled him away. "Let's get some air."

Sitting in the Jeep, Zelly sucked deep breaths while Fergus held his shoulder. Fergus assumed the reaction was from fear of Himmler. "He's dead and no threat to you."

"You don't understand. Without that man, I'd never have survived. He provided my job at Peenemünde and my promotions. Whenever someone investigated or verified my credentials, they found his black band on my folder. I owe him my life."

"If he had discovered your identity, he would have shot you. You aren't beholden to him."

As Fred's head cleared, the nausea subsided. "Have you learned anything about your brother Danny?"

"The Red Cross has confirmed his death and located his body. The Army will take him home to Knockbreda, and he'll rest in the parish burying grounds."

"My deepest condolences," Zelly said.

"I'm sorry," Fred said.

"I'll miss him. Now, I need a new brother, and I want it to be you." Fergus put his arm around Fred's shoulders, but Fred thought the words were only soldierly camaraderie.

"Shall we visit Meg?"

Fred's heart leaped until Zelly added a thought.

What will she think when she learns what we've done?

CHAPTER 22

Exit

24 May 1945—An orphanage in Lüneburg

Once Himmler's identity was confirmed, Fergus drove for a few minutes to the Kaltenmoor district of Lüneburg. He stopped by a building beside a Congregational Church and led Fred to an orphanage. Children from tiny babies through about age five filled several rooms.

As soon as they entered, Fred's eyes were drawn to Meg's red hair, as bright as ever, pulled back beneath a white nurse's cap. Time had softened her freckles to render her gorgeous. Holding a baby, she moved toward him. He thought she was planning a hug, but she handed him the armful.

"He's Guenther."

"Hi, little man," Fred said into the wrappings, where a small face grinned and giggled.

"He's got a dirty nappy." When he tried to return the bundle, she said, "No, you do it."

Fred was at a loss. While he handled his share of nasty farm chores, but he'd never faced the challenge of changing a diaper. Fred unbundled him, removed his clothes, and opened the safety pins. "Yuck, Guenther, what did you eat?" The yellow and green goo between his legs was revolting and stank. The boy kicked and reached, smearing both hand and foot. When his filthy hand approached his mouth, Fred intercepted by wiping with one hand and disposing of the mess with the other.

Zelly flashed to the Jewish child flailing in the snow. Though I didn't stomp, he died anyway.

The vision pulled Fred up short. Soon, Guenther had a new diaper pinned in place and grinned with satisfaction.

"You might make a father yet," Meg said.

Fred held the baby like a football as he gazed at all the children. "When Fergus said you were a nurse, I figured a military hospital."

"I served in one until the war's end when the Army didn't need me. I volunteer here."

"You mean you can leave?" Fred asked.

"For a month."

Fred couldn't think of a reason anyone would stay in Germany. Every soldier believed like Judy Garland—'There's no place like home.' "Why didn't you?"

Meg's mind raced, struggling with what to say and wondering about the consequences of her words. Her face was a mix of emotions, unsure whether it would break into a smile or tears. "Fergus said he found you, and it couldn't be anybody else."

When Fred hugged her, she kissed him, a light peck on the lips. A dark pall lifted from him, like the bluebird over Dover's white cliffs, when he returned her kiss.

"I've prayed a long time for that," she said.

"With all the cribs occupied, what should I do with him?"

"Love him."

He couldn't tell if her sentence was a statement, a question, or an order.

Her next words hit Zelly like Peenemünde's bombs. "He's mine."

"Yours?" Shocked, Fred raced to a conclusion—*I've kissed a married woman.* His face telegraphed his thoughts.

"Not that, dumb-ass, Meg's adopting him," Fergus said.

Filled with confusion, Fred asked, "Why?"

"Guenther's Lebensborn, a program where they kept young, racially pure women to birth children of the Nazis. His father was an unnamed SS officer, and his mother was a Germanic girl from the Netherlands. When our army liberated the home, the citizens stoned her for collaboration, so Guenther's an orphan—one of ten thousand."

As Meg combed Zelly's fingers through the baby's silky blond hair, he remembered Trudl and her fling with Stengler to produce a baby for Hitler.

Guenther smiled, a playful glint showing in his beautiful eyes.

"He resembles you," she said. "How about a movie, Bing Crosby starring in *Going My Way?*"

"Who?" Fred asked.

Fergus tried to help. "The guy from the road pictures with Bob Hope— *Road to Singapore, Road to Zanzibar, Road to Morocco.*" When Fred's face showed no recognition, he said, "Boy, are you lost?"

"*Pennies from Heaven,*" Meg said.

"The singer?"

"Don't suspect he played much in Germany," Fergus said.

"Come at five?" she asked.

The cribs were still full, so he asked, "What about Guenther?"

"Take him along for an afternoon with the boys."

Fergus drove south of town to where the Ilmenau River flowed through the sandy heath. They found a stand of tall junipers amidst coppiced shrubs. Grass ran up to the riverbank, and the glistening green water drifted slowly. Fergus tossed a blanket, and Guenther studied the clouds flying and the treetops swaying. Fred blew Himbeeren on the baby's bare belly, as his father had once done on him. Guenther's chortles echoed over the landscape.

Beer bottles cooled in the stream. When Guenther cried for his bottle, they guzzled theirs with him. Fred managed a baby burp, and they supplied their own.

They swam in the late afternoon, and Guenther didn't mind going diaper-free while he splashed. Exhausted, he fell asleep between them on the blanket.

"He'll be a lady killer since his dick's twice the size of yours," Fergus teased.

Guenther rolled to his side and snuggled against Fred's chest.

Out of Germany's desolation, such a fragile life begins.

He deserves to be cherished if only to show that some things are more important than war.

To atone for the child who died that first day in Brenner.

I could be a fantastic father.

At five o'clock, they picked up Meg and parked Guenther in a crib. They ate at the British HQ mess. Fred held her hand through the movie until she rested her head on his shoulder, and he draped his arm around her.

She nibbled on Fred's earlobe and blew in his ear. Her caresses caused a physical reaction, which inspired her giggle and Zelly's grin.

Early the following day, but still in darkness, a dozen gravediggers buried Himmler without fanfare. They left the grave site unmarked and unrecorded so that the location couldn't turn into a shrine or a place of pilgrimage. Himmler couldn't become a Nazi martyr like Zelly's cover story father.

Zelly was the only one present who could have been called a friend by Himmler. He said no prayers, shed no tears, and offered no remorse. Jeeps packed down the dirt above the plot, and workers raked dry sand and leaves over the surface. No trace of the burial reached daylight.

As often as duty allowed over the summer, Fred bunked with Fergus and visited Meg. A relationship blossomed, and Guenther's grin was infectious.

****

24 August 1945—The Wellendorff

Three months after reconnecting with Meg, Fred took a chance. On a weekend pass, he checked out a motor pool Jeep and drove to Lüneburg, carrying in his trouser pocket a small box containing something that belonged to Zelly.

His hand rested on the bulge, and when he shifted gears, his fingers returned there. Apprehensive, he considered turning around out of fear of rejection. The dilemmas were still unanswered when he reached the foundling home.

Meg was in the playroom with Guenther near her feet as she bottle-fed two other babies. "Hi, you," she said. "Sit on the floor and see what happens."

He sat about a yard away and gazed at her. "You're missing the show." He followed her eyes to Guenther, who slithered over the carpet on his stomach like a soldier in basic training.

When Fred reached for him, Meg said, "Just wait."

Soon, the little boy climbed onto Fred's lap, stretched across his legs, and chortled.

"He'll crawl any day. When is his birthday?" Zelly scooped him up, laid back, and pressed the baby's body like a weight.

"February 22nd."

"That's mine," Zelly said, lifting the giggling and squealing infant through three sets of ten.

"What's in your pocket?" Meg asked.

Fred blushed. "A present."

"For me?"

"No, silly, for him."

"Why don't you give it to him?"

With the bluff called, Zelly opened the box as Guenther's eyes sparkled. The baby reached for the shiny thing. "Guenther, may I have your permission to ask your mommy to be my wife?" Zelly handed her the gift with jittery hands and waited for her to open it.

She examined the ring, gasped, and dropped it like a hot potato. "How could you?"

Crushed, Fred picked it up and took a knee, balancing Guenther on a hip. "Please, Meg, marry me?" He expected a negative answer coming like a Russian artillery shell.

"How did you afford a Wellendorff with fifty or more diamonds?"

Fred hadn't examined it since the housewife on the train gave it to Zelly. The thought of proposing with a second-hand band embarrassed him, but he hadn't enough money for anything else. Remembering how Zelly smuggled it through allied lines in his rectum turned him crimson. "I'm sorry."

She fell to her knees with the ring on her finger. "Yes."

He embraced and kissed her.

"Guenther, say hello to your new daddy."

"Da Da Da Da," He said and giggled.

"Meg, I'm a rather complex guy," Zelly said. "There could be two of us in this body—one German and one American. I won't hold it against you if you decide differently." He told her the story of Germany without holding back gruesome details.

When he finished, Fred described the psychological diagnosis and explained the relationship between the two personas.

After some time, Meg understood, but her choice held firm.

****

14 November 1945—Nuremberg

Almost three months after proposing to Meg, orders came for Zelly to arrive promptly at 7:10 AM at the Palace of Justice in Nuremberg. He'd read of war crimes trials taking place there. At the specified moment, he entered the wood-paneled room to find a silver-haired man at the prosecution table with two stars perched on his shoulder.

Zelly approached from behind. "General, you sent for me?"

When the man turned, Fred recognized William Donovan. Wild Bill raised a salute before dropping his hand for a handshake and a hug. "You survived against all the odds. I'm both glad and proud."

"Thank you, sir. I did my best."

"We followed your excellent performance from Panzer pictures and rocket drawings to the Peenemünde map. Dr. Otto made heyday with the Jewish stuff, and Professor Koehler loved the rocketry and bomb reports. But discerning your identity as the mythical Austrian sergeant was challenging."

"An idea from the Polish resistance," Zelly said.

With a smile, Donovan pulled some papers from a stack. "Seeing you would have overjoyed Roosevelt."

"Vinny didn't come back, but I tried to find him."

The general slipped an arm around his shoulders. "Lots of boys didn't return."

"Did he have another mission—the atomic bomb? He died of radiation poisoning."

"You gave him a target of opportunity, and he acted. Though we won the race, it was a closer contest than the government will ever admit. Vinny's contribution was indispensable, and so was yours." He handed Fred the pages.

The top one was travel orders for sailing on the *USS LeJeune* with the 29th Infantry Division, leaving Bremerhaven on the day after Christmas. "I'm going home?"

"This ship is a lot like you. She used to be a German passenger liner, the *Windhuk*. When the Navy captured her, she took on a new name. She's part of two worlds with two names, like Fred and Zelly."

"You read the psych evaluation?"

"Yes, and the reports tell me you're getting better. No one will understand the trauma you've endured. Knowing what I do now, I unfairly asked too much of you. But without your exceptional service, outcomes would undoubtedly be different."

"Thank you, sir. I often wondered if I was doing enough."

"Keep working in the OSS and learn Russian because America needs spies more than ever. I won't be leading the organization because Truman has taken a dislike of me."

"May I ask some questions?" Fred asked.

"Vinny warned me you have plenty."

"How huge was the conspiracy?"

"The Great War's peace wasn't the way the U.S. wanted. We didn't want to punish Germany, but the French and the British insisted on reparations— taking Alsace and Lorraine, weakening the enemy, demilitarizing the Rhineland. They created the circumstances for the Nazis to rise, and some, like Roosevelt and me, anticipated the outcome."

"So, you planned my entire life—even my birth?"

He stood. "Sorry, but our time has ended. You must leave— and no one can find you here."

Fred didn't budge. "Sir, I need… deserve… an answer."

"Read the second page."

Zelly found a ledger of war criminals, and, near the page's middle, he found his name. 'Frederich Zellner, Ebensee, Accessory to mass murder, at large.'

I followed orders.

You're a criminal.

"A trial will start soon, and I don't want a sharp-eyed survivor to spot you." He pointed Fred toward the door.

Fred walked until his hand touched the doorknob. "Please, sir, I have to understand."

"I expected you to have everything figured out by now. Ask yourself, in those seventeen years, why hadn't your parents learned English? In the depths of a depression, how did they afford the hundreds of electrical parts you requested?"

The door opened, and people pushed inside. Bucking the crowd, he left the building unnoticed.

****

6 January 1946—Fredericksburg, Texas

The taxi from San Antonio dropped Fred off at the mailbox where 'Brown' was scrawled on the side in his childhood penmanship. He walked up the driveway, remembering every step, as his house loomed before him, and the dormer window beckoned with a wink.

Assuming the Lutheran minister was long-winded, he expected the house was empty. He hadn't called or cabled because he wanted the return to be as much of a surprise as the departure. He propped his drab duffel bag near the door and found the grave of Beans, his trusted Irish setter, in the pet cemetery. Memories of a small cross beside a Wittenberg barn flooded Zelly. He teared up as Fred rocked on the porch swing.

Soon, Da's pickup lumbered down the road and turned to follow the ruts, like the Army staff car years ago.

Ma opened her door. She seemed old—hair entirely gray, worry-lines furrowing her brow and sagging cheeks, but her eyes were still bright. She spotted his uniform on her third step and expected unpleasant news. "Dear God," she said in English, which had replaced her favorite German expression.

Da rounded the truck with fear filling his face as he steadied her. "Your heart?"

Fred moved to where she always greeted company. "I'm home."

Da spun, not recognizing the voice, and Fred rushed to meet them in the yard. As Ma's tears flowed, he hugged her. Da tried to usher them inside, but she wouldn't move until she had kissed Fred a dozen times. Da bussed the other cheek.

When they stepped into the front parlor, Fred relaxed into an easy and serene sense of normalcy. "I have news. I'm married to Meg, a beautiful Irish girl, and we have a baby boy, Guenther. You are grandparents." He offered a handful of snapshots Fergus had taken.

"She has such red hair," Da said.

"Look at that diamond!" Ma gushed.

"Here's Guenther with his Uncle Fergus." Fred gave them the picture.

"He looks like you." She touched the photo to her lips. "I'm a grandma—God has so blessed."

"He's so big. Will his hair change color to be like his mom and uncle?" Da asked.

"He'll stay blond, I'm sure," Zelly grinned.

"When can I meet them?" she asked.

"Next month. Fergus is coming, too, and he can farm. Can they live here?"

Da nodded. "I'm fetching steaks from the freezer, for the prodigal son has returned."

"Since when—?"

"The Army took care of us," Da said.

"And you. They've been putting your salary in a savings account." Ma rummaged in the parlor's roll-top desk. "Here's your passbook, and we often went to the bank to have it updated." Her voice quivered. "That was the only way to hope you remained alive."

Fred checked the balance—more than enough for college. "Is Jimmy around?"

Da's head shook. "He was a Marine, killed on Iwo Jima."

"The scout master—I have some items to discuss with him."

"Moved away not long after your court of honor," Da said.

They chatted in the kitchen while Ma prepared lunch. Fred told them about meeting Meg, and Zelly relayed the story of Fergus saving him with a song.

"Quite a tale," Da said.

Acid bloomed in Fred's gut. The thought of spoiling the homecoming was terrible, but the questions would inevitably spill.

Why not now?

Guy, I've got to understand. We deserve it.

"I've uncovered a bigger story," Zelly said.

"What?" Ma opened a Mason jar of corn.

"This family used to be Jewish. You escaped Germany to avoid persecution and settled here with all the Lutherans. You weren't the Browns—likely the Zellners, like August and Freida in Wittenberg, or something else. They had a little boy, Frederich, murdered by Nazis. I was his replacement." Zelly pointed to the Eagle Scout picture hanging near the hearth. "They published that in a 1938 magazine. Two years before, the staff car drove up the driveway."

Ma started crying at the word Jewish and bawled throughout.

Da's shoelaces were so interesting he couldn't raise his eyes. "When I enlisted for the Great War, I wanted to be less German, so we became the Browns."

"Ma, I don't want to hurt you," Fred said. "I will love you forever, but that day, you got my pictures too fast. You had them ready."

"Don't blame Ma," Da said as tears streamed down his face.

Fred said, "I'm not angry and I love you both and nothing you tell me will change—"

"—But I want… **need**… to understand," Zelly said.

Da came to Fred's chair and reached toward a shoulder. "It was my idea." Before the touch arrived, Da slumped to the floor. His head landed in Fred's lap, and he sobbed. "I offered them my only son."

Fred stroked the few remaining wisps of Da's hair. "Now, I realize how much you cherish America."

"Not only a Purple Heart, but all your heart," Zelly said.

Ma draped her arms around him like a necklace. "Are you upset?"

"So many parents have sacrificed sons like Jimmy's," Fred said.

"I'm proud to be the first," Zelly said. "When did it start?"

"San Antonio Air Show when I was twelve," Fred guessed. "When Amelia Earhart took me up, she didn't give others a ride."

"Earlier," Da admitted.

Zelly nodded, accepting the historical revision of his childhood. "I'm not the boy I was. I've done and witnessed too much to stay the same. Honestly, I'm wanted in Germany for war crimes."

"Pshaw," she said. "Of course, you're not the child you used to be. You're a man."

"I'm so glad you returned," Da said. "The farm is your home and your family's. One day, soon, it will be yours. We have a new litter of puppies in the barn and Guenther can choose."

"Irish setters?" Fred asked, and Da nodded.

Zelly winked at Ma. "You've learned to speak English."

He didn't have the heart to say he would continue working as a spy. In homage to being both American and German, Fred kept the last name of Zellner and hyphenated it with Brown with Zelly as his nickname. The OSS became the CIA, and they gave him many aliases. He stayed a spook until a paperclip summoned him.

EPILOGUE

12 September 1962—Houston, Texas

An invitation arrived, hand-addressed in German script. The double-s in the Mission Street address used the Eszett (β). The envelope had no return information, but the invitation was for Zelly to listen to President Kennedy at Rice University's football stadium.

He arranged for Gunther, who had dropped the e from his name in America, to miss school in the first days of his senior year. With any luck, he'd be in college next fall. Tall, blond, and handsome, he sat beside Zelly in the folding chairs arrayed on the field.

Zelly and Meg were proud of their son. He was a straight-A student, excelling in science and math, and a leader in his class and on his sports teams. Gunther was an only child. They hadn't conceived, probably because of the testicle injury from fighting Bart at Fort Sam Houston. They never told Gunther about his true birth circumstances. He thought they were lovers as the war came to a close, which delayed marriage vows.

Gunther interrupted Zelly's thoughts with an elbow. "Guys on the dais are staring."

"No. They're viewing Kennedy."

"Are not. At us." He was right. They were German, and their stares targeted Zelly. He recognized them all—Wernher von Braun, Otto Hirschler, Helmut Hölzer, and more.

"Sh. Listen to the President."

Kennedy spoke. "But why, some say, the moon? Why choose this as our goal? And they may well ask, why climb the highest mountain? Why, 35 years ago, fly the Atlantic? Why does Rice play Texas? We choose to go to the moon. We choose to go to the moon in this decade and do the other things, not because they are easy, but because they are hard because that goal will serve to organize and measure the best of our energies and skills because that challenge is one that we are willing to accept, one we are unwilling to postpone, and one which we intend to win."

When the speech ended, Hölzer strode to Zelly, hand extended. As he shook it, Zelly said, "This is my son, Gunther."

"A fine boy." Hölzer handed over some paper-clipped pages, turned, and walked away.

"What are those?" Gunther asked.

Zelly held a job description from the new space center NASA was building southeast of Houston. In the margin, someone wrote: 'This one's for you. When you call, mention the paperclip.'

Zelly called Thursday morning.

"I'm sorry, but we're not hiring," the lady said.

"I was told about the position at Kennedy's speech," he explained.

"Like I said, we have nothing open."

"The document said to point out the paper clip," Zelly tried.

"Can you start on Monday?" she asked.

He rejoined the old Peenemünde team, working to fulfill Kennedy's vision of a man on the moon. He remembered October

3, 1942, when the A- 4, painted with a girl in black stockings—the Frau im Mond—launched into outer space.

It was my dream long before it became Kennedy's.

Mine, too.

****

On July 20, 1969, Fred manned a station in NASA's Mission Control when Neil Armstrong radioed, "Houston, Tranquility Base here. The Eagle has landed."

AUTHOR'S NOTE

In 1991, I met the old man who claimed to have lived this story. As we sat overlooking Galveston Bay, he astounded me with this tale. When I suggested he write a book, he smiled. "I promised the government I never would, but you can after I die." We spoke several times, and I ended up with 22 pages of notes.

Following his death in 2010, I investigated through official American and British sources but received only rejections. Frustrated, I sought verification on my own by traveling to Germany in 2011 to check details against reality.

Whether things were true or not, the tale was compelling by itself.

I took the "Ruins of the Third Reich" tour from Tony Cisneros at Alpventures, and he got our group into Peenemunde, one of the first groups allowed to visit the closed facility. At Wewelsburg Castle, we ate in the Ottenshof where carved swastikas on the booth ends and the basement beehive fireplace perfectly matched the man's description.

At Peenemünde, I could navigate the base from the information in my notes. Parts of the old Strength Through Joy camp remained. I located the foundation stones of the women's dorm along the beach. Kai, a docent at the museum, showed us a display of the various tinnies, and I surprised him by asking why the gold one was missing. In the cemetery commemorating those killed in the bombing, the tour group helped me locate the tombstones for Trudl Ehle and Helmut Dotzel, proving those characters once actually breathed. For the book, I used their real names as a homage but invented the events of their lives. In Berlin, I located the dedication plaque on Albert Speer's labor headquarters building, where Vinny hid his apartment key. I left Germany believing in the tale.

One fact troubled me. In the official history, the British claim some fishermen reported Peenemünde's importance while the old man claimed the information came from three Polish workers. When I researched, I found Józef Garliński's book *Hitler's Last Weapons: The Underground War Against the V1 and V2* (1978), claiming the knowledge came from Polish partisans. I've wished I could have told Mr. Garliński their names.

I have endeavored to keep the novel as historically accurate as possible. Most events portrayed fit historical records, including the flight of various rockets, the surrender in Fern Pass, radio broadcasts, and Himmler's death and burial. Major William "Wild Bill" Donovan was active in the pre-war years with President Roosevelt and Secretary of the Navy Frank Knox in attempting to prepare the U.S. for the conflict. Douglas Waller's biography of Donovan does not put him in Texas as in this story, but White House records confirm his attendance at the Southern Fried Chicken dinner on September 25, 1940, with FDR, Knox and two unnamed people.

The Design of Audio Amplifiers Using Regeneration exists as a doctoral dissertation. Its author taught at Rice University, but I have no proof the author ever played the role I described.

A copy of *Hilf Mit!* of 6/1938 hangs on a wall beside me as I write. I was shown a copy of the Eagle Scout Court of Honor invitation with the same picture in 1991, but I do not own it. I have no explanation, other than this story, of how the image appeared in both places. I have attempted to find an original or negative of it in the German archives, to no avail.

Other characters that populate the book are of my creation. Stengler is an amalgamation of various Gestapo officers. By combining them, I made the antagonist of the novel more sinister. Vinny, Bob, Carl, Kurt, Kris, Katchen, and Greta are my imaginary cast. I invented the Stengler family in Zinnowitz, the McAuley family in Knockbreda, and Zellner family in Wittenberg to fit the name and roles played in the story. The martyr's badge is also imaginary.

Fred Brown or "Zelly" Zellner are not the character's real names. The man working in the OSS and CIA owned many personas. I'm unwilling to expose them.

I deviated from the original story in several ways for drama, primarily because the factual tale had an unhappy ending. The psychotic break never fully healed. Reunification with Meg, marriage, and Guenther are the most significant departures. In truth, the man never married. Though he lived a productive life, I sensed a deep melancholy about him. He suffered from trust issues, surprising me by telling me of these events. Discovering so many lies about his mission, his family, and himself had to have been traumatic. For the novel, I wanted to give him an escape from the palls of war.

ACKNOWLEDGMENTS

I have a host of people to thank. Most importantly, the old man by the bay who entrusted his story to me.

Professors Sarah Harris Wallman, Eric Schoeck, and Charles Rafferty of Albertus Magnus College led me through the first two drafts as part of my Master of Fine Arts in Creative Writing. Arianne 'Tex' Thompson workshopped a section over beers and encouraged me to persevere. Dr. Kirk Wetters, Yale's Professor of Germanic Languages & Literatures, helped me with the *Hilf Mit!* translation and the quest for the original photograph. Kai, from the Historisch-Technisches Museum Peenemünde, answered my correspondence and dug for details.

Ryan Steck, The Real Book Spy and author of several thrillers edited the novel and offered hundreds of wonderful suggestions. He is as good as gold.

Mary Helen Lowry, my partner, read this book dozens of times more than she would have liked. I suspect the book has contributed to her dislike of war stories and violence. Many other friends were alpha and beta readers, and I owe them my thanks.